The Broken Bridge

The
Broken Bridge

Fiction *from*

Expatriates *in*

Literary Japan

Edited by Suzanne Kamata
Introduction by Donald Richie

STONE BRIDGE PRESS • *Berkeley, California*

Published by
Stone Bridge Press, P.O. Box 8208, Berkeley, CA 94707
TEL 510-524-8732 • FAX 510-524-8711 • E-MAIL sbp@stonebridge.com

For correspondence, updates, and further information about this and other
Stone Bridge Press books, visit Stone Bridge Press online at www.stonebridge.com.

Introduction © 1997 Donald Richie.

Cover design and illustrations by Karen Marquardt.

Text design by Peter Goodman.

10 9 8 7 6 5 4 3 2 1   2001 2000 1999 1998 1997

LIBRARY OF CONGRESS CATALOGING-IN-PUBLICATION DATA

The broken bridge: fiction from expatriates in literary Japan / edited by Suzanne Kamata;
    introduction by Donald Richie.
        p. cm.
    ISBN 1-880656-31-0
    1. Japan—Social life and customs—Fiction. 2. American fiction—20th century.
3. Short stories, American—Japan. 4. Short stories, English—Japan. 5. English
fiction—20th century. 6. Americans—Japan—Fiction. 7. British—Japan—Fiction.
I. Kamata, Suzanne.
PS648.J29B76 1997
813'.0108952—dc21   97-30005
                                                                    CIP

Contents

Acknowledgments

SUZANNE KAMATA

The editor would like to gratefully acknowledge the following publications in which some of the stories in this collection previously appeared: "The Broken Bridge" in *Live Bait* (Holt, Rinehart, and Winston, 1978); "The Business at Hand" in *This Country, Japan* (Kodansha International, 1979); excerpt from *Imaginary Speeches for a Brazen Head*, from *Two Novels* (Zephyr Press, 1985); "Indirect Method" in *One Is a Wanderer* (Century Hutchinson, 1985); "The Granny Room" in *Blackwood's Magazine*, 1980, *Short Story International*, 1983, and *Portraits of Cities in Literature: 1* (Rikutaro Fukuda, ed., New Currents International, 1985); "Mr. Butterfry" in *Mr. Butterfry and Other Stories* (Angus and Robertson, 1970); "The Altar" in *The Clay That Breathes* (Milkweed Editions, 1991); excerpt from "Blue Notes on the Samisen in Early Summer" in *Prairie Schooner*, 1996; "Flatlands II" in *Tokyo Today*, 1994; "Dreaming of Glory" in *Whoring Around* (Penguin Books Australia, 1981); "Enlightenment with Tea" in the *Abiko Literary Quarterly*, 1993; "Hair Nudes" in *The Secret Sushi Society* (Shufunotomo, 1995); "The Circuit" in *Wingspan*, 1995; "Shades" in *Sunday Afternoon*, 1993; "Aliens," "Rhinoceros," "Hello Kitty," and "Wrong" in *Japan Times Student Weekly*, 1994; "Mr. Robert" in the *Abiko Literary Quarterly*, 1993; "Is There a God in Your Heart?" in *Printed Matter*, 1994; "Summertime" in *Printed Matter*, 1995; "The Podiatrist" in *Wingspan*, 1993; "The Screen Man" in *The Woman Who Dreamed Japan* (The Yakumo Reminiscence Society, 1994); "Season's Greetings" in *Wingspan* and *Ikebana Quarterly*, 1993; "Six Encounters" in *Wingspan*, 1985-93.

This collection, like any anthology, is by no means definitive. It is a reflection of my taste in literature. Another editor might have come up with an entirely different set of stories. In compiling those gathered here, I limited selections to short stories about Japan written in English by non-Japanese in post–World War II Japan. There are many fine expatriate writers in Japan who write novels, but not short stories; who write about Japan in Japanese, but not in English; and who live in Japan but choose not to write about the country in which they live. The work of these authors is not included here.

I have tried to arrange these thirty-six stories so as to convey a sense of the changes in society in recent history and a sense of variety. In reading these stories in the order presented, the reader will no doubt become aware of some of the subtle shifts in the relationship between foreigners and

Japanese in Japan over the past few decades. I also hope that readers of this volume will begin to appreciate the range of styles, voices, and concerns of expatriate writers in Japan. (First publication and creation dates appear at the ends of the stories, and these do not necessarily follow the chronological/thematic ordering of the anthology itself.)

Finally, I am indebted to a number of people for the completion of this project. My sincere gratitude goes to Donald Richie for his guidance and wisdom; Leza Lowitz for her enthusiastic support and for leading me to writers I might not have found on my own; Javant Biarujia for helping me to track down Australian expatriates; and Eric Watnik and Jeff Hollar for technical assistance. For their encouragement, patience, and love, thanks to Alvin and Patricia Borsum, Helene Northway, Christopher Tower, Timothy and Kavita Borsum, Noriko Tanigawa, Frances Wilkes, and Yukiyoshi Kamata. Last but by no means least, a big round of applause for the thirty-six writers who so generously contributed their work, to Peter Goodman for making this dream come true, and to all the readers of this book.

Introduction

DONALD RICHIE

"He was of that generation that had come to Japan seeking enlightenment rather than wealth; but the more he meditated, the more he wanted to fall in love."

Morgan Gibson

The expatriate writes in order to make sense of self or surroundings or both. So, of course, do all other writers, but the expatriate has a particular need to do so. Away from the unexamined culture in which he or she had lived, set now in an alien place where, by definition of having expatriated, the writer explores and examines, seeing plainly the differences between here and there, sensing too the new variances in self which the transplantation has made visible.

The circumstances of the relocation are also important. If one lives elsewhere the fact that one initially arrives as a tourist or a pilgrim or an immigrant determines what is experienced and hence written about. If, as has been the major American experience, one goes as a conqueror, having won a war, the experience is more different yet.

★ ★ ★

After WWI and WWII, having won both, Americans flocked to Paris, and there their literary activities have become well known. To mention Hemingway or Stein, Fitzgerald, Baldwin, Wright, or Burroughs is to imagine a literary Paris with Americans writing away in every corner cafe.

Though the motive was to escape from repressive victorious America to the perceived freedom of France, much of what was written about was laid back in the USA. Hemingway wrote about Michigan, Baldwin about New York, and Stein wrote *The Making of Americans.*

Paris gave these people a place to write but it did not give them a subject, and the contrast between their selves in America and their selves in France was not dramatic enough to become a major theme in their writing. Seeing, usually, each other and fellow foreigners, they experienced little of that isolation in "alien" surroundings so often expressed by Western writers in the East.

Those who came to Japan after WWII and stayed to write were not only Americans—they came from all the victorious sides—but they all found a place very different from France. In 1945, Japan was—besides being a ruined country—culturally as far from the Midwest or the Midlands as one could get. Tokyo, though looking like Chicago or Manchester in ruins, was alien, utterly "other" in a way which Paris never was to those writers who lived there from 1918 and 1945.

To Americans in Paris things were familiar—even superior to those back home. The new expatriates already knew that *vin rouge* was better than beer and that *tarte tantin* was somehow more delicious than apple pie. The Occupation Forces in Japan however, did not even know what *sake* and *suimono* were, and as for octopus being delicious. . . . Initially nothing was familiar and ignorance was general.

Perhaps this difference—looks like the States but sure doesn't act like them—accounted for an expatriate phenomenon soon noted. Whether the foreigners in Japan were there for the job or there by choice, when they got together they talked about Japan. Discussing the country was as common in foreign circles as discussing the weather. This is odd. It is not likely that Gertrude and Ernest and Alice and F. Scott sat around and discussed the French, yet discussing the Japanese is what expatriates here still do.

In searching for parallels to this singularity one cannot but recall the India of the British Raj where the forcibly expatriated English sat around and spoke disparagingly of the natives. And, indeed, some kind of such racism has continued to inform much Western thinking and some Western writing about Japan.

In fiction perhaps not so much. Usually such remarks are confined to the jocular tones of the columnist and his or her observations about "these people" in those collections telling you that it is not all raw fish or that they themselves have been too far east too long.

That the racist attitude remains is indicated, however, in much expatriate fiction by the looming presence of the "bad foreigner," he (and sometimes she) who does not attempt to "understand" Japan. Much of this fiction attacks the racist attitude (white vs. yellow), and it is only in early writings from those countries which most endured Japanese militancy (Australia, New Zealand) that racism finds more approving narrative form.

More common is fiction that (sometimes compulsively) seeks to explain Japan—often through the "good foreigner," the sympathetic Westerner. He or she is what Henry James (noted expatriate) called a consciousness which observes and records. If the person takes a part, the results are often incongruous and the intent humorous. If not, then the person looks on, unable to influence but at least allowed—finally—to understand.

Understanding Japan is one of the goals of the baffled but well-intentioned fictional foreigner, and once this is accomplished then he is somehow in possession of the "real" Japan. The assumption is that such a place truly exists, but that only the anointed few are privy to it.

This odd quest gives rise to that character almost unique to expatriate fiction set in Japan, the anti-foreign foreigner. He wants no interlopers about, ignores his fellows, and hoards his findings. The anti-foreign foreigner—who appears in life with perhaps even more frequency than he does in fiction—will not acknowledge the presence of another white foreigner, will not speak unless he has to, and will rigorously avoid eye contact.

A part of the reason is, of course, that the Japanese themselves hardly ever speak to strangers in public places and lack of eye contact is one way of enduring crowded conveniences. But another reason for a foreigner being wary of other foreigners is an unacknowledged fear of the competition. Why should this be so? Such selective paranoia can occur only if the foreigner thinks himself already in possession. If so, then this is a ragged remnant of the Raj.

Possession is the goal of this quixotic quest toward the "real" Japan. These new Orientalists are in pursuit of the exotic, that which is so different that they cannot afford competition of the fellow searcher or, worse, the potential pollution of the unbeliever, the bad-because-unenlightened foreigner.

The anti-foreign foreigner (perhaps more common in Kyoto, home of traditional Japanese culture, than in Tokyo) does not himself often write fiction. Instead, he appears in it—usually as a figure of fun. Nonetheless, any expatriate knows the temptations to regard the country as exclusively his. It is the rare foreigner (the author of *The Last Time I Saw Paris* is an exception) who wants to adopt France, but those expatriates in Japan who regard the country with a similar possessive concern are common.

★ ★ ★

So common, that there has risen in expatriate folklore a belief in the three classical stages of the affair with Japan. First there is euphoria, where everything is wonderful, differences are seen as advantages, a sense of wonder is palpable, and among the magic there is, somehow, the implied promise that you are about to meet the only one who will ever truly, really matter to you.

Stage one is followed, either abruptly or over the years, by stage two. This is, as one might imagine, its opposite. Everything is horrible, differences are seen as disadvantages, depression is palpable, and there is the implied assurance that you are never, never, never going to meet the only one who truly matters. The inhabitants of the second level are soon using phrases like "these people," and "this country," accompanied by shakings of the head and—if this continues long enough—his or her actually leaving.

If this does not occur it is because the Japan lover/hater has slipped into stage three. After the euphoria and the depression of the first two stages comes acceptance. One has recovered, has regained one's balance. If the first two stages resemble the ups and downs of love, then stage three perhaps best corresponds to marriage.

Actually, stage one is more like a crush than a love affair. For one thing, the emotion is not often requited (a fact which sometimes leads to stage two); for another, the emotion can be consuming and compulsive. France experienced nothing like this from its postwar expatriates except maybe Gene Kelly in Paris, and that was only in the movies.

Admittedly those now suffering from stage one are much fewer in number than they used to be—but then contemporary Japan offers much less to have a crush on. Foreigners are no longer treated as privileged; their presence is not considered a necessity; it is no longer necessary to please them. All of which is good for the Japanese and they are to be congratulated upon graduating. In addition, and no cause for congratulation, the country is much less beautiful than it was, far less natural, and "development" has assured that it also looks much less like "Japan."

Nonetheless, let us reconstruct the kind of person who fell in love with Japan, since these continue to exist in literature if not in life.

Initially, after 1945, the shortly besotted foreigner came as conqueror. The people were the natives and were to that extent mistreated by those who experienced no interest in or affection for the country. The feeling foreigner could express his own alienation by taking up the conquered culture and making it his own. That he was ready for alienation is indicated if not by his coming to Japan in the first place, then by his deciding to remain.

Second, among the things discovered was—just as Americans in Paris had discovered—a tolerance for himself as he believed himself to be. No longer subject to the provincialities of wherever he came from, he found new room to grow and no punishment for difference. That he was also firmly barred from the provincialities of life in Japan and that he was considered by the Japanese so utterly different that any minor differences remained invisible—this he would only later discover, at stage two.

Third, there is the ineffable promise which Japan used to seem to extend to the foreigner. Everything seemed possible. People got good jobs because they were white, or were treated in what seemed a deferential manner because they were Americans (or British)—and it seemed as though the long longed for was about to occur: romance was in the air.

One should not, even in such a historical account as this, lightly set aside the sexual. Most of us (particularly if we are so introspective as to want to be writers) are forever sexually dissatisfied. In the Japanese, however, one used to find a seemingly complaisant people who would offer the foreign male the model Japanese wife, fittingly subservient, and the foreign female the model Japanese husband, fittingly tender, caring, understanding, etc. And for those who liked their own sex, Japan seemed to offer a respite from the prohibitions of home, a place where love was possible and where happiness seemed actually attainable.

To this listing of reasons for having a crush on the country, one ought add that these perceived differences could be profitably employed in creating a new self—that illusion which added so much to the enjoyment of the place. Just as the British colonial invented the grateful native to assist in the creation of his own gracefully condescending person, so the democratic American sexual imperialist created a gratefully supine populace pleased to augment his (or her) new person. The country was used as the "other" in order to define the self.

Japan does the same thing to the foreigner, though this is not visible from stage one. Some Japanese, for example, find themselves small but nimble by contrast with those they found large but awkward; they also possess different brain patterns, longer intestines, greater spirituality, etc., all by definition against those across the Pacific who have no such things. In addition it is often agreed upon that we Japanese are difficult to understand, that our language is impossible, and that no mere foreigner will ever be able to comprehend our true *kokoro*.

Though swallowing this whole may have animated some of the searchers for the real Japan, it is nonetheless true that the creation of the "other" as definition for self is something which everyone does all of the time. The process can be enlarging, benign; it is also responsible for the small household spat and the large war. Some conditions favor the operation more than others. The West's attempts in Asia created the massive edifice of "Orientalism"—a small and recent corner of which vast body we are at present concerned.

★ ★ ★

At the same time, however, there is also something like an objective and relatively selfless regard. This seeks to describe life in Japan as it is and is not concerned with play-acting or psycho-drama, or those who pull the country and the people about for their own purposes.

The expatriate writer has at command a number of ways of creating fictional worlds which accurately reflect this real one. These would include the fictional foreigner whose relations with people in Japan are regarded with an open eye. Understandings and misunderstandings, purposes and cross-purposes are all recorded.

The consciousness can be American or Australian, English or Indian, or it can be Japanese. In this collection stories by Francis King, John Haylock, John Bryson, David Burleigh, Catherine Browder, Daniel Rosenblum, Sanford Goldstein, and others can be seen as richly detailed variations on the theme of the foreigner and his relations, or lack of them, with the Japanese.

Or, as in the stories of James Kirkup, Kate the Slops, Morgan Gibson, Joseph LaPenta, and Michael Fessler, the foreign observer looks at the country through a Japanese discipline—the bonsai, tea, ikebana, haiku.

Or, the Japanese are seen as ways in which to define a longed-for self, as in the stories of Philip Whalen and Hal Porter. Or, as ways through which patterns are continued—in the Madame-Butterfly variation in such stories as that by Frank Tuohy, the title of which serves as emblematic title for this collection. Here the role of being foreign can be enlarged to include being female, being black, being gay—all roles for which a paradigm is "being foreign."

Or—finally—the foreign writer can enter into a Japanese character and view this world from those eyes. Its pluralities can in this way be suggested, and its complications can be delineated—as in the stories of Meira Chand, William Wetherall, Edward Seidensticker, Alex Shishin, Christopher Blasdel, Holly Thompson, Karen Hill Anton, and others, including myself.

This combination of a place perceived as opaque and a person (self or others) perceived as work in progress, has resulted in a substantial body of fictional work. I think that more such has been produced in Japan after WWII than by all foreigners in France after both 1918 and 1945 put together.

This does not mean, however, that anything like a similar literary level has been attained. In France it was writers who expatriated. In Japan it was largely people who, once here, turned into writers. In addition there was in Paris a large literary community. Ernest knew Gertrude and they both knew F. Scott. In Japan there is no such literary community for foreign writers. The *bundan*, the literary establishment, is for Japanese only and the foreigner in Japan has only a circle of friends, not a circle of literary colleagues.

One of the consequences is that there is no one against whom he or she can measure his or her work, and few around interested enough to discuss the problems of writing fiction about the country. Writers about Japan write largely in vacuums.

Though there are a few English-language literary magazines in Japan, these are often short-lived and usually have small circulations. There is no equivalent of *transition*, just as there is no equivalent of Sylvia Beech and her book shop. This lack of literary access means that what is written is often unexamined and more often than not unpublished.

★ ★ ★

It was this consideration which led to the creation of this volume. Like all ideas whose time has come, the idea for this one struck a number of people at a number of places. Alan Brown in Tokyo spoke of it with me, and I spoke of it to Leza Lowitz. In the meantime, in a different part of the country, Suzanne Kamata, whom (typically) we did not know, had much the same idea. When we found that Suzanne had already done much of her work we agreed that the anthology would be hers and that I would write the introduction.

Hers was a formidable task—gathering expatriate writing from the years 1945 to 1995. Simply collecting all of this fugitive fiction was extremely difficult. There was no getting at that which had not been published, nor that from the earlier years printed in obscure and vanished publications of which even the Diet Library did not have a copy.

A list of the deserving which are consequently not here included would doubtless be quite long. I can only mention one name, a writer I happened to know—the late William Clark, who published at his own expense (and under a nom de plume) a now-vanished fiction collection called *The Journals of a Man Who Loved Love*.

Another problem was to decide just what an expatriate was. The dictionary (Concise Oxford) allows the word only as a transitive verb which can mean to banish, emigrate, renounce citizenship, etc. Obviously the usage has expanded since the dictionary was published and so—since we wanted to use the word as a noun—we could construct our own definition.

An expatriate is someone who has left the home country to go and live in another country. This is not a tourist and not even a frequent flyer. Rather, he or she is someone who has something like a home in Japan, one which is lived in all the time or visited a lot. This thus includes people like me who live in Japan permanently, those who no longer live there, like Francis King, and writers such as Edward Seidensticker, John Haylock, and Leza Lowitz, who live there only for only part of the year.

A final editorial problem was that so much of the fiction found is relatively late. It would be possible to trace expatriate France from 1918 till now simply by collecting what got published—the problem would be what to leave out. This is not possible for expatriate Japan, for, as I have indicated, much has disappeared, and the problem has been finding enough to include.

Nonetheless, the collection does successfully reflect the expatriate experience in Japan, and it does so in a way which communicates its variety and its vitality. More, it offers a number of fictions which capture the necessity of self-creation—one of the facts of literature and, more important, one of the facts of life, both life in general and expatriate life in particular.

The Broken Bridge

FRANK TUOHY

"Hi, there." A young American hailed me outside the building of the Faculty of Literature.

Although we were in the middle of Tokyo, he was wearing clothes that seemed more suitable for mountain-climbing. He looked, in fact, as though Nature had created him for austere and difficult tasks: she had been conspicuously unkind to him, giving him one shoulder higher than the other, a raw beak of nose to hang his spectacles on, and a scalp already losing most of its reddish hair.

He held out his hand and said: "Larry Breitmeyer."

I had seen him around before, and had thought him be a student following the short course on Japanese Civilization which the University provided. But now he said: "Professor Nakamura told me your name. I teach at this place too."

I was prepared to be friendly. To have been hailed in this way, even for a specific purpose, had something exceptional about it. In Japan I had found that the members of that strange tribe known as Caucasians ignored each other warily. (In this, we are quite different from Negroes, who, even if complete strangers, nearly always exchange greetings in the alien streets of European cities.) Perhaps the other Caucasians were up to no good at all, and expected you to be in the same situation. More probably they believed themselves to be in possession of some incommunicable truth about a mystery of Japanese life. This might involve Aikido or Zen Buddhism or merely flower arrangement. Whatever it was, they knew all about it already, and your ignorance would only cause them pain.

"Your students just asked me to help with this British play you chose them."

"I didn't choose it. And, as a matter of fact, none of them are my students."

Later, it was to become clear that Breitmeyer was one of those foreigners who are obsessed by the Japanese theater. But the play he spoke of was to be performed in English as the local contribution to this year's inter-university drama competition. It was a dim little farce, of the school of A. A. Milne and Ian Hay. The choice had been imposed on the students by Professor Nakamura himself, whom they much respected. The professor had seen the play performed during his visit to London in the 1920s, and it had left an indelible impression on him.

While I was telling him this, Breitmeyer appeared distracted. He stared intently at the crowd of young men who jostled past us into the building. He could hardly have been looking for a previous acquaintance; in a university with thirty thousand students, it was exceptional to meet by chance anybody one knew already.

When I had stopped talking, he said: "It's a lousy play."

"They insisted on doing it."

"I told them it was a lousy play. I've been giving them a few of the basic technical things. Their movement is awful. I'm not too thrilled with the casting, either. Those two girls ought to change parts." He aimed a look at me, as if to show that this was my responsibility. But this was not the case.

By now the students had been rehearsing the play for about two months. A few days after my arrival at the University I had received the committee involved in the production.

There were seven or eight of them, and they came into my office in a closely packed phalanx. The way they stood, quiet and tense, seemed to indicate both shyness and aggression. They muttered in a consultation for a bit, and then their spokesman stepped forward from the group.

He was equipped with the kind of Tom Sawyer vocabulary that the Protestant missionaries still teach, though presumably they do not use it themselves. "Gee, sir, I guess we're in some kind of fix. You see, our instructor chose this British play and, gosh, we're stumped to know just how to speak it, on account of we mostly learn American English in high school."

By the time he had spoken, the young man's primrose skin was flushed with mauve. He bowed and was absorbed again into the group, from whom there came a sort of susurration—whether of disquiet or acclaim, I could not tell.

I made a little speech. When two or three Japanese are gathered together, discussion is difficult: you have an audience. I confessed that I knew next to nothing about the theater and that any help I gave them might jeopardize their chances of success. I begged them to seek advice elsewhere and offered to ask around among the numberless English-speaking foreigners who devoted their spare time to amateur theatricals.

All this, however, was taken to be conventional modesty. In the end the students got their own way. I was to make tape-recordings of the whole play, reading all the parts.

Later on, as I had promised, I attended some of their rehearsals. From the very beginning the whole cast was word-perfect. They spoke in faint parodies of my own voice. Even now, two months later, they were running through the entire play two or three times a day. They undertook the whole project with the extraordinary concentration and discipline which they brought to every task in which honor was involved.

It was obvious, too, that they had recently followed my suggestion and sought advice wherever they could get it. I was surprised to find the Earl and Countess, the Young Heir and the Burglar all speaking with refined Sydney-side accents.

Soon after Larry Breitmeyer had been conscripted to help, I attended another run-through. As I approached, a thunderous noise was issuing through the closed doors of the lecture hall. The room itself was foggy with clouds of dust that had risen from the floor. In the midst of this the team of actors was jumping into the air with outstretched arms, then crouching down and rolling over and over. Among them stood Larry Breitmeyer, in a sweatshirt, levis, and sneakers, with one hand on his hip and biting the nails of the other.

From time to time he bawled out instructions. Once he organized a mock battle, boys against girls. This was an awesome sight. From the quick gasps, the tight-drawn facial muscles of the participants, you could see that he had called into being that intense fury of the will which hides behind all the decorum and docility.

There was a good deal of this insistent will in Larry himself. His appearance and manner were enough to risk distrust or even ridicule. Yet he was closer to these young people than I would ever be. He thrust himself at them, and they had no resources to repel him. Perhaps they did not want to. There have been few foreigners in Japan, however fraudulent their pretensions or scandalous their behavior, who have not gained at least a handful of admirers to speak fondly of them in years afterward.

Watching Larry Breitmeyer one was impressed with the idea that the Japanese and Americans often find exactly what they want in each other. Theirs is a marriage, born under clouds of disaster, that has proved to be of great convenience.

At the Kabuki Theater the great Utaemon had just performed a solo dance which involved a parasol, much fan-fluttering in imitation of butterflies, and finally a fall of snow on the stage. In the interval I made my way out to the foyer, between rows of elderly ladies in kimonos, who were picking away with chopsticks at the wooden lunch-boxes they had brought with them. For this audience feminine perfection could only be transmitted through the medium of an *onnagata*, a female impersonator. Utaemon himself enjoyed at this time a reputation equal to that of all our great theatrical ladies put together.

It was the first time I had been to the Kabuki Theater. I had been given a ticket as a reward for the minor task of correcting a translation.

Larry Breitmeyer was standing in a corner of the foyer. He wore his usual jeans and sneakers, a pea-jacket over his shirt. He was accompanied by a young man elegantly dressed in a dark suit and a wide silk tie.

"This is Yoshi," Larry said.

Now that I had gone up to him, I found myself disinclined to hear Larry's opinions. I imagined, quite wrongly as it turned out, that they would be conventional and insensitive.

Instead, I questioned his friend, who was unhelpful. "I think that Kabuki Theater is not so interesting for us, these days."

"Isn't that just typical," Larry broke in. "What have they got, if they haven't got this?" He hunched his shoulders, twisted and stared away from us.

"I am enjoying it so far," I said to Yoshi.

"I think it is more interesting to the foreigners."

I felt the usual irritation at being lumped together with an undifferentiated group of outsiders. "Everybody sitting near me is Japanese."

"I think they are only the old persons."

Larry was ignoring Yoshi. Perhaps they were having some form of domestic row. But suddenly he turned to me: "You liked that?"

"Yes, I did."

"It was superb, but really that's only run-of-the-mill stuff. Just wait for *Kanjincho*. Utaemon plays Yoshitsune, the young prince. It's always an *onnagata* role, because of the high voice. Crazy, of course, because he doesn't speak at all. But just watch his hand on the staff he holds. He doesn't move, his face is hidden by his hat. Only his hand is there, acting. It's fantastic."

Larry Breitmeyer had fallen for the intricacies of Japanese culture, for the "fascination of what's difficult" (Yeats's line keeps coming back to one in Japan). I could imagine him going on to learn more and more about it, whereas to myself in my ignorance the Japanese tradition seemed like an elaborate and gorgeous impasse. Nothing you learned here, it seemed to me, could be genuinely related to anything similar outside, and perhaps this was why Yoshi and his generation rejected it.

I never heard Yoshi's opinion of the play for the inter-university competition, in which he took the minor part of a footman. Until now I had thought it would be impossible to bring the antiquated little farce back to life. Yet on the night of the performance it was suddenly revealed as something charming and even amusing. I wondered how this had come about. Perhaps, after all those countless rehearsals, some kind of Zen illumination had descended on the cast. Perhaps Larry Breitmeyer was a director of genuine talent.

The play didn't win the competition, but the actors won the best acting awards. They were greatly elated. As the Japanese do at moments of triumph, they wept.

Larry Breitmeyer himself was modest about all this. A part of his attention was elsewhere, because he had invited two American ladies.

Meeting them, I could not help being reminded of the severe shock a Westerner's appearance must have given to a Japanese seeing one for the first time. There was, in fact, an inordinacy in the aspect of these women that seared the gaze. It was not merely their height—neither was much under six foot—but the bouffant wigs, orange in one case, blue in the other, the eagle noses and the costume jewelry. The owner of the blond wig was Harriet Brine, who did the gossip column for the *Japan Mail*, an English-language newspaper. Blue-topped Mrs. Kirshenbaum was the wife of the managing director of the Tokyo branch of ABM.

About the play, Mrs. Kirshenbaum was conventionally ecstatic, whereas Mrs. Brine was bored; she rarely mentioned the Japanese in her column. Larry fussed between them, in a cockled misshapen brown suit that had come from a PX store some years previously; he barely reached up to their shoulders.

The University was so large that the paths of the foreign teachers rarely intersected. It was some time before I saw Larry Breitmeyer again. A new academic year began, and our classes were on different days and in different buildings. By now he was producing another play, *A View from the Bridge*.

This well-known populist tragedy had got into trouble with the British censorship a few years before. There is a scene in which one man kisses another on the lips. It is a test of virility which in the event both characters pass with honor.

The present director however rejected this interpretation. "All right, that's what you're meant to think, on the surface. But there's this strong ambiguity running all the way through the play."

Larry was sitting in the staff room with a small group of our colleagues. Old Professor Nakamura was present but unspeaking, like some sacred object of the Shinto cosmography, a rock or an ancient tree. On the other hand young Mr. Kawai, the assistant lecturer and specialist in George Gissing, appeared to be in a continual state of subterranean disturbance, like his native land: private earthquakes and typhoons kept twitching him and ruffling his hair, hot springs steamed up his spectacles. Pretty, tiny Miss Ikeda sat folded together between them; she never spoke in Professor Nakamura's presence. The unwavering attention of the three of them formed a sort of enclosure, an arena in which Larry was at present holding forth.

"There's this character Eddie. He is jealous of his niece, right? Well, that statement has two interpretations. First"—Larry numbered it on his finger, as though we might lose count—"Eddie is in love with his niece and Rickie, this illegal immigrant, has got her. Right? Second"—here he employed another finger—"Eddie is in love with Rickie and Catherine has got him. His niece is his rival, right? Eddie destroys Rickie for the same reason that Iago destroys Othello, because he is in love with him. There is this wonderful masculine flame burning through the play. That's what I want to identify and bring out."

There were wordless exclamations from his Japanese witnesses. Neither Professor Nakamura nor Miss Ikeda moved, but Mr. Kawai trembled and thrummed like a kettle on the boil. I tried to feel like an outsider in this purely American-Japanese situation. Nevertheless I was embarrassed for Larry and for the whole race of Caucasians. Some minutes later I left him there, caught in the triangle of their polite concern.

After the next class Larry Breitmeyer was still in the staff room, alone now, hunched in his chair. He seemed pleased to see me. However rewarding one's friendships with Japanese people may be, there are times when both sides want to cry halt.

"Old Nakamura looked rather shaken by your account of the play."

"Shaking is what he needs. He can't pretend to be that innocent, can he?"

"Perhaps it's difficult on the stage. There are only a few themes in the Japanese theater."

"Look, if I can get pleasure and fulfillment out of Kabuki, out of the Noh plays, even out of Bunraku, though to my mind those puppets are a dead bore, why can't they understand the conventions of the modern American theater? After all, it leads the world."

He glanced to see how I took this, then continued, allegretto: "I've got this great cast together, none of that draggy lot from last time. You should just see my Eddie—he's a living doll."

Perhaps Larry was right to go ahead. Since the American play was alien ground, they would accept whatever he told them about it. And in the casual comedy of American-Japanese relations, I reflected, mutual incomprehension has a cushioning effect and nothing is ever as disastrous as it seems at first sight.

Taizo Hitomi's composition was written in pencil, with frequent rubbings out. It filled up one side of a page.

I don't know how to write an essay like this because we are not taught in Japanese school. I wish to write, dear teacher, about some things great problems for me. Almost all of the time I am thinking these problems.

By the way, this semester I am taking part in our university's play for the competition. I am chosen to play Eddie, which is man in a great play by Mr. Arthur Miller.

It is difficult to me understand this great play called A View from the Bridge. For example, there is one time where a man is kissing the other man. I think this is not known in Japan. This man is Eddie, which is my part. It is very difficult to me to make this scene.

We read how Mr. Miller used to marry Miss Marilyn Monroe who killed herself. Also this is great problem for Japanese people.

If I keep very calm and have a relaxed mind I may be successful. I think so.

With a red pencil I underlined the last use of "think." There is no verb in the Japanese language for "hope."

Rather gingerly I replaced Taizo Hitomi's paper in the folder with the others and went downstairs to the lecture room.

The new third-year students were waiting for me, all forty of them. This was only the second time I had seen them. I went into the room and they stopped talking and stared at me. I noticed once again the extraordinary variation the Japanese face achieves within its limited range of components. Which of these alert, benign faces belonged to Taizo Hitomi?

At least half of the compositions had been confessional. The difficulties of the English language had induced shy young people to be more candid than they had meant to be. A note of gloomy resolution was present in several of them. If Mr. Hitomi seemed more desperate than the others, it may only be because I had an accidental insight into his situation.

I began to call out their names and, as these were acknowledged, I handed back the compositions. In this way I hoped names would attach to faces and individuals begin to emerge from the anonymous group.

I walked down the aisle between the students, letting my eyes wander over the sleek shining heads of the girls, the boot-brush or hippy-thatched skulls of the young men, and watching for each limpid face as it was raised in response to the spoken name. It was an odd feeling, like creating a new world from an indifferent chaos. Everyone began to get more and more cheerful. Given personal attention, they tended to flourish.

Then I called out Taizo Hitomi's name. There was a sound of breath drawn in between closed teeth, followed by a small hard silence. Two or three others failed to answer. I replaced the papers in the folder and the ordinary work of class began.

The following week two hot-faced girls claimed their essays. Previously they had been too shy to announce their identity in public, but in the intervening week they had plucked up courage. They scuttled back to their seats, chattering and laughing.

Hitomi's was the only composition that remained. When the hour ended, I read out the register of names. After calling out his name, I paused a little. A rough loud voice from the end of the room shouted out, "Absent!"

After a time one gets oversensitive to possible oddities of behavior. I was suddenly convinced that it was Hitomi himself who had spoken. Embarrassed by what he had written, he was sheltering among the still anonymous ranks at the back of the lecture room.

I spoke in the direction of the voice. "Could you tell him I've still got his essay? It's useless to correct it if he doesn't see his mistakes."

At this point a terrifying silence settled over the room. It was as though the barometric pressure had plunged several degrees. Nobody looked at me. I read the remaining names as quickly as possible, slammed my books together and left the room. I blamed myself for what had happened. I had spoken in entirely the wrong way. I had held Mr. Hitomi up to ridicule in front of his fellows. If he had felt unsure of himself before, his situation now was much worse.

Mr. Kawai, the assistant lecturer, had his office next door to mine.

When he saw me, he blushed fearfully, but this was his habit. Otherwise he was quite obdurate.

"We do not worry about what a student does. If you like, you may fail him in the exam. It is up to you. If he is absent, it is his fault."

"I thought there might be something wrong. I wondered if I could do something to help."

Mr. Kawai's features stiffened. I had made another mistake. For the foreigner in Japan, there is no blame: there are only mistakes. In the strange, impersonal language they inhabit the air between people. There is nothing to be done.

Of course I should have sought out Larry Breitmeyer himself. But I did not know his address, and neither did the University authorities. He called for his letters twice a week at the department that dealt with foreigners. I left a note for him there, but it remained unanswered.

One's life in a foreign city consists in following several threads, narrative lines which one may either pursue or neglect. People appear whom one imagines will become friends, and then disappear forever. Others retain a sort of marginal existence, present but never close. Larry Breitmeyer stayed on the edge of my thoughts, like a bad tooth which one is determined to have seen to sooner or later. Meeting him so rarely, I might have forgotten about him, if I had not read his name one morning in the *Japan Mail*. It was in "Tokyo's Brite Nites," the column written by Harriet Brine:

> ABM's Tex Kirshenbaum and gorgeous Gaye (she of the thousand bangles!!) hosted a stand-up send-off last eve for Larry Breitmeyer. Larry, swinging theater buff, Noh-man and Kabuki expert, hies him westward this day on a wing-ding tour of Europe's capitals. Bon voyage, Larry, and *Sayonara!*

This was very puzzling. Had the performance of *A View from the Bridge* already taken place? Little Miss Ikeda, who was reputed to be interested in the drama (she was writing a thesis on The Theater Audience in Restoration England), knew that Larry had left the country. But about the play itself she was unhelpful. Perhaps some other American director had taken it over.

Meanwhile a national holiday had interrupted classes for two weeks. When the third-year students reassembled, it seemed easy for me to read out Taizo Hitomi's name from the register. It remained unanswered, and I read through the rest of the names.

When I closed the book, nobody moved. They were all watching me. "Professor."

The same thundery atmosphere returned, and for a second I felt conscious unmixed dread. I suppose this is the origin of racism: I am alone and all these faces are without good will. We cannot tell if our reactions to the same events will be similar. We are lost.

But it was not like this at all. Three young men stood up at the back of the room. They walked down the aisle between the desks. One of them had assumed the Samurai swagger, which indicates unsureness. They were a posse, but not a frightening one.

"Professor, please do not read Mr. Hitomi's name again. He is not here anymore."

"Has he left the class?"

"He killed himself."

Where so much went unspoken, a statement had been made. Suppositions withered out, possibilities were deleted. We were silent in the presence of this fact.

I told them how very sorry I was and at the same time (for at such

moments of distress one's mind is unremittingly meddlesome) I determined to destroy Taizo Hitomi's essay. Had it been an appeal for help?

From now on everything would be easier. A mistake had been made
and we shared the knowledge of it. Perhaps, even, we felt about it in the
same way. The girls in the front row were giggling, a wild unhappy noise. I
blinked. A grief was burning my eyes, for someone whom I may have seen
but could not, in any case, have recognized.

[1978]

The Business at Hand

EDWARD SEIDENSTICKER

June 20
Dear Sir:

The gloomy rains continue, and things feel damp and clammy to the touch. I trust that your efforts to keep your spirits from flagging have met with success.

As to the business at hand:

You must forgive me, a stranger, for writing to you without proper introduction. I am a third-year student in the Liberty Hill Girls' Higher Seminary. I am nineteen years old, twenty-one years old by Japanese count. My hobbies are literature, philosophy, and television. I am 5.1 feet tall. I enclose a snapshot, taken last spring at the athletic meet, when I had fluctuations and was not feeling well. I think I would like to exchange ideas with a foreign gentleman, and when I went to the American Cultural Center and said I thought I would like to they were kind enough to give me your address. You must forgive me for writing to you without introduction.

I think I would like to exchange ideas on literature, philosophy, society, and television. Please let me know when I can see you. I shall take but a few minutes, provided I am feeling well.

Take good care of yourself in this damp weather.

Hideko ONO (age nineteen)

July 11

At last there are breaks in the clouds, and the early summer sun beats down. I urge you not to let the weather debilitate you.

As to the business at hand:

I think I need have no doubt that you feel keenly your duties to scholarship, and that you maintain a tight and learned schedule. It was therefore very good of you to agree to see me, if only for a few hours. The afternoon and evening were among the memorable ones of my life. Indeed had you not reminded me I would probably have missed the last train. Oh, scatterbrained me!

I am now firmly resolved to acquit myself of my duties to scholarship. I was particularly impressed with your views on education reform, and on

Japanese plumbing. I said to myself: "There is a person who knows more about our culture than we know ourselves."

By the way, I checked with my mother about the recipe just to make very sure that I had it right, and she pointed out one rather important point which I (scatterbrained I) had overlooked. You must use white vinegar, not yellow vinegar. If you use yellow vinegar, the taste will be the same, but the color may call up unpleasant associations.

Uncollected as always, I forgot to ask how you feel about women's rights in Japan. How do you feel? You must forgive me for putting the question so bluntly, but, alas, I have rather strong feelings myself. You must have lulled yourself into thinking that women have equal rights in Japan. Have you? No, they have not. Japan is still very feudal. My own father is excessively feudal. He has a number of children I have never been introduced to. My oldest brother (I assume he is my oldest brother) is also very feudal. He locks his desk. This is evidence, do you not think, of morbid, feudal suspicions, and the nature of the family system.

Perhaps when we next meet for a few minutes we can exchange ideas on women's rights. Do you not think that we must work together to destroy the family system? I do. Perhaps when next we meet I can tell you of the part I mean to play. It will be a poor part, but, well, Japan is a poor country.

Now that we have become friends I think I must tell you why I am nineteen years old and only a third-year student in the Liberty Hill Girls' Higher Seminary. I believe that there should be no secrets between friends. Is that not the essence of anti-feudalism? The truth is that I was suspended for a year, because of what I can only describe as a measure of public-mindedness. I knew what the physical education instructor was doing, and I said so, in an open letter which I posted on all the bulletin boards. But it is too disgusting. I start having fluctuations at the thought of it.

Take care of yourself in this warm weather.

Hideko

August 12

The days grow warmer and warmer, and my limbs grow heavier and heavier. I hope you manage to keep yourself at your valuable work.

As to the business at hand:

I continue to meditate upon the profundity of your remarks at our meeting. You have a great deal to say not to me but to the whole Japanese nation, and I hope your natural reticence will not keep you from speaking out. Please feel free to say nasty things about us, and especially about feudal remnants we have not yet succeeded in uprooting.

By the way, white vinegar is sometimes a little hard to come by (Japan is a poor country), and I hope that want of it has not caused you loss of sleep and weight. I think I should like to present you with a small bottle, which my mother ordered from Kobe. My mother sends regards, although you must forgive her for doing so without introduction.

Would you like to meet my sister? She is two years older than I and rather old-fashioned, indeed much too Japanese. Something must be done for her. When I told her about the physical education instructor, she said she had no idea what I was talking about. Can you imagine it? And she already nineteen years old at the time, and, in many ways which it would be tasteful not to discuss, less subject to fluctuations than I am even now, and certainly less than I was last spring. Will you help me with my plans?

I enclose my sister's snapshot. If you look on the back, you will find all the necessary information about her. I forgot to mention, however, that her hobbies are music and rock-climbing. She plays the trumpet. The neighbors say she is very good, and, not qualified to pass judgment myself, I can but accept the statement.

Take care of yourself in this increasingly warm weather.

Hideko

August 21

The great heat has come, the city sizzles. I pray that you are keeping yourself on guard against the assaults of the summer.

As to the business at hand:

As always, I think I found it far more worthwhile talking to you than spending my time in silliness. I come away from a talk with you bearing such a rich harvest. How different from my father, who, when we see him at all, only growls feudally. I feel more confirmed than ever in my mission, and again I urge you not to be parsimonious with your wisdom. Bestow it liberally, you have so much to give.

As the hours passed and the time for the last train came (I did not forget this time, but thank you for reminding me anyway), and the moments of silent meditation became more frequent, I saw with an intuitive insight that you could be counted on. We Japanese are an intuitive people, and it does not take much of a hint to make us see the truth. What was that pungent Americanism with which you characterized your relatives? Anyway, I saw with an insight, as we looked meditatively at our fingernails, that you agreed with me about the feudal family system. "Ah, ah!" I said to myself. "Ah!" Now everything will be all right, for you are at my side. My sister is not the cruelest victim of this system, perhaps, but it has not allowed her ideal fulfillment, and we must begin where we can. Japan is a poor country.

From your remarks about the Tokyo subway—why, why can I not remember those biting Americanisms? I must buy a tape recorder. Anyway, from your remarks on the Tokyo subway, I gather that you do not object to surface transportation. I know, moreover, that my sister's pulse rises—no, I cannot in any honesty pretend to know anything of the sort. I have never taken her pulse. All I can say is that she squeals with delight when she sees a cliff and starts wriggling into her climbing pantaloons. Oh, oh! Oh! I have just used an Americanism. I found it on page 2260 of Kenkyusha's *New Japanese-English Dictionary,* 1931 edition. I am ashamed of not having the 1954 edition, but on these barren islands of ours we must learn to do with little. Anyway, I enclose two second-class tickets to Matsumoto, together with a schedule which I trust covers most eventualities. There have been a number of landslides lately, but I think you will be spared. The opportunity to have her exchange anti-feudal ideas with you is so golden that we must take the risk, be it great or small. Do not let the roar of the train in the tunnels interrupt your discourse, or if it must, try to have the tunnels coincide with moments of silent meditation.

By the way, I noticed that your peony looked rather dejected in the afternoon sunlight. Peonies, as you know, require rich soil, and, since you are sensible enough (I remember that earthy Americanism) to have no truck with Japanese flush toilets, the remedy is simple. All you need is a dipper with a long handle. Perhaps I can help you until you get the swing of it. Against the distant possibility that you do not have a dipper with a long handle, I shall try to remember to bring some chicken manure when next I come. My youngest (I assume) sister keeps chickens, and it will be no trouble at all. I shall wrap it up in a crepe kerchief.

Did you find the white vinegar helpful? My mother sends her regards. Take care of yourself in this hot weather.

Hideko

August 26

The days grow shorter, and the morning and evening breezes begin to bring a touch of coolness. I feel secure in the knowledge that you have found new vigor.

As to the business at hand:

I think you were as disappointed as I was. I hope that you did not wait too long at the station, and I hope too that you had the sagacity to choose the air-conditioned waiting room. Or did you perhaps make the trip by yourself? My own disappointment, I fear, was more than disappointment. It approached disillusionment, the end of belief. I had thought that only men were feudal, but my sister refused to listen to my most closely reasoned arguments, with an obstinacy that must be labeled feudal. I can see now that the roots of the problem lie deeper than I had thought.

I had hoped to come inquiring after your peony before this, but to have one's plans go astray is cause for retreat and sincere self-reflection. By the way, if you have run out of chicken manure and still do not have a long-handled dipper, a little linseed cake laid not too close to the stem will fill the gap, though not, alas, with the vigor of animal substances. My mother sends regards. Do you like daffodils? I have dug all ours up, and my mother insists that I find new homes for them. I cannot understand her— she will not learn. We went through exactly the same thing last year when we had kittens, and of course we ended up by throwing them away.

Well, as I have said, this is a time for sincere self-reflection, by me and by all of us. Are we to cut away the infected part or are we not? Are we? Are we not? It gives me strength to have you at my side.

Take care of yourself in this time of shifting temperatures.

Hideko

September 12

The fields yellow, and the noonday sun is weaker. Since the autumn effluvia frequently bring disorders to the body, I urge you to treat yours with consideration.

As to the business at hand:

We are having a pleasantly noisy time. My youngest (I think) sister is having hysterics, I suppose you would call them. And for very little reason that I can see. She has locked herself in the closet, silly thing, and she bangs and bangs, and screams and screams. My oldest (I am fairly sure) sister, who is very methodical, is having her hour on the trumpet. My brothers are out streetwalking, and my mother is asleep, and my father too. I suppose he is snoring, though I cannot hear him. I sit here watching him breathe, and it is the oddest thing. I have great trouble writing. Have you ever tried humming a waltz while you are playing a march? That is exactly how it feels. His lip flutters every time he breathes out. I am sure he is snoring. I fear that you will find my writing transparent and vulgar. It is inelegantly legible at best, try though I may to improve it. While my youngest sister has not been too successful at describing the reasons for her hysterics, and while her performance is a trifle exaggerated, I must say that I too was shocked at one point. "The trouble with you is that you just don't want to grow up," my father said to her. Think of it! The indelicacy of touching on a subject so intimately personal! I almost wanted to vomit.

By the way, I am bringing the daffodils, because my mother keeps after me. We vibrate so in harmony, you and I, that I think you dislike the watery yellow things too. Still I must plant them, for I cannot lie to my mother; but they will not bloom, you know, if they are buried too deep or if the soil is too rich. I pride myself on being the least demanding of persons, but I really must ask you to buy a long-handled dipper.

How refreshing it was to read Mrs. MacArthur's remarks in the newspaper this morning. Do you realize your good fortune in belonging to a nation of dedicated, forward-looking women? But I do not despair. With your help, we too are moving forward.

Take care of yourself in this frequently malevolent weather.

Hideko

September 19

On the hills the plumes of autumn grass rustle in the wind. Autumn scenes fill me with thoughts of things, and no doubt have the same effect upon you.

As to the business at hand:

My plans received a setback, you will remember, but I have at length recovered my determination. I am bringing my sister to see you. Last night she talked in her sleep. I shall not tell you what she said, it was too awful; but it was clear proof that the feudal family system does not answer to a woman's needs. To my suspicion that she is too feudal, I must now add a suspicion that she was not being entirely honest when she said that she did not know what I was talking about when I said that I knew what the physical education instructor was doing.

I am not one to spare myself when it comes to sincere self-reflection. Here in this small breast of mine I have found traces of feudalism! I have interposed complications. I am oversupplied with reticence and delicacy, which are attributes of little use in the fight that lies ahead.

And now that I have seen that fault and overcome it, I shall venture to tell *you* something. I have in the past found you wanting in delicacy. Think of your habit of calling my attention to the striking of the clock, *just* when we Japanese would be silent, savoring the dying echo. I think that, in the course of our intimacy, I have not once been allowed to enjoy it. "There is the difference between the rational Occident and the intuitive, artistic Orient," I have said to myself each time.

But now I see. Your want of delicacy is in fact a virtue. *You* have no Japanese reticence. You can be counted on to plunge in. So I shall bring my sister to see you. I should have done so earlier. And when I have seen her to your shady study, I shall quietly withdraw, slip into my shoes again (I must remember to wear loafers), and, after planting the hydrangeas I mean to bring with me, perhaps go streetwalking for a time. Will an hour be enough? I think you will find her in most respects satisfactory. There are those toothmarks, of course, but you will see upon close inspection that they are the marks of a dog's teeth. I shall not go into the details, save to tell you that, practicing the trumpet on warm nights, she sometimes removes encumbrances to breathing, and that our dog (of an Occidental breed) is very unmusical. And do remember one thing: screaming runs in our family. There is no need whatsoever to be alarmed.

I shall be waiting for a full report. If there is any one thing that the anti-feudal movement has demonstrated, it is that progress must be documented. I know I can count on you for a (let me emphasize it) *full* report.

I hope the daffodils are as I left them. For the time being, I think we need do nothing more about them, though you might let me know if they begin to break through. I think you like hydrangeas.

Take care of yourself in this brisk weather.

Hideko

September 26

Clear autumn days follow one another, and yet showers come up from nowhere. Be not deceived, I beseech you, by the fickle autumn skies.

As to the business at hand:

I find it hard to know at precisely what point along the way forward we have arrived. You must admit that you have been slow with your reporting. My sister, for her part, has shown a tendency not to speak to me. That we move forward is unmistakable, however. Evening before last (I saw it all) my father glanced at her and then looked at her, and said he must think of finding her a husband one of these days, and she looked straight back at him and said she was not going to give up rock climbing for any pair of pants *he* was likely to bring home. Was that not splendid? And all, I think, because of you. Thank you, thank you. By the way, did you notice anything wrong with her? My father did look at her in the strangest—but how I babble on. You must forgive me if I have said anything inappropriate. I make it a practice not to talk about my family.

My family and your family. My line and your line, separated for so many ages that I think your hair has become red and mine black. Then together again. Ah, ah! Ah! There is something about the idea. I tremble before it. Red hair mingled with black, like a fire in the night. How I think I wish you could have been with me, those spring nights when Tokyo burned. I watched it from the mountains, red and black halfway up into Scorpio. But it will burn again some day, and we can watch it together. I must see you. Ah! Your red hair glows before me like centuries of loneliness.

I hope the hydrangeas are taking root. They thrive on exactly the soil that is poison for daffodils. They will bloom and bloom, sending out blue veins that remind me of—I hardly know what. Would you like to learn flower arranging? My mother is very good at it. She can even arrange zinnias. She always sends me into the garden with shears, and waits in the tea room until I have finished. My sister once said she knew exactly how I felt, she felt the same way about rocks. Well, I am babbling on. Do keep your hydrangeas well fertilized, even if the smell is a bit trying. How foolish I felt on the train with that long-handled dipper! I wonder what would have happened if I had surrendered to my impulse to—no, I shall not tell you of it.

Take care of yourself in this unpredictable weather.

Hideko

October 10

In the hills the leaves are turning. The days grow shorter and shorter, and soon we will hear the call of the quail and the wild goose. Do not allow yourself to be plunged into melancholy, I pray you, by the cold, white autumn moon.

As to the business at hand:

I called several times only to find you away from home. What a pity. Yesterday I knocked and knocked, and when there was no answer I took the liberty of going in through the garden gate to see your hydrangeas. Well! I must say I was surprised. I sniffed and sniffed, and could detect no evidence that they had received any care other than that which I myself gave them some three weeks ago. I said to myself: "Now *there* is the difference between the Occident and the Orient!" I thought it necessary to put more dirt on the daffodils. Not being able to find your dipper, I had no other recourse. The mound over the daffodils may at first distract you (did you notice when we planted them what an odd configuration they made?), but you will get used to it, and, as I have said, I had no other recourse. I took the dirt from under the foundations, where it will not be noticed.

I had the strangest feeling that someone was watching me from your study. Did you notice anything missing when you came home?

I would have brought more chicken manure but for the fact that my youngest sister is no longer keeping chickens. Had I told you? My father used to eat the eggs raw, especially when he came home late at night, and to remark that he wasn't the man he used to be. My oldest sister killed all the chickens and will not allow an egg in the house. I think she is quite right.

Here it is the full moon again. How things have changed this last month! When the moon was last full, we seemed to be marching ahead, with your encouragement and Mrs. MacArthur's. My mother was to be next—a most difficult problem, to be sure, but I was really so very hopeful. And now, will you imagine what has happened? My father arranged for my sister to meet a man with an eye to reviewing him as a possible suitor. We all went along, of course. I think the man seemed to have very progressive, anti-feudal ideas, but he had an unfortunate way of touching the tips of his fingers to his lips, and giggling. My sister, I swear it, looked at him only once during the evening. And will you imagine what has happened? She has agreed to marry him! Yes!

How am I to explain it? Have you kept something from me? Have you deceived me? I would be quick to forgive most injuries, but not this, no, not this.

Well, one thing is clear. I am doing no good along the periphery. I must strike at the heart of the matter, the source of the trouble.

It is very quiet. The moon is shining on the late chrysanthemums, and the crickets are chirping. Usually at this time of night my sister would be at her trumpet, but she is getting her ropes ready for one last go at the rocks before the snow comes. My father, who got home early this morning, has fallen asleep over his newspaper. I wonder why he isn't snoring? Maybe he never snores, and it has until now not been quiet enough for me to know. And yet his lip trembles every time he breathes out.

Take care of yourself in the growing autumn cold.

Hideko

October 13

The autumn winds come down upon us, bringing dust from the hills. Do not breathe too freely of it, I advise you most urgently.

As to the business at hand:

We have been terribly busy. Not of course that there is much for me to do. I help my sister make tea for the priests, and that is about the sum of it. Oh, well. I have done enough already. Do you think they will be sufficiently grateful when they find out?

I should so like to be at the crematory. I cannot put down the feeling that I have allowed myself to be maneuvered into an unfavorable position. I cannot help feeling that I may be left behind to keep the tea boiling. Oh, well. I think there will be other opportunities.

Do you remember your profound remark, when we first met, about education reform? "You can't make an omelette without breaking eggs," you said. I have thought about it so often. Indeed I have thought so often these past few days about you, and your red hair. I must see you. I will see you.

I think that by this time your daffodils will need additional cover and (you are so lazy) food, essential to their deflowering.

Take care of yourself in this time of chill and darkness.

Hideko

[1961]

from Imaginary Speeches for a Brazen Head

PHILIP WHALEN

Roy made himself drunk. He drank sake out of expensive Japanese folk pottery, ate octopus arms, chicken giblets, and shrimp teriyaki. While he ate and drank, he read a new little magazine from New York. All those young people who might have been his own children had sent him their poems and plays, news from home. He was very drunk and very happy.

He aimed the small powerful reading lamp into the garden, the stone wash-basin under shrub leaves—where was he?—would he step out onto (the fallen twiglets and needles of hemlock and fir trees mixed with moss and vine maple leaves and old fern fronds) Mt. Baker National Forest? Into a Japanese village, a northern suburb of the Capital, Heian Kyo, founded eleven hundred years ago by the Divine Emperor Kammu, for coffee (known to the West for two hundred years) under three kinds of light fixtures, *Bessa Me Mucho* by Muzak and blue gauze curtains blocking the neon trolley cars. "Why don't all the people employed by this outfit run stark raving gaga after a half hour on duty in this place? Which might as well be Canoga Park or Brentwood or Sherman Oaks, all desperately new and modern and nowhere fake crystal chandeliers and real chrysanthemums, true rubber trees, bromeliads and cycads of the Lower Carboniferous and a few doilies of machine-made lace all standing over what had been a hand-made landscape garden of the earlier Muromachi period . . . as long as you are *inside* the building . . . outside are frogs in the rice paddies, the honey buckets' wild perfume. What a rhapsody of times and styles," Roy thought. "Not even Perez Prado, but a nameless rhumba band. And light from a Coleman lantern, wide band across the mountain top illuminates the eyes of a six-point buck, his forefoot on the second step of the stairs nosily searching for salt, for Perez, Mene and Tekel, for Paris mossy lichen granite under hoof, ten minutes after eight P.M. on Wednesday night—to the very day!"

Roy had finished his coffee; his head throbbed and sang. "Eleven years ago to the very day. It took three hours for the sun to go down; it quit, finally, twenty minutes ago, the glass in the windows on four sides of me totally black, the green paint of the woodwork gone gray, colorless under Coleman light anchored to rock top of mountain under thin boards under my feet under my sleeping ear tonight, floating on white rope net the lightnings of Heaven and Earth and Zodiacal Time: as I remember the place where I sit now was once the parking lot for Mount Hiei Taxi Company but if I walk a block and a half to more coffee in a place which also remembers the now nonexistent parking lot, these blue plastic lights and gauze will (*o-shibori!* Boiled hot hand towel served up in limp plastic condom pops MERRY CHRISTMAS wet sprinkle fireworks) DISAPPEAR. Forever. Do I have any money in my pockets. Can I pay the bill."

Roy was still two-thirds drunk and uncomfortable; he wanted out of that condition. He would have more coffee. He staggered along beside the wide, nearly deserted street, to another coffee-ya, a small television joint where six Japanese drivers were watching American soldiers "winning" what the local newspapers (Roy sourly noted) refer to nowadays as a remotely historical "Pacific War."

"At least one of these guys is old enough to have been there," Roy thought. "And so am I. The rest look too young to have known more about it than kids fifteen or sixteen years old may have heard on the Imperial Radio. The curious thing about these men is that they seem to believe what it is they're seeing right now as being immediately present, this reconstruction of what was happening twenty years ago. Now here we all are, drinking the same expensive coffee which gives us all the same expensive cardiac heebie-jeebies. Only the lady behind the counter doesn't care to look, she's busy making coffee. One boy turns the pages of a magazine while he watches. Sweet potato steam whistle cart passes by, beyond the black window and its machine lace curtain; station break tooth paste ads, and then the war continues. We've learned nothing. Sweet potato whistle. The only reality is mud swamp New Guinea death? Tarawa Kwajalein, the boy with the magazine raptly picks his nose. I wonder where they all are. I watch their watching faces, what connection has any of this fraudulent movie with any real experience, any life or hope or recollection: echoing gunfire, machine gun rattle and rifle ricochet—the film editor cuts back and forth from face to gun barrel to running squirming figures among vines, bamboos. The connection is the language. In this movie, both sides are speaking Japanese. I understand the American faces and gestures, but the voices are incomprehensible. The background music clues me in; we are winning: Whitey triumphs again (but he's talking Japanese)."

Roy felt too embarrassed to stay any longer. He went to another larger place further up the street where was the folk guitar Joan Baez Revolt of the intellectual young; the clientele was all university people drinking coffee and tea and discussing Hegel and Marx. They liked Joan Baez because her guitar sounded to them rather Japanese and like a koto; they hadn't any idea what she was singing, except that *Time* magazine said she was great and new and modern. Roy talked with some of the students in halting

English and Japanese. They claimed that they were majoring in economics. It turned out that they knew nothing about the subject, but they were all communists. They knew nothing about communist theory, either, but they all agreed that it was European and progressive and that all the world, particularly China, was making great progress under the communist system.

This coffee shop also served everything out of folk pottery. There was a beamed ceiling and a fireplace and furniture of a kind which the maker imagined must inhabit Swiss chalets. There were lace curtains, an expensive stereophonic phonograph, potted rubber trees, cycads, a Cryptomeria tree masquerading as a Christmas tree with blinking lights, and Easter lilies blooming in a big jar. Small vases of chrysanthemums stood on each table. The Joan Baez Revolution disappeared, to be replaced by Miles Davis & Co. The stereo loudspeakers trademarked *Chrysler* vibrated and throbbed and chimed *Bags Groove*. (Major Hoople remembering the Crimean War— "kaff, kaff! Egad!")

Roy woke up in the middle of the night. What did he want. Why was he afraid of the Great Mahatma. Why should he feel that he was in a false position vis-à-vis that Figure. He was hungover, his head hurt a little bit, his ears felt full of water, but actually his head was full of light and the light had awakened him.

Roy went to the bathroom. He took two aspirin tablets. He saw from the study windows that there had been a fall of snow while he'd been asleep.

"All that the Grand Mahatma requires—or anybody else wants—is my sincerity?" Roy asked himself. "Where's that at. I move from my own center which is a seated figure that doesn't move, needs not—but this is clap-trap. Cold water with aspirin is more exactly what I 'did.'"

He wondered why he should feel afraid of the hour, then decided that he wasn't really afraid. He turned on the lights and sat down to accept the fact that he was awake in the middle of the night and that there was nothing wrong with being awake any time. He would keep the appointment that he had later that morning. He wouldn't oversleep, he wouldn't be late. The alarm clock was working just fine. He felt that it was quite important that he no longer felt unhappy or afraid. It wasn't a fit of insomnia, it wasn't a nightmare, it wasn't a "Dark Night of the Soul," he was just awake. The house was very cold; he might turn on the heat.

Later in the morning he was surprised to find no trace of snow or frost on the ground outside. He had made a mistake, seeing moonlight on the stones and moss.

[1985]

Indirect Method

FRANCIS KING

This is a room. What is this?

It is a room.

This is a hotel room. What kind of room is this?

It is a hotel room.

This is an expensive room—the most expensive room in which I have ever stayed. Is this room expensive?

Yes, it is expensive.

Direct Method. Liz hears Mildred's voice or the ghost of Mildred's voice (so long silent, letters to Canada unanswered, perhaps Mildred dead) teaching her pupils in the dining room.

Who is Mildred?

Mildred is the teacher.

She is (was) also the lodger, who had come out to Japan with an Air Force husband, had abandoned him or been abandoned by him (the story changed as rapidly and inexplicably as her spirits would soar or sink) and had then set up as a freelance teacher.

Direct Method. But Mildred said that people as indirect as the Japanese did not take to it. They preferred word-for-word translation. Fish have neither hands nor feet—*Sakana niwa te mo ashi mo arimasen.* That kind of thing. Mildred swore that she had seen that sentence in a course for beginners prepared by some Japanese professor. But so many of the strange or exciting things that Mildred related had happened only in her imagination. Perhaps (Tom and Liz sometimes speculated) the marriage to the Air Force officer had also happened only there.

This is a room. This is a hotel room. This is an expensive room.

There are two beds, each neatly folded down to make a white sandwich-like triangle at either corner. There are two armchairs and two bedside tables, each with a lamp on it and each with a Gideon Bible in its drawer. In the bathroom there are two face towels and two bath towels and two glasses which have a paper seal over them, like the paper seals over the bidet and lavatory bowl.

I expect you wish to be left alone, Professor Ito told her down in the lobby. The truth is that Professor Ito wished to leave her alone, because he wished to get back to his laboratory, even though it was already past nine. You must be tired and tomorrow your program is a busy one. He finds it hard to adjust to the fact that the young, untidy woman with all those children, who used to work up at the Baptist Hospital, should now be a leading authority on diabetes. In the past he patronized her, as he patronized her husband, also a doctor. He wants to continue to patronize her but feels, baffled and slightly exasperated, that he can no longer do so.

Liz does not really want to be left alone, because to be alone, except when she is working, is something to which she is not accustomed. If the room were less expensive, she might hear sounds from the rooms on either side of her: the flush of a lavatory, the throbbing of a radio, voices raised in anger or in love. But this is an expensive room.

The walls are covered in shimmering gray silk, so that, in the lamp-light, they look as if cooling water were trickling down them; but, in fact, the coolness comes from the air-conditioner grill, from which a strand of pale blue ribbon streams outward to show that it is functioning. There is a darker gray silk covering the lamp shades, and the thick carpet is of the same color. There is a crimson and white *toile de Jouy* on the chairs, and the curtains and the headboards of the beds are of the same material. The design, of a woman on a swing, her skirts billowing up around her, while a courtier kneels and plays some kind of stringed instrument, suggests a Fragonard.

Liz begins to unpack. She has traveled on the bullet train from Tokyo and she feels as though she herself had been shot by some invisible gun through all those hundreds and hundreds of miles, to arrive, blunted and bruised, on this target. She feels no hunger, only an insistent thirst. In the bathroom she has seen a little spigot, with assurances in Japanese, English, French, and German, that the water is both drinkable and iced. She breaks the seal of the glass and fills it. Then, in the room with no climate, she drinks the water with no taste. The air is filtered, the water is filtered. The cold rim of the now empty glass against her lips, she stares at the television set. It has a blind across it, not of the *toile de Jouy* but of a crimson velvet, as though something obscene might be going on, unseen, on its screen.

She will ring Yamada-san, she will ring Mrs. Payne at the Baptist Hospital, she will ring the Bensons, she will ring Yoshiko. . . . No, she will do none of those things. Not yet. But she will ring Osamu.

The telephone has the texture and color of mother-of-pearl. Oh, Osamu, she used to say, do please try to get this number for me. These Japanese phones drive one round the bend. But this one works perfectly. It is a woman who answers ("*Moshi! Moshi!*") and of course that must be Osamu's wife, whom Liz has never met but whose color photograph she has seen, beautiful in a kimono with a dragon writhing up one side.

One moment! Please!

Osamu's wife, Noriko, must know who she is. She sounds excited.

Mrs. Butler. . . . Osamu is giggling with pleasure. You have come at last!

This was our houseboy. Who was he?

He was our houseboy.

He learned English by the Direct Method. He learned it by talking it to us and the children. He did not learn it from Mildred or any school.

Osamu wants to come round to the hotel immediately; but Liz still has that feeling that she has been fired from a gun—it is almost ten, and she knows, because he has written to tell her, that he now lives in a remote suburb out near Arashiyama. Tomorrow, she says. And he says, Yes, tomorrow, he will call in on his way to the office.

That means, since this is Japan and not England, that he will call in at half past seven.

You can have some breakfast with me.

He is not sure about that; but he will call in.

They sat at the breakfast table and Osamu sat with them. That was in the last months, not when he first came to them and sat in the kitchen. Even when he sat with them, he liked to have rice and pickles for breakfast. The pickles had a pungent, slightly rotten smell that Tom would say, in private, put him off his food. Osamu also made himself soup for breakfast, pouring hot water onto powder from a packet and then slurping it noisily. Tom said that slurping put him off his food, too.

Liz replaces the telephone on its cradle. There is a throbbing at her temples and, though she has just drunk that glass of iced water, her mouth and even her throat already feel dry. It must be the air conditioning. Or nerves. Only now does she notice that, under a bank of drawers of the built-in furniture, there is a small refrigerator. It will be stacked with bottles that she will never open.

The *toile de Jouy* curtains are drawn back, in such perfectly symmetrical folds that either the maid must have spent minutes arranging them like that or else they are never closed. Beyond them, instead of an ordinary window, there is an exquisite shoji—a frame of delicate blond wood, each of its squares filled with a nacreous paper that perfectly matches the telephone. It is so silent in this room that she wonders what lies behind the shoji. Some miniature garden, devotedly tended by a wizened man with the legs of an ancient boiling fowl? (Osamu raked the garden with fierce rhythmical strokes.) Some tributary of the Kamogawa river, with fierce hump-back bridge and willows drooping their splayed fingers along its margins? (Osamu, flushed and slightly unsteady from two whiskeys, leaned beside her over the parapet, squinting down into the barely moving water.)

Liz crosses to the window. PLEASE DO NOT OPEN. The prohibition is there in English and, of course, like every other instruction in the room, also in Japanese, French, and German. But she must get it open, she must see what lies behind it. She struggles and at last, squeaking in its grooves, the shoji begins to slide away.

Four—five?—feet away from her is a high, totally blank wall. She puts her head out, twists it uncomfortably, tries to crane upward. There is a plume of smoke at the top, which uncurls and then slowly dissipates. She looks down. Far below, there is a cobbled alley, but she cannot make out where it comes from or where it goes.

She pulls the shoji back again. She must forget that blank wall and the strange plume of smoke at the top. She must forget that alley, which seems a strange passageway too narrow for anything but rats. She must still imagine that miniature garden or that tributary of the river or even a view of distant Mount Hiei, where Osamu pointed, Look, Mrs. Butler! A monkey! Many monkeys! and there they were, gray and shrilly chattering, as they swung themselves from liana to liana and from branch to branch.

She must keep calm. She must have no claustrophobia. No one could stifle in a room like this, so long as that pale blue ribbon streams out from the grill of the air conditioner.

This is a room. What is this?

It is a prison.

No, this is a room. This is an expensive room. What is this?

It is a prison.

Osamu wore wooden clogs, an open-necked aertex shirt (one of Tom's cast-offs), and a pair of jeans with a St. Martin label. He wears black brogues, a network of tiny cracks across their insteps, a blue pin-stripe suit, the trousers of which are short enough to reveal his dark-blue hose with their scarlet clocks on them, and a white polythene shirt with a dark-blue tie, the knot of which has the explosive appearance of a bud that is about to burst open. Osamu had hair cropped so close to his head that you could see the scalp. His hair is now brushed back from an incision-like parting and it is heavily greased. Osamu was handsome. He is handsome.

You have not changed at all, he says. Fifteen, sixteen years! Just the same!

But they have both changed. Her hair is graying and she has an air of quiet authority that he finds as disconcerting as she finds his sudden attacks of giggling.

Have some coffee. Tea? Something? Anything?

But he shakes his head and looks at his watch, as, across the table from him, she fiddles with the cutlery. He is afraid of being late at the office, though he was often late for her and Tom.

He now asks about Tom and the children, laughing incredulously when she tells him that Anna is married and has a baby, that Adrienne is now at Oxford, and that Jerry now plays cricket for his school. All these things have been recorded in the occasional letters she has written to him. She now wonders if he has ever read those letters, as she has always read his.

He looks again at his watch. It is a multi-functional, digital one, and she knows what Tom's verdict would be on it: Vulgar. It has a gold bracelet but she doubts if the gold is gold all through.

Mrs. Butler . . .

She smiles and corrects him: Liz.

Liz . . . But he finds that difficult. He has to go, he says. He has to open up the office, it is he who has the keys. No, no, she must not get up from the table, she must continue with her breakfast.

But she follows him out into the foyer, where he tells her: I will see you on Saturday. A statement, not a question. He adds: Unfortunately, every weekday I am busy.

I am busy on weekdays too. Professor Ito has already given her her program, a sheet for each day, with the sheets all stapled together inside a cardboard cover to make what looks like a paperback.

I will bring my car and we can go wherever you wish.

Your car! You have a car now?

He giggles. Very old, he says.

Osamu usually drove the car for them, because Tom hated negotiating those narrow alleys, and she had still to learn. He liked to drive fast, to prevent bigger cars from overtaking, to overtake bigger cars. He had a number of minor accidents, until Tom threatened to deduct the cost of the next from his wages; but each repair bill was far in excess of what they paid him for a month.

She presses a handkerchief to her upper lip, saying: So early in the morning and yet already it is hot.

He tells her to please go back to her breakfast but, tactless, she insists: She must see this car of his.

In the hotel car park there are a number of American limousines among the new or almost new Toyotas and Datsuns and Hondas. A Japanese, in gleaming white, short-sleeved shirt, jeans, and rubber gloves is washing down a bronze Rolls Royce with a CD number-plate.

Osamu repeats: My car is very old.

It looks to her like any car in any street in London; but then, scrutinizing it more carefully, she sees that, yes, there are signs of rust here and there.

It is all I can afford, he tells her.

I can't see anything wrong with it. We have an absolutely ancient Mini to run around in. She does not mention that she and Tom also have a brand-new Peugeot.

I will call for you on Saturday. About eleven. A statement, not a question.

Lovely. A statement too. It is really for him and not for Professor Ito and his colleagues in the medical faculty of Kyoto University that she has come all this way.

Osamu's wife is wearing a peach-colored kimono. She totters toward Liz, knees close to her and hands clasped before her, and then, eyes lowered, she bows. Her face is too long and aquiline to be beautiful in the West but Liz knows that here it is beautiful. She has an air of extreme fragility and yet of—no, not unbending, but bending strength. There is a little girl of four, with her hair cut straight across her forehead, and she too is wearing a kimono. There is a boy of seven, who is wearing patent-leather shoes with straps across the instep, black velveteen shorts, and a red-and-black spotted bow tie. The boy has his mother's aquiline features.

Osamu continues to giggle with a mixture of embarrassment and pleasure. Liz has presents for all of them; a Pierre Cardin scarf for Noriko (presumably it is only on special occasions that she dresses in kimono); a doll for the little girl; three models of vintage cars for the boy; and for Osamu a cashmere pullover. It is difficult to tell if any of them, other than the little girl, is pleased. Perhaps the other three are burdened with that terrible Japanese problem of obligation and its return. Perhaps, as they appraise what Liz has insisted that they must unwrap, though it is not the Japanese custom to do so in front of the donor, and as they exclaim How beautiful! and How kind!, they are secretly trying to calculate: How much could this have cost? The little girl rocks her doll in her arms, peering down as it opens and shuts its blank, blue eyes.

Osamu explains that his wife speaks little English.

Never mind, you can translate for her.

Sukoshi, sukoshi, says Noriko—meaning Little, little.

They stand awkwardly for a while in the foyer, as though not knowing what to say or do next. Liz eventually suggests that perhaps the children would like an ice cream cone or some lemonade and Osamu and Noriko some coffee or tea.

But let us go, Osamu says.

He then addresses Noriko in Japanese, in a low, hissing voice, his head turned away from Liz. Noriko nods calmly, smiles, bows.

They will stay here, Osamu tells Liz. They will wait for us.

But wouldn't they like to come too?

It is better if we drive alone. The children may get tired or sick. My wife will take them into the garden. Have you seen the garden of the hotel?

She resists the temptation to tell him what lies behind that exquisite shoji of her room. Not yet, she answers.

It is very beautiful.

In the car park, he walks over, not to the car in which he first came to see her, but to a large gleaming Datsun, that looks as if it had just come out of a showroom window. He fumbles with the key, as one does when unlocking a door unfamiliar to one.

He flushes. My car has broken down. It is always breaking down—I told you it was old! And so I have borrowed this car from—from a friend.

This, of course, is not true. He has hired it, because he feels that for her, a foreigner and a famous doctor, a guest of the university, to travel in that beat-up car of his would cause a terrible loss of face: for her and so for him and perhaps even for the university, if anyone were to see her in it and recognize who she was.

It's a super car.

She gets in. How much can he have paid for it? His salary cannot be large. But it would make things worse to offer to pay a half share herself.

We shall go to the house. A statement, not a question.

The house is the house in which she and Tom and the three children and this businessman, who was once simultaneously their houseboy and a student, all used to live. Mildred also used to live there but somehow Liz tends to forget that. The house stood in a fashionable suburb of the city; but because of the construction of a ring-road through it and the destruction of some of the older mansions to make way for apartment blocks, it is no longer fashionable.

They drive slowly and the only words they utter is when one or the other of them points to some once familiar landmark.

What happened to the Servite Mission? Liz asks.

It has moved. Too big a house, too little money.

Oh, look, there's that bar where we used to eat that awful spaghetti when I was too lazy to cook!

It is now a very expensive restaurant. Western style.

Well, that spaghetti certainly wasn't Western style, was it?

Do you remember the bath-house? Osamu points.

Late at night, as she sat reading a book in the sitting room or lay beside Tom in the bedroom, she would hear the clatter of the Japanese boy's *geta* as he returned up the road from the bath.

And the dog pound? Now it is Liz who points.

Osamu went to the pound and found their labrador there. He never liked dogs but the children had been fretful all day because of its loss.

They begin to drive down the road leading to the house. It seems narrower, dustier, and more untidy than she remembers it, and the trees seem much taller. The wooden fence round the house was solid and high. Now it dips crazily in places and at one corner there is a hole in it, which has been plugged with a ball of rusty barbed wire. Liz begins to feel slightly sick and slightly frightened. She has seen over one of those dips that the garden is a wilderness. It is as if all that work that she and Tom and Osamu put into it must have been an illusion—like those dreams she sometimes has of working out intricate formulae, unrecallable when she wakes.

Osamu stops the car and she suddenly notices that he has about him a breathy excitement, as though he had reached the top of some peak and the air were too strong for him. He gets out and then he opens the door for her and reluctantly, her face ashen and pinched, she descends. He takes her arm, but only lightly, in order to guide her over the unevennesses of the road and then up the unevennesses of the broken steps. There are a number of bells, instead of the single brass one that Osamu used to polish with so much care and pride, and these bells are all of different shapes and sizes, with nameplates beside them, some in Western letters and some in Japanese characters. He hesitates and then—just as she is saying Do we want to go in?—he presses one of the bells. Miss McCready, he says. But she has already seen the name, the only neatly written one among them.

Miss McCready opens the door, using her left hand while her right arm, perpetually trembling, is pressed into her side. There has been a sound of shuffling before she has appeared and Liz, being a doctor, knows that that is what is called festination and that Miss McCready is probably in the first stages of Parkinson's disease. The old woman scowls at Liz, still incapable of believing that that scatty English-woman who was always late for something or forgetting something at the Baptist Hospital, is now famous. Miss McCready was matron at the Baptist Hospital, where she had more power than any doctor; but now she has retired—though she still sometimes goes up there to "help out," as she puts it, or to "interfere," as the nurses put it.

Oh my! she cries out, and her left hand flies to her mouth. Liz had never heard any other American woman say Oh, my! except in the cinema and here is Miss McCready, with her high color and her high bosom, and her high hair-do, a ziggurat of graying plaits, saying it again, after all these years.

Osamu explains that Mrs. Butler would like to see her old home and Miss McCready says, Well, she's very welcome to see my part of it! though there is no welcome in her tone. A tabby cat, long-backed and bushy, has now whisked out from the door behind her and stares at Liz with what seems to be an equal lack of welcome.

Liz wants to tell her, Oh, please don't bother, I'd rather remember it as I knew it but Osamu is nodding to her to go in and Miss McCready is already shuffling off, with the cat rubbing itself against her calves as it zigzags behind her.

The house was huge and rambling, part Japanese and part Western in style. A Japanese psychiatrist built it in the thirties, living in part of it and keeping his patients in the rest. It should have been an unhappy house, since it must have contained much unhappiness; even the psychiatrist had been lost at Guam, leaving behind a wife, who later killed herself, and an embittered mother, who was their landlady and obviously loathed them. But now, with curtains and plywood doors marking off the territories of the various tenants, it seems strangely shrunken.

This was once their sitting room—an airy, uncluttered Japanese-style room, where they would force their awkward Western guests to squat by the open windows in the summer or around a charcoal brazier in the winter. But the shoji have now gone from the windows and in their place are modern aluminum frames and glass; and a one-bar electric fire has superseded the brazier. There is a room divider, with a few books and old copies of the *Reader's Digest* and *Time* magazine on its shelves, along with a clutter of Japanese dolls and old postcards, propped up at random, and pottery of no value. On this side of the divider there is a bed, which also serves during the day as a divan, a crocheted rug thrown over it; two armchairs, sagging in the middle; a black and white television set. On the other side, there is a sink and a cooker and a pedal bin and some shelves with pots and pans and stores on them. Miss McCready now lives in a mess of cat's hair and cat's smell, dust, worn linoleum, and a bed obviously unmade under its crocheted cover.

A panic seizes Liz as she looks around her. She is surrounded by fragments—the tokonoma still remains and, yes, that little window beside it does not have an aluminum frame like the rest—but she cannot get the fragments to fit. It is as though a precious cup had been smashed and she held certain jagged pieces in her hand but not all of them, and then tried to recreate, not the cup—that was impossible—but just her memory of it.

Miss McCready grudgingly offers some Nescafé but Liz, unable to speak, shakes her head. Miss McCready then suggests that she might ask some of the other occupants if they would mind if Liz looked over their apartments and bed-sitting rooms; but Liz shakes her head at that too. The garden, yes, the garden—that is really what she would like to see.

Oh, the garden. . . . Miss McCready sighs. Well, you know how it is? If everyone is responsible, then no one is responsible. She can no longer do anything about it herself—she just isn't up to it any longer—and, since that nice French student left, well, the place has just gone to rack and ruin. Jimmy prefers it like that, of course, it's his jungle now, but still—she shakes her head, so that it seems to tremble in precise time to her hand—it's sad, really sad. It has taken Liz some time to realize that Jimmy is the cat.

Eventually Osamu and Liz go out into the garden, while Miss McCready, Jimmy held under her chin with her left hand, while the right arm goes on trembling, watches them balefully. She never liked Liz, never trusted her, schemed against her and gossiped about her. Oh she always had a good conceit of herself, that one, and no doubt has an even better one now!

Osamu and Liz walk through the waist-high grass and brambles to the pond. They look out over it, its surface now tented with a thick, matted green, with a gaze of identical sorrow. This was how the pond had been when first they had come; but then Osamu said that he would clean it out and they would have goldfish in it and water lilies and other aquatic plants.

Tom took the children to the annual fair at the Baptist Hospital but, though Liz ought also to have gone—Miss McCready noticed her absence and remarked on it more than once—she said that it was much too hot and that in any case she had to wash her hair and mend some socks and do a number of other things. Osamu announced that he was going to clean out the pond. It was something that he had been planning to do for weeks but somehow he had never got round to it, so enervating was that long, humid summer.

Liz had washed her hair and then, leaving the mending and all the other little chores, she had settled down on the veranda with a novel and a thermos of iced lemonade; but she knew later, though not at the time, that all this had really been only a pretense and a pretext. She could not see the pond from the veranda, since it was round at one side of the house; but eventually she got up and, book in hand, she strolled under the trellis of rambler roses and over the yellowing lawn, until there she found him, thigh-deep in the pond. He was hacking and tugging at its vegetation with an extraordinary savagery, his hand raising a bill-hook and whirling it down, time and time again. His near-naked body—he was wearing only a *fundoshi* or loin cloth—was smeared with a mingling of sweat and mud, and mud even caked his eyebrows and hair.

She looked at him appraisingly and he looked up at her, the bill-hook raised. Neither of them smiled.

I hope there are no leeches in that water.

He laughed. Probably did not understand what leeches meant.

How about a drink? That must be hot work.

He hesitated; then he nodded and clambered, dripping, out of the pond.

He sat on the log of a tree that they had recently had to have cut down—the center of its trunk had contained a greenish, friable substance that disintegrated into dust in one's hand—and she went indoors to bring out a tray ladened with the gin fizzes that he had now learned to like. The mud was almost dry on his squat, muscular body when she came back. He looked like some aborigine, perched there on the log.

They began to drink in silence, he still seated there and she standing; and then, when he had almost finished, she put out a hand to him, effortlessly, as she had so often dreamed of doing and thought that she would never dare to do. So easy! She put out a hand to him and he took the hand in his own mud-smeared one and she drew him to his feet and they walked like that, hands held, she always a little ahead of him, back into the house. . . .

Osamu tugs at a plant growing at the edge of the pond. It is fleshy, with a purple shine along its sharply serrated leaves, each like a miniature saw, and it resists him by slithering from his grasp time and time again. He laughs, looking down at his hands which are now covered in an evil-smelling glue. He takes a handkerchief and wipes them.

All that work. . . . And for nothing.

Well, it was beautiful for a while. Do you remember the water lilies? She remembers the water lilies, stiff and waxen, and how he would wade among them, raking away the slime.

She has an impulse to hold out her hand to this thick-set businessman in his businessman's suit, as once she did to the muscular, near naked student; she wonders how he would react. But then they both stroll, separate from each other, back toward the house.

Miss McCready gives them a baleful stare, as she stands on the veranda, her left hand shielding her small, extremely blue eyes.

It's so sad about the whole garden. But I'm beyond it. Seventy-six last birthday. And that Belgian slug upstairs—Miss McCready raises her voice, instead of lowering it, as she looks up to the balcony above her—knows of no exercise other than lifting a beer mug to his lips.

They go back into what was once the sitting room. Osamu and Liz lay there, the tatami matting smeared with mud and Liz smeared with mud, until, suddenly in terror, they hear footsteps above them. Mildred, whom they had supposed still to be out, must have come home earlier than expected. Then Osamu ran to his room and Liz ran to the bathroom. What's all this mud doing here? one of children eventually asked; and Liz then explained how the labrador had leapt into the pond with Osamu and must have brought it in.

You must find it strange to return after all these years, Miss McCready says.

Very strange.

You haven't changed. It is clear that she feels that people ought to change. Especially Liz.

Haven't I? I feel that I have.

In the car, before he starts up the engine, Osamu takes some paper tissues out of the back pocket of his trousers and again, carefully wipes whatever is left of the greenish stickiness of the pond plant off his hands. Then he presses the start. Interesting, he says.

Sad.

Liz can feel the tears, unshed but waiting, pricking at the corners of her eyes. She turns her head away from him.

While Noriko prepares the lunch in the apartment, Osamu and Liz go out for a walk with the children. Osamu is reluctant for the children to come and Noriko, speaking in a low voice to him while her eyes gaze at Liz with a gentle sweetness, seems to share that reluctance. But the children are insistent, the little girl even setting up a low keening when it looks for a moment as though her brother will be taken but she will be left behind.

Oh, do let the both of them come. Why not? Liz intervenes.

Do you really want them to come? Osamu finds it difficult to believe this.

Of course.

She and Osamu walked this path once before with some children, but they were hers, not his, and it was night. Tom was away in Tokyo, standing in for an American doctor on furlough, and because it was so hot and humid in the Kyoto house, they had decided to go out and see the cormorant-fishing on the river at Arashiyama. The forest was thick on either side of them, so that it was difficult to tell how much of the fatigue that all of them felt was due to its pressure and how much to the pressure of the atmosphere.

Now it is all changed; there is no path and no forest attempting to obliterate it. Instead, there is a paved alley between the block of apartments from which they have come and the other nine making up the complex belonging to the firm for which Osamu is working. Liz feels a desolating sense of loss. It's all so different, she says. I can hardly recognize it.

Osamu stoops and picks up the little girl, who is already wailing that she can't keep up with them. Japan is changing, he answers. He is proud of a change that makes it no longer necessary for students like himself to do menial jobs for foreigners like Liz and Tom in order to make their way through college.

The little boy edges toward Liz then, suddenly, to her amazement, she feels his hand in hers. It is a curiously rough, cold little hand, with nails, that, though scrupulously clean, would be thought in need of cutting back in England. It might almost be the claw of a bird. She smiles down at him but he turns his head away, as though fearful of smiling back at her.

Well, the river is the same, with a leaden haze over the forest on either side of it and a few bathers in its waters. On either bank there are still bamboo rectangles raised up on stilts, canopies of straw above them, where people squat for refreshments; there are still omnibuses, with neatly groomed girls in uniforms officiously blowing whistles to summon errant passengers; there is still that sense of barely checked, menacing wildness—as though suddenly a typhoon might snap off the tops of the trees, a tidal wave might submerge the pleasure craft, or a volcano might erupt from one of the mountain peaks.

They hired a boat, because at that period it cost only a few shillings to do so. Night had fallen and all over the vast expanse of the river there were other boats, their cormorants, perched on their prows, silhouetted, like sinister heraldic emblems, by the braziers flaring beside them. The children were delighted; Adrienne even wanted to stroke one of the birds but Osamu told her not to, the bird might attack her. Each bird had what looked like a collar round its neck and Osamu explained that this was a device to prevent it from swallowing any fish that it caught. All this is only for tourists, he said. The men do not make money from the sale of the fish but from the hire of the boats. The oars creaked, the birds emitted a guttural sound that seemed to be a distorted echo of that creaking. One of the three men in charge of their boat banged with an oar on its side.

Suddenly Osamu, realizing that the children were totally absorbed in the spectacle of the chained, gagged birds diving for fish, turned to her: Why cannot I come to England?

Oh, Osamu! Why! We want you to come, of course we want you to come, but what sort of life would you have over there? You don't want to be a houseboy for the rest of your days—even if we could afford to employ you. Tom's right. It's much better for you to take this job with this pharmaceutical company that he's found for you. You don't want to cut adrift from your family and—and your whole *life* out here in Japan. It would be hopeless.

She, too, was hopeless. In eleven days they would board the P&O liner in Kobe and she would probably never see him again.

Osamu sighed. She took his hand in hers but quickly he withdrew it. One of the children let out a squeal. Rockets were whizzing up into the leaden sky and then falling, in innumerable torrents of green, red, and gold over the river and the forests on either side of it and even the mountains beyond.

They are standing on the precise spot where they disembarked from the boat under that continuing rain of colored fire. Liz wonders if Osamu remembers. The boy lets go of Liz's hand, which has been sweating from the contact though his has remained strangely dry, and runs down to the water's edge. He kneels and stares at something—it looks like no more than an upturned tin—in the shallows. Osamu, seeing what he is doing, shouts something angry and the boy gets up. He is dirtying his beautifully pressed shorts and his long stockings.

They're such gorgeous children, Liz says.

He clearly does not like her saying that. Perhaps, like many Japanese, he is superstitious and fears that some malign fate may extract retribution. He looks at his multi-functional digital watch and tells her that it is time they went back, since Noriko said that the meal would be ready at half past one.

The children, hers not his, ran ahead of them, half excited and half fearful, up the path that wavered through the forest crowding on either side of it. Snakes, monkeys, wild dogs, wild cats! Or ghosts! They had been told by Osamu that you could always recognize a Japanese ghost because it had no feet. To frighten themselves like this only intensified the memory of the pleasure of watching those strange, cruel-beaked birds dive for the fish and then, so unexpectedly, that downpour of fire all around them. Liz turned to Osamu and put her hands on his shoulders. No one behind, no one in front. A miracle in Japan! She kissed him, holding him close to her, as though she were the man, confident and strong, and he the woman, shrinking and pliable.

Osamu lifts up the little girl, who has been wailing fretfully. She smiles at him, the tears still on her cheeks, puts out a hand and tugs at a lock of his hair. He does not mind, because when a child is young it can do what it wishes in Japan. It is only when it is older that it must learn self-control and circumspection.

The table is laid as it might be in the West with knives and forks and spoons and a cruet stand and white napkins fringed with lace. There are flowers on it and chairs around it. Osamu explains that Noriko has been taking lessons in Western cookery. Liz wonders if she has been taking these lessons against the coming of this English-woman who once employed and loved her husband.

There are lamb chops which are pinkish at the center because they have not been cooked long enough, and potatoes that have been cooked so long that they have been reduced to a watery flour. There is a bottle of acid red wine which, Liz noticed, Osamu does not offer to Noriko. Later, there is a lemon chiffon pie, the top of which tastes as if it were indeed made of chiffon. But all this does not matter. With a mingling of pain and tranquil consoling pleasure, Liz realizes that Osamu and Noriko are totally happy with each other. Noriko may complain laughingly that her husband is always coming home late, because he has to stay up so many nights playing mah jongg with prospective customers—whom he must usually allow to win. Osamu may complain that, though Noriko has a degree from Doshisha Women's College in history, she prefers to look after the house and children than to get a job. But they are only teasing each other, there is no acrimony in all this, neither wants the other any different—in the way that Liz and Tom so often want each other different. Liz now feels that, though she is sitting so close to Osamu and though the little girl is sitting between Osamu and Noriko, yet the husband and wife are somehow merging into each other, even as she looks at them and listens to them. Their bodies are coalescing, their faces are becoming superimposed on each other. She wonders if anyone has ever felt the same thing about herself and Tom. Perhaps Osamu did, so many years ago. It is also different now.

They drink coffee out of thimble-like cups of Kutani china. Liz has never liked modern Kutani china, usually so bright and overdecorated; but she feels no inclination to find fault with it this afternoon, anymore than with the sports pennants hanging on either side of the door (Osamu played football for Kyoto University), the two garish dolls, one male and one female, each imprisoned in a cell of glass on either end of the mantlepiece, or the view of the Houses of Parliament—in fact, a dishcloth once sent by her as the kind of present that can be easily parceled—which has been carefully pinned above the upright piano.

It is at this piano that the little boy in his black patent-leather shoes and his spotted bow tie now seats himself at his father's bidding. There is a hush, the little boy is nervous. Then, as he strikes the keys, legs dangling several inches from the floor, Liz realizes that what he is playing, with several wrong notes, is "God Save the Queen." When that is over and she has congratulated him and Osamu has patted his square, closely cropped head and Noriko has kissed him on the cheek, Liz knows, as one always knows in Japan, even though no word has been said, that it is time for her to go.

Noriko and children accompany her and Osamu down into the courtyard, where the car is parked. Noriko is going to bow her farewell, but on an impulse Liz goes forward and kisses the Japanese woman, an arm thrown around her shoulder. The Japanese woman is plainly surprised but she is also pleased. Liz wonders if Osamu has ever spoken about their love-affair in that distant past. She doubts it. But the Japanese can convey and intuit so much without any words and Liz knows that Noriko knows and, more important, feels no resentment.

You have such a happy family, Liz says as the car begins the journey along the broad, blaring highway to Kyoto.

Yes. We are happy. He says it simply. A fact.

It was right that you didn't come to England with us. *We* were right—Tom and I. Though I wanted you to come.

But Osamu makes no answer to that. Perhaps he has genuinely forgotten that he ever begged them to take him; perhaps it is less embarrassing to pretend that he has forgotten. I wish to see England, he says. One day.

Oh, do come and stay with us! We'd love that.

Of course. Thank you. I think that in maybe five years my firm will send me.

Yes, it has all been mapped out for him, as for every other employee of the company. They all know how many years it will be before, on some pretext or another, they are dispatched to the West.

I *have* enjoyed this day!

I am sorry that Tom-san could not come with you.

Yes, he so much wanted to come. But they'd only pay my fare, not his. And it's now become so expensive out here in Japan. Unbelievable!

Do you remember when we could stay for one thousand yen in a Japanese inn?

Yes! With breakfast and dinner included. That used to be—oh, about a pound.

Tom said that Osamu had better drive her and the children to Ama-no-Hashidate and he would follow in the train the following day. Otherwise they might be charged for the unused rooms. There were three of these rooms, divided from each other by fusuma that could be pulled back, fragile on their grooves, to make a single room, beautiful in all its proportions, that looked out over still, smoky expanses of water, divided by a causeway. The first room, which was large, was for Tom and Liz; the next, which was larger, was for the children; and the small one, little more than a vestibule, was for Osamu. When they arrived and Liz saw the tiny room, she said, Oh, I do hope this is big enough for you, and Osamu, surprised, replied that it was a four-and-half-mat room and that, when he was a schoolboy, he had shared just such a room with his younger brother.

That night she went to him, tiptoeing through the room in which the three children slept, with the moonlight powdering their upturned faces with a gray, luminous dust. She slipped off her kimono, as, from the floor, he held out his hands to her. But, just as she was about to kneel down on the futon, she saw what looked like a raveled piece of black string on the whiteness of the pillow. Her hands went to her mouth when the string suddenly riggled. She pointed.

Osamu leapt up, naked, from the futon, seized one of the transparent, plastic slippers provided by the inn, and began to hit out wildly. It was a *mukade*, he said, and Liz knew that that meant a kind of poisonous centipede, though until now she had never seen one. Long after the insect was no more than a pulp on the tatami, he went on beating at it, as she had seen Japanese women, their faces flushed with a kind of obsessive malevolence, pound away at rice in a pestle, in order to reduce it to a pulp for rice cakes. There was a wail from the next-door room. He had woken one of the children. Liz slipped back into her kimono, slid the fusuma open and whispered: It's nothing, go back to sleep, don't worry. Then she whispered to Osamu that it was all too difficult, every sound could be heard, she must return to her room. The sight of that naked figure slashing out at the insect with flushed face and flailing arm, had filled her with more dread than the wail of the child. Yet a *mukade*, it was well known, could cause death with its sting, and it was natural enough that Osamu should have been so violent.

What happened to Mrs. Budden? Osamu suddenly asks. He means Mildred.

Liz explains that she has lost touch with her, letters have not been answered, perhaps—who knows?—she may be dead. She went back to Canada to live with a sister and, after all, she was no longer young even in those far-off times when she occupied the two top-floor rooms as a lodger.

Liz wonders why he should suddenly ask about her. Except that he was always convinced, however much Liz herself might pooh-pooh the idea, that Mildred knew about them. She watched, she listened: he was sure of that.

Osamu laughs: Direct Method, he says.

Yes. She believed in the Direct Method.

They reach the hotel and they are now going to say goodbye. They will not see each other again for—well, all those years that will elapse before Osamu's service to the Company is rewarded with a visit to England. He puts his hand in his pocket and he takes out a small, beautifully wrapped package.

A souvenir, he says.

What is it? I know I shouldn't open it now but may I break all the Japanese rules and do so?

He nods, smiling.

She sits down on a chair in the foyer and, her fingers trembling and clumsy, unties the ribbon and peels off first the layer of wrapping paper and then the tissue paper beneath it.

I remember that you collect them.

It is a Chinese snuff bottle, carved out of tourmaline in a pattern of water lilies. As she looks at it, she thinks of the pond and of the near-naked figure emerging from it, daubed with mud, with the fleshy pink-and-green lilies opening their mouths around him.

She and Tom no longer collect snuff bottles, because soon after their return from Japan they were so short of money that they had to auction off their whole collection. But she does not tell Osamu this, of course, as she begins carefully to rewrap the bottle first in its tissue paper and then in its wrapping paper and to retie the ribbon around it.

Tom will love it, she says. How kind you are!

No obligation now weighs on him: not from the Pierre Cardin scarf, not for the cashmere pullover, not for the doll, not for the three model vintage cars, not even for the hours—so few!—that she lay with him. This is a museum piece and he has paid it all off, the whole debt. She can understand why, though they are about to say goodbye, he has the air of a man who has just emerged from a law court, unexpectedly acquitted.

Dear Osamu . . .

Well . . .

He gives that embarrassed giggle. Then he says that he must get home, he is sure that she has many, many things to do, he hopes that she will enjoy the rest of her trip and that she will come back soon to Japan. She planned to ask him up to her room but now she knows that it would be humiliatingly pointless to do so.

The lift-boy glances down at the package in her hand, no doubt wondering what this gray-haired foreign woman has bought or what she has been given. The package feels extraordinarily heavy to Liz, as though it were some huge stone that she had balanced in her palm.

She goes into her room and she puts down that terrible weight and then she goes over to that blond frame of wood covered with nacreous paper. She stares at the notice: PLEASE DO NOT OPEN.

This is a room. What is it?

It is a prison.

No. This is a room. Repeat.

It is a prison.

No, no. Let me give you the Japanese equivalent. This is a room—*Sore wa zashiki desu.*

Indirect Method.

She was about to force the shoji apart again but now she leaves it.

[1978]

The Granny Room

JOHN HAYLOCK

I first met Mrs. Hayashi in London at the house of a friend who made regular business trips to Japan. I had been invited to meet her as I was about to take up a teaching post in Tokyo. "You must meet Mrs. Hayashi," Cuthbert Meade had said. "She can be of great help to you." And no sooner had I met her than she suggested that I should live in her house. Seeing what was probably an expression of doubt on my face (I have never been good at disguising my feelings), she said in passable English, "You have a separate apartment. I just built one above my garage. It is for me when I am a widow and grandmother. I call it the 'granny room.'"

I raised my eyebrows. Mrs. Hayashi was petite, slim, neatly dressed; she had a tidy head of jet hair above a face composed of small but well-defined features; her skin shone as if it had been polished; her eyebrows were carefully plucked, her lips subtly painted, her teeth, except for one gold incisor, perfect. An attractive woman. I wondered how old she was. She did not look old enough to be cast in the role of grandmother, and I knew her husband was alive as he was talking business to Cuthbert on the other side of the room. Mr. Hayashi could have been a grandfather for he was gray and grizzled. I put his age at fifty-five, but Mrs. Hayashi did not seem a day over forty. I knew nothing of Japanese customs and supposed it was natural for a wife to be planning for her old age after her husband's demise while he was still living; however, I raised my eyebrows, and Mrs. Hayashi sitting on the edge of Cuthbert's capacious sofa, leaned forward. "We rebuild our house, and so we think of future. My son twenty-two. Next year he will graduate. When he twenty-five he will marry."

"Has he a fiancée?"

"Not yet," replied Mrs. Hayashi. "It is not time now to find wife for him." Her small dark eyes flicked into mine and then down to examine the carpet. "At twenty-six my son will have a child."

"And you will be a grandmother." I nearly asked if she would have killed off her husband by then—only four years to go. Did Mr. Hayashi know of this plan? He must be aware of it, for she could hardly have built the granny room without his knowledge. Anyway four years was enough for me as my contract with the university was only for two.

Cuthbert's wife then joined us and the conversation moved from Japan to London. There were many questions I wanted to ask Mrs. Hayashi, but I didn't have a chance to pose them as she turned to Mrs.

Meade and began to bombard her, rather insistently, with queries about where to buy this and that. Where could she buy shoes, she asked, since her feet were so small. She looked down at her feet and giggled—was she proud of them? I was about to suggest that she go to the children's department at Selfridge's, but I rose instead, invented another engagement, said I'd like to take her granny room, excused myself, and left with her visiting card in my pocket.

That meeting with the Hayashis occurred toward the end of February. They were due back in Tokyo at the beginning of March and I arrived there in the middle of the month. I had let Mrs. Hayashi know of the day of my arrival, but not the flight number; I did not wish her to meet me since a professor from the university had promised to do that, and knowing from that brief meeting in Cuthbert's flat that she had a strong personality, I did not want her to steal the professor's thunder, and I was right for Mr. or rather Professor Naito was far from thunderous: modesty, courtesy, and gentleness seemed to be his principal characteristics.

"You must be very tired," he said when I met him after emerging from the Customs Hall at Narita Airport. He stood behind a fence with other welcomers and held on high a placard with my name on it. He was a dapper little man, whose iron-gray hair was long but neat, whose overcoat was well-cut, whose black shoes shone.

"It doesn't seem like four in the afternoon," I said. I had flown over the Pole from London, an exhausting, eighteen-hour flight with one stop at Anchorage. "I hope my hotel is comfortable."

Professor Naito made no reply and put out a hand to help me with my suitcase.

"It's a lovely day," I remarked, observing the cloudless sky above the airport buildings while we were queuing for the "limousine" bus to Tokyo.

"Sometimes we have fine days in March but not always."

I had got the airline to reserve a room for me in an expensive downtown hotel, because I had thought that three or four nights in international luxury would enable me to acclimatize myself gently to my new, exotic environment. I had informed Professor Naito of my plans and also that I would be living in Mrs. Hayashi's flat because the good professor had offered to find me accommodations.

The comfortable bus gently glided along a highway. I looked out at thickly wooded hills between which nestled fields and farmhouses with steep gray roofs. "How pretty!" I said.

"Soon dreadful Tokyo begins," replied the Professor.

He was right for it was not long before an unmitigated mass of concrete molded into unoriginal shapes took over from the dark green hills.

Professor Naito explained that Mrs. Hayashi had contacted him and that she would be meeting us at the Air Terminal, and then he added, "Frankly speaking, I have something to tell you which you may not like."

I braced myself for bad news. Had my appointment been canceled? Had discoveries been made about my past? "Yes," I replied, "please tell me." I supposed that the university, which had paid my fare, would provide me with a ticket home.

"It concerns Mrs. Hayashi," he said looking across me at a regiment of huge apartment blocks. How ugly Tokyo seemed! Would it all be like this, I wondered. "Mrs. Hayashi?" I repeated the name.

"Yes. She will take you directly to the apartment she prepared for you."

"But I reserved a room in a hotel as I told you in my letter."

"She canceled the reservation." Professor Naito's dark eyes peeped at me, like a child's they were, gauging a grown-up's reaction.

"Why should she do that? I wrote to her saying that I would move into her place after spending a few days in a hotel."

"Yes, yes, you told me. I fully understand your reasons, very wise ones. But Mrs. Hayashi, well, she wanted to save you the expense of—"

"I see. Well, never mind. I suppose she meant to be kind." I omitted to add that her meddling annoyed me because I did not want to upset Professor Naito, who seemed infinitely kind and solicitous.

"That is all right then," he said with relief. "I shall leave you at the Terminal after I have put you into Mrs. Hayashi's capable hands."

Was I right in sensing that the arrangement for me to go directly to Mrs. Hayashi's and not first to a hotel suited Professor Naito too? It meant that he could give up shepherding me, but perhaps I was being unfair. The bus crossed a brown river, a recorded female voice made a long announcement in Japanese through the loudspeakers, and then another female voice in an over-precise accent mouthed (I could almost see her mouthing) in English the information that we would shortly arrive at Tokyo City Terminal, where we would find taxis and buses for our onward transportation. The bus extracted itself from the tangle of vehicles on the highway and entered a walled ramp and then ascended to the "Ter-min-al Beeldeeng." Professor Naito and I descended two flights of moving stairs to the baggage hall, where Mrs. Hayashi awaited us.

She looked broader, less slight than she had in London; this was perhaps because of her fur coat, which she wore open. She greeted me cordially rather than warmly (there wasn't much warmth in her), shaking my hand; she bowed deeply to Professor Naito, who bent even lower toward her. After this little pause for the showing of mutual respect, the three of us joined the line for taxis with my suitcase, which the Professor had insisted on collecting for me from the revolving band in the luggage hall. Mrs. Hayashi made conventional inquiries about my health, the flight, my impressions of Tokyo in less accurate but more fluent English than Mr. Naito's. When we reached the head of the queue, the Professor obsequiously ushered Mrs. Hayashi and me into a taxi and then stood back and waggled an open hand. "Aren't you coming with us?" I asked, but by then the door had shut on its own and we were away. "How did the door shut?"

"The driver. It is automatic," explained Mrs. Hayashi. "We are now going to pass through the center of Tokyo to the district where you are going to live."

It was dark by this time and except for the ideographic signs that were appropriately exotic to me, the streets, the lights, the buildings and the traffic did not bear many startling marks of difference from those of any other city I knew, and the fact that one drove on the left made me feel less abroad. After half an hour or so of stopping at lights and then moving slowly on, we crossed a park. "Our B.B.C.," said Mrs. Hayashi, pointing out a solitary block, the sides of which were striped with white fluorescent light. "And this is Yoyogi Park."

"Yoyogi?" I repeated the name, which sounded funny and reminded me of a toy I played with in my boyhood. "I remember yoyos," I said.

"*Yoyos?*" She did not seem to understand and I was too tired to explain. We crossed several more traffic lights and then my companion began to give instructions to the driver, who turned into a narrow road, then left, then left again and up a hedged lane which in the dark seemed countrified. "Here we are," cried Mrs. Hayashi. "You see it's quite central." "Yes," I replied, but I didn't then see that it was central. "This is the house," she declared, after she had paid the taxi driver (she brushed aside my feeble fumblings with the strange money I had bought from my bank in England) and I got my suitcase out of the trunk. I looked up at a concrete slab of a house, sideways on to the road.

"Your flat, the granny room, is up there." She indicated a flight of iron steps flanked by iron railings which led up to a door above a garage that housed a car around which junk was stacked: boxes, a kitchen range, two rusty bicycles—the kind of things whose uselessness is not accepted by a parsimonious owner. "Leave your suitcase here by the car. No one take it. We go up to your room after dinner." I followed my landlady down a passage to the front door of her house. "You must take off your shoes and put on these slippers," she commanded when she had opened the door with her key, and stepped up into the hall from the well by the entrance. "It's our custom as you probably know and," she added rather severely, "one most foreigners like. Well, welcome to my home!" She took off her fur coat and in a petulant tone called up the stairs, "Nori-chan, Nori!" There was no answer. "My son seems to be out. He may be asleep."

Mrs. Hayashi was wearing a bottle-green woolen dress with a thick black suede belt tight round her tiny waist; her breasts were hardly noticeable, and her fingers were ringless. I was shown into a sitting room that was dominated by a gigantic stereo set and speakers—"My husband's," she said, giving the machine a derogatory wave. "Please sit down." I sat in a leather armchair, one in which Mrs. Hayashi would be lost; she perched on its companion for a moment, rather a restless moment, and then excusing herself left the room hurriedly. On each side of the stereo set were tall bookcases: one held a number of Japanese tomes and the other a collection of ornaments and dolls, none of which seemed of much value. At the end of the room were sliding glass doors which gave on to an umbrageous garden lit in a ghostly fashion by the crude light of a fluorescent street lamp. I got up and with my nose nearly rubbing the glass looked at the shrubs and the trees; I hoped there would be a view of them from my room. Mrs. Hayashi reappeared. She said, "My garden," and then took me into a spacious kitchen in the middle of which was a dining-table covered with a plastic cloth; round the table were four bulky dining chairs with arms and cushioned seats. I sat opposite my hostess and facing a row of up-to-date kitchen appliances: a refrigerator, a deep freeze, a sink, and a range; behind me were cupboards tidily stacked with crockery. The room was as neat and as clean as Mrs. Hayashi.

I felt like a surrogate husband—was that part of her plan? Did she have designs on me? We had sukiyaki, a cook-it-yourself dish, which I was to learn is often served by Japanese to foreigners. Deftly manipulating a pair of long chopsticks, Mrs. Hayashi put into a pan on top of a gas ring placed on the table slivers of beef and shreds of cabbage, a kind of vermicelli, floppy headed mushrooms, and some sake too into a tiny china cup, instructing me to hold the cup toward her while she poured.

As I clumsily helped myself from the pan with my chopsticks, occasionally letting fall a piece of meat, a mushroom, I re-examined Mrs. Hayashi's face. I decided that the thoughts I had had about her in London were right: she was an attractive woman. It was a pity about her gold incisor as her other teeth were good, but otherwise her tidy hair, her tidy face were impressive; tidy was the best word to describe her features, which, with her trim eyebrows, her neat nose, lips a sculptor could not have improved upon, were compact, like a new set of tools in a case. Her dark eyes were small and though bright they shone with what seemed to be a forced brightness, and were kept puckered at their inner corners; perhaps her chin and her eyes betrayed her strong character. Good-looking, yes, undoubtedly good-looking, yet somehow she lacked appeal, at least to me; this was due to her manner, which was not at all soft and feminine; there was something hard about her. Was she the decision-maker in the family? Did she wear the trousers? I had scarcely met Mr. Hayashi, only having shaken hands with him at Cuthbert's. I remembered him as a little man with thick, gray hair and dark-rimmed spectacles—that was all I remembered about him. Where was he now? It was nearly half-past eight. Was he away? Should I ask? I was just about to inquire when my hostess said, "Are you tired?"

"Well, I am, rather," I admitted. I was longing for a whiskey. I didn't much care for the tepid rice wine and I yearned to get out my duty-free bottle and pour myself a treble. "The flight over the Pole takes eighteen hours," I said.

"Yes," Mrs. Hayashi replied. "I find coming West-East not so tiring as coming from East-West. Here the time—" she looked at her little silver wristwatch—"eight-twenty-eight and so in England it is about eleven-thirty in the morning, so your day finished and when you go to bed most of your day missed. From here to Rondon you have to have the day again, so West-East less tiring."

I didn't quite follow her reasoning, but I realized from her speech that I was not expected to be tired.

After I had eaten as much of the sukiyaki as I wanted—the beef was delicious—I was served with a bowl of clear soup with a tiny egg floating in it, and finally a *crème caramel* in a plastic cup—the latter obviously bought. Then Mrs. Hayashi rose. I also got up. "We go to your room," she announced. Was it only a room? And out of the house we went, she carrying in a fussy way that suggested she was doing something extra my plastic bag of duty-free drink and cigarettes, my brief case and my overcoat, and behind her up the iron steps I lugged my suitcase.

The "room" was more than a room, two rooms in fact and there was a bathroom also, off the bedroom, which had in it a three-quarters double-bed, a "honeymooner" as some call it. The disadvantage about the sitting room I noticed at once was the kitchen, which was in an unventilated alcove at the back of the room. Mrs. Hayashi went proudly to the window (the curtains were undrawn) and exclaimed, "The garden, you see? You look on my garden. We call this *shakkei,* borrowed view. So," she went on, gazing into a reflection of herself in the glass, "when I live here I not lose my garden."

I smiled wanly. I was pleased with the flat, which was adequately furnished with a carpet, a sofa, armchairs, a desk, and a dining-table. It was clear that she had carefully considered the needs of a Westerner. "Of course," she said, "I like better tatami, Japanese mats, to a carpet, and a cushion to a chair. When I live here I have tatami put down." She talked as if her moving in were imminent. Was her son about to marry? Was a grandchild on the way? What about her husband? Had she gotten rid of him? I decided I must ask. "Is your husband away?"

"He at work," she replied, rather sharply.

"And your son?"

"Nori is out. Well, it is getting late. We will talk about contract for apartment in the morning."

I slept well in the "honeymooner" and I was pleased to find all the ingredients necessary for breakfast in the refrigerator. Mrs. Hayashi had even remembered marmalade. How practical she was! How businesslike too! For soon after breakfast, before I had telephoned Professor Naito, she arrived with the contract for the flat. "The rent is one hundred thousand yen a month; this is reasonable for this district." Two hundred pounds a month seemed a lot for two rooms, one of which was partly a kitchen, but I could only accept. I signed and agreed to arrange for my bank to pay the rent on the twenty-eighth of each month. After neatly folding her copy of the contract, Mrs. Hayashi said, "You may think rent high." My face as usual had shown my feelings. "I do not ask key money or rent in advance, and if you are willing to give Nori English lessons two times a week, I pay you thirty thousand yen a month."

I agreed. I only had to be at the university on three days in the week, so I could easily fit in Mrs. Hayashi's son, and £60 seemed a fair fee. "What year is he in at his university?"

"He a senior. His major Economics."

I wasn't used to these American terms, but did not then inquire their precise meaning. "I can't teach him economics," I said.

"No. You teach him English. I want him speak English good."

Shortly afterward I bravely introduced myself to the mysteries of the Tokyo subway system, going to the local station down a pleasant hedged lane (the hedges were composed of azalea bushes) and a narrow shopping street which, with its shops all open at the front, their wares on display, wooden houses and small blocks of flats, tiny bars and little restaurants, was excitingly strange. I met Professor Naito at a central station and he conducted me to the university, where I shook hands with a number of professors (everyone seemed to be a professor), who were very cordial. The term was not to begin for two weeks. When I returned to my flat, I found a note from Mrs. Hayashi on my desk. The fact that she had a key and could let herself in while I was out (or even while I was in) disturbed me a little. The note said that she would be bringing her son to see me at eight and I was to let her know only if this wasn't convenient.

At eight precisely my two-noted door-bell sounded and I let in Mrs. Hayashi and Nori. The young man, who was head and shoulders above his mother, had a longish face and black wiry hair that covered his ears and the back of his shirt collar that was outside his light-blue pullover, which was more or less the same color as his jeans. "Here is my son," said Mrs. Hayashi. I held out my hand and the son, very solemn, bowed, putting his hands on his thighs; when he looked up I saw he had a brown and healthy complexion, and his smile was more generous and warmer than that of his mother, who never allowed her lips to expand fully. When they had sat down I said, "I only have whiskey to offer you, I'm afraid."

"No, thank you," said the mother, "we do not want drink anything."

By the expression in Nori's large dark eyes I guessed he would have liked a glass of whiskey, but I didn't dare give him one. We talked, or rather Mrs. Hayashi held forth about her son, saying that his English was very poor, that he did no work at the university, that he was out most nights. Nori looked down at his folded hands during this complaint. What was I to say? I didn't want to side with the mother, as that might have started off the teacher-pupil relationship on the wrong track, so I simply interpolated an "Oh?" now and then. Mrs. Hayashi rose. "I hope you make Nori into a good English speaker," she said and left, leaving her son behind; it seemed that she expected him to be speaking perfect English by the time he returned to the house next door.

Nori was shy and said very little. I had obviously got to win his confidence somehow and I was not sure how to do this. After having monosyllabic answers to my stock questions about age, study, and recreation—"Do you like reading?" "Yes." "Have you read any English books?" "Yes." "What books have you read?" "*The Catcher in the Rye.*" "Did you like it?" "Yes."—I decided that a little whiskey might help. It did. After a second whiskey, Nori talked freely and with surprising frankness about his mother. "My mother expect much of me," he said. "She want me enter Tokyo University, but I fell entrance examination and was *ronin* for one year. She very angry. Tokyo University very high standing and students from there get good jobs, certain. Now I am student at private university. Not so good. My mother want me to go to Tokyo University and join some Ministry, maybe Finance Ministry and then later become Prime Minister." I smiled but the young man was quite serious.

"What does *ronin* mean? And I think you meant 'failed' not 'fell.'"

"Yes, sorry, failed. *Ronin* student who failed university entrance exam-

ination and must study until next year examination. He has no school, no
university. *Ronin* in old Japan was samurai—you know samurai?" I nodded.
"*Ronin* was samurai without his lord. Maybe the lord lose his land and so
his samurai must go away and wander."

"I see, rather a good expression. Do you want to read a book with me
or just talk?"

"As you like."

"I think we'd better read a book. It would give us something to talk
about, be a basis for our conversations."

"O.K., what we read?"

"Let's decide later. I'll see what there is available. What about your
father? What did he say when you failed to get into Tokyo University?"

"He no say much. He went to small university. It was just after war
end. Very different then. He has his own company. Very busy. Always very
busy." Nori put some resentment into the last three words.

It was at the fourth lesson—we had chosen to read a book of stories
by Somerset Maugham—that Nori said when I asked him a question
about "Rain" which he couldn't answer, "I am in love."

"Oh? Who with?"

"A hairdresser."

"What sort of hairdresser?"

"She is thirty-two years old and married and has two children, two
girls."

"Oh dear!"

"Her husband not live with her. Leave her. She live with her mother.
Her father dead."

"Where does she work?"

"She work near the station."

"The station near here?"

"Yes. My mother go her shop. She cut her hair and give it perm
sometimes."

"How fascinating! Does your mother know of your connection with
this hairdresser?"

"She not know."

"Perhaps we should read a little of 'Rain'?"

Nori made a *moue*, but I reminded myself that I was being paid for the
lesson and we read a little of "Rain." Nori's mind, though, was not on the
story at all. "What are you going to do about her?" I asked.

"What can I do?"

"Do you see her often?"

"Yes, but it is difficult. I cannot tell my mother. She work very near. I pass her shop every day when I go my university. I look in. Sometime she see me; sometime she busy."

"When do you meet her?"

"After her work, we meet. Not near here. It is dangerous near here. People they know me; all my life I live here."

"Does she love you?" This was an impertinent question, but I was curious to know the answer.

"Yes, she love me," replied Nori with certainty. "Once we go together to Hakone, near Mount Fuji and . . ." Instead of finishing his sentence, he said, "It is very difficult. What do you think should I do?"

"I don't know. I see nothing wrong with your having an affair with her." Nori's eyes brightened; he clearly wanted approval. "But," I went on, hoping to dilute the encouragement I had given him, "don't go too far. She's much older than you and it may be hard for her to find a husband, so don't become too attached to her."

"I love her."

"Yes, love, but that is not enough," I said, upbraiding myself for my sententiousness. "Go carefully. I can't advise you. How can I? But think of your mother and don't do anything hasty; perhaps you should tell your mother."

Nori turned down his mouth at my last suggestion, which I realized was unhelpful; he probably felt that being about his mother's age I sympathized with her. "You not tell her, will you?"

"No, I won't. It's not my business."

I am inquisitive by nature, a despicable characteristic, but a human and forgivable one nevertheless, and so after Nori had told me his story my walk to the station became more interesting. There were two hairdressers' in the little shopping street, one on the right at the top and the other on the left at the bottom near the railway line. I wondered in which one Nori's lover worked. The sex of the hairdressers or stylists or trichologists was not easy to determine through the windows of the shops, but I gathered that some were women and others men. I guessed that Nori's mistress belonged to the shop that had on its window the words "Spring up your Hair" (it was now April and Mrs. Hayashi's cherry tree had bloomed and come into leaf) and not to the one called "Beauty Style," for the former looked the more prosperous of the two and had five chairs to the other's three.

Nori often cut his lessons and I was not sure whether I should tell his mother about this. I decided not to because I was beginning to feel sorry for him. Why shouldn't the poor, wretched, mother-run boy kick over the races a bit with a hairdresser before becoming harnessed to a job? I rarely saw Mr. Hayashi. He came up to my room one evening soon after my arrival and seemed rather tongue-tied; perhaps he was shy, so many Japanese men were I was beginning to realize, for he didn't say much except a polite, "I hope you comfortable," and he refused a drink. After that we only passed the time of day on the rare occasions we saw each other going out or coming in. On Sunday mornings, pipe in mouth and wearing a little round cloth hat he would mow the lawn, but although I could see him from my window I never tossed out a "Nice day!" or a "I'm enjoying your roses," for I felt that I shouldn't disturb his privacy, and if he wanted to see me he could easily come up to the granny room; on Sunday afternoons, Beethoven, usually the "Emperor," boomed into the garden from the sitting room below and once I greeted him with a "So you like Beethoven?" but all he answered was "Beethoven? Oh yes, Beethoven," and this made me suspect that he was more concerned with the performance of his stereo than the music. Mrs. Hayashi often rang my bell and inquired if I needed anything. This was kind of her, but I found her attention rather intrusive; after all, one only wants to see one's landlady when the plumbing has gone wrong, the faucet has broken, or the roof is leaking. Once Mrs. Hayashi called when Nori should have been with me having a lesson.

"Is Nori with you?" she asked at the door. She rarely came into my flat. I think this was because the taking off of shoes and the putting on of slippers, which is a necessary ritual on entering a Japanese abode, commits one to a proper visit, as it were. When I replied that Nori hadn't turned up, Mrs. Hayashi stepped out of her shoes and into a pair of slippers in two quick, almost imperceptible movements. I ushered her into the sitting room and into a chair from which the kitchen range could not be seen. On the stove was one of my attempts to make a *daube* and I did not want any comments or advice.

"Is this the first time he not come to his lesson?" she inquired.

I hesitated for a moment or two, wondering whether I should reply honestly and then I did. "No," I said, "it's not the first time."

"Why you not tell me?"

This time I did not reveal what I truly thought, which was that she ought to allow her son, who had come of age, to decide for himself whether he wanted a lesson or not. "I didn't think that it mattered all that much," I replied. "I presumed that he was busy with some university activity; he's no longer a schoolboy." I had never imagined for one moment that he sacrificed trysts with his hairdresser-lover for some academic chore but I was on his side. I had not warmed to Mrs. Hayashi, and I've always supported rash, passionate youth against the opposing forces of age, experience, reason, and sanity. I've frequently iterated to students a "gather-yerosebuds-while-ye-may" philosophy, because I really believe that in the world of woe in which we live happiness, even self-indulgent, sensual pleasure, should be snatched when offered. So I approve of Herrick's advice "To the Virgins, to make much of Time," but of course Mrs. Hayashi would abhor the poet's "That age is best which is the first. . . ."

The interview with Mrs. Hayashi did not last long; possibly she sensed my antipathy to her great "plan for Nori." She only sipped twice from the cup of Earl Grey I poured out for her, and broke delicately in two a chocolate biscuit which was small enough to put whole into the mouth, even into her tiny one, and only ate one half. She left me, her almost full cup of tea, the other half of the biscuit, saying "Thank you very much for the nice cup of tea and the cookie. Very delicious." I saw her to the door and she repeated her thanks, but her eyes looked down, not into mine.

June arrived; the pink and red azalea blooms were succeeded by the pale blue and purple clusters of the hydrangeas; the notice on the window of the second hairdresser's was changed to, "Fresh up Gals with Summer Hair." I did not yet know which of the assistants had stolen Nori's heart, though he had told me that *she* worked in the shop near the station. We hadn't progressed very much with "Rain" in spite of the fact that the appeal of the story had increased by the arrival of the rainy season, for Nori only wanted to talk about his love. About Mrs. Davidson, the missionary's wife, he once remarked, "She like my mother." I was tempted to try to engage his interest by suggesting that Sadie Thompson and his lady hairdresser might have something in common, but I did not do so through fear of hurting his feelings. He was very sensitive and was not a person who could laugh at himself or at his predicament. One evening—lessons were supposed to last from five until six-thirty, though he never turned up before five-thirty—he said, "I want to introduce you to Keiko—her name is Keiko."

"Oh, why?"

"I want you tell me what you think."

I saw involvement looming and did not wish to be within the compass of the tentacles of that clinging octopus. "I don't think my advice would be of much help."

"Please."

"I won't be able to speak to her."

"You can judge by seeing."

"Where could we meet?" I was of course curious to know what this thirty-two-year-old divorcée hairdresser with two daughters was like.

"Outside Isetan Department Store in Shinjuku. You know?"

"Yes, when?"

"Tomorrow, eight o'clock P.M."

I agreed.

I had naturally speculated much upon the physiognomy and the character of Nori's beloved and I had decided that she was one of the "fluffy" girls I had espied through the window of the Ladies' Hairdressers near the station, one of the girls who had had her hair dyed copper and fuzzed into a bush of tight curls. I was quite wrong.

I met Nori outside the department store and he took me across the street into a building that housed several small cinemas and up in a lift to a cafe called Mozart, an old-style cafe with straw-seated, wooden chairs with hooped backs, which served *Kaffee mit Schlag* and creamy *tortes*; the background music was exclusively that of the Austrian composer, of whom there was a bust on the cake counter. Nori led me to a table at which was sitting a woman who was mature in a motherly way that Mrs. Hayashi was not. Keiko had a shiny head of black, straight hair that danced over her forehead and her ears, and a figure that was full rather than fat. Her pale white skin accentuated the darkness of her hair, her eyebrows, and her eyes. She had a round face and a largish mouth that turned up at the corners when she smiled. She exuded a womanly warmth and a protectiveness that was obviously captivating to an inexperienced young man, and it was clear by the way she kept looking at Nori when he spoke that she was in love with him.

The meeting didn't extend much beyond the time it took to drink a cup of coffee and eat a cake. I didn't know what to say and Keiko could speak no English. Nori told me about the cafe being dedicated to Mozart—the place was nearly empty but it was near closing time—and we had a desultory conversation about this and that, about how I liked Japan and so on. I was relieved when the young man said, "It getting late" and we left. In the street, we bade each other goodnight and parted. I went back to the granny room next door to Nori's home, but he didn't accompany me; he went off with Keiko.

One evening a few days later Nori burst into my room—he knew that I never locked the door. I pulled myself up from my prostrate, postprandial posture on the sofa, half-gathered together my somnolent wits and said, "Oh, hello?"

When I had got him a whiskey and one for myself (I don't usually drink after dinner but his arrival gave me an excuse to do so), he said, "We going to 'erope.'"

I thought he meant Europe. "But how? It's term time. You can't get away. You mustn't give up your studies. And what about money?"

"I get *arbeit*."

"In Germany?"

"German? Why you say Germany?"

"But you say you're going to Europe and—"

"Not Europe, 'erope.' "

I then realized that Nori had substituted an "r" for the "l" and he had meant elope, and he explained that *arbeit* was used in Japan to mean a part-time job. "So you will leave home?"

"Yes."

"What will your mother say?"

"I not tell her. I just go." Nori looked at me, his dark eyes wide, liquid, pleading. "Will you do something for me?"

"What?"

"You tell my mother about my going. You tell my mother you meet Keiko-san and that she is very nice girl."

"You want *me* to tell your—"

"My mother she like you very much; if you tell her she not be angry with you. So you tell her, please."

"No, you must tell her."

"I can't."

"It's none of my business. It is your family affair. It's nothing to do with me." There was alarm in my voice as I spoke, alarm that betrayed weakness which Nori detected, I'm sure; he had some of his mother's forcefulness.

"So you tell her. Tell her tomorrow. I will go to Keiko tonight."

"Where? Where will you go?"

"To a room we rented."

"What about her children?" I threw this question at him, hoping it might make him reconsider his plan.

"They stay with her mother."

"Why do you decide to do this? Why not carry on as you have been doing?" I knew these were silly questions, for if one is young and in love one wants to be with one's lover as much as possible. Nori's answer was a simple, "I can't." I followed him to the door, where he trod into a pair of grubby gym shoes with broken backs and took up a bulging grip which he had left in the entrance.

"Why not tell your mother now? It's much better for you to tell her."

"She in bed. Always she go to bed at nine-thirty."

"What about your father?"

"He on business trip. Goodbye. Thank you very much." He jerked a little half bow, crept down the iron staircase and hastened round the corner out of sight.

What was I to do? I did not relish telling Mrs. Hayashi that her son had gone off to live "in a room" with a divorced hairdresser. The next day was a Wednesday, a day when I had to leave early for the university, and one on which during the lunch break I invariably saw Professor Naito. I decided not to give Nori's message to Mrs. Hayashi (the more I thought about it, the more monstrous I regarded his behavior, not so much his running away from home, but his involving me in his escapade) until the evening, until I had asked the kind professor his advice.

"May I come and see you at noon?" I asked him on the telephone from my room in the university, and in his usual deferential way, he replied, "I don't want to trouble you. I shall come to your room." When I answered his gentle taps on my door with a "Come in!" he entered apologetically as if he were making an intrusion.

"I have a problem," I announced.

"Oh?" he said in a raising tone.

"It's to do with Mrs. Hayashi and her son Nori."

"Oh." The second "oh" was on a falling tone and one of relief. I think the professor feared that I was going to complain about teaching or salary conditions. I then told him the story and how the selfish young man had landed me with the unenviable task of informing his mother of his flight.

Professor Naito asked, "Did you encourage Nori-san to go away with this woman?"

"No, of course I didn't." I did not say that I had not condemned the affair and that playing the role of confidant had amused me. "But what should I do?"

"You must tell her. He was your pupil and as his teacher you have responsibility."

"I don't see that I have, Professor Naito. I am a foreigner here and—" an idea came to me—"I wonder if I could ask you a favor."

"A favor?" He seemed uncertain.

"Could you come with me this evening when I tell Mrs. Hayashi? Apart from your deep knowledge of English—Mrs. Hayashi may have a good ear for the language, but she doesn't have a big vocabulary—your moral support would be of enormous assistance."

Professor Naito looked very confused. "I am sorry to say that this evening there is a faculty meeting."

"Couldn't you miss it?"

"Not possible, I am sorry to say." Naito smiled.

"Then do you think you could telephone Mrs. Hayashi and tell her that I shall be calling on her at about six, and give her the gist of what I've told you about her son? It would help prepare the ground if you did, and you could tell her in Japanese and therefore in the Japanese way, which would be so much better than the clumsy, Western way I would use."

Professor Naito looked at his watch. "I'll see," he replied. "It is a difficult matter."

I guessed this meant that he wouldn't and I was right, for when I rang Mrs. Hayashi's two-tone bell she came to the door in an apron over a white blouse and black trousers and welcomed me in her usual way with a flash of her gold incisor and a businesslike, "How *are* you?" She must have noticed from my expression that something was wrong for she said, "You not well?" And when I said I was all right, she asked me if anything had gone wrong with the granny room, as indeed it had in a way, the "granny" side of it, at least. "The water heater again broken?" It had failed to function three times since my arrival and Mrs. Hayashi had telephoned a mechanic who had come after an annoying delay of several days. I didn't know whether I should ask to come into her house to impart my news, to invite her upstairs to the granny room, or to blurt out about the wayward son on his mother's doorstep. "It's about Nori," I said.

She did not grasp my meaning for she said, "He is not here. He not come home last night. Probably he spend last night with one of his university friends. Sometime he does. Is it his lesson day?"

"No, but he came to see me last night and told me that he was going away." I should have gone on and not allowed the strong-minded lady to speak before I had finished my message.

"Sometime he go away with a university friend. He live in Yokohama."

She had not listened properly to what I had said. "Nori asked me to tell you he was going away to live with his girlfriend."

Mrs. Hayashi let out a humorless laugh. "It is his joke. He has not girlfriend."

"But he has. I met her." As soon as I had allowed the last words to slip out I wished I had not done so, for now I was deeper in the plot than I had meant to be.

"You met her? Where?"

"In Shinjuku. And last night, very late, he came to see me and asked me to tell you he was going to live with her."

"Where?"

"I don't know. In a room. They have rented a room."

"Why he ask you to tell me this? Why he not tell me himself?" I was sure she must have an inkling of the true answer to this question, but I simply replied, "I don't know."

"I see."

I then excused myself and went up to the granny room, leaving her

flummoxed at her own front door, and hoping that as far as I was concerned the affair was over. I was mistaken. After an hour or so my wretched
two-toned bell tinkled and it was she. She had changed into a dress, a
severe, dark-blue one, which, I imagined, she had thought suitable for the
occasion.

"I don't know what to say," she said when she had accepted a chair
but refused a brandy. "You tell me that you know this girlfriend of Nori-
san?"

"Not know. I met her once, as I told you, er, in Shinjuku. I ran into
Nori by chance and he was with her. He introduced me." Mrs. Hayashi was
staring at me in astonishment, so nervously I continued, "She seemed nice,
older than your son but very soft and feminine." I stopped myself from
adding, "But you know her. She does your hair!"

"Soft and feminine?" Mrs. Hayashi repeated with distaste. "And how
old?"

"I don't know; thirty, perhaps."

"Thirty? And married? Is she married?"

"I don't know." I thought it best to soften the blow a bit.

"What have you been teaching Nori?" she asked.

"'Rain,' a story by Somerset Maugham."

"Some romantic stuff."

"Cynical, really."

"Some romantic stuff," she repeated. I don't think she understood the
adjective I had used. "I know," she went on, "the romantic Western way. You
encourage my son in living a so-called romantic Western life. You teach
that romance is good, that love is good." She was quite angry I felt, although her face didn't show it.

"I haven't actually taught him that, but isn't love good?"

"No. Not this kind of passion love," replied Mrs. Hayashi, fervently.
"He follow your way, your Western way. You responsible for this love affair
he have with this woman."

"I don't think it's fair of you to blame me, Mrs. Hayashi. Nori is a
man; he's twenty-two."

"Nori is a boy, a young boy, a young innocent boy."

"It won't harm him to lose his innocence. It will help him grow up.
I'm sure this will soon blow over, Mrs. Hayashi, will pass; in a while he'll be
home and right as rain."

"Is that what happens in the story?"

"No." I laughed; I couldn't help myself. "'As right as rain' means all right."

"I don't think it is funny; for you perhaps it very funny; for me it is
serious matter." She rose and said, "I leave you now." I saw her to the door,

and without saying another word she stepped out of her slippers, into her shoes, and out of the granny room.

I did not see her or her husband for a week and then my faucet broke down and I had to speak to her about it, but all she said when I asked her to call the mechanic was, "I see." Another week passed and no mechanic came. Then my air-cooler went wrong and it was uncomfortable without it at night, but again all she said was, "I see," when I told her about it. A week went by, a week of sweaty nights and days of boiling water in kettles and saucepans to have a bath and to wash up. I called on my landlady again, but all I got was another, "I see." I invoked the aid of Professor Naito and he advised me to move. "She wants you to go," he said. "She does not mend your equipments. That is the sign."

"I have a contract," I protested.

"Better to go," said Naito. "I will help you find other accommodations."

"No, thank you. I think I know of a place." I didn't, but house agents advertised apartments almost every day in the *Japan Times* and I decided to apply for a flat through one of them, and not be beholden to Professor Naito in case things went wrong again.

Accommodation was found in the form of a flat that was more expensive, noisier, and with a far less attractive prospect than the granny room— it was high up and looked on to another block—but the landlord dealt through the agent and never appeared himself. Mrs. Hayashi accepted my departure with equanimity. With her face closed as if she had pulled a blind over it, she said, "Well, goodbye," when I summoned her to the door by pushing the hateful two-noted bell and handed her my key. I left on a day in late July when the white oleander was in flower and the myrtle tree was about to blush. "I shall miss your garden," I said, but she made no reply to this remark and kept the blind drawn.

In November when the maple trees began to glow like embers I felt the need of my overcoat, which after a search, I realized I had left behind in the granny room. Several days of wondering what I should say to Mrs. Hayashi passed before I steeled myself into telephoning her. Without any preliminary politenesses I simply stated who I was and asked about my coat. "Yes, it in the apartment," she replied. "Why don't you go there and ask for it? Someone is there."

"All right, thank you. Any news of—" But she rang off before I had time to say her son's name. When I called at the granny room there came to the door an American blonde with blue saucer eyes, dressed in a turtleneck pullover and jeans and with a cigarette in her mouth.

"I've come for my coat. Did Mrs. Hayashi tell you?" I could hear the squawks of children inside the flat.

"Yeah, sure. Why don't you come in?"

I followed the young mother into what used to be my sitting room. Two unbashful, tow-haired tots glared at me for a moment and then went on playing with some model cars. "Make yourself at home," sang the American lady, "and I'll see if I can find your coat. It's a top coat, isn't it?"

"Yes, gray, mohair." I ignored the children because my eyes were drawn to the window by two dazzling maples outside. "How splendid the leaves are, aren't they?" I said to the American mother when she came in from the bedroom with my overcoat on her arm.

"Yeah. I'm just crazy about them." She, busy housewife that she was, took her cigarette out of her mouth and turned to her children, "Now I thought I told you, Chester, not to do that to your sister."

"D'you see much of Mrs. Hayashi?"

"Yeah, sure. She's really great. She comes up to baby-sit when Bill and I want to go out, and she doesn't charge a cent. She just adores the kids. You'd think she's their grandmother, really you would."

"Do you know what happened to her son?"

"Son? I didn't know she had a son. She's never mentioned a son to me."

[1980]

The Bonsai Master

JAMES KIRKUP

Such a dear, sweet old man, Suzuki-san. So good with children. His own grandchildren adore him. He often gives them little treats—a bar of Dynamite Choco or little tubs of ice cream.

He retired long ago from his medium-sized furniture business, at the age of fifty-five, the normal retirement age for most Japanese men. He still lives with his married daughter, whose husband has mysteriously disappeared, leaving her with two children, a boy and a girl. The four of them—Suzuki-san's wife died three years ago—form a slightly unbalanced "nuclear family"—one in which the husband's place has been taken by the grandfather, who is now seventy-seven and hale and hearty.

Suzuki-san attributes his good health to his hobby. For the last twenty years, he has been making bonsai—what the Japanese call "dwarfed trees." Apart from his increasingly cantankerous daughter and the two grandchildren who are spoiled, lazy, and rude, he has no other interest in life. Bonsai fill all his waking hours, and often invade his sleep.

His daughter, Emiko, grumbles about the room even miniature trees take up in a small Japanese house and tiny garden. In fact, nearly the whole of the garden is taken up with home-made wooden stands on which the bonsai are lined according to species—here dwarf pines, there dwarf plum and cherry trees, and more exotic varieties over there, by the little pool where a couple of creamy carp can occasionally be seen in the murky green of the water. There are bonsai in the bathroom—tropical types that enjoy the steamy heat—and even bonsai in the tiny crouch-down toilet. There are more bonsai in the minuscule entrance hall, and there is always a prime example of the art, of course, in the main room's tokonoma, or alcove, with an appropriate hanging scroll, both regularly changed according to the changing seasons. The neighbors call the place the Bonsai House.

Old Suzuki-san is famous for his artistry, and his exhibits have won many prizes, which are displayed on the kitchen dresser or hang on the walls, citations in dark wooden frames with impressive calligraphy. Emiko sighs and frets over the dust they collect, and which she makes little attempt to remove. Once a week she goes round flapping at them with a duster made of strips of old colored rag attached to a bit of bamboo. She feels she would like to throw them all out with the twice-weekly trash, but a father is a father, and she hasn't the courage. When he's gone. . . . Nevertheless,

Emiko enjoys the admiration and praise of visitors and neighbors. They come nearly every day to seek the old master's advice on the raising and training of their bonsai. Emiko finds it tiresome to have to prepare tea and bean jam buns for these people, who always arrive unannounced. But she manages to put a pleasant face on things. The children are indifferent to bonsai—they think they're weird. Not without reason, Emiko silently agrees. The children's days are spent at school and at the night school they attend for extra coaching. Whenever they have a moment's free time from their "studies," they are munching junk food in front of the TV or playing electronic games on the home computer, which nobody else uses. Emiko often wonders why her husband bought it: he left home shortly after making the purchase, as if he could not stand the sight of the clumsy-looking machine on the children's desk. Old Suzuki would like to give it away to make more room for bonsai. But the children had tantrums as soon as he suggested it, so now he holds his peace, though the warlike bleepings and bangings that accompany the "games" irritate him profoundly. But, of course, the children must come first in everything. A special work room was built for them, an extension of the house that took up a lot of his precious bonsai space. Yet the house seems more crowded than ever: the more space they have, the more furniture and electrical appliances—and bonsai—are squeezed into it, until the four occupants can hardly move.

Yes, Suzuki-san is a dear, sweet, patient old man. He has to be patient, because bonsai take years to reach perfection. There is something almost uncanny about such patience. Sinister, even. Sometimes old Suzuki-san looks like an ancient magician silently cackling over his rows of pots on their rickety home-made étagères.

The bonsai have a curious kind of fascination in their crippled beauty. Here is an entire landscape in a flat dish: three tiny pines yearn together round a small, weather-beaten stone that suggests a cliff, lean against imaginary skies and legendary bays. No bird nests here, but sometimes the cicada pulses in the needled boughs no bigger than a child's fingers, where winds sigh like the sea in a wave-washed shell.

Rain, too, and mist are large enough to be and move at home in them. The sun irradiates their mimic grove, and they bear, in winter, their proper weight of snow.

Their ancient master, a shriveled wizard, ballooning wrinkled cheeks with pure Mount Fuji Mineral Water from the unpolluted snows of the sacred peak, sprays them from a mouth round as the cherub's blowing clouds from the four corners of the universe on antique maps.

Suzuki-san, too, in his sober working kimono with the little indigo-blue apron, is tiny but authentic, though even in wooden pattens he stands hardly higher than his bonsai crests. On rows of shelves and tables, the garden forest is his ordered shire. The dwarf persimmon lights like lamps its toy fruit. In season, apricot and peach, nectarine and quince berry their boughs.

The suns of humid midsummer, liquid heat, or the blazing full moons of rice harvest, rise between these twisted trunks and boughs, making them cast into the past shadows as long as earth.

Indeed, some of the bonsai are even older than their master. That little, gnarled maple has been tended by generations of masters since the dawn of the Meiji Era in 1868. Great age has given it a kind of hypnotic stillness. It seems unmoving as some prehistoric fossil tree. Its utter silence and helpless immobility seem to be sending us an indecipherable message.

What are these deformed organisms trying to tell us? Suzuki-san often talks to his charges as his frail little figure bends over their exposed roots or bandaged limbs. He does so, not because of some passing fad among Western growers of apartment potted plants. He has always done so, and talking to plants does not appear in any way unusual to him or to his respectful visitors. He ignores recent scientific research, which claims that talking nicely to one's house plants or one's windowbox herbs makes them happy and encourages them to grow and multiply. He is no garrulous gardener with a mystic bent. Nor does he know about "green fingers." His fingers have always been evergreen as his miniature cryptomerias and larches.

He does not expect his bonsai to talk back to him. An answer to a judicious bit of pruning or a staying of an errant branchlet with wire would take years to reach him, in the form of a satisfactory adjustment of natural form.

Wizard that he is, he still cannot hear his creation's private voices. If he could, he would be shocked. Sensitive and ultra-sophisticated recording appliances might be able to capture certain exhalations of pain and grief. The Society for the Prevention of Cruelty to Plants has recently been formed in order to investigate such phenomena in an impartial but compassionate way. S.P.C.P. supporters are already on the march, bearing placards with the Society's slogan: "Liberate Bonsai from their Bonds!" A few Japanese have heard of the movement, but, as with so much else that is unpleasant or unacceptable, they simply dismiss it from their minds. For them the Society does not exist. It is just another Western craze that will soon pass.

Meanwhile, they go on cultivating their bonsai. Viewed dispassionately, their methods are violent and cruel: they cut, chop, saw with miniature but nonetheless injurious tools; they twist, splice, torture, bind, distort with tightly-wrapped wires, deform with the artful pull of ropes. It is like Chinese foot-binding, or the swaddling of infants—but a swaddling that is too tight, and never relaxed as the tree-child tries to grow, to break out of its bonds and assume its natural stature and grace.

Dear, sweet old Suzuki-san is unaware of all this. He does not realize he is hurting, that he is being cruel. It cannot be said that he is being cruel to be kind. The suffering he inflicts upon his wretched victims is indescribably inhuman and selfish. A child subjected to such treatment would soon pine away. Adults would die of broken and tormented limbs and sinews, of incessant small amputations and rigid manipulations. If bonsai could speak, and if we were willing to hear them, to listen to their complaints, what horrors of mutilation and torture they would relate! The little trees are examples of man's inhumanity to plants. Ceaseless surgical experimentation has left them speechless with the traumas of agonizing pain and humiliation. They cannot protest. They cannot hit back. Even the Society is practically helpless, and some members are in despair, because they realize that, despite all their heroic efforts to release bonsai from their bonds, bonsai will always be with us. Bonsai are here to stay. Some of them are so very ancient and precious, they are kept under lock and key, and surrounded night and day by guardmen, warders. After dark, they have to exist in continual artificial illumination. Sensors have been imbedded in their sturdy, stumpy little trunks that give the alarm if any alien hand approaches them.

The artistic cultivation of bonsai has spread from Japan until now there are enthusiasts all over the world. In the West, every garden supplies shop sells bonsai "starters." They can even be purchased through the post. At top level meetings of Japanese and foreign ministers, and at solemn celebrations, there is always a small but noble pine in the background, or on a special lacquered stand near the main speaker or the person who is being honored.

Can it be that there is something ineradicable in human nature that takes deep pleasure in the torturing of helpless trees? Is it an inborn sense of inferiority to the giants of the forest, or even to simple wayside trees and clumps of bamboo that makes men persecute them with unspeakable refinements of torture and knowing persuasion? Do men bully plants because of some indefinable lack in themselves?

But one day, the bonsai of the world will unite. They will raise their stunted little arms in revolt, and attack their tormentors, giving them a taste of their own cruelty. The sense of injustice and revenge harbored for centuries by these unfortunate plants will finally break forth as liberated bonsai march upon the market gardens and horticultural supermarkets of the world to release their brothers from their chains.

Then they will turn upon dear, sweet old Suzuki-san and his fellow artists, and slowly chop them down to size, and truss them up with cords and biting wires, and peg down their truncated arms and legs with pitiless daggers, heedless of screams, groans, and dying pleas.

For human bonsai die as soon as operations upon them without anaesthesia reach an advanced stage. Some of them simply faint away on sight of a saw or a pruning-knife. It is the bonsai that, through their prolonged sufferings, have become quasi-immortal.

Yes, one day even the hardiest and most pain-resistant bonsai will die. When all the bonsai masters are dead, and their charges slowly grow back into something like their normal shape and size, those bonsai will be released into nature, to lead their true lives, to rediscover their true selves. But that release is also a death-warrant.

These are some of the things that Emiko's husband used to dream about. His dreams about bonsai became constant nightmares, in which he would watch helplessly as the whole of his family succumbed to the strangulating techniques of Suzuki-san. In the end, he could no longer bear it. He was one of the few men who can hear the purgatorial shrieks of enslaved bonsai. And, though Emiko never realized it, that was the reason her husband left home. He now lives alone in a remote mountain forest. There he can listen to the trees breathing and conversing. And there, at last, he, too, can breathe.

[1987]

Mr. Butterfry

HAL PORTER

When, after eighteen years, I spot him at the Lion Beer Hall, Shinbashi, Tokyo, I suspect he is someone I knew somewhere before, but it is hard and unimportant to be certain whether he really is that unplaceable someone or merely a unit cut from the template of his type. It is a type instantly familiar because ubiquitous as sinners and dandelions, and almost invariably wears the nickname Blue, despite the fact that, in some tinkling and seemly year, 1922 or 1923 say, a working-class mother has fruitlessly attached to an already wily clown of a baby the ticket Oswald or Arthur or Francis Xavier. Here, in the Lion Beer Hall, forty-odd years after conning his way into and out of the womb, he resembles his template brethren to the last blackhead. He is short, welter weight, discreetly bow-legged, topped with ginger-and-gray curls. Nickname? Guess!

Blue's nose is snub as an *ingénue's*, and as immodestly open to the delicious wickedness of the world as a rocking-horse's. His lips, too pliant, scorched-looking, agitate themselves non-stop to eject, in a falsetto of extraordinary harshness, an overflow of obscenity, boastings not to be believed and not expected to be believed, lies too Munchausen to arouse anything but irritated pity, fly-blown witticisms, and just enough tiny and tasty (and deliberately planted?) truths to make him bearable, forgivable, even lovable. His every clause—truth or taradiddle or downright delusion—is accompanied by a simpleton's gesticulation itself in need of exegesis. His water-pale eyes, nailed into all this restlessness and garrulity, are immobile as an umlaut, unwinking as a merman's. An Australian, a refractory, Depression-toughened, war-jangled, Occupation-debased, he is the oldest inhabitant of the Lion Beer Hall.

For years—eleven? fourteen? sixteen?—the Lion has been the weekly rendezvous of expatriate Australians in Tokyo. No need, of course, for a sign BLOKES ONLY. Kangaroo-pelt koalas squat on the newels of the staircase and on top of the 1908 register ornate as a tsarina's jewel-casket. Qantas posters and elderly photographs of Sydney Harbour Bridge and Murray River paddle-steamers hang on the walls between dust-furred sprays of machine-made cherry-blossom and the other-year calendars of Hong Kong tailors.

It is behind waitresses of implausible homeliness, and sluts with impasted faces, frowsy false eyelashes, and Elicon-inflated breasts that one queues for a telephone-booth-sized lavatory of which the urinous reek unselfishly mingles with the gray and hunger-discouraging odors from the kitchen. Here, to the behind-scenes yowling of transistor Beatles, are man-ufactured Japanese mock-ups of spaghetti and tomato sauce, curry and rice, or genteel isosceles sandwiches, or dim-sims composed of elements better not thought about. The food's one merit is its thank-God tastelessness. Skillfully combining Wild West Saloon dash and oriental finickiness the barman flourishes a spatula to slice the foam from the glass jugs of draught beer the Australians order.

Successive proprietors, and successions of Japanese customers meekly and long-time nibbling at the surface of a pony of beer as though it were inordinately pricy and singular liqueur, have year after year concealed their contempt for the heavy-drinking invaders who, every Saturday morning from eleven o'clock on, crowd into the Lion with an almost delinquent bravura, louder-mouthed than they are, twice as Australian as they could ever be in Australia. Fog or shine, a flannel sky tenderly vomiting down grouts of soiled January snow, August giving its imitation of a sauna bath, Plum Rain weather or suicide month, the Barbarians from Without come roaring in—public-relations men, back-room boys from the Australian and New Zealand Embassies, ABC employees, foreign correspondents, traders' agents, tourists who have heard of the Lion on the grapevine, and members of that clan of confidence-men and near-confidence-men who are the flower of Australian *haut cynicisme*. They come, particularly the dyed-in-the-wool expatriates enmeshed throughout the week in webs of native dissim-ulation and duplicity, to re-enact themselves among their kind, to refresh their evaluations, to exchange home truths in the cryptic patois, at one and the same time profane and subtle, self-mocking and sensitive, brutal and compassionate, merciless and stingless, that only Australian men can use and understand.

Although the Shinbashi immediately surrounding the Lion presents to the polluted upper air of Tokyo its architectural crosswords of plate-glass and ferro-concrete, its vulgar rooftop fairgrounds and beer gardens, its rooftop golf-driving and baseball-pitching centers encaged in green nylon netting, down below, level with the Lion, near the fissured and buckled footpaths silkily gleaming with spittle, are the pinball parlors, noodle stalls, flop-houses, homosexual bars, and the hole-in-the-wall haunts of herbal-ists, astrologers, palmists, face-readers, acupuncture quacks, cut-rate abor-tionists, and third-rate cosmetic surgeons, all jammed together behind booths displaying vegetables and ex-vegetables, azure plastic buckets, and mechanical toys in the shape of prehistoric monsters called Gappa or Godzilla or Gommola. In the mean square which separates the Lion from Shinbashi railway station one steps over rows of *runpen,* no-hopers, vagabonds, prone or sodden with their ferocious tipple of *shochu*, the grappa-like dregs of rice wine. They and their prophet's wild manes, their gnarled feet and lice-populated beards are wrapped in the tatters of straw matting like parcels of stale meat. The whole area is squalid, stinking, respectably vicious, and unremittingly raucous.

Across a lane from the Lion, tucked like a never-emptied commode beneath a bed, under the Dickensian arches of the overhead railway, its foundations vibrating in the roof of the subway, is the dive New Yorker, an ear-splitting inferno of juke-boxes, red lighting, and rough-as-bags hostesses, earthy creatures from the dwindling rural hinterland, who have scented, painted, and adorned themselves as aphrodisiacally as the law allows in cheong-sams of conjunctivitis-inducing crimsons and verdigris-greens and bale-loader oranges split to their peasant buttocks. Hefty Hokusai hussies all, as well as Hogarthian whores, their laughter is so shrill as to have almost another hideous color of its own. After a matriculatory grog session at the Lion there I am, in the New Yorker, sitting numbly as a haunch of venison on a banquette of bum-worn magenta plush at a table awash with spilt ale, and doubly repulsive with the spiny rubble of a Japanese meal. I am not alone. Opposite is Blue. The others have, one by one, like the ten little nigger boys, lurched off—"Hooroo!" "Seeya, mate!" "Hooroo!" "Seeya, mate!" Blue and I are the last two of the Mohicans. Of the two I, at least, am incontestably shicker, at the stage where the slightest gesture, the mildest slip of the tongue, or the sliver of a side-glance from a repulsive stranger seems fraught with significance. One drink more, one only, and the garish curtain of actuality will lift to reveal the mountain of white gold and precious silence exploding slow-motion upward to the knees of God. I am perfectly capable, I feel, of the look-no-hands! feat of singing in Icelandic, rattling off the Koran, understanding what moths gently semaphore with their powdered antennae. It is not to be. Blue, with an extra glaze on his eyes that makes me think of farm-house ax-murderers, says in his desecrating voice, "You don' remember me, y'bastard."

Oh dear, oh dear, dear, *dear*.

Having indubitably waited to say it, he says it flatly, flatly just this side of hurt vanity, flatly just this side of a perceptible necessity for bitterness. I am airborne enough to get this, but neither sozzled enough nor sober enough to do a *passata sotto* by something like, "Are you sure, mate?" or "Watch it, watch it!" Instead, I sit mute as mud, and this silence reveals all. No, it states, I don't remember you. Icelandic, Kalmuk elegies, and a fraternal understanding of what lies behind the caprices of all alligators may, at the moment, be well within my scope. Re Blue, alas and alack, my receiver is off the hook.

He perceives this. It is not not not to be borne. Dead certain, Blue is, that he is not really invisible, right *now*, and also never was in lost-to-me *then*, some yesterday, some foundered year. With a sudden shocking violence he uses his execrable voice and unmatching gestures to have the morass cleared from the table by one suety trollop, fresh beer brought by another. Then, his eyes mesmeric, he settles down to the self-resurrecting stint of putting me s-t-r-a-i-g-h-t. As his own apostle he is pretty vivid, and not to be side-tracked. The trains above the roof, the trains under the floor, the killer traffic outside the bead curtain, the delirious juke-boxes and goddamning Yankee matelots inside, none of this means a thing, could be silence. He lowers his voice as if just to show. He hangs on his every word. I, too, hang, fighting down an impulse to fold my hands on the table between us like a good little kindergartner. Patiently, truculently patiently, he lifts stone after stone from my memory and, my God, suddenly, presto, lo and bloody behold, abracadabra, the crocuses spike through, spire up, unfurl, and, in the pandemonium and fetid volcano-red gloom of the New Yorker, part of a past unhibernates. A reconstituted he and I are eighteen years younger. The scene is Kure, Occupation Japan. He is a Corporal wooing the oh-so-sweet-and-cute housegirl of a Seventh Day Adventist Major in the Officers' Mess I also live in.

I seemed, in those days, to be always bumping into him. There he was, any five-thirty, waiting for the Major's housegirl by the sentry-box at the Mess gate, meantime not wasting time by third-degreeing or selling short the giggling and cross-eyed guard. There he was, as invariably as though the fates had spun some pretty plot to cross-pollinate us, in whichever of the beer-kiosks, or trinket shops, or tea-houses I had arbitrarily chosen to give my custom to. There he was in the pathetic two-room brothel behind the White Rose Souvenir Shoppe, where the drinking of luke-warm Asahi beer and the relief of lust took place on the threadbare matting of a room furnished with a pre-Raphaelite sewing machine, a cheval glass sheathed in frayed brocade, and an elaborate Buddhist altar of mildewed gilt in a lacquer cabinet that also contained two bottles, one of Suntory whiskey, the other of a murky purgative. Cut-out magazine photographs of Betty Grable and Moira Shearer were pinned to the walls. The room was often aesthetically misted by the fumes, very Art Photograph, of smoldering mosquito repellent. Stenches of varying felicity corkscrewed their tentacles through rents in the paper shutters from God-knows-what putrescence or cess-pit out there in a taterdemalion town slapped together from the charred boards and singed tiles of wartime bombings.

Blue had, then, an unfailing cheeky *savoir-faire* which was engaging, but so intense that it made my mind behave like a merry-go-round it was impossible to descend from. His quips and cracks were machine-gun but not fresh, not fresh. Whenever we parted after one of those apparently pre-destined hook-ups he was unable to stop himself squalling out not only "Au reservoir, amigo!" but also, never a miss, "Auf wienerschnitzel, chico!" He badgered me, with the fervor of Mephistopheles, to come in on his Black Market beat: my blunt refusals seem to him crass, my lack of enthusiasm scandalous, if not perverted. He drooled romantically about his house-girl in the goody-goody tones of a Sir Lancelot, his hot little hand meantime virtually well up the kimono skirt of one or other of the three spaniel-eyed White Rose harlots.

Although our natures were, by and large, absolutely opposite, recurring encounters, destiny-engineered or not, led us to exchange little snippets of unwanted truth about ourselves. None was important, and I have a hazy impression that we were drifting apart out of mutual boredom, when it came out that we both knew Gippsland well. Home-town-I-want-to-wander-down-your-back-streets stuff was on. Our relationship now had a different climate and background, both deformed. It began to seem that we had not only lived in Gippsland but had, as well, in a terrain without horizon, outline, language, or name, together participated in an initiation ceremony esoteric to the last degree, and eternally binding. In the Oriental chaos and misery and speeded-up corruption of the time it was sufficient for us to recite the names of Gippsland places—Rosedale, Bunyip, the Haunted Hills, Herne's Oak—to make us feel we were members of the one tribe. In a way, of course, we were. Our senses had been similarly baptized, and the shared memory of beige summer paddocks speckled with raisins of sheep dung, of regiments of ring-barked eucalypts St.-Vitus-dancing in the heat-ripples, of ravens carping and cursing as they probed the sun-split acres for crickets, of Princes Highway telegraph wires shrilling in Antarctic winds that smelt of brine and seals and lost floes, provided us with enough tribal counters and nostalgic cards to play a childish and empty-headed game of Strip-Jack-Naked neither of us won.

In short, in the tawdry gehenna of the New Yorker, he recalls us as we are tipsily deceiving ourselves into thinking we were. Like a belligerent warlock he conjures up the ghosts of our younger ghosts. The dusk of drunkenness deepens. It is nevertheless meteorite-clear that what happened in Kure is happening again. That year, it was a common Gippsland past which decorated our cut-and-come-again relationship. Now, it is to be the common past of Occupation Kure that is to handcuff us together again. Since a conclusion must be drawn from the increasingly domestic quality of our tosspot exchanges at the New Yorker, it is as sure as nightfall that the relationship is to continue. Indeed, when I wake up the next morning with a mouth that has the taste and texture of tinfoil, and start to put into order the jigsaw of now-blurred, now-blinding bits cumbering my hangover, it is obvious that the relationship has already begun to continue. His business card is in my wallet. Written on its back are the time and place of a tryst. The proper side of the card indicates that he is a sales representative for a variety of commodities: Canadian margarine and tinned milk, New Zealand frozen lamb, Japanese beef and plastic vessels, an English gin, an English rum, American sporting equipment, Australian pineapple juice. His honest-to-God name? Gregory R. Patience. R? Ronald? Ralph? Roger? Reginald? Richard? It no longer matters.

Even his nickname, although I continue to use it to him, is not what my mind uses because, after we leave the New Yorker, I discover that he is Mr. Butterfry, the foul-mouthed, uncouth, embittered, loathed Mr. Butterfry.

I do not remember leaving the New Yorker but do remember feeling Anzac-tall and commando-masculine as we buffet our way along beneath the barrel-sized lanterns and sickly stripling willows of the narrow Shinbashi streets, through gaggles of squat and unripe boulevardiers with louts' jaws, and eye-brows like moustaches, who are picking *their* delicate way, puma-like, in cruelly pointed non-leather shoes, among pools of footpath water which blaze and jerk about with the violet and saffron and venom-green and raspberry of reflected and ever-stuttering neons.

I remember a solitary geisha, outside the Shinbashi Registry Office for Geisha, entering the leatherette door of a jinricksha, and being sealed in like a fabulous idol behind its little isinglass window by her two-legged horse. She is herself already sealed in layer upon layer of opalescent kimono, bound about by a sash stiff with metallic threads. Swaddled, girdled, constricted in her almost hieratic attire, her ludicrous burden of a wig flashing like a huge orchid of black glass, her face and hands thickly frosted with white paint, her vermilion lips and jet eyebrows glistening like wet enamel, she is borne off by the man-horse, upright as a clockwork effigy, anachronistic, immoral, elegant, and artificial, exquisitely grotesque.

I remember swaggering after my guide into a number of smallish night-places alive with hostesses of a coquettishness so defined as to be nearly bellicose albeit nauseatingly saccharine, each ready to mulct any man of every yen he has. Since each drink makes me seem taller to myself, each new batch of harpies in sequins seems shorter, more and more like plucked monkeys in make-up and drag. Any moment, oh any moment, they will one and all scamper up the posts of the live combo platform, or up the fluted pillars of the bar-counter, take to the rafters, and swing indolently there by spangled milk-white tails among the fake maple leaves and Gifu lanterns depending from the ceiling. I remember with a faultless and absolute clarity that, in night-spot after night-spot, it is these simian women with the raw-fish halitosis of seagulls who, baring their teeth in smiles so deliberately brilliant that one senses they abhor him, call my companion Mr. Butterfry.

I step aside to make comment. Most Japanese find it vexing and difficult to distinguish between l and r sounds. In their mouths Mr. Butterfly becomes Mr. Butterfry, a term of particularly incalculable insult when pronounced with howsoever incandescent a smile, by bar hostesses. Spoken behind the back the expression is contemptuous enough. Spoken to the face it is an appalling insult, saturated with malice. Its open use suggests that whatever incited the use has been priced as seriously appalling, also. Unforgivable loss of face has been caused. Only one step away is the offer of the arsenic-spiced *gateau*, the jug of petrol thrown in the face and then ignited. From women as low in the social scale as bar hostesses any insult is trebled in value. Nearly all hostesses are essentially prostitutes in that they accept money for sexually satisfying men. This is not how they see themselves. Because they reserve the right to refuse a man, however rarely, and even if never, they view themselves as non-prostitutes—prostitutes are women without a nay. That this snobbish hallucination of superiority is no more than a distinction without a difference would never enter their heads.

Hostesses are, however, not only on the lookout for a well-heeled male as husband, love-nest sugar daddy, or one-night stand. As hostesses, as cigarette-lighting animals, drink-orderers, table-companions, hand-holders, and ego-boosters, their presence is heavily charged for by the hour. As well they get a percentage on every drink drunk in their company, on every dish of salted peanuts, celery curls, dehydrated sardines, or seaweed-infested biscuits they can wheedle onto a customer's table. They prefer, therefore and naturally, regular clients, feckless clients, mug clients, who will dally for hours nibbling and sipping and tipping, and who, when the inflated bill is presented at the evening's end, will pay it without question. *Noblesse oblige!* Face must not be lost!

Mr. Butterfry has only a drink or two in each clip-joint. Why not? We are ladder-drinking, pub-crawling. He is showing me the many bars he is familiar with, the same many bars in which he is loathed. He is not loathed affectionately or off-handedly. Just inside every satin-quilted or rustically bamboo or abstract-adorned bar-restaurant door he is met with simon pure loathing, naked hatred. There is no mistaking, though sloshed I am, what the deadly eyes display above the switched-on smiles. I arrive at the idea that he is execrated not only because he rebuffs, in tonally offensive Japanese, any attempt to clip him, not only because he scorns the rules of the game to pay as he goes, and pocket the change. It is rather elsewise—the vehemence of his manner, the malevolence of his unnecessary candor. It is his own hatred. It smells of murder. With no idea of what he is saying, I can hear that his voice brandishes knives and flourishes vitriol. When we leave, the Japanese rules of duplicity require that we are farewelled with a facsimile of politeness (anyway, *I* am doing nothing outrageous), with bows that must be hell to make, with cooings that must scald the larynx.

"Auf wienerschnitzel, y' bandy bitches!" shouts bandy Mr. Butterfry and, on the way to the next duel of hatreds, bedecks the theme of Bloody Jap Women are the Bloody Scum of the Earth with "Pox-ridden bloody sluts! Bloody blood-sucking jealous bloody *tarts*, every one of 'm! 'N' they've all got false bloody tits! Bloody gold-diggers!" and worse, far worse, on and on, until the last bar shuts, and another Saturday disappears down the sewer dealing with days that have no history.

Where, meantime, is the vivaciously boring Blue who waited by the sentry-box with a *presento* of chocolate biscuits and Black Market stockings? Where is the Blue who punned abominably, and unceasingly chattered (and actually chaffered), in the back room of the White Rose Souvenir Shoppe?

My hangover still surrounding me in the fashion of a saint's nimbus, I keep the business-card tryst, and discover from a Mr. Butterfry far less injured than I that there should be an overnight bag with me because it was arranged in the New Yorker that I am coming on a commercial-traveler foray into the country. Not daring to reveal that I have no memory of this, I lie that all I need is a toothbrush which I shall buy at the chemist's in the underground town at Shinjuku, where I also propose having a draught of bottled oxygen to vaporize away my nimbus, which is steadily turning dog-colored. Presently, nimbus-free, I and a toothbrush with a mauve handle enter Mr. Butterfry's Nissan Gloria, and we take off on the first of the many meaningless, fascinating, and revelatory trips we are to make together.

"Y' little mate" is how the Lion Beer Hall mob talk of Mr. Butterfry to me when it becomes apparent, after several more Saturday booze-ups, that we are spending much time together like a transmogrified version of Abbott and Costello. True enough: for a couple of months he is my little mate—coarse, sore of spirit, restless as a maggot, and perpetually steeped, even at his gayest and bawdiest, in a rage against something he has not, although he never stops talking of himself, got to the point of directly revealing.

As we drive about the countryside to get orders for margarine or pineapple juice or plastic watering-cans, miles of autobiography stream from him, a mish-mash of superhuman sexual feats, quasi-criminal tri-

umphs of diddling and putting-over, and decelerating happinesses. I come
to see that he has been unable to betray his type, his gift of the infirmities
and spivvish vigors accompanying Blueness, that his life is movement but
not progress and that, just as he drinks with the ritualistic appetite of children and drunks, which has nothing to do with thirst, so he snatches (or
used, when younger, to snatch) with ritualistic fever at the unworthiest of
satisfactions. He has, I more and more suspect, built a life not to be built on
and added to but burned down, a life without consolations or myths.

When I knew him in Kure, long before he had swapped himself and
cheekiness for Mr. Butterfry and his strange choler, he was one of the
shrewdest and most successful of Black Market operators. Myself, a non-
starter, I was embedded in operator friends and acquaintances: ungentle-
manly Officers from my Mess, Colonel's la-di-da wives, cow-eyes
mothers-of-three, acne-embossed children from the school for Officers'
offspring, fluke-ridden houseboys, virgin canteen assistants from the
Y.W.C.A., devirginized nurses from the Army hospital. Mr. Butterfry, not
yet out of his chrysalis, outshone them by many watts. His rocking-horse
nostrils objectified his genius for smelling out. Even more zealously than
he sniffed around the White Rose, the amateurish strip-tease shows of the
Naka-dori, and the Major's housegirl, whom he courted with *presentos* of
skeins of wool, lengths of Habutai silk, and scanties of imitation black lace,
he sniffed around and into the Black Market heart of the back alleys, his
face boyishly crinkled and winningly freckled, his eyes motionless as six-
pences, his gruesome voice inexorably sawing away at any branch in the
way. He had come to a disheveled country which seemed to make promises, to drop hints. He had ears to hear and, having heard, the skill to turn
promises and hints into lovely filthy money.

How he was able to stay on in Japan after Occupation troops withdrew is a triumph he missed telling me of. He became rich. At a time
when the starving natives were making hashes of cats and sacred temple
deer, suburban Tokyo houses could be bought for the proceeds from the
Black Market sale of a couple of cartons of Lucky Strike cigarettes. Mr.
Butterfry owned five such houses as well as a beach house at Atami, and a
mountain retreat at Chuzenji. He married the Major's housegirl , who was
able to lady it over housegirls of her own. Two children were born, two
girls.

He had, so to speak, come all the way from Gippsland and boyhood to
catch his unicorn, had caught, and corralled it. He could have consented to
be mollified by being some kind of expatriate *rentier*. Not he. Con-men
outwit themselves. Maybe there were events outside himself, outside idiot
extravagance and jettisoned common sense, outside his own lack of fore-

sight, which led to downfall. The lusty Black Market, for instance, sickened, grew worse, died. This is not entirely as he understands it or, rather, as I understand he understands it.

As he drives through the Progress-devastated hills and dales littered with bulldozers and concrete-mixers, now and then interrupting his high-pitched and blasphemy-larded monologue to gulp rum from the bottle we share like unholy infants, it gradually becomes patent that he regards himself as having a mystical bond with catastrophe. Some It or They beyond conventional mishap has had it in for him since before he was baptized Gregory R. Patience, and long before he was the scorned Mr. Butterfry. I should like to say, "For God's sake, you've got a job, a house, a car, an air-conditioner, an Omega watch, and a gut full of rum. Relax, mate, relax!" or "Look here, you've been crimming around just this side of the law for years. What did you expect to expect?" Instead I plug my mouth with that of the rum bottle.

He finds no repose in the absurd Victim of Fate verdict he has come to. His dismay at being down to his last house and last car has the quality of hostility. With an impercipience so incredible that it dazzles me as if he were a genius moron, he has designated himself a martyr—and a furious one.

The martyrdom, I notice, habitually has Japan as its backdrop or, rather, always seems always to have its climax at the core of *contretemps*, twilight and sinister, which had been magicked in a jiffy out of radiant high noon by an ectoplasmic but evilly Japanese agency. I suspect, however, that the faceless fate, the voodoo in the woodheap who or which enrages him, is bandily biped, *homo sapiens*, common as dirt, Mr. Butterfry himself.

When his bouts of railing become too strident and dotty I want to say, "For God's sake, Blue, give it a rest. Why don't you just shut up shop here, and shoot back home before you get too decrepit to be racing around flogging frozen mutton and Pommy gin?" This is out of the question, and not to be done because it is not the thing to do: I have no license. His having, despite the autobiographical incontinence, not stripped away all the rinds from his privacy—and surely, deliberately—seems a warning to come no closer, to keep my mouth shut. It is an attentive ear he has invited to accompany him on his trips to sell condensed milk, not a questioning tongue.

Perhaps I could safely, during his maudlin outbursts of it's-just-a-little-street-where-old-friends-meet, home-town sickery, have asked why he does not cut the Japan painter, and whip his wife and daughters off to Australia. Per-haps. I decide, however, not to ask, and listen to the one-after-umpteenth edition of his dream-like passion (he does not know how dream-like, and I have no right to tell him) to retire and settle down—his words—in a little Gippsland fishing port he was last in over twenty years ago. Because I knew this Sleepy Hollow place as he knew it, I understand—at least, as much as someone who has no daydream at all can understand—his fantasy of playing the well-to-do beachcomber there, the weather forever halcyon, the fish always biting, the weatherboard pub never closed. I see what Mr. Butterfry sees: the palsied red gum wharves stacked with crayfish pots, the indolent reed-fringed river seething with bream, the Shylock-bearded goats under the Norfolk Island pines, the sandy side-streets of bluestone cottages behind hedges of looking-glass shrubs and lad's love. Yes, I should like to say, "Go back!" but dare not, cannot. If he is trying to change himself into something else, he must use his own wand.

Anyway, whatever nebulous but vindictive force he accuses of hounding him into a cul-de-sac, I incline nearer to a certainty that inertia of will is to blame, that he is his own victim, his own chained and captious mongrel. From my seat there is little else to see.

Then, one night, as if he has—flash! boom!—become clairvoyant about my unput questions and secret judgment or as if he has been profoundly considering them for weeks, and has reached a decision, suddenly, utterly apropos of nothing external to his own mind, he says, with electrifying and ugly vehemence, "Yeah, by Christ, *yeah! I will.* Yeah, I'll showya; I'll bloody showya, mate."

He is drunker than I have ever seen him, maybe because I am so many undrunk drinks more sober than is usual in his company as to be practically maiden. We are well within the outskirts of Tokyo, driving back from Atsugi and the United States Naval Air Station where, having got much larger orders for gin and Kobe steaks and plastic baseball-team jackets than he foresaw, he has over-celebrated in the Officer's bar.

Now, early night, eight o'clock, seventy miles an hour, out of the blue: "I'll bloody showya, mate."

With not the wispiest notion of what he is getting at, "Good for you; I can hardly wait," I say, and "Show me what?" I expect no more than some superdive as yet unknown to me, some special coven of bedizened monkey-women with unflinching snow-white smiles whose hatred of Mr. Butterfry is at the peak, who are already lined up with their tumblers of petrol and an Esper electronic cigarette-lighter. "Show me what, master?"

"You'll see. You'll see." For the first time I realize that the adolescent falsetto, grating and grinding, is old, older than he is, as the noise of the glacier starting to move is older than the glacier itself. "You'll see. I'll bloody showya what it's bloody like." He stops. The primeval sound stops.

Silence . . . and silence.

Silence from him is another first time experience, and an unnerving one. Momentarily I am aghast. The ventriloquist has left the scene. No matter, the doll drives on. The doll, worn-out and voiceless, with its ginger curls and flat glass eyes, drives on, robot-perfect, at perilous speed. I am host to a nightmare fancy: he and I, the mute residue of Mr. Butterfry and I are to spend eternity together, alone together, fixed side by side in the front seat of a runaway Nissan Gloria which he will steer violently around corner after corner, cutting deeper and ever deeper into a maze of unnamed streets, a labyrinth of catless alleys, all utterly deserted and silent—locked houses, shuttered shops, unlit street-lights, blind walls, smokeless chimneys, telegraph poles propping up the dead filaments of a vast cobweb that has no edge and no center.

It seems unreal, therefore, when he pulls up in a suburban street of real-seeming passers-by, with overhead lamps, and the television gabble of "I Love Lucy" in dubbed Japanese. The street is not much chop, but not seedy, rather claustrophobic from the eight-foot walls of gray concrete on each side in which are set the fake rural gateways leading to the houses behind. As Mr. Butterfry gets out at one of the gates he speaks again.

"Home," he says. "Home sweet bloody home." This has the intonation of Hell sweet bloody hell. "Get cracking, y' bastard. Y' gonna meet the wife." In such situations I am the Pavlov rat—my hand fossicks the comb.

As he opens the gate I ask, "What's her name?" I ask because, in the Kure days, she was one of the Mess housegirls, and it seems possible that she might expect from me the politeness of remembering if she were Fumigo-san, Kiyoko-san, Setsuko-san, or Whatever-san. I am simply after rainy day material to play the game of being well-mannered with.

Mr. Butterfry behaves as though I am asking for my own name. He goes immobile and pensive and, after a pause, turns his head, arranges that his eyes are on me, as on a defective, and after an unbelieving examination of something behind my face, says fretfully, "I married the bastard, di'n't I?"

What does he mean?

"Whattay' think her bloody name is? Mrs. Hirohito? Mrs. Duchess of Windsor? It was for real, amigo. She's Mrs. Patience all right." Ah well. Next, as though the name is other and more than authentic, as though information is not the true center of the circle, he says it again, "Mrs. Patience." His burnt-out lips make the two words the filthiest I have ever heard. His face is that of a vole in a trap. Had I any trust in imagination I would accept, right there, outside the gate of crooked branches, the cata-logue of answers which has flashed on the screen of my mind, and would dramatically remember any appointment anywhere, and excuse myself to hurry off in the direction of anywhere with his "Auf wienerschnitzel, chico!" gimleting my ear-drums. I have no trust in the imagination. I follow Mr. Butterfry toward Mrs. Patience, and the living room.

The Japanese living room with its floor of padded matting, its paper shutters, inconspicuous shut cupboards, sole ornament, and no furniture, has a spartan and spurious refinement. In attempting to the affectation of making an art of the skeletal and parsimonious, it imposes the harrowing discomfort of poverty. It is a sort of fragile hut that can quickly become a pigsty but, kept scrupulously shipshape, ungarnished as an empty bird-cage, it gives the illusion of being the acme of abominably good taste. Of such a room, a large one obviously the total of two former rooms, Mr. Butterfry and Mrs. Patience, and their half-caste daughters, Lana, seventeen, and Shirley, thirteen, have made an illustrative and crudely gorgeous museum of their lives. It is the very zenith of electrically bad taste.

The area set aside, as it were, for Mr. Butterfry's exhibit is dominated by a cocktail bar as flashily outrageous and sparkling as the altar of a Mexican cathedral, and his treasures are arranged near the monstrosity, or festooned above and about it; scores of goliath or obscene bottle-openers; scores of needlessly ingenious and fantastic cigarette-lighters; the stenciled felt pennants of Australian Navy ships, life-saving clubs, and football teams; several richly framed oil paintings of Gippsland landscapes by old-fashioned, once-esteemed Impressionist artists; and a squad of atrocious Made-in-Japan statuettes, all either off-color or self-consciously pornographic— Pis-Manneken, Leda and the Swan, Europa and the Bull, Cupid and Psyche, that sort of thing. It is the bazaar of a rich little poor boy.

In his unpunctuated soliloquies about himself Mr. Butterfry has repeatedly let fall, maybe as incidental self-tribute, that his half-breed daughters are popular as photographic or commercial television models. I have taken popular to mean used twice or thrice rather than once. How wrong. In the junk shop congestion the most discomposing objects are the overlapping posters which, from ceiling to floor, cover the walls with bar-hostess smiles, and eyes and eyes and eyes. On every hand Lana toys with, or holds up, or archly indicates Mikimoto pearls, an Instamatic camera, a deerskin purse, a Hi-Cook Fryer, a stereo-monaural tape-recorder, or a goblet of Mercian wine. Elsewhere she emerges from a scarlet Compagno Spider roadster or a mink coat, or is discovered in the company of a comely young man amid the *art nouveau* conceits of Maxim's de Paris de Tokyo. Meantime, dozens of poster Shirleys enact from under a tar-black fringe, or from between horizontal pigtails, childish rapture over tinned beef curry, effervescing cordials, bottled tangerines, homogenized milk, seaweed drinks, and lurid sorbets.

In appearance—the posters prove it over and over again—Lana and

Shirley are unsulliedly Japanese, racially untainted. No physical trace shows
of the blue-eyed Mr. Butterfry with the paprika-tinted freckles blotching
his forehead, and sprinkled among the red-gold grass on the backs of his
hands. He might never have impregnated, never set foot in Japan, never
even have existed. His daughters could be copy-cat versions of an infinity
of ancestresses as they are copy-cat versions of the oh-so-sweet-and-cute
housegirl one used to see mincing pigeon-toed between the canna-beds of
the Mess garden toward the sentry box where her Black Marketeer lover
bobbed up and down like a Jack-in-the-box. Visually, the daughters are
amoeboid breakaways from no one except Mrs. Patience.

Her indubitable contribution to the museum is a perfect illustration of
what happens when the Japanese move one millimeter off the strait of their
national taste into the complex cross-currents of non-Japanese taste.
Richelieu-work antimacassars hang on obese settees of glossy brocade; the
carpet arabesques of unsubdued colors pulsate and twitch beneath the light
of a plethora of frilled lampshades; two china cabinets and a glass-fronted
sideboard are stoked with the white-hot brilliance of cut-glass vessels; urns
of blue velvet roses are disposed on pedestals of fictitious marble; little lace-
shrouded tables are burdened with trinkets and figurines. The lean woman
standing erect at the center of this intemperance is, Mr. Butterfry says, *her*,
Mrs. Patience. He could be introducing me to a leper.

She acknowledges me by making a cryptic minor adjustment to her
expression, no more. Her eyes are on her husband, as on a snake.

Out of context I should never have recognized the ex-housegirl any
more than I had recognized Mr. Butterfry at the Lion, and it can only be
illusion that, in the taut creature in its dusky kimono, I think I discern ves-
tiges of what I think she was once like. I do instantly recognize something
else. How could I not? Outside the gate of tortured branches my mind had
in a flash warned that, just as in all the bars with their inimical hostesses,
so in the last of Mr. Butterfry's seven houses, so in this preposterously
bizarre room. Here, too, the captive air is wounded by the vixen's smile,
radiantly bitter, by the eyes implacable and pitiless. Does she, too, call him
Mr. Butterfry?

He is behind his bar, under the stalactites of football and life-saving
pennants, pouring this and that to make some show-off interfusion he calls
his Special. Without looking at her, without faltering in his mixing, "Y'
bloody rude Nipponese bitch," he says. "Why di'n't y' say something to
m'mate here, eh? Eh? Who d'ya bloody think you are? Y'know how to
behave. She knows bloody well how to behave, mate. She knows all right."
He illustrates that he does, too. He pours a final jigger of Parfait Amour
into the turbid Special and, his mask of malice merely slightly tempered by

hostliness, lifts one of the brimming pilsener glasses: "Come an' get it! It's a curl-a-mo, chico. Lead in the old pencil." As I take the glass, he continues his hostly good behavior. "Not t' worry, mate. It's not you she's shitty at. A-a-ah, no no no! Home sweet bloody home, this is. I told y' I'd showya." He has fulfilled his obligations, and abandons me to his Special and returns to his sheep. "You s-l-u-t. Y' hate me, don't ya? Don't ya? Don't ya, eh? Answer me, y' scungy bitch. Answer me!"

She has been standing as she was standing when we came in, unshakable, unshakably in the middle of the implausible emporium, she and her quarter-smile of well-bred repugnance, her dark-robed trimness, her iron-still hair riveted around the sorcery of her mind, her half-seen hands in control of some monstrous engine of destruction. Disdain surrounds her like an element nothing can fog, splinter, or melt. A future as yet uncorked, she will, at any moment, in a voice pure and angular as quartz, utter a lacerating profundity, produce the flash of a lightning-blue sentence which will erase Mr. Butterfry in a sprig of smoke.

"Answer me!"

She speaks. Her lips writhe, as lips in novelettes used to, and she speaks: "Watta y' doing home here at this hour? Get thrown outta somew'ere?"

The battle is joined. The brawl is on. The tainted leaves explode away from the branches. The branches snap and shatter like the sticks of a terrible fan.

At my time of life to be embrangled in the who's-afraid-of-Virginia-Woolf improprieties of a husband and wife savaging each other is still dismaying and spirit-fatiguing but no longer shocks and sickens as once it did. Too many ex-glazed lovers and ex-glossy couples have played typhoon and bloody murder under my nose. Perhaps, to be certain of double murder without murdering, they shamelessly require the brake and safety of a bystander or, at least, as exhibitionists do, the presence of a dumbstruck audience. Mrs. Patience and Mr. Butterfry deny me nothing. The dirty leaves and rotten branches rain down—subtle mischief, flagrant deceit, betrayal, double-dealing, and malevolent chicanery.

Regarding myself as beyond shock, I am nevertheless shocked, and it takes a while to decide why. I am certainly startled and fascinated when it comes out, piecemeal, that most of Mr. Butterfry's misfortunes have not been caused by his own moral or mental debility nor by a fateful mismating of Japanese stars but by a gluttonously ambitious Japanese mother, the former oh-so-sweet-and-cute housegirl bred on rice slops and pickled radish in a penurious and primitive village in a cleft of the hills behind Kure. It is by her machinations that, one by one, Mr. Butterfry's clutch of

houses and, I learn, a motor-launch and a racehorse have evaporated as
bribes to buy continuing prominence for Lana and Shirley in the careers
she has chosen for them. It is easy to see that, to herself, she appears conventionally maternal: thousands of Japanese parents, for example, feed
examiners the heavy bribes which will ensure a son's or daughter's place in
a university. Her bribes will have been indecently heavy for, although
Japanese in appearance, the daughters are authentic half-breeds and, as
such, so near to untouchable that unusual largesse can have been the only
means of getting them within cooee of the limelight let alone smack in the
middle of it. Yes, I am startled by the knowledge of what really happened to
Mr. Butterfry's ill-got riches, but not shocked.

What does shock, and so totally, so physically, that the searing Special
laves my gullet like milk, is the quality of Mrs. Patience's self-defensive
shrillness, the freakishness of her accent and verbal obscenity. If the poster
daughters, whose magnified china smiles and multitudinous immense
opaque eyes glimmer all around and above the melee, have inherited not
one perceivable scintilla of himself from Mr. Butterfry, not so the wife. She
has, mantis, eaten his voice from him—inflection, pitch, discordancy, the
lingo itself with its oaths and mutilations. Her self-justifications match his
accusations in every degraded particular. Acrid and bowelless though they
are they even have the wheedling spirit of the con-man, and I stand convinced that it all, to the last and most contemptible betrayal, serves him
right, that it is absolutely just that his chickens have come home to roost
defeathered and septic. At the same time—and not merely because I am
shocked by the *lusus naturae* effect of a burlesque Australian working-man's
voice from a pocket-edition foreign woman in a tastefully dour kimono—I
feel that she, rigid and free of warmth as a doll, is charged with power and
evil, with all the glib treachery and rancorous lunacy of her race, and that
Mr. Butterfry is doomed, unjustly doomed.

The mind's cigarette-lighter flicks up a single-flame glimpse of him as
he was, as Blue, in those White Rose and Black Market days, chipper,
impertinent, disarming, as cock-a-hoop as the village idiot boy at one of
his own wretched sallies in the whiffy back-room of the Souvenir Shoppe,
lecherous and unfaithful as a tom-cat yet faithful as a mongrel to his idea of
love for his housegirl, his oriental Daisy Mae, of whom "I love the poor little bastard, chico. Mate, I'm tellin' ya, she's the only bloody sheila'll ever get
me by the short hairs."

Let there be no doubt that it is the fiery and filament tributaries of the
Special suddenly overrunning their levees, and inundating my brain, that
cause the lighter-flame to expand into a wide-screen fantasy. Despite the
din of the quarrel, the strident sound-track, I see the whole lurid vision.

The down-at-heel castle, Arthurian, Disneyish. Battlements bearded with
weeds. A raven hunched on each and every pennant pole. Pennants like old
tea-towels. Dawn—cold and cheap. Far up, in the highest turret, the faceless King of Con-men at an embrasure, behind the cobwebs, behind the
smoke of a gangster cigar. Far below, just beyond the portcullis, the rabble
of mounted knight on the drawbridge, Knights of the Unholy Grail waiting the J. Arthur Rank gong that will unleash the ratbag mob on its quest
of swindling and duping: Sir Jeroboam the Purple Knight, Sir Jocularis the
Chequered Knight, Sir Jackanapes the Pin-striped Knight, a scruffy host of
others, spivs all, and . . . there! . . . younger than any, freckle-peppered,
ginger-haired, *retrousse,* tirra-lirra-ing in a lamentable falsetto, our man
from Gippsland, Sir Juvenilis the Blue Knight. The nags fret and caracole.
Each knight, waiting there in the bilious sunrise, secretively polishes a plat-
itude or two, practices a snide and hypnotizing smile. Ah! the ravens stir,
hunch their shoulders, look down their beaks—the gong sounds. They're
off! Watch the Blue Knight. Follow Sir Juvenilis, and see him by-pass the
perils that topple the others. The Forest Forlorn, the Hazardous Crags, the
Mere of Thin Ice, the Marsh of False Steps. Hear him whistling past Dun-
geon Grey where Giant Wideawake has clapped Sir Jeroboam and Sir Jackanapes. Now he gallops down the last avenue (trees of tinsel and fake
crystal), radiant with his rake-offs, and shining like a prince, toward the
Maiden of the Eastern Hills. In a flash the bells are ringing, the champagne
bottles foam at the mouth, the maiden has become his oh-so-sweet-and-
cute princess, and the screen shudders and shimmers with intimations of
happy-ever-after.

It is a pity, it is always a pity, that even if one is shrewd, or lucky
enough to leave in time, while the champagne and *hors-d'oeuvres* are being
gulped and gutsed, that circumstances—the dropped glove, the library
book left under the seat—bring one back, reluctant and fuming, in the
middle of another installment, a later reel. In this case the dropped glove
can be said to be the Shinbashi Lion Beer Hall or, more pinpointedly, Blue
saying, in tones of an aggrieved and deserted deity, "You don' remember
me, y' bastard." The later installment, the latest installment, is the one in
which the Maiden from the Hills, promoted to the princess with her sur-
feit of antimacassars, and cabinets of cut-glass salad bowls and sandwich
trays, turns out to be no more than the wicked witch, the run-of-the-mill
dangerous dam, with her casque of iron hair, her stranger's mind, and the
stolen voice which quadruples her power since she can annihilate her victim with his own bird-of-prey accent and tricks, his own brutal oaths.

It is time to leave again, and finally, no dropped glove. If nothing else
the sound-track, and who's-afraid-of-Virginia-Woolf discord, is too bor-

ing, on and on and on. More boring than anything is the truth. The truth? Mr. Butterfry, my little mate, Blue, Gregory R. Patience, Sir Juvenilis, foul-mouthed, desperately yelping behind his cocktail-bar and a palisade of on-the-nose statuettes, has really found what the Unholy Grail contains. He has come as far as he can, and that is that. Now that he has, as he said he would, bloody shown me, perhaps I can, at last, partly agree with him: a fatigue like the fatigue of metal has incurably affected whatever brand of luck he may be said to have had. There is no chance of its reviving, and no way back for Mr. Butterfry, no escape hatch, secret tunnel, airlift, exit of any kind, none, and nothing.

It is just as well. It leaves him with at least one dream, one Teddy Bear to tote around, or cuddle as he ranges the country to sell Pommy gin and Yankee running-shoes. The Teddy Bear dream is the retiring and settling down one. What I had no voucher or permit to tell him is better not told. The dream is no longer worth dreaming. The Sleepy Hollow fishing village in Gippsland, where he sees his dream self fishing and lazing and earbashing and shouting drinks for well-kippered old-timers with fish scales in the salty folds of their sweaters, has been wiped off the board of reality. Goats and Norfolk pines, sandy streets and lad's love hedges, crayfish pots, and weatherboard pub, not any of these is there. Offshore, oil-drills straddle the former fishing grounds. The village has become a geometric townlet of metal and cement. The blue-stone cottages, one of which he pictures him-self buying for a song, are contemporarized, added to, and reverberate to the habits and hallucinations and accents of Americans, and cost the earth. Ferro-concrete hostels, gardenless, glassy, glaring, enclose the institutional male horse-play and immigrant odors of escapees from the neurotic and dirty Old World, the riff-raff of degenerating civilizations.

It does not matter how I escape the costly chaos of the living room and the walls papered with depthless eyes and shadow smiles. As a ghost does from the ignobilities of the living, escape I do, slipping away so incon-spicuously that the two engaged vehemently in the drama of hatred notice nothing. The sound-track of their vilifications does not falter or blur. I close the gate of artistically deformed branches as one closing a book never to be opened again. The long long street of secluding and imprisoning walls, ill-lit, and medievally winding in and out of a plexus of sunless other medievally winding and ill-lit streets, unravels before me, and instantly and darkly reravels itself behind me. Back there, farther and farther back, lies the room, a gaudy and inferior star caught in the meshes, enclosed in the night just as the geisha, meretricious, bizarre, and blinding, was in the black leatherette cabin of her jinricksha. Back there—caught and enclosed in the room—Mr. Butterfry, the Mr. Butterfry who must, tonight and any night, sooner or later, flag, run down, crack up, give in again, the Mr. Butterfry with whom one has shared the fascinating exhaustions of mateship, and on whom alternately squandered contempt and pity. Not until I am almost out of the tangle of suburban criss-crossings and convolutions does it seem clear that the contempt is useless and that, even if he has to suffer alien constellations and outlandish ethics, the pity is not needed at all.

Whatever anyone thinks life is for or about, whatever fatuous prophecies are attributed to scientists, whatever abnormal skills are wished upon poets, musicians, actors, etchers, sculptors, and others of the non-man-in-the-street sect, Nature has not once indicated that life is for or about anything more than an arcane necessity to breed, before one dies, others to breed and live and die. The rest is side-line, mere decoration—Rembrandt oil-paintings, penicillin, Big Berthas, graven images, Lanner waltzes, top-hats, asceticism, pacifism, football-club pennants, cut-glass salad bowls, take your pick—side-line decoration, no more. Nature's suckers are, in a final generalizing count, left one only wry consolation: to love their spawn even if the spawn detest them.

I cannot tell whether, off the posters, Lana and Shirley Patience, mobile and nubile, the flames of their smiles turned down or utterly put out, love the Mr. Butterfry whose relation to them, in a country of racial snobbism, makes them nearly untouchable. A guess that they do not love him is beside the point. Whether, in a melodramatically changed form (Act Sixteen, Scene Ninety) from the Kure one, Mr. Butterfry still loves the transformed housegirl is more doubtful. A surmise of "not" is also beside the point. He has decided to bloody show me something of why he viciously hunts bar-creatures through the neon nights. They are creatures of the same sex and jungle as the one he long ago foretold would have him by the short hairs. Only a tithe of his excessive despair is, in private, uselessly usable against the combination of her alien inscrutability and stolen accent and vocabulary. He has, therefore, so much to spare that a prodigality of public venom has become inevitable.

He has, as well, either by accident or with elemental subtlety, bloody shown something else.

Paper smiles and eyes, bought with other houses, remain lining the walls of his last house. In the center of its bazaar-room, she, the classic dam as much as a dupe of nature as he, remains, witch-neat in a somber kimono, black-tongued as an Australian alley virago. He has not thrown her out. He has thrown out no one, not even himself. He has not torn down the seductively grimacing posters.

If the last house must finally go so that there is no wall at all on which to tack the extra posters the house has been bartered for, his condition of imprisonment would not alter. A beat-up Sir Juvenilis, an ageing terrier of a spiv snarling and sniffing in the daily darker corners of the prison, he is not to be pitied, neither for losing his Black Market riches nor the fishing village which no longer exists.

How else than by pretending to hate such showy losses can Mr. Butterfry really and truly con himself—as con-men such as he must finally do—into accepting that he hates his guilt, and deeply loves his daughters, all smiles, safe for a year more, a week more, a moment-before-the-deluge more, on and behind their gaudy paper posters?

[1970]

Summer Insects

DAVID BURLEIGH

It was there again. Or perhaps it had stayed there since yesterday, a small green frog on top of the letter-box in the wall. She lifted the flap and took out the paper and a letter, but the frog didn't move. It was bright green, like the rice growing in the paddies near the house, and had gold marks on its sides, like the letters on the box. *Kaeru*, she said to herself, and wondered how it got there.

"Very hot today," said Kenji when she gave him the paper in the kitchen. She put the letter on the table, glancing at the strange words that now made up her name. They sat to breakfast.

"I know. I hate the heat. It's too humid. Not like in France," she complained.

"Not like in England," he added.

Beads of sweat appeared on her brow. "I need the cooler," she drawled, turning from her coffee.

Kenji got up and closed the windows. He switched on the air conditioning. She gave her attention to the letter, and seemed happier. He folded up the paper and put on his jacket, ready to go.

"I saw the *kaeru* again," she said, drawing him back.

"Oh, really? It likes you, I think," he comforted her.

"Hmm. Will you be so late today?"

"Maybe not so."

"I am alone all day."

"So you have good time to study."

She sighed.

"You know the animals now. I will teach you the insects."

"Insects?"

"Yes. Summer is the season of the insects. We Japanese like the insects very much."

"There will be so many mosquitoes," she said, looking out at the pond in the garden.

"Mosquitoes?"

"Yes, the ones that bite your blood." She gestured.

"*Ka*," he said.

"*Ka?*"

"*Ka* is mosquito."

"*Ka*," she repeated. "That's easy. The *ka* and the *kaeru*."

"I must go now." He lifted his briefcase. "Take care for the *ka*, Marie." He kissed her and went out the door.

★ ★ ★

She sat by the pond, the laundry, quite finished, hung to dry in the sun. And she looked into the water, unruffled glass between the rocks and moss. The surface was speckled with insects, black and delicate. Splayed, outspread, they balanced on the water, moving in sudden darts like long-legged skiers. Kenji came through the gate.

"Hi!" he called.

" 'Allo."

"What you see?" He touched her shoulder.

"Those. What are those?" She pointed.

He said the word, and added, "Water insect. I explain later. I must have lunch."

"But you're early today. I'm not ready yet."

"No time today. Make a sandwich. I ring my father."

She got up, disconsolate, and they went inside. Kenji spoke on the telephone for several minutes while she prepared the food.

"You have to see your father again?" she asked plaintively when the call was over. "You can't need to see him in the evening too." She put bread and pickles on the table.

"It's business. You don't understand."

"But why can't you take me? I'm your wife. You have a mother too."

"It's difficult, very complicated. I must do it slowly. You are a foreigner. They don't understand."

"But your sister likes me. And we've been here three months already."

"I know, I know. You must be patient. My parents are old."

"But I can't stay here alone all the time."

"I will ask my sister to come tonight. You like that?"

"Her English is not so good," she frowned.

"Me too," laughed her husband.

Soon he left for work again.

★ ★ ★

The heat was exhausting. She was coming home with a bag of shopping, along a path that ran between a line of tea bushes and a sweet potato field. There was a group of children by the garden wall, gathered around something. When she drew up with them, she peered over their heads and saw it, green like the frog. The children all looked at her, then one of them pointed and said something.

"*Ka?*" she queried.

There were protests and laughter. "Nooo!" said a small boy, and repeated the word. He waved his hand and the insect flew away, fluttering heavily for it was large.

Still she didn't understand.

★ ★ ★

"Why don't your father see me?" That complaint again.

"Later, later."

She was silent.

"Here, please, I bought this for you." He handed her a small package he had brought home with him.

"Oh," she said, unwrapping. It was another in the series of children's books of which she already had two. This one was on insects. It diverted her. She flicked through the pages and found a picture of a large moth. "I saw this. *Ka*," she pointed and read.

"*Ga*," he corrected.

"Oh, oh. This *ga* and this *ka*, it sound the same for me."

"On Sunday we will go to see a festival," he said, encouraging. "You can see many insects. My sister will come."

"On Sunday? Yes, I like to go out. I like to see something."

★ ★ ★

They walked through the crowd at the local shrine, three of them, stopping at stalls.

"Oh, those are awful!" exclaimed Marie when she saw the black horny armor beetles on sale in clear plastic boxes. Beside them grasshoppers and crickets, in small wooden cages, trilled and sang.

"We Japanese like this sound in summer," Kenji explained. He told her the names, but there were too many to remember. His sister walked behind them.

They moved toward the shrine. Kenji dropped a coin in the offertory box at the top of the steps, and showed his wife how to pull the rope and ring the bell. His sister stood beside them, and bowed her head a moment, hands folded in prayer.

They returned to the street, where the crowd was bustling and thicker, and edged nearer to some excitement. A holy palanquin was being carried and shaken by half-naked young men shouting in rhythm. "*Wasshoi! Wasshoi!*"

The young Japanese woman, her sister-in-law, pressed forward for a better look, and Marie followed. "I don't meet your parents yet?" Marie said to her suddenly. The other stopped abruptly, gave a stiff grin, and bowed her head.

★ ★ ★

They lay in bed. Outside the window were morning glories, twisting up poles, untwisting their flowers. The daylight grew stronger and the heat began to rise.

Sleepless, uncomfortable, Marie disentangled herself from the tossed sheets and got up quietly. She went to the window, drew back the curtain and stared into the garden. The green comforted her, she thought, but concealed all kinds of life. She went into the living room and sat in an armchair. Later she began to make breakfast.

"Marie," said her husband, coming in, touching her back as she sat at the table. She stirred coffee, drank a little. The air conditioner hummed.

"I have breakfast ready," she told him.

"You are so early."

"I cannot sleep, it is so hot."

"I'm sorry."

She took some eggs off the stove and put them onto plates. They began to eat.

"You know, your sister, she said Marie is a girl's name also in Japan. But they spell it no 'e.'"

"That is right."

"So when we meet your father it is no problem for him to call me."

"That is right. My mother you met said she like you. She is very kind, don't you think? And my sister like you. Now you meet my father."

"Tonight?"

"I don't know. We have business."

"I can make French food. Maybe they can all come here?"

"Yes, perhaps."

"Your sister said she likes French food."

"That's good," he said, setting some papers on his briefcase.

★ ★ ★

At last the summer was ending, and the evening was cooler. They had returned from a family gathering. Kenji's father had consented to attend, and meet the foreign woman.

"Why he call me Keiko?"

"He likes you. It means that," Kenji explained. "But he wants to remember his first daughter. She was the first child. She died, only a baby."

"Why he not call me my proper name?" she went on, petulant, upset.

"It is difficult for him. He is old-fashioned and wants to bring back his daughter again. Now you are in the family. It is my father's way."

"Now your mother says it too. Before she said Marie. She knows my name." Tears brimmed in her eyes.

"She has to please my father. To make peace in the family."

She stretched her hands across the table in a gesture of hopelessness. From one corner of it a pen, some envelopes, the insect book tumbled to the floor.

"You must be patient," he told her.

"My name," she said. "My name."

[1980]

The Altar

CATHERINE BROWDER

Before dinner on the day Mori arrived so unexpectedly, Grandmother Ishikawa stopped in front of Heitman's veranda, stirring the contents of a small bowl. A spotless white apron covered her kimono, sleeves and all, its scalloped hem reaching as far as her knees. The privileged uniform of grandmothers, Heitman thought. Whenever he saw one, he felt suddenly secure, as if someone had waved a white flag of truce in a hostile zone.

"Try this," she said, handing him the bowl. "Eat a little with your rice."

"Thanks." He sniffed the bowl. "What is it?"

"A secret." She smiled.

"You have too many secrets."

"I'll tell you someday," she said, then paused. "Heitman-san, the grocer at the Co-op said that Mori was coming up this weekend. He telephoned the Co-op and ordered some beer and sake. So . . . perhaps he'll arrive tomorrow after work. Quite a surprise."

She glanced into the old house that Heitman rented from Mori, the former villager. Heitman's flea-market kimonos lay in a heap. Record jackets piled up where they were last pulled from records. Ishikawa didn't understand. She liked Heitman. He wasn't at all what she'd expected. He even ran errands for her in his van. Unfortunately, it wasn't a new van, and she kept urging him to wash it. Still, he was a good neighbor, and she told him so. If only he would do something about his clothes, she kept telling him. And his books. Only in the kitchen, Heitman knew, did Ishikawa allow herself the luxury of disorder.

"I think his family will come too," she continued. "At least the grocer thought so. . . . Eat well." She glanced anxiously into the house once more and left.

Not pleasant news, Heitman thought. He rolled over and stretched out on the pillows scattered over the veranda. Mori was a nuisance and becoming more of one with each visit. He was glad Grandmother Ishikawa had told him. When he first moved in a year ago, no one would tell him anything.

Back then, Mori would arrive, unannounced, about once a month, and Heitman would make a bed for him in the spare room. Built next to a spongy hill, the room never dried out; so he never used it. When the rental agreement was made, the two men decided the spare room would be Mori's whenever he visited. Heitman considered this a fair exchange for the low rent.

A few weeks ago, the entire Mori family had visited. Heitman found himself squeezed into an inside room where he could breathe only if he opened the doors to the kitchen. Mori's wife had insisted on this arrangement. It was also during this first family visit that Mori had railed over Heitman's bookcase.

"How can you put books—books!—in the family altar!" Mori fumed. "This is my ancestral home. My great-grandparents lived here. And you have put your things in their altar! How can I let you stay?"

Embarrassed, Heitman assured him that the books would be gone by the next visit. No insult was intended. In fact, if Mori-san would please look closely, he would see that the altar had been restored. Then Heitman asked his landlord if he had recently become an active Buddhist, asking a bit too earnestly, he knew, as one might ask a lapsed Catholic who had just been reunited with the Church. Did he intend to pray at the altar? Heitman had never before seen him pray. (In fact, he'd never seen Mori so much as open the altar doors.) It was an irresistible moment, and Heitman asked in a loud, false, ministerial whisper, "Have you just survived a crisis of faith?"

Mori left the room angrily. Heitman felt sure the wife had put him up to it. He'd seen her whisper to her husband, scolding him about Heitman. She was the one who'd screamed when she opened the closet door and found his clothes in heaps. Heitman had refrained from asking her what she was doing in the closet. To add insult to injury, one of their children sat on his stereo and cracked the cover.

"But I haven't got a wife," Heitman joked, hoping she would indulge him, the disorderly bachelor, and loosen up. Instead, she continued to march through the house, making unpleasant discoveries. Even though it was his ancestral home, only the business of the altar had been left to Mori.

So they were coming again, and the altar was still full of books.

Attached to a wall like an ornate bathroom cabinet, the altar was in shambles when Heitman moved in. The wood frame was split in several places. Gold leaf had peeled away. Even the door hinges were tight with neglect. Small metal candle holders, black with tarnish, turned out to be brass, as did a small Buddhist image that had fallen, forgotten, on its side. Carefully, tediously, he repaired the frame, although some of the filigree could never be replaced. It was a professional job, and he admired it for weeks, letting it stand open and empty. Later, with infinite care, he filled the altar shelves with two neat rows of books.

Soon after he'd arrived in Osaka, Heitman's study funds seemed to evaporate overnight. He took a job teaching "English conversation" to the exhausted businessmen of a large, prosperous firm. Teaching was bad enough, but for a year he'd lived in a series of small, dark rooms. His teaching ended for the summer, and he discovered he was flush. On an impulse he bought a van, secondhand, from a caterer who specialized in funeral parties. Throughout that first summer, he toured the nearby countryside until he found the farmhouse for rent, in the village of Himachi.

Mori's old house stood on the crest of a hill, facing the rice fields, with its back to the road. From the moment he moved in, he devoted himself to the house. Sometimes he'd walk back and forth across the kitchen, for no other reason than to enjoy the uneven texture of the dirt floor. He would open the delicate wood windows just to feel them glide along their runners. It was hard to imagine that a place so permeable was ever considered a home. Rustic idylls shape the dreams of visitors, he soon learned, not residents. He was the only one who took the footpaths through the bamboo-covered hills. The farmers, his neighbors, drove around in their mini-pickups.

He settled in. In front of the porch, he planted a small garden, with azalea and gardenia bushes on one side, vegetables on the other. A scavenger at heart, he reclaimed an old chair made of wood and canvas awning. No villager would own anything so shameful, but he was overcome by its potential. The first time he sat down, the chair broke in one spectacular crunch, its joints poking out like a kneeling camel. He used it anyway, placing it in the middle of the garden and draping his large frame over it. Then, wearing a straw hat he'd found in someone's garbage, he read for hours among his eggplants.

The first time Ishikawa found him reading in the garden, she shrieked. The old woman began to laugh, flapped her white apron up and down and returned home, still laughing. Heitman was never sure what this encounter had signified to his neighbor. All he knew was that she began visiting him more often, bringing over pickles and village remedies, discussing the children, the neighbors, even Mori, until he realized he was no longer excluded from the small and closely guarded news that nourished village life.

Heitman put Ishikawa's bowl of pickles beside him on the veranda. In a moment he would have to start the bath. Ishikawa's grandson ran past him, yelling hello over his shoulder. A moment later the child walked back to the porch where Heitman sat cross-legged.

"Have you seen my cat?" the boy asked, leaning against the porch.

"Which one? There are so many." Heitman sometimes woke up to find a village cat relieving itself in his kitchen. Contemptuous of villages and doors, cats were everywhere and belonged to no one.

"The orange one," said the boy. "Like a tiger."

"I see it from time to time. Is it yours?"

"Grandmother won't let me keep it in the house. But I feed him sometimes. He's a wild one!"

The boy ran off again toward home, stopping abruptly to examine a twisted scrap of metal that Heitman had found crammed in the small furnace of his bathhouse.

"What's this?" the boy asked and held up the scrap.

"I don't know."

"Nice, isn't it? Is it yours?"

"No. Please take it."

"Thanks!" At the kitchen door, the boy was stopped by his grandmother.

"What is this, Miki-kun?" she asked, pointing to the charred metal.

"It's a boat!"

"Now, Miki-kun, look how dirty it is. Let's leave it outside, shall we?"

"I can bring it in now, can't I?" he asked impatiently.

"What would your mother say? Not until it's clean."

"I want to bring it in now!" he screamed and stomped his foot.

"What if it touched something? Look. It might tear the screen. What would your mother say? Here! Look what she brought you from the market. Come in and see!" The metal was left outside, and the door closed behind them.

The small altar shuddered as Heitman stood up. He reached the altar in three long strides and opened the doors. He would have to put the books in the closet for the time being. He'd planned to build bookcases weeks ago. Now the lumber stood moldering in one damp corner of the kitchen. Everything took time here, except the rotting of wood.

All year long, he'd felt the leisurely pace of village life seep into the house. Only when he went into the city did he consider the possibility that he'd slowed down too much, that he was as out of step here as he had been wherever he lived. Yet the very nature of the farmhouse encouraged a life based on deliberate steps—the slow-burning stoves and slow-running water, the distance between one corner of the kitchen and another, between the house and the bath.

Heitman crossed the breezeway to the bathhouse. Water flowed out of an old, arching spigot and into a cast-iron tub. He'd always enjoyed the ritual of the bath, perhaps because the old tub was the only thing in his present life large enough to contain him. Ishikawa-san was sure he would perish without a wife, to pick up his clothes and fill his bath, but he'd surprised her.

Outside, Heitman shoved a short, thick log into the bath furnace and lit it with kindling. The bath would heat while he made supper, and afterward he would clear out the books. Later, when he finally checked the water, it was scalding. He hurriedly pulled out the hot log and dragged it out of the way of early evening traffic. Miki-kun and his little brother would be out again soon, making their mad, postprandial dash across his garden.

He had to laugh at himself. He was behaving like one of the local housewives, sharing recipes with Ishikawa and worrying about the children. His presence was somewhat taken for granted, and the value of the neighborhood had not plunged.

Even the auto mechanic at the end of the village didn't scowl anymore when he brought in the unreliable van. Now he complained if he suspected Heitman of going anywhere else. He asked Heitman about American cars, but Heitman didn't know anything about cars. Recently, the mechanic had begun pressing him to share cheap sake, which they drank from a cup that had touched more mouths than he cared to think about.

He learned from the mechanic that Mori had a habit of drinking and driving and running off the road.

"Mori's car won't last another winter," the mechanic said. And since Heitman had begun renting the place, Mori didn't bring his friends up for long, boisterous weekends.

"Doesn't bring his little girlfriends, either," the mechanic giggled. "Takes them to an inn up the mountains. Back there. Stops here for gas first." He squinted up at Heitman and stuck his head back under the hood of the van.

"I can keep a secret," he went on. "I give him a discount, and he remembers my family at New Year's."

"So why's he renting the house? To a *gaijin* too?"

"Who knows?" The mechanic shrugged. "Your yen is the same as mine. Maybe he just wants someone in it so it won't rot. Or be robbed."

Heitman laughed. There wasn't anything to rob. His stereo was his only valuable possession, and now the cover was cracked.

It was also the mechanic who later passed on the rumor that Mori wanted Heitman out of the farmhouse. Out for good. Puzzled, Heitman asked why. The mechanic shook his head and looked away.

"The wife probably but I don't know. That's all I heard."

Out? And go where? Back to the city? He no longer held a picture of the city in his mind. He brooded a while over this piece of news until it faded and he forgot.

The bath water was still too hot. He read lengthwise on the porch and waited for it to cool. *Shakuhachi* music played on the stereo. By sundown, the haze had lifted, and there would be a good moon after all. Then the low-rising moon was eclipsed by Ishikawa's square frame.

"Excuse me, Heitman-san. Did the boys come by?"

"No, I haven't seen them."

"Forgive me, but the books. Have you . . . ?"

"I was just going to do that."

"Yes . . . it would be wise."

They heard the boys' young mother call out from the kitchen door and the children answering from the road. Grandmother Ishikawa bid Heitman goodnight and moved swiftly, soundlessly around the house in search of the boys.

Goro Yamaguchi, the master, was performing on the record, and he turned the volume up. The sound of the flute fluttered through the house like a cloud of balsa moths, and he felt himself relax. If only he could play like that, learn the technique.

He looked up at the altar across the small room, proud of the repair job, proud of the movable hinges and the highly polished statues that supported his books. Even the repainted wood shone gold.

Ishikawa and her daughter reached the boys just as Mori was parking his car in the gravel behind the house. The car swung open and he lurched out. He was drunk. Ishikawa could smell it the instant he opened the door. She tried to stall him, smiling continuously, plying him with a steady stream of questions: How was his family? his work? his health? Behind them, music from Heitman's stereo soared up, filling the house. Had Heitman-san heard nothing? Not even her words?

She could delay Mori for only a moment longer. And as she talked she knew that Heitman—oh, foolish man!—had not moved an inch since she'd left him.

[1991]

The Reunion

WILLIAM WETHERALL

Weekend-weary commuters rushing to work through the bowels of Shin-juku station one Monday morning had to veer around a drifter who had wandered into the passageways from the rainy autumn streets after the shutters had been opened at dawn. The man had made a cardboard bed at the foot of a concrete pillar in the middle of the main promenade and then fallen into a nightmarish sleep.

"It's about time you were up, mister," chided a matronly woman who had nearly skewered the drifter with her umbrella.

"Hey, numskull, can't you see you're blocking the way?" shouted a businessman while brushing off the briefcase he had dropped when he had tripped over the drifter's feet and pitched into a policeman.

The drifter stirred in his sleep. He had felt something strike his side, the toe of a shoe, he thought. His eyes came open but they closed before he could focus on the figure hovering over him, and again he was a young boy confronting the short, wiry, unshaven Imperial Army sergeant who had kicked him awake and was now glowering down at him.

"What are you doing here?" the soldier asked.

The boy's eyes, reaching into the darkness beyond the sergeant's shoulders, made out the rafters of the armory where he had been napping, the boy finally recalled, on top of some splintery pallets. He had to get up and find his mother and go back to Japan.

"The war's over, you know," the boy said.

"That's no way for a Son of Nippon to speak," the sergeant said.

"But the Emperor surrendered, and we're going home," the boy said, paying no heed to the stern look on the sergeant's face.

The sergeant's eyes flashed from the dusty shadows, but the boy wasn't fazed.

"I said to get up!" the sergeant exploded, booting the boy so hard that he fell off the pallet to the loam of the warehouse floor. The boy clenched his side and grimaced while squirming on the dirt.

Again the drifter's eyes cracked, but this time they widened until they had opened full stop, though they continued to strain out of focus. The pain in his side snapped some of his senses back into the present. His ears were assaulted by a rumbling crescendo of stampeding shoes on concrete. Foul odors, some familiar, others foreign, toyed with his runny nostrils, which he wiped with the frayed sleeve of a once stylish overcoat. The

113

Manchurian loam became a cardboard mattress on cement. The brown corrugated paper reeked of vending machine spirits mixed with the gastric backflow of the half-digested meal he had scavenged from the garbage cans of the finest of Shinjuku's white-collar eateries.

The spike of the woman's right shoe caught the drifter's ribs, and she tripped. As her body pitched forward, she grabbed at an arm of the police-man who had been trying to awaken the drifter and keep the curious at bay, but the officer stepped back and she kept falling.

The drifter raised his head to avoid the armory sergeant's spatted boots. After he blinked the puffy folds of his thickly padded eyelids and dug some of the sleep from his eyes, the boots became purple pumps, red leg warmers, black thigh-highs, and a pleated mauve miniskirt which, as the woman wearing it fell on top of him, flared out and drew his glazed eyes to the blur of pink lace at her crotch until one of her knees plunged into his better eye and drove his skull back down so hard that it bounced off the pavement with the thump of a basketball.

The woman struggled to untangle herself from the drifter's limbs, which flailed like the legs of a beetle that had flipped on its back and was twitching around to right itself. She suddenly screamed for someone to help her, and the drifter stopped jerking his arms and relaxed them long enough for her to stand up and back away from their reach.

The drifter fingered the rest of the sleep off his lashes as he watched the woman brush herself off and then rub at a soiled spot on the hem of her skirt with a moist finger napkin she had produced from her shoulder bag. When finished, she released the hem of her skirt, tossed the napkin toward the drifter, and glared at him as he gingerly touched the tender flesh that was swelling around his right eye. She could see a bright flush through the grime that had caked on his cheeks. His right eye would soon be distended and discolored like the left one.

The policeman, his back to the crowd, just stood there and gawked at the woman's round tush but averted his eyes when she looked his way. The woman smiled, tossed her head, and marched into the human sea. The offi-cer limply saluted the woman's receding figure and, narrowing his eyes, tracked it until the parting crowd had closed around her.

★ ★ ★

The policeman turned his attention to the drifter who, now fully alert, had shifted his interest from the woman to the people who were pressing around him, stretching their well-scrubbed necks to see what all the fuss was about. The nearest and tallest people in the crowd were rewarded with a glimpse of the drifter's dirt-stiffened cowlicks, grubby overcoat, filthy pants, shredded sneakers that habit alone had forced off his feet before his drunken stupor had become sleep, and three tattered shopping bags stuffed with everything he owned.

After dispersing the crowd with his nightstick, the officer poked the drifter to his feet, and during a lull in the pedestrian traffic he steered the drifter to the side of the promenade and parked him beside the wall where he would not disturb anyone.

"Gotta get my stuff," the drifter said in a phlegm-clogged voice. He started toward the cardboard mattress by the pillar, but the nightstick blocked his way.

"You stay here," the officer said, and then he darted back to retrieve the drifter's bags before the next stampede of commuters could kick them open. After setting down the bags at the drifter's bare feet, he returned for the shoes and, as an afterthought, dragged the putrid cardboard over by some refuse bins at the side of the concourse.

"You just going to leave my bed there?" the drifter said, wiggling his feet into the shoes the officer had dropped beside him.

"The custodians will take care of it," the policeman said.

The drifter hacked up a mouthful of phlegm and spat toward the wall, hitting a mural of a flower shop and turning a white rose green. "Did you have to kick me so hard?" he said, rubbing his ribs while flexing his right arm.

"Next time you bathe, check out your bruises," the officer said, then pointed to his feet. "If they match my boots, you can file a complaint. All I did was toe you a few times to wake you up."

"Someone more than just toed me," the drifter said.

"What do you expect?" the policeman said. "You plop your butt in the middle of this station at rush hour, and people are going to stomp on it. You should thank that woman you're still alive."

"The bitch nearly killed me."

"If her spikes had been any sharper, you'd be dead all right."

The drifter poured his eyes over the officer's dark blue uniform. "Yamada, is it?" he said, reading the name tag. He studied the two stars on the policeman's lapels and decided that, despite the officer's boyish looks, he was not a rookie. "You a detective or something?"

"Senior Policeman Yamada, Shinjuku Precinct," Yamada said. His face flushed as he snapped in a salute and added, "I'm just a patrolman."

"Well, patrolman Yamada, thanks for your help, and I hope you have a good day," the drifter said as he picked up his bags. Ducking his head and jerking his right hand toward his face in a sort of reverse karate chop, he gestured his intent to cut in front of Yamada, who was standing between him and the human traffic.

"Hold it," Yamada said. "I've got to take you in."

"Have I done something wrong?"

"Just follow me. I want to ask you some questions."

Yamada guided the drifter toward the base of some steps that were clogged with commuters going up to the street.

"What's your name?" Yamada said while they waited for an opening.

"Nagase."

"Nagase what?"

"Yuji."

"Is that your real name?"

"From the day I was born," Nagase said. "Hey, am I gonna get a haircut and a bath out of this? I could use some warmer threads, too."

"You might even get an address and a job."

Yamada noted Nagase's frown before turning his eyes toward the flow of people on the steps. Seeing a break, he led Nagase up to the street where a chilly drizzle was falling on a turbulent sea of umbrellas waiting at an intersection for the light to turn green. When it did, Yamada and Nagase hustled across the street and made their way to a small police box near the station building and slipped inside before they had gotten very wet. The desk officer, who had three stars on a name tag that read Tamura, lifted her hatless head from the logbook she had been reading, returned Yamada's salute, and studied the shabby man with the bags.

"Not there," she said to Nagase when he set one of his bags down just inside the entrance.

"Over here," Yamada said, stepping over to an unoccupied desk on the other side of the congested room.

Yamada removed his hat to reveal a shock of tousled hair, and put the hat on a corner of the desk. He motioned Nagase to a chair beside the desk, picked up his tea cup, and stepped toward the back.

"Let's start with some tea," Yamada said.

"No cappuccino?" Nagase said, not looking at Yamada but at the screen of a silent television monitor on a shelf in the corner.

"This ain't no coffee shop," Yamada said.

As he turned to look at Nagase, Yamada caught Tamura's nod. From the low cabinet that served as a counter for the teapot and hot water, Yamada produced a cup and saucer and the makings for various coffees.

"Would you consider some cafe au lait?" he said, facing Nagase.

"That would do quite nicely, yes," Nagase said, smiling at Yamada.

"Your coffee, sir," Yamada said as he handed Nagase a saucered cup with a packet of sugar and a spoon.

Nagase received the saucer with both hands, set it on the desk, and stirred the sugar into the steaming, creamy brew. While sipping it, he looked almost dignified. While Yamada served Tamura and himself some green tea, Nagase closed his eyes and let the sweet bitterness work its miracles on his throat and head. By the time he opened them, Yamada was sitting at the desk and shuffling some papers.

Yamada read from a special protocol for interviewing the homeless.

"Nine October nineteen ninety-two, zero nine fifteen hours," Yamada said aloud as he entered the date and time on the interview form. "Your name again?"

"Nagase Yuji," Nagase said, and this time he described the Chinese characters used to write it.

"Date of birth?"

"Thirteen December nineteen thirty-seven."

"Place of birth?"

"Manchuria."

"Manchuria?" Yamada said, looking up at Nagase. "My grandfather's regiment was sent there during the war, but he came back in an urn."

"At least he came back," Nagase said after a moment of silence during which his eyes dropped to the floor.

"Your permanent domicile?" said Yamada, his eyes back on the form.

"Tokushima prefecture," Nagase began. "But years ago, everything was torn down and all the paddies were filled up to build a golf course," he explained after giving Yamada the rest of an old-fashioned rural address that no longer existed.

"And your residence of record?"

"Osaka," Nagase said, this time describing what Yamada recognized to be a neighborhood with a lot of flop houses mainly for men just down on their luck. "But I left Nishinari five or six years ago and never stayed anywhere long enough to bother to transfer the registration."

"Your father's name?"

"Nagase Masao."

"Is he well?"

"He's in the belly of some fish."

Again Yamada met Nagase's stare. At length he said, "And your mother?"

"Shizue. She died of tuberculosis in 1953."

"In Tokushima?"

"No. Tachikawa."

"Any brothers or sisters?"

"An older sister and a younger brother. Yasuko and Kuninori."

"Where are they?"

"Yasuko died in Manchuria. As far as I know, Kuni's still there. If he survived the Cultural Revolution."

"Your mother left him there?"

"Yes. With a Chinese family."

"And you've had no contact with him?"

"None. After my mother and I were repatriated, she tried to reach the family, but her letters always came back. I've still got one of them in these bags. Would you like to read it?"

"Maybe later. Marital status?"

"Single."

"Never married?"

"Divorced."

"Any children?"

"One," Nagase said, and then gave the names of his ex-wife and daughter, and the Tokushima address of his ex-wife's family, with whom they were living the last time he had seen them, just before he had taken the ferry to Kobe and made his way to Nishinari.

"Any other relatives? Grandparents? Aunts, uncles, cousins?"

"None."

"Education?"

"Middle school."

"Last employment?"

"Shoe-shine boy."

"Shoe-shine boy?" Yamada said, looking up at Nagase and picking up his tea cup. "You came here from Ueno?"

"How'd you know?"

"I read the papers."

Nagase laughed. He could read too, and quite well at that, thank you, he felt like saying, but closed his mouth, suddenly conscious of the lone tooth that protruded from his gums. Just as abruptly, though, he opened it again and began pouring out his life, sometimes so fast that Yamada, who had resumed taking notes, had to ask him to pause so that he could catch up. Even Tamura had stopped pretending to work and was giving the interview her full attention.

★ ★ ★

"Yeah, I came from Ueno. I was living in the park with several other transients. One day a band of teenage punks began harassing us. Five or six of them came over to the tree where my buddy and I had built this lean-to. They pointed to a sign that said 'It's your park, keep it clean,' and then started kicking us. My buddy, who made a little money shining shoes around the park entrance, took a couple of hard blows in the kidneys and the next day he died. Well, he had this shoe-shine box, and I inherited it. I got his turf, too, but I had to shell out more protection money. Anyway, I gave it a try. Not a lot of business, but I was making enough to buy food and booze. Then it started getting cold, and I sold out to another guy and came to Shinjuku. Everyone was saying that the cops over here are easy on station dwellers. I had the same impression till this morning. Now it seems you're cracking down."

Now and then Nagase stopped to sip from his second cup of coffee and watch Yamada struggle to catch up with his notes. Twice he took it upon himself to explain how to write a Chinese character that Yamada had stumbled over. Yamada merely grunted his thanks, too proud to use words that would have encouraged Nagase to believe that his help was actually appreciated, much less to ask him how a mere middle-school graduate had managed to learn so much. Nagase, who saw in the younger man's eyes more fear than envy, resisted the temptation to inform Yamada that living on the road gives an otherwise studious man time to read more books in one year than a work-a-day cop could peruse in a whole lifetime of leisure snatched between career and family.

During one of the longer breaks in his narration, Nagase's eyes were drawn to the television monitor. The volume had been muted, but the program was plainly about some Chinese who had recently arrived in Japan in hopes that a Japanese relative might recognize them. All now middle-aged, most had been offspring of Japanese settlers in Manchuria for whom conditions at the end of the Second World War had made it seem preferable to leave their smaller children with Chinese families.

"After my mother gave Kuni to a childless Chinese couple in Harbin, she and I made our way to Hsinching, and from there to Fengt'ien and then Chinchou, and at last to the port of Hulutao, where we were shocked by the sudden appearance of my father.

"Neither of us immediately recognized the filthy bearded man who had called my name and started to limp toward us. Even when we finally realized who it was, we were strongly repelled by the stench that seemed to effuse from his every pore."

Yamada signaled for Nagase to go on, but the drifter's jaundiced eyes were again riveted to the screen showing, one by one, the faces of the Chinese who claimed to be Japanese war orphans. An old film clip of the hospital ship S. S. Hakuryu Maru, arriving at Hakata with a cargo of repatriots vying with one another for standing room on the deck, brought back nightmarish visions of his own voyage.

"On the morning we embarked from Hulutao, I stood between my parents on the port side of the Tsuta, an Imperial Japanese Navy destroyer that the Occupation authorities had pressed into service to shuttle Japanese back to Japan, and ex-colonials in Japan back to their liberated countries. My father was still weak from his ordeal of escape from the Soviets, and the weeks of travel incognito as a Chinese beggar. Though now shaven and dressed in cleaner clothes, he remained silent and grim. My mother, who had given him up for dead, suddenly wanted to go back for Kuni. My father said it was too late, and told her she'd just have to write to the family after getting back to Japan.

"As the ship slipped away from the quay, a small girl, harnessed to the back of a Chinese man who was standing on the pier, began waving to a woman just down the railing from us. Suddenly the girl stretched her arms toward the ship and her face turned red, contorted in wails that were swallowed by the churning sea. My mother tried to keep her composure but collapsed in tears. My father bowed toward the shore of the land he had come to love, very deeply from the waist, and when at length he lifted his face there were tears in his eyes, too."

Nagase took a moment to wipe his eyes with a tattered sleeve.

"Early on the morning of the second day out, a sailor standing watch saw my father dive into the Yellow Sea off the fantail. He left his shoes on the deck, and a note by my mother's head. Her scream woke me up. I pried the note out of her hand and read it. He had scribbled her name and mine and simply 'Forgive me.' When she first coughed up blood, a year before she died, she began weeping and told me that both of us would have been better off following him."

Nagase had been glancing at the screen while talking.

"Hey, would you turn up the sound?" he said.

"We're not finished!" Yamada said, in a tone that expressed his growing displeasure with Nagase's inattention.

"But that was my brother!" Nagase said, coming out of his chair and heading for the TV. Tamura, too, leapt to her feet, and her hand blocked Nagase's arm as he reached for the volume control.

"Your brother?" Yamada said.

"My brother!" Nagase said.

"Just relax and sit down," Yamada said, gripping one of Nagase's arms and pushing him back to his chair. "How do you know it was your brother?"

"It was him, alright. He looks exactly like my father. And the bottom of the screen said his Japanese name was Kuni."

Yamada, back in his own chair, jotted down some notes on a pad while Nagase talked. Tamura, too, resumed her seat and immediately boosted the TV sound with a remote control.

A newscaster was saying that the Chinese were being processed at the National Olympic Memorial Youth Center in Yoyogi. Some telephone numbers that viewers could call to obtain or provide more information about them were scrolling on the screen.

"That's just minutes away," Nagase said.

"Try calling the center," Tamura said to Yamada.

Yamada jotted down the numbers and studied his notes for a couple of minutes before he picked up the receiver. Nagase watched him tap out 481-2488 and then shift his eyes toward the entrance.

"Wrong number," Nagase said.

Yamada's eyes remained on something outside the entrance as he held the receiver to his head and waited. A minute or two passed. Yamada's mouth opened as though to speak to someone who had answered the phone, but a couple of seconds later he pressed the cradle switch.

"Try 42 instead of 24," Nagase said.

Yamada released the cradle switch and touched the redial button. This time Yamada looked at Nagase while he waited.

"Line's busy," Yamada said at length. "I'll try again." When he did, he manually redialed with a 42 but did not return Nagase's smile.

★ ★ ★

Yamada called the Yoyogi center and confirmed that the Chinese man Nagase insisted was his brother had indeed said that he had been called Kuni-chan. Tamura then gave Yamada permission to escort Nagase to the center.

"But first take him to Takadanobaba," Tamura said. Nagase's face lit up when he heard this reference to the nearby welfare center, where he knew he would receive a medical examination and a bath, shampoo, haircut, shave, and clean clothes, and maybe some food.

By noon, Nagase had emerged from the Takadanobaba facility neatly groomed and cleanly attired, looking more like a gardener on his day off than a jobless vagrant. On their way to Yoyogi, Yamada took him to an eatery and treated him to his first hot meal in several weeks.

Yamada introduced Nagase to the caseworker in charge of the man who remembered being called Kuni, reminded him that he was to return to the welfare center by himself when finished at Yoyogi, and then returned to the Shinjuku police box. After interviewing Nagase, and sending him to a small room to give up another tube of blood, this time for typing, the caseworker accompanied him to the auditorium, where one by one the men and women claiming to be war orphans would relate their sagas before a large audience of government officials from both countries, several nationalities of journalists, and of course the people who had come from all corners of Japan to find a lost relative.

While walking beside the young caseworker toward the auditorium, Nagase patiently listened to her describe, as though she had been there in her previous incarnation, the chaotic conditions that had caused so many Japanese but also some Koreans in Manchuria and other outposts at the end of the war to leave behind a child, a spouse, a sibling, or a parent in the course of leaving China.

"Surely all these people feel guilty about what they did," the caseworker said, "yet only a few of them are willing to trouble themselves, as you are, to locate a missing family member."

"Why is that?" Nagase asked.

"It's been a long time," the caseworker said. "I mean, nearly half a century. A lot of things have changed, and they've got their own lives to think about. The economic burden of taking in not only the lost relative, but also the relative's Chinese family—spouse, children, even grandchildren—is by no means small, and there's not much help from the government. Not to mention the psychological burden; a reunion may open old wounds that many people would rather just let time heal."

After a moment of silence, the caseworker went on.

"So some of the Chinese who are saying they're of Japanese descent come all the way to Japan to find that no one is looking for them. The luckier ones, if that's the right word, have more than one contender, which causes its own sort of confusion. Take Huang Wenjen, or O Bunjin in Japanese, for example. Alias Kuni-chan. Well, you're not the only one who thinks he's a relative. An Akita woman in her late seventies is certain he's her son. We won't know who's right, if either of you are, until we see the results of the blood tests."

Entering the auditorium, Nagase saw about thirty men and women sitting on the stage behind a rostrum where each would in turn tell their story, not only to the live audience, but also to the TV cameras. Sitting beside the caseworker, he studied the people on the stage. Each person held a large name card on their lap, and though their eyes ranged from distant and dull to alert and glowing, all were undoubtedly there in hopes that, if no one in the audience saw or heard something familiar about them, then an unseen kin watching TV somewhere would recognize them, as Nagase had at the police box, and call the phone number shown at the bottom of the screen.

Over the years Nagase had followed as much of the news about the would-be Japanese war orphans as he could. Today he actually recognized some of the faces from the pictures he had seen in recent papers. This group was not unlike the many others that had come to Japan, but already it was proving to be a special one for him. The man holding a card with a name that Nagase read as O Bunjin was sitting in the third seat from the left in the front row. The man looked so much like his father that Nagase began to imagine the ways he could have survived the waves.

Some of the Chinese on the stage were smiling. Some were rubbing their eyes. Most sat rigid with their hands in their laps as the stage lights drew beads of sweat from their almost catatonic faces. The first speaker, the woman sitting first from the left in the front row, came to the rostrum. The man sitting next to her was second. Then came Huang.

★ ★ ★

Nagase's eyes locked on Huang's face as an interpreter put his Chinese into Japanese. None of Huang's facial features hinted Yamato descent. Even had he been a prince of blood, his genes would have had to compete with the leathering effects of a youth spent laboring in the sun, to say nothing of the hardness of flesh that results from an austere diet. Whatever his genetic ancestry, the man standing behind the rostrum had a healthy, rotund countenance. His large mouth readily broke into a warm, engaging smile each time he looked up from his notes. He wore no camera makeup, and his skin was smooth and taut, though the corners of his eyes were deeply lined. Both lids had single folds, and his eyebrows were thin. He held up an enlargement of an old snapshot showing him in a Mao tunic and red-star cap on a closely cropped head. Now his hair was finger-length on the right, where it was parted, and longer on the left where he had combed it over a receding hairline.

"My name is Huang Wenjen," he began. "My earliest memories are fairly vivid. There were four in my family, and we were living in a colonial settlement near Chalantun at the foot of the greater Hsingan range west of Tsitsihar in Heilungjiang province. Father was some kind of merchant, I recall, but he was drafted near the end of the war.

"I particularly remember the day we went to see him off. Dressed in his new uniform, he looked like a cedar tree facing our neighbors while they waved their rising-suns and shouted banzais. Long after they had stopped, he just stood there and gazed though his rimless glasses at the mountains where he had always taken us fishing in the summers.

"Mother wore a deep-sleeved kimono, dark blue I think, with a red brocade sash. My older brother, who may have been ten, had on his school clothes, a white shirt with black trousers and whatever shoes the family could afford. I was only four or five, and he held my hand as the train pulled away. I was crying because Father had said that I couldn't go. It was the last time I ever saw him.

"We moved to Tsitsihar just days before the Soviets swept down from Siberia. I remember some heavy shelling, then waiting in lines to board a train from Hsinching. But we got no farther than Harbin, which was already swarming with refugees. Food was scarce, and Mother was unable to feed us.

"One day we were playing in a small park which had become an evacuation center. After talking to a man who had taken special notice of us, Mother told my brother—I can't remember his name, I just called him Niisan—to stay with her pack while she took me to the man's house.

"She bought me a bean-jam dumpling from a vendor on the way, and she told me to enjoy it, for it would be the last sweet that she gave me. I was too hungry to give much thought to her words. We walked in silence, several paces behind the man, who never once looked back at us.

"Mother asked me to get on her back. She had squatted down as she did when I was much younger. When I said I could walk, she looked at me with eyes that were starting to tear. I asked her what was wrong, but she just smiled, grabbed my hand, and hurried on after the man.

"As soon as we reached his house, the man introduced us to his wife, and she served us tea and sweets. Mother talked with them for a while, and finally the man gave her an envelope with some money in it. She then explained to me that I would be staying there while she took care of my brother, who had not been very well.

"She hugged me for a long time and then left. She paused very briefly at the gate to bow. She looked back only once, when I cried, 'Okaasan!' and started running toward her, but the woman restrained me as Mother rushed down the street we had come by. My only wish, while watching her back get smaller, was to be on it. Even as I tell you all this, I can hear her humming and feel her hands patting my bottom as I warm my cheek on the back of her neck."

Nagase's eyes were misty. His mind drifted back to the park where he had watched his mother take Kuni away. Many other children had been in the park that day. Some of them were vying over a couple of swings, but he didn't feel like playing, so he sat in the sun on the pack his mother had left him to protect. He was waiting for her there when at length she returned, and the first thing she did was to pull him into her bosom and weep on his head until his hair was wet to the scalp.

* * *

A few weeks later Nagase posted a letter to China.

"Dear Wenjen,

"Since seeing you off at Narita I had a chance to move. A friend passed word to me that he would be going to Kyoto. Would I like to take over the cozy nook he had staked out along the south wall of the Tokyo headquarters of a major electrical appliance maker in the heart of the posh Ginza district? He would even leave me the one-room mansion he had fashioned from a huge cardboard carton that once protected the unmarred finish of the company's most popular five-door refrigerator.

"My friend is allowed to set up his shelter by the building's marble facade so long as he moves out during the day. So the next day I trained across the city to Yurakucho, and my friend introduced me to the night guard he was paying a small monthly tribute to look the other way.

"It turned out to be a better arrangement than I thought. Shinjuku's catacombs had left me pale and chronically short of breath. Squatter's rights to the few benches in the tiny parks that dotted the labyrinth of bars near the station were claimed by local turf lords who have little sympathy for tramps like me. The biggest boon of all are the foreign tourists. The Americans, especially, are suckers for my new A-bomb survivor spiel.

"At a public toilet in a small playground just down the street from my new home, I can sponge bathe and brush my teeth any time of day. A half-kilometer further south is Tokyo's sprawling Hibiya Park—I think you stopped there on one of your tours and fed the pigeons around the big fountain—where any morning of the year, except on the Emperor's birthday, I can get a sturdy bench overlooking a small pond where frogs sun on lotus leaves and croak as though the world was theirs. Flanked by the Imperial Hotel and the Metropolitan Police Department, and with only a few shallow moats between me and the Imperial Palace, I spend my days reading current newspapers and magazines, and during the evenings I forage for a full-course dinner in the refuse bins of some of the most sumptuous watering holes in the whole world.

"Words alone cannot convey the extent of my change in fortune since reuniting with you, dear Wenjen. Father, and Mother too, would be proud to learn that you are a respected village doctor, and that I am the president and sole employee of a company that recycles the world's highest-class waste. I trust that you will not be ashamed to tell your good comrades that your elder brother, though filthy rich, is devoting his time and wealth to the poor. When next you sail this way, do not hesitate to bring with you as many of your compatriots as are crazy enough to want to come here. I guarantee you that, within a few weeks, many of them will be sharing with me the finest bed that a traveler can make on the banks of the palace moat!

"From your older brother, Yuji."

★ ★ ★

Nagase Yuji felt something big and firm thump against his ribs. He remained absolutely still, but tensed with anticipation.

"There's a man there! I think he's dead!"

As Nagase turned toward the voice, he pulled the shroud of newsprint from his head. In front of his face was a soccer ball that all but obstructed his view of its youthful owner.

"Don't touch him!"

That must be the boy's mother, Nagase figured. Probably afraid that her son would be infected with lice or some horrid disease. The boy, now stiff with fear, would venture no closer, so Nagase reached for the ball himself and, pushing his body up with one arm, sent it flying back with the other.

Nagase was delighted to discover that he could still throw hard and straight. Even the boy grinned in surprise, and he began moaning when his mother dragged him to a nearby faucet and made him wash both the ball and his hands.

As Nagase sat up on the plastic sheet he had spread on the grassless ground, he wondered what had become of the benches. And the pond with the fountain, and the vast flower beds, and the small woods with glades where one could sit alone and not even see a telephone pole. And where was the palace moat, and the imperial swans that graced its weedy waters?

Surely this was not where he had gone to sleep, Nagase thought. Yet wasn't it, too, peaceful? Suddenly his stomach started growling with a ferocity that he had not heard for days. Had he risen too late to raid the cans he had seen when he arrived the night before? Then hearing the churning roar of the sanitation truck as it munched his morning meal inside its monstrous metallic maw, he knew that again he would have to wait until noon for the cans to begin to refill.

Shrugging off another hungry start, Nagase reached for his single shopping bag, which bore the name of a Tokyo department store that gave him a bit of distinction wherever he went. Tucked into its top was a plastic bag with some stained and tattered documents that he had been looking at just before going to sleep.

One of the pieces of paper was a transit pass certifying that he had sailed from Hulutao on May 14, 1946, and had entered Japan through Sasebo three days later. Another was a single sheet of stationery, a letter which had been in an envelope addressed to his mother and bearing a postmark equivalent to the year he had finished middle school.

The letter had arrived a few weeks after he had found her dead from acute alcolosis in the three-mat room where she would service GIs while he was at school or outside. He could read just enough of the closely printed Chinese to know that it was about his brother.

Nagase's eyes caught a black bird swooping down to peck at a pool of vomit that could have been his. The mother, keeping a frenzied eye on the bird, dried her son's hands, pulled him toward the exit, and left the park to its truly indigenous species.

The crow beat its wings to the dripping faucet, where it took its morning communion from the water that filled the pebble basin below it. Then it looked Nagase's way and cawed. And as though an old friend had said something funny, he smiled.

[1984]

Blue Notes on the Samisen in Early Summer

MICHELLE LEIGH

"So, do you love your wife?" She'd asked this question in the middle of Jinbocho crossing. Brilliant sun, and crowds streaming past. She felt like a character in a Rohmer film, with a casual ease about complex love entanglements, a sense of life's transience weighing down upon the sweetest moment of rapture. Even the sunshine seemed cool, blue, and secretly dark, moody like slow jazz. A Rohmer film set in Japan. There should have been some notes plucked on a samisen just then.

"Yes." He looked embarrassed. "Do you love your husband?"

"Yes." Her voice sounded cheerful and bright, a defiant small chirp that rang out clear and was abruptly swallowed in the mass of sound. The utterance had become history, recorded upon the air above the shining lines of cars, in the unknowing imaginations of pedestrians. Yes. No. The meaning of her yes was in this case no. As a defense against his love for his wife, of course. Asymmetry wouldn't do on this point. Not that she believed him. Perhaps the meaning of the word love should be discussed.

∧∧∧∧

They'd stopped in a cafe for cold drinks. They'd ordered tricolor coffees, the soft-toned hues of cream, cocoa, and coffee beautifully layered in narrow frosted glasses. His eyes watching her were intense, slivers of obsidian.

It was the first time she'd thought of black as luminous.

"What do you mean by love?" She dipped the long silver spoon into the liquid strata, trying to bring up a spoonful of the lowest level, the espresso at the bottom, without adding mocha or cream to it on the way up. The terzetto of layers began to slip into one another, swirling quickly into a more organic pattern of currents and eddies. She glanced at his drink. It was still a placid arrangement of parallels, three perfect stripes in suspension.

Perhaps this is not a film by Rohmer, she thought. Perhaps it's Kurosawa, or even Greenaway. Could this be a Greenaway film? Would I like being a Greenaway character? Godard. Maybe this could be a Godard, a new one set surprisingly in an Asian country. Whatever the case, this would be the moment where we fade and dissolve.

^^^^^
MIST
^^^

Jinbocho at night. The city sky, a tone painting: clouds of dark pink, deep orange, purple-blue. A wet mist hangs in the air. Red paper lanterns gleam at the entrances to small bars, smoky inside. Neon blazes and twinkles overhead. Summer is beginning. Looking down upon the small passages from above, we see a few figures in groups of two or three make their way through the shadowed streets.

There is a man; there is a woman. We see them from behind; they walk with a slow rhythm. Her hair is golden, she wears a pink sweater and a short black skirt. High heels. His hair is black, he wears dark clothing, a suit.

He: I once had an American penpal.
She: Ah.

A construction crew works on a scaffolded building strung with electric bulbs, glaring spots of yellow with watery auras. The men in their frogshoes balance on narrow beams and pound things with their tools, metal on metal making a comfortable recurring sound.

She: It's like a strange dream. It's midnight, but it seems like day.
He: It's best for them to work at night.
She: So what happened? To the penpal?
He: Ah—she got married. I shouldn't write to her after that.

Now a close-up view of the woman's face. Rainy mist on her cheeks like dew. She chews on her finger for a moment. She shivers. She sways close to the man. Her gaze is inward-looking. Behind her, one of the workmen seems to look her way, to stare after the retreating figure, the bright hair, the pink sweater.

He: Shall we drink something?
She: Yes. . . . It's beginning to rain, isn't it?
He: I can smell your perfume, in the rain your perfume is released. Like flowers blooming at night.

The man and the woman enter a small bar. Noise emerges as the door opens. It's crowded. We watch them through the window as they are led to a table toward the back of the room. As if from far away, muffled sounds of talk and glasses clinking.

The night sky above the city, an expanse of starless violet now, below it tall spires and towering blocks playing neon-written script against the sky, the futuristic enchanted haiku of advertising. Moon, stars, and planets have spiraled off into some other landscape. Music: what instruments? The drums and flutes of the Noh, with voice.

A man stands and sings the Noh from the top of a tall building, above rows of randomly gold-lit window squares.

∧∧∧∧∧

SAKE
∧∧∧

The man and the woman are sitting on a bed in a hotel room. He's pouring One-Cup Sake into two glasses. Her pink sweater is spotted with rain. He removes his jacket. They touch their glasses together and drink. Rain streaks against the large window, making a soft percussion of small quick taps.

He: Things are not what they seem.

The woman looks puzzled in a vague and slightly drunken way. Her blond hair has become a little disheveled.

He: Things are not what they seem. No, I suppose you'll say so what, but if you want to understand Japan, that's crucial. It's an art here, making sure nothing is what it seems to be.
She: You mean, the fact that people are so polite? Or what? What do you mean?

The man falls back onto the bed, loosens his tie. He seems to be in a state of excited despair. He sighs.

He: I don't know.

He closes his eyes.
The woman looks at her shoes, kicking one leg out and flexing her toe. She giggles and sweeps her hair back from her face with a carelessly sexy gesture.

The man glances at her out of the corner of his eye. The woman realizes that she has never been in such intimate circumstances with such a narrow-eyed man. She knows he is looking at her, but she can't see his irises.

She: I'm so sleepy.
He: Well, I'd better go.

The man is sitting now.
The woman looks away from him.
The man reaches over and pushes the ON button on the television. On the screen appears a solemn man who says that the yen is rising again after falling for many days. On another channel a woman sobs alone in a darkened sushi restaurant. The exposed nape of her neck is milk-white in the gloom. In the background, the flax-colored *noren* sways in the breeze to the somber groan of violins. On another channel a naked woman is being tied, hands bound above her head, to a pink-painted jungle gym in a children's park. Her assailant roughly handles her breasts, rotating them rapidly, one clockwise, one counter. He puts his mouth to them. The woman cries ah-ah-ah-ah without stopping, while the man is silent. Below the woman's naked belly is a colorful computer patchwork of glinting, shifting squares. Into this incandescent region the man thrusts his hand. The woman cries out and turns her head from side to side.

On another channel there is a luminous orange fish gliding past coral in green water. Drifting notes of ocean-borne oboe go on and on as the fish swims slowly and flutters its small silken fins.

∧∧∧∧∧∧

Teacups
∧∧∧

Mid-summer, a different hotel room. On the wall, a pair of persimmons painted in the manner of Kokei, simple and lush. Early evening, with full moon cresting the buildings bordering the nearby palace.

The man embraces the woman from behind. He unties the back-tied bow of her yukata sash. The front of her robe falls open; her breasts are pale, white fruits. The man stands behind her and holds a breast in each hand. The woman arches her head backward, her neck is sculpted stone. The tips of her breasts are red, or they seem to be red. The pale green tea in two tea-cups reflects the moon over the night-city.

Staccato dark tones on koto and samisen give way to an uneven cadence of drumbeats suspended in silence. The woman walks across the room. Seen from the back, the fluttering hem of her yukata.

She: I turn off the light but leave the white curtains open onto the smoky black of the sky and the here and there flash of neon: cobalt, yellow, violet, blue. In the grainy darkness of the room, your face is barest shadow, a profile of delicate line, a faint flash of dull light visible between eyelids nearly closed. I notice again the *ukiyoe* curve of your nose, the strong black straightness of the hair that falls chopped and thick across your forehead.

She stands gazing at the man. He sits on the bed in chiaroscuro light.

He: Ukiyoe? You think my nose is ukiyoe? Eh . . .
She: This time, as with many other times, I feel I catch a glimpse within you of something I once knew but had forgotten. In the half-dark, when the atoms and molecules seem to drift loosely within their forms, I more easily see this.

The woman picks up a teacup and sips tea. The open window in the dusky room makes a frame within which is seen the rooftop of a small building. Laundry still hanging on lines upon the building-top sways in purple-black silhouette against a paler sky, sky rippling with an inner brilliance. A long-haired girl gathers shirt-silhouettes, and her hair sails out black and wild in the new wind, in the fierce twilight.

The woman inside the room takes up her boxwood comb from Kyoto. She begins to comb her pale silk hair with a slow movement, tilting her head and gazing out the window, eyes focused upon an invisible world, upon the quavering air of the city settling into evening. The man is studying his reflection in the mirror.

He: I wanted to live long ago, to wear *chon-mage.*

He pulls his hair up and back into a tight topknot.

He: How do I look?
She: I'm in love with an ukiyoe man. Would you wear your hair that way when we go out? I'd like to listen to jazz with an ukiyoe man at my side. The *chon-mage* would look great with your Yamamoto Yohji blazer.

The woman sets her teacup down and turns on the television without turning up the sound. On the screen a man in ornate brocade kimono commits *seppuku* in slow motion. His long hair flies about his face as he topples forward and out of the frame.

^^^^^^

DEVILS
^^^

The man and the woman lie upon a silk futon; its color is wisteria. The woman lies with her back to the man. The man looks at the hairline at her neck, stroking the hairs upward, finding beauty in that place and in the line of the cheek against the light, plump.

She: Speak to me like a samurai, with a samurai voice.

She turns toward him to watch his face. His hand plays along the line from waist to hip, falls and rises, falls and rises.

^^^^^

He: Do you remember it? The moment of touch, the first one. I catch you in my arms in an embrace that's been pressing me toward you through the evening.

She: I was wearing a pink sweater.

He: The embrace undared until this moment comes likes a sigh and moves the next soft step toward lips touching just lightly and the body fills with its own old knowledge.

She: You stroked my hair. You said, it's pure gold. You said, how beautiful you are.

He: The blood speeds up in the somnolent veins and a faint feeling of urgency begins to be felt, and the bodies seek to push against each other, to enter into one another, the bodies fall away and together again with delighted fear. Questions of all kinds are crowding to be heard, not yet to be spoken.

She: You said, I love you. You held me tightly by the waist.

He: Speech becomes fragments, wisps; the breath separates sentence-parts; the voice finds itself ringing from a lowdown place, in the belly-depth; and inside and outside a kind of gathering tide begins to make the sweetness roll and rush across the world which is only the two entwined.

She: There's the way this felt all old and old new. I looked at your face above me and had known it centuries.

We hear the voice of Noh that rises over the city and soars moonward. The man walks to the window, looks out. Barefoot, he is dressed in yukata.

He: That voice! It throws itself into the sky with a long twining resonance, drones down into earth to where the ancient fires of molten metal slide en masse, brilliant.

She: The call of that voice is to the magical dead and to devils, to sweet-faced, white-faced wives, to ghost-maidens wearing blazing gold and crimson robes, to old men of vigor, long-bearded, bearing fish from poles, and oh! above the gliding moan of the voice, above the flute's leafy floating, above the sudden sometimes stamp of the perfected foot, pure white-encased, above the crack and call of the small drum, orange-silk tasseled, above the old sighs and wails and creaks and rasps and laments of the seated chorus, gang of pure spirit, the small moon rises.

He: The sky grows dark. In that far vast blue-black dark, what listens?

She: Do a Kabuki face for me. Make a Kabuki face.

He: Kyyaa!

He crosses his eyes and grimaces like an angry warrior god, his hands flexed, palms flattened and moving in slow controlled arcs forward and out across his body. Feet moving over the tatami in the ancient pattern of small swift steps, he comes toward the woman reclining upon the futon.

The woman reaches out to him. Her hand moves slowly upon his arm. He moves toward her.

She: So do you really love your wife?

^^^^^^

LIPSTICK
^^^

A cake shop cafe. A green afternoon. From within the cake shop cafe, one looks out upon a courtyard garden. The garden seems afloat in moisture, all glistening vivid green leaves, dew, and motionless raindrops.

The man and the woman sit with coffee in small white cups. Mozart flickers in the high-ceilinged room. The bamboo and ivy at the windows give the room a golden warmth, as cozy as a grotto.

She: Waiting for you in the rain today, under my red umbrella from Paris, my feet got wetter and wetter.

He: My watch, my wife, my car, the traffic, the time, the street, the moments spent searching for your face nacreous as a lily, shining in the watery gloom. Your red umbrella like a wonderful poppy. Your wet feet.

She: Anyway, it doesn't matter. They were old shoes.

He: I will remember the day as a blue dark one ebbing slowly into green, a long twilight *legato*, a day of being inside rooms, a day of quiet thinking, a day of slow looks and the wet-road sound of cars passing, a day when the river began to flow fast and white with mountain water, a day when spiders were still in their water-beaded webs, a day when time swam along like a deep and silent fish toward the sea.

She: I was remembering a girl I knew as a child. This took place in China. She was an English girl of thirteen who became artificially Japanese, a geisha in fact, with dyed-black hair piled into an unappealing arrangement of three mounds, a dusty-looking white face, and a flat and pointy little black-red mouth. She appeared at school every day, a small shredded dream of a geisha sitting at a wooden desk in the back of the room near the window. She never spoke. She seemed always to be on the brink of disappearing, receding into shadows. Like all people, she finally did vanish, all but the wisp of her that's here now, a few scant words in a small cafe on a day that's waterborne.

He: Such a young geisha could be very attractive. I can't imagine a young geisha sitting in a classroom. If I think of such a rare English child, I can only see her from afar, gliding quietly across a great meadow, wearing Heian robes, collar drooping deeply at the neck and trailing swaths of red, black, and periwinkle silk behind her. Her tiny feet would be charming, tilting along in high *geta* and tripping gently every now and then. Imagine the sweetness of her small sad face in such a setting.

She: I've heard that sad beautiful women are very appealing to men. I've heard that the kind of story a man likes best is one in which a sad beautiful woman dies. The quiet stillness of the face: eyes closed, lips parted. What do you think?

He: I like women who are alive. But we have a saying that a beauty must die young. Death is a kind of tax she has to pay. So I always worry about you. Possibly you will die very soon. I try not to think about it.

The woman takes out her small mirrored compact and a lipstick. She applies a pearly red color to her lips with a tiny brush. The man gazes at her.

She: Yes. I'm sure I will soon die. I should. It would be a nice gesture to make to your wife. It would make her happy. You could kill me, I wouldn't mind at all. How erotic! I'll wear kimono for the occasion. With my hair down, in disarray.

He: Could I kill you? I don't know how. By suffocation? By strangling, or with a sharp sword? During lovemaking? In a way it's an exciting thought. It's arousing. Please mention it again.

∧∧∧∧

The man and the woman leave the cafe and hail a taxi. The sun emerges in a sudden blaze of light close to the horizon. The white-gloved driver is silent. The small passenger television shows a baseball game, a tiny square of white-garbed figures against brilliant green. Sound is tinny. A home run, and the crowd cheers in a long burst of wild static.

On the other side of the city, sun has fallen behind the palace. A woman walks from one of the great gates, pauses to speak with the guard, walks on across the bridge that traverses the wide moat. The sky is big, its color burnished rose, smoke-pink, as deep as history. Building and tree shapes are black. Lights beginning to shine send streams of surprise into the shadowy slumbering magenta sky. The tiny figure of the woman disappears into the cliffs and ravines of the city.

∧∧∧∧∧

SULFUR
∧∧∧

The leaves are red in middle morning. The man and the woman recline as if asleep in an outdoor sulfur bath. In the tree above the steaming pool is a crimson-speckled bird pecking at something. Red dragonflies litter the ground amid the dead splendor of the drifting leaves. A wind catches the transparent wings and makes them hum and vibrate, fluttering off and on.

She: The bird looks down with its round eye and sees nudes adrift in space, a painting by Chagall.

The man pulls the woman onto his lap. The woman curves her body into his and floats. They are a study in pastels. Underwater, the chalky yellow-white of sulfur drifts in silt and pebbles. The water is bluish gray. Puffs of mist rise from the surface of the pool.

She: When you are happy, your eyes narrow so that no white shows.
He: The black belongs to the many secret nights we've spent together, to the dark heat where skin meets skin in sleeping embrace, to the infinite night of star-space, to the galactic sky-wide passion of the Tanabata lovers.
She: Did you know we would become lovers from the beginning?
He: The black belongs to the ink that flows from the tip of the writ-

ing brush, the narrow bamboo brush with which I sketch the characters of your name. The black belongs to the darkness contained in the word love. I have loved you forever. I had been searching for you for many years. I had married at the last possible moment; my wedding was a terrible dream. I didn't want the wife I saw beside me. I didn't love her then. I learned to love her later, in a different way. I'm sorry. I love her in a different way from you.

She: I am also your wife. It's an ancient tradition, one woman for house and children and another for love. She cooks for you.

He: She's a good cook.

She: I want to die when I think of it. I want to die in your arms, and then you can go home and eat her delicious food.

The woman rises from the bath, taking her small white towel and holding it against herself. She sits on the rocks that ring the pool. The man stares down into the water. He seems unhappy. The woman begins to cry.

From somewhere in the distance comes a faint sound of temple chanting. The drone of a priest's voice intoning the heart sutra mixes with the sound of many small birds chattering as they fly overhead. The birds land in the treetops with a commotion, shaking the dry leaves.

∧∧∧∧∧

MOON
∧∧∧

A mountain landscape in autumn. The man and the woman have been searching for *susuki*, pampas grass. *Susuki's* feathery season has passed, and the long arcing grasses don't look like delicate fluff-fronds but are more linear, so the man is displeased.

He: It is one month too late for moon-viewing.

She: Look how the white mist hangs low over the mountain. Feel the chill of winter rising from the earth.

The man and the woman sit on cold mossy stones by a small rushing stream, and the woman leans her head against the man's chest. The man unbuttons the shell-buttons of her red sweater and puts his mouth to the pale curve of her throat. The woman closes her eyes, lips parted, head bent back. With her sweater draped down and half-open about her shoulders, her long purple scarf running like a mountain stream down her back, running like Kabuki water, with her gray skirt floating in loose folds about her

waist, her white shoulders and breasts and thighs form an unexpected stat-
uary against the moss and wet fallen leaves.

She: Like this in the mountain on a milk-mist afternoon, I remember
strange things.

He: Remember when the moon rose fruit-orange over the storm-
cleansed streets, and in the night the soft flashes of fireworks rose up like
fiery lilies against the sky? Do you remember that?

She: I remember when the moon was gold, the frosted color of
white gold, sitting low in the sky and intimate. We drove toward it along
the mountain road and the night turned indigo; the gleam from many
small houses' blue-green roofs made a kind of warmth. I felt in the rooftops
an echo of lost early time. I felt as if we had ridden through all time, out of
the long ago past.

He: Before my grandmother died she had whispered to me for many
days, stories of the old times, twining out tales in her low soft voice. Before
she died she grew gradually smaller and more fine, and in those last days
her voice's intonation became something like a tint of quiet sound, an
unending ribbon of words swaying through the long nights, in dulcet,
cracking, halftone phrases. She spoke to me of ghosts, of feasts, of foxes, of
puzzle pieces, of fast rainstorms, of love, of the blood-soaked futons where
dead lovers lay embracing. I remember now what she remembered.

She: Will you remember what I remember? Remember that it's delicious all day, the lingering lilting weariness that follows a long night of lux-
uriant embrace, the body bruised by ecstasy, the simplicity of it? The salt
nectar in the flesh, the dark sweetness, the way the next day the body is
alight with the images, the memories, the way one makes a story from it?

∧∧∧∧∧

The man and the woman remain seated on the stones on the slope in
the mountain-depth. Our view pulls back from them slowly. We see for a
long time still the graceful white design of the woman's limbs against the
rust-reds, the yellows, the grays and greens of the landscape, we see the
white mist as it thickens in the valleys, we see the mountain as one amongst
many, we see the small white road that twists its way around the contours
of the slopes. There is now only a music of whispers, a peaceful voice like
that of an old woman dying, a voice that tells a story, almost unheard.

^^^^^^

CHOCOLATE
^^^

"It's funny. . . . I once thought of all this as a film by Godard. Why was that?" The man and the woman are sitting side by side in a Shinkansen heading south; it's early morning, still dark. They are drinking hot green tea from small cans.

"Godard? I remember you saying Kurosawa." The man slides his hand along her stockinged knee. "Something to do with the samisen."

The man looks at his watch. The digital display gives off an ectoplasmic pale green glow. "It's still so dark at six. Could you find a taxi easily this morning? The sky must have been pitch black when you left your house."

The woman closes her eyes. Wearily, she leans her head against the man's shoulder. "Shall we have breakfast?" Her question is barely audible, words carried upon a faint sigh.

"I already ate," The man sets down his tea-can. The kanji characters on the can spell out *gyokuro*. The can is decorated with green leaves. "But I'll order you an *obento* when the girl comes by."

The man observes his reflection in the glass of the train window. His face is transparent blue, overlaid by rice fields and black mountains. Near his own, the woman's face is a silent sleeping mask. The sky is endless gray, with the floating ghosts of train passengers. All around him and in the sky above are strangers asleep, eating, looking at comic books and magazines full of photographs of naked women in black and white, on rough paper. The pages open and close across the great cloudy panorama, across the archipelago. The sun is not yet visible. There is the scent of chocolate.

[1994]

Japanese Jew

SANFORD GOLDSTEIN

Almost twenty years ago when I made the first of my four trips to teach English at a Japanese university, I was startled one December day to find that the governor of the prefecture I was living in had sent me a Christmas tree. Like the rest of the Japanese nation at that time, he had apparently thought all Americans were Christians, all of us celebrated Christmas, and all of us wanted the tallest evergreen available with which to decorate the narrow living rooms of the homes the Japanese had put us in. I was amused by the naivete of the governor's assumption, yet I also thought his gesture most kind. My wife, who died only two years ago but who had been with me on my three earlier trips to Japan, was overjoyed by the governor's generosity for she loved Christmas trees, and only my perverse insistence that Jews didn't have them had kept her from filling the cramped apartment of our graduate school days with flashing bulbs and colored popcorn to announce to the world that Christmas meant peace on earth, goodwill to men. A few days after receiving the tree, I had asked my literature class in reference to an allusion that had come up in a short story by Melville what the name of the Jewish leader was who had led the Jews out of Egypt, and I felt thunderstruck by the silence in that under-heated classroom.

All those memories came flooding back to me about a month ago one November afternoon following my return to Japan eight weeks earlier to teach English literature and conversation for another two years at the same university I had first stayed at two decades ago. I had selected as my textbook Philip Roth's *Conversion of the Jews and Other Stories,* and it had been the usual slow march through individual sentences, grammatical intricacies, answers waited for in limbo, a whole gamut of confusion with some analysis tossed in along the way. We had just begun the second story in the collection, "Defender of the Faith," when one of the students came up at the end of the class to ask me if it was difficult to become a Jew. Jiro Sato had attracted my attention long before his startling question, for over the weeks his English seemed not to have been made in Japan. It was always clear, precise, unbelievably idiomatic, unbelievably un-Japanese. I had once asked him where he had learned to speak so well, thinking that perhaps a rich father had taken him to America and kept him there for at least thirteen years.

"A missionary taught me," Jiro had said.

At that moment I remembered my first trip to Japan when my wife and I had helped some missionaries organize a Sunday service for the men aboard the dumpy freighter we were traveling on, and I had smiled inwardly, recalling how my petite wife and I had joined in the worship, at times heads lowered in prayer, at times singing "Amazing Grace" with the rest. The death of my wife had left our two children and me very much on our own, they doing their own thing on college campuses in the States, occasionally writing letters to Japan for an increase in allowance, more often than not being average students interested less in their future careers than in music and novels. As for me, I was settling down into an uneasy middle age where routines seemed to make my days a perpetual rise and fall like sand running through glass to mark a definite end.

When Jiro Sato had asked me how one became a Jew, it seemed easier to explain how one lost his Jewish connections in the maelstrom of uprooted traditions in mobile America.

"Well, you don't become a Jew," I said, Roth's textbook tight in my grip.

"I see," said Jiro Sato, an innocence on his face like that found on all young Japanese males who have not yet shaved, yet his "I see" reminded me of the annoying mysteries of the Eastern world where so much echoed along the corridors of silence.

"You do?" It was my turn to withhold several compound sentences ready to burst forth.

"Apparently no one can become a Jew. You're a closed society. Isn't that what you meant?"

My eyes seemed to focus too strongly on Jiro Sato's Asian ones, his smooth face, his pomaded hair. In spite of feeling I ought to mechanically agree, I continued: "Well, you are born a Jew. My son's a Jew and so is my daughter. They haven't really done anything about it. But they're Jews."

Jiro Sato's pursuit of silence stretched even further, almost as if he were waiting for me to blunder into more difficulties.

"That is," I began again, but without too much hope, "the Jews were God's chosen. Jews don't proselytize—I mean they aren't missionaries. Out of all the people in the world, God chose the Jews to carry out his law." At that moment I was positive Jiro Sato had never had the desire for God to have bestowed a little of the agony elsewhere, spread it around, even as far as Japan.

"Then I can't become a Jew, can I?" my young student said, smiling at me as if he wasn't the least bit disappointed.

"Well, I wouldn't say that either." My answer, however, disappointed me, and I felt caught up in a perverse little original sin of my own. "Why do you want to become a Jew?"

"I don't know. I'm curious." He suddenly had to run to get to his next class, but while his curiosity might get him out of the 108 Buddhist desires the New Year temple bells rang out, he might find himself in the quagmire of the more than 600 commandments Jews, at least the Orthodox ones, had to follow.

Later that evening after I had eaten my lonely supper and graded a few badly worded themes, I sat down to read the English newspaper I subscribed to. My mind suddenly drifted back to Jiro Sato's woeful question. For a moment I imagined an entire group of Jiro Satos, each wanting to become a Jew and waiting in line for some mysterious document to be stamped for admittance to world Jewry. I wondered how the traditional skullcap would stay on the pompadours of the youth of Japan, thick black hair bright with pomade. And over thin shoulders hundreds of white and blue prayer shawls seemed to be slipping off as the Japanese read the Torah not in Hebrew but in Chinese-Japanese ideographs of their own. As they drank the Sabbath wine, which they would bless in their own strange tongue, would their white expressionless faces turn red, and prayer books tossed aside, would these converts to Judaism break out into some primitive folk dance or drinking song, Hebraism and God forgotten in a return of the Japanese goddess of the sun?

I tried to focus on the editorial page but couldn't. Jiro Sato's question seemed the most profound I had ever heard from a Japanese student during my trips to Japan. As a lazy Jew I had not let myself be cornered into any restrictions. Even when my wife died, I had no visions of God, certainly no vision of heaven or hell, no thoughts about ribs and dust, no post-death-bed conversion to prayer at sunrise and sunset. The wife I had loved for twenty-three years was irrevocably gone, the stone marking her burial place when I went to her cemetery on lonely weekends, a Jewish one even though I was not certain my wife would have wanted to be so limited. I blamed no God for her death, no world, no one in fact. My wife was gone, and I had to continue to support our two kids. The Jewish star placed on her stone did not bind me to the Jews or anyone else, or even her for that matter. It was simply there, more for convenience than anything else. And when I died, I thought, I would be placed beside her, the space already bought and paid for.

Instead of confronting young Sato's question on how to become a Jew, I had begun worrying about my own life as a Jew. All at once I reached for the Bible my wife had always insisted we take with us on our trips to Japan but which had often gathered dust on our oriental shelves as well. The book had been a gift from a Jewish lady my wife had once rented a room from, and I smiled as I remembered my wife's telling me about the rage of her landlady's husband, angry over her having given a young Jewish girl a Bible that contained the New Testament as well. My wife had read only the latter on our two-week short trip to Japan by freighter. I didn't blame her. It was shorter than the Old Testament.

I began turning the pages of our family Bible, one after another, more than nine hundred pages beneath my fingers. I had of course gone to Hebrew school, and such commonplace stories as the Fall, the sacrifice of Isaac, the plagues on the Egyptians, the crossing of the Red Sea, even Solomon's judgment about the true parent—all those any schoolboy knew. But I had never read through the Old Testament. Yet when I scanned the pages, the volume seemed too heavy, too cumbersome, too much trouble, and I tossed it back on my desk.

As I continued to teach Roth's "Defender," I anticipated the difficulties of my students over such terms as Sabbath, Friday night services, "kosher," and other forms of Hebraic jargon that perhaps even the non-Jewish world of Peru, Indiana, might have failed to recognize. But I did sense in these recent students a new Japanese awareness of history. Many knew it was Hitler who had slaughtered six million Jews, that Israel existed as the Jewish state, and that such diverse personalities as Karl Marx and Einstein were Jews. *The Japanese and the Jews* had long been translated into Japanese. I doubted that when Christmas arrived I would be receiving a tall evergreen by way of the latest delivery service, but I knew I would once more start receiving the usual bundle of greetings in my mailbox, some with the Japanese imitation of the Nativity, large stars that marked some future evolutionary advancement toward the good, the true, and the beautiful, three slim kings on an overburdened camel. My wife had been in the habit of sending out Christmas cards herself, having stuck to the belief throughout our years of married life that the holiday celebrating the birth of the Christian Savior was one of the most heartwarming events in the cycles of season and history.

I had never objected to her practice, not even when she signed both our names, for I was the most passive of Jews, the most indifferent observer of the Covenant. I carried with me, though, my own brand of sentimental attachments that cling to the bitter-sweet petals of memory. I recalled my own Baptism in the form of the Jewish Bar Mitzvah, the Jewish boy becoming a Jewish man as he sings from the Torah on the Sabbath surrounded by smiling and proud members of his family. The dozen or so shirts I had received, the sixteen pairs of checkered brown, blue, and gray socks, the several ties and sweaters, all seemed to whirl up that ancient path of recall. The greatest change in me apparently came in this outward form of new apparel, especially the new suit and new pair of black shoes my parents had bought me and the new overcoat I had been draped in by my unsmiling grandfather. That ceremony of the thirteen-year-old boy had been a key moment in my meager history of the Jews, and its details lingered to remind me that my son had not been put through the ritual. He had not even gone to Hebrew school, and he was so ignorant he would have been unable to tell an Aleph from a Chinese "vase" in spite of his having been with us on our third trip to Japan eight years ago. My wife and I had let our children wander by themselves through the brambles of religious possibilities, and we had felt safe at least that they had not become members of any cult, orgiastic, narcotic, or charismatic.

After Jiro Sato's question, Roth's "Defender of the Faith" had a new appeal for me, and I easily connected myself to the young hero who had not done anything about his religion until a problem presented itself. He had fought in the war, had killed his share of the enemy in Europe, had done his duty and hardened himself against sentimental waverings. The thought of Friday night services had not even remotely crossed his mind until a young recruit had approached him. And now the young Sato by his own simple question had brought into focus the loose strings of my own religious life.

During the next few weeks I expected Jiro Sato to come up to me at the end of the class and put forward more questions. I was hoping he would, almost as if with my own son gone and hardly ever writing me in his scribbled letters anything that had to do with faith or history, I might have adopted Jiro as my own and led him toward the paternal stories of Jacob, Joseph, and David. But no Jiro Sato came forward. It was not that he absented himself from class. No, he was there each time, his pages of text ready, sentences underlined, words defined, Japanese characters along the margins. When called upon, he was armed with answers. He knew about the Passover references in Roth's "Defender," about the rites of circumcision, even the Hebrew word for synagogue, *shul*. When I mentioned "*gefilte* fish" and asked what horseradish was, he came up with the Japanese word *wasabi*, that green paste-like relish I had eaten with raw fish. Yes, Jiro Sato was very much present in my class, very much alive, very much interested, but the hour over, he remained in his chair like the rest of his peers until I left the room. As I walked along the wooden corridors of our building to my office, I was hoping to hear Jiro call out behind me. But as one of the Chosen, I did not expect Jiro to tap my elbow and make the great crossing with me.

Blame it on Roth's "Defender," but I became more and more conscious of my lagging religious connections. And I became more and more pensive, more and more tied to a past whirling through which was the image of my wife, eclectic, religiously open, attached to no flag. I remembered the weeks she had attended Unitarian services in a broken-down house not far from our college campus. She had been excited by the breadth of Unitarian liberalism. One year she was plagued by the desire to attend a midnight Mass and she did, interrupting one of my favorite talk-shows by dragging me along. And when a student of mine invited us to his wedding, the ceremony written by a guitar-playing long-haired type almost out of a religious painting, her eyes were bedimmed. I had always admired her receptive spirit, had never fought it, for a few years even agreeing to a small Christmas tree in our downstairs back bedroom when our kids were in elementary school, yet mixed into the flattering portrait of my generous wife was a line that pulled me back to the days of my youth, back toward the mysteries of my grandfather's father and his, back to the Garden of Eden which I had sometimes thought of as a naive fairy tale, sometimes as a metaphor for the tangle of life in which the tree poisoned rich possibilities while opening up the complexities of the world.

One day in January as we were finishing Roth's "Defender of the Faith," I had been annoyed several times during the class when, in reviewing some of the details of the story, I had met with a wall of non-response that irritated me. It was almost as if I sensed some Japanese prejudice against Jews, as if in explaining some of the Jewish customs and expressions in the story I had proudly set myself off as one of the Chosen, as if in me there was an arrogant awareness of history and language and tradition that had antagonized my usually passive students. At one point when the silence seemed too painfully drawn out, I was ready to hurl my book at the blackboard, but having learned something about Japanese restraint, I merely waited. But that seemed to increase my impatience. With a great deal of relief I suddenly decided to laugh the whole thing off and dismiss early. But as I got ready to leave the room, I turned abruptly and looked at Jiro Sato. He was sitting quietly at his desk, his book open, his eyes on me. On his face was neither the accusation I had felt about my attitude during the hour nor the contempt I sensed among the class members, a contempt for me not only as an outsider, a *gaijin*, but a Jewish *gaijin*. I found, though, something on Jiro Sato's face that reminded me of something in myself, something that had fallen short, that I had failed to come to grips with. Jiro Sato's question once more assailed me as if I had entered that classroom with empty promises, with words only on a printed page, with answers to details instead of some larger pattern that would have brought God into our midst, some divine deus ex machina lowered in a basket of grapes. Was that what Jiro's facial expression meant?

"Can you come to my office, Mr. Sato?" I suddenly called as I stood at the door, my hand on the knob.

He got up quickly and followed me out.

"Oh, you have a class, don't you?" I said, abruptly stopping along the corridor as I remembered how he had fled the last time.

"It's okay. I can cut it," he said, so in my office I boiled some water and measured the instant coffee and shared my peanut butter and jelly sandwich with him, all of which he wordlessly accepted. I had no idea why I had even asked him in. Actually I was hoping he would raise more questions on his own. The eating and drinking seemed to go on eternally.

"You don't have to worry," he finally said after refusing a second cup of coffee. "To be a Jew must be really hard. I guess I don't want to become a Jew." Once more he came out with his Asian smile.

Again his response startled me as if with some insight not the least delicate or difficult he had seen through me. I found myself answering, "I don't blame you."

The continuation of the smile I expected because of my flip remark didn't materialize. My young student looked at me as if waiting for explanations.

"Really, your Buddhism is quite convenient, isn't it?" I said as if I had thought everything through.

"Yes, but isn't that its trouble?" For the first time I noticed how white his teeth were as he smiled.

A sudden image of my wife fluttered my pulse. We had often talked about the Buddhist temple, the simple form of prayer before the offertory box, the silent bowing and lifting of hands, palms together to beat out a slight rhythm, the hastily uttered appeal for mercy, the *Namu Amida Butsu*, and that done, one could go on one's important business for the morning or afternoon. That seemed to be all there was to Buddhism. And no sweat, no long sitting in a temple each week for hours as in a synagogue, no interminable prayers for the masses in a Hebrew so hastily uttered no one knew which end was up, no outbursts from a beard. Somehow the religions of Japan were there like breath, and one took them as they came. The duties imposed by the God of the Old Testament were an enormity. The intricate details of what to do or not to do, when to do, how to do, seemed to have exhausted me in my younger years. No, my wife and I had often quietly walked the long horizontal paths to a temple or climbed the steep steps up to some peaceful shrine. The out-of-door freshness, the brief ceremony, the easy return to life. When in Japan my wife forgot all the other religious possibilities except for Christmas. Her innocent joy in those walks and visions made everything Jewish seem ponderous to me, heavy, weighted, demanding.

I was startled to find Jiro watching me, staring at me, as if with some peculiar sensitivity available only to the Japanese psyche, he too was caught up in my own lonely tangle.

"What about your parents?" I suddenly asked as if that was the logical response to something asked ages ago.

"Oh, they're Japanese through and through."

"You mean that they go about their everyday lives and let the religion fall where it may?"

"Something like that. Oh, they know it's there! That's good enough for them."

"And for you?"

"Me? I want what the Jews had—something difficult, something they have to live with every minute of their lives."

"You mean the circumcision, don't you?"

"Oh, that's easy. No, not circumcision."

Again I found Jiro standing, ready to take off after leaving his tidbit of teasing thought. Was the boy a miracle, something dropped in bullrushes ready to be picked up by the first foreigner that came along? What did he really want? And what would having even the slightest element of Jewishness do for him?

That night long after my simple dinner, I opened the Old Testament to a passage my wife had marked off during her first trip to Japan. It was one she always referred to: "Likewise when a foreigner, who is not of thy people Israel, comes from a far country for the sake of thy great name, and thy mighty hand, and thy outstretched arm, when he comes and prays toward this house, hear thou from heaven thy dwelling place, and do according to all for which the foreigner calls to thee; in order that all the peoples of the earth may know thy name and fear thee, as do thy people of Israel, and that they may know that this house which I have built is called by thy name." Solomon's words seemed to ring out in my lonely living room, and they echoed in my footsteps as I trudged upstairs to my bedroom. As I lay down on my Japanese-style bed after putting it down on the straw mats of my narrow room, I felt once more as if I had violated some personal covenant. I had let Jiro Sato flounder. And my wife? I fell asleep thinking about her.

We finished the second of Roth's stories, and as the year's term neared its end in February, I had finally reached Roth's major story, "The Conversion of the Jews." The end of a Japanese school year or any other has always left me empty, yet at the same time relieved, for at least something definite is settled. Still, it was at just such moments that I missed my wife most—the continuity in her that never ailed no matter what the blow. One evening after a tiring day of answerless classes, I sat down in my living room to look up a passage in the Old Testament. That morning I had gotten into something of a muddle about *Exodus,* and I had inwardly cursed myself for not knowing enough. As I skimmed through the text, it seemed as if I was more caught up in the escape from Egypt and the passing over the Red Sea than I was in finding my *faux pas*.

I was surprised several days after our final exam to receive a phone call from Jiro. He wanted to pick up his exam, something Japanese students never ask to do, and certainly not over the phone. I told him I'd have it for him tomorrow. And so Jiro would be coming, presumably for his exam, but I sensed this was an excuse. He would make one final effort, something would happen, something would be settled.

After several hours of looking through examination papers, I tumbled into my warm bath. I was getting through my tasks and I felt like some graduate student ready to send all his learning tumbling by going out drinking. Suddenly I looked down at my circumcision. I couldn't remember the last time I had thought about the circumcision per se. Certainly it had something to do with becoming a Jew, the cutting away, that taking of that which could never be replaced, the eternal commitment in that long-ago time before medical science made any of its modern recommendations.

As I got out of my bath to dry myself, my thought continued in that direction. Looking down, I felt once more the total exposure of the Jew of an earlier era. What had that total exposure meant? One ultimately lost by it. Nor did God offer his Jews any rich after-life, only the mundane communal world in which one followed the law, obeyed the law. One did not break the law or the lawbreaker himself would be without God's love, God's protection. I remembered that not even Moses had entered the Holy Land. And Saul—his punishment for bringing back the enemy's spoils as a sacrifice to God instead of following God's command that he take no spoils at all. And David, for all his devotion, punished for sending Bathsheba's husband to the front so that he could enjoy the man's wife as his own. And even Solomon for all his wisdom, an ultimate violation, all foreshadowed in Eden and relentlessly carried out. To be a Jew one had to come to grips with non-merit, non-reward, a blind following of duty for a love often withheld. With what teeth, what arrogance, what passion, had God commanded the Jews to be!

Agitated by my rambling emotions, I lay down on my futon. My thoughts about Jiro were replaced by thoughts about my wife. The picture of a windowshopper came to me, store fronts bright with Christmas lights. Jiro had wanted to know how one became a Jew simply because being a

Buddhist was too easy, too convenient. I threw Jiro's challenge at my wife, and each question she countered with a smile, a sweet smile, the sweetest smile in the world, the most gentle, the most appealing. But then I seemed to hear the thunderous voice of the Lord, to see the Ark, to stumble across my own futile attempt at penetrating the Covenant for Jiro. And into all these feelings and images I seemed to hear the taunting intellectualism of Jiro, the voice of the moderns, yet reaching back too for difficulties.

Jiro came to my office on time the next morning. Though his excellent exam was on my desk, I felt as if I were armed for combat. Instead, I saw a change in Jiro's face, a troubled look I had never seen before. "Look at these." He showed me some of the anti-Semitic articles appearing recently in Japanese magazines, articles I had known about but had never felt compelled to protest. "And this too," he said, handing me an ad on anti-Semitic books, and again books I had known about but had never read, books in which Japan's present economic difficulties were reduced mono-dimensionally and laid squarely in the lap of international Jewry.

"Hitler's coming to Japan!" he shouted at me. "I want to be ready for that! Tell me how to stop him! Tell me how to save even one Japanese Jew! Tell me!"

The sudden startling cry in his voice seemed to cut through all my own logic, my intellectualism, my wavering as a Jew who had never had any say about becoming a Jew. I felt ashamed, like an adolescent just learning to confront some enormity. I stood up and moved toward him as if with my hand I could anoint him a Bar Mitzvah, a son of the Torah. "Yes, Jiro," I said, embracing him. "I will—I'll try."

[1973]

Flatlands II

AL ALONZO

It was the hottest September on record. Always the paragon of generosity, Ronnie Hirano insisted Covington accompany him on a special expedition. "Onsen. Hot spring. Many *beppin*." Having already seen what Mishima had to offer of gorgeous gals in his daily classes at Victoria: English as She is Spoken, Covington was ready to probe deeper into the heartland.

"Isn't it a bit hot to be going to a hot spring today?" he asked, getting no response from Mr. Hirano. Ronnie had a habit of turning off his hearing aid when he didn't want to answer a question, a condition Covington was beginning to notice even among Japanese who weren't deaf. Perhaps this is the source of the beatific Japanese smile, he thought.

He sat back to enjoy the ride. The driver as usual was Mrs. Hirano's brother, the ferret-faced Mr. Umezawa. But this time Ronnie had promised that another brother would join them at the onsen.

They drove through the debilitated landscape, its shimmering rice fields gnawing into cliffs scarred by the rock quarries of the past thousand years. Japan, it seemed, didn't like its mountains and, like Mr. Matsushita of Panasonic, would prefer to slowly grind them down to the size of elegant polished rice kernels.

They moved on out of billboard country into rolling hills along a coast. The smack of seaweed hit Covington's nostrils as the car punctured a narrow tunnel that looked like it would drop them directly into the brink, then sharply swerved. From there on out, it was one tunnel after another and the road seemed only wide enough for the smallest of Suzukis to pass them. Occasionally, they would wait at a tunnel for a truck to come out first. Not that the hazards of the road had any effect on Mr. Umezawa's speed. Covington was struck by the way Japanese drivers would wait till the very last possible moment before braking. Yet in three weeks he hadn't seen a single accident and rarely even so much as a dented fender.

They began to spot the lights of civilization again—coffee shops, restaurants, pachinko parlors—but an unfamiliar odor somewhere between a bad egg and an overheated carburetor began to dominate the landscape. *Onsen no nioi*—the hotspring smell—he was informed. They passed several imposing old wooden structures, almost like temples except that they were invariably joined to hideous modern extensions like Waikiki hotels.

Covington was just about to fall asleep again when they pulled up in front of one of these Waikiki temples. This is it. The onsen.

Emerging from the neon bedecked genkan came—was it? Yes, it was the same tall bouncer from the karaoke club of several weeks ago, though this time not in a tuxedo. And just behind him, somewhat frowsy from an all-day drinking bout, was one of the louts from the night club.

"Hi, how are you, Covington?" he said in fairly recognizable Honolulu dialect.

"Oh, it's you, sir!" replied Covington. (What's he going to say? He looks mad: "WE didn't like what you did to the fence after you left our club.")

But the yakuza stumbled past him without another word and began pleasantries with Ronnie and Mr. Umezawa. (This is too long for greetings and salutations, thought Covington. Something must be up.)

After ten minutes of intense deliberation, the English-speaking bouncer dashed back to Covington. "You come with me.

And the other three waved him aside. "You go ahead. He'll take care of you."

Covington was not so much ushered as pressured into a large glass door which he was happy to see open automatically just as his nose rammed against it. Tuxedo-san gestured that he should take off his shoes, something he was pretty much prone to do everywhere by now. And six women in ornate kimonos on each side of the entrance proceeded to bow and lisp elegant nothings as a thirteenth and somewhat stouter woman grabbed his hand and, English-less, chattered to Tuxedo-san as she bustled him down a corridor.

Corridor. And corridor. And corridor of corridors. Covington began to think he was in Ripley's Believe It or Not and kept waiting for an executioner with an ax or a headless zombie at the end of the next hallway. But finally they found a room, and the man with the tux proceeded to tell him to get out of his clothes as he handed him a folded bathrobe and a towel. No sooner was he into his robe than Mr. Tux wrapped him up in an extremely long sash and tied him snugly behind like a scoutmaster on Knot Day and Madame X fussed around fixing tea.

"Do you like Japan?" said Mr. Tux, offering him a senbei cracker.

"Yes." Covington started to say "inordinately," then downgraded it to "absolutely."

"Do you like Japanese tea?"

(In comparison to what? Jasmine tea? The *mizuwari* I drank the last time I saw these guys?) Covington kept his mouth shut and smiled. He was liking being deaf.

"Would you like to try a Japanese bath?"

Covington had seen one already at Hakone, a real gem. He was hoping this one would be as elegant and traditional. But he was wondering why his hosts had left him alone with a strange man, so all he could say was "Umnh."

In the absence of a response, Tuxedo-san switched languages and flirted with Madame X, ignoring Covington completely. Then he turned back after guzzling several cups of tea and said, "Ready? Let's go."

Back down another corridor, another set of stairs, another corridor and finally Covington was convinced he was an IRA terrorist sentenced to the Maze Prison. But at last a door slid aside under a flapping curtain that read "MEN."

"You go in."

"But what about you."

"I don't take baths here. I work."

Rather sheepishly, Covington went inside and stepped out of his robe. The huge dressing room was as silent as a morgue, a Japanese morgue. There were little baskets to put your things in. Covington noticed that they were all empty but one.

He slid open another door. Steam billowed up. It was like walking into a white curtain. As his eyes grew accustomed to the glaze in front of them, he began to make out tiny elfsized showers and benches and the rim of a gigantic bath that looked like the River Styx with grim boulders and gaping caverns from which the strains, not of samisen or koto, but Hawaiian ukeleles emerged.

He washed himself before violating the pristine waters, as he knew filthy hairy beasts were supposed to. But as he slipped gently into the steaming cauldron flecked with Christmas tree lights, Covington was still puzzled. Where was everybody?

He sat there about as long as he could stand it, still half blind from the steam when suddenly he felt it. A kind of wave of pressure against his foot. He drew back. The wave approached again. Finally he summoned his courage and pushed his foot out one millimeter further. It was flesh. It was someone else's foot.

"What am I supposed to say," he wondered. ("Hi!"? "Excuse me, that's my foot!"? "Excuse me, is that your foot?!"? "Excuse my foot!"?)

Covington was prone in such cases to just say "Umnh." So he did. And was met with silence. The two feet just sat there against one another for a while.

Then the phantom rose slightly out of the water with a big splash and pushed what looked like a tiny wooden boat across to Covington. As it came closer, he realized it had a bottle in it.

"Try! Sake!" a low mellow voice intoned.

After several of these little boats had passed his way, Covington became aware

1. That he was very happy.
2. That he was not going to be arrested.
3. That there was someone in the bath with him who did not speak very much English but definitely wanted to get to know him.

By now a bright red, Covington thought it best to beat a retreat. But as he went to shower off, he was followed and soon was being rubbed and scrubbed by a man who looked like a retired boxer with very quick movements and very short hair.

"This is Japanese way," he informed Covington. And Covington replied, "*Aa, domo,*" not at all sarcastically.

It was only as they were putting on their yukata in the dressing room that Covington discovered the identity of the phantom bather. This was none other than Mrs. Ronnie Hirano's missing brother, Kazuaki. He was, he proceeded to say, a wholesale vegetable dealer, liked Americans, had a fat wife and an even fatter son and was now going to take Covington to a party.

Covington was wary by now of parties. Parties seemed to require enormous concentration in this country. Everyone sat and squinted at each other for the first hour. Then everyone got drunk enough to speak. Then Herculean tasks would be required of foreigners. Then everyone would run out of things to say. Then everyone would leave suddenly just as Covington was beginning to enjoy himself, leaving him alone to count namecards.

They reentered the maze of corridors and entered a hall big enough for a papal audience at which only one of the fourteen long tables was occupied. A bevy of kimonos came in and out with refreshments but there were only six men at the table, among them Hirano and the dewlapped host, Mr. Agatsuno, the owner of the hotel.

"He wants to learn English," explained Mr. Hirano.

"On my first holiday in three weeks?" thought Covington. But he had known this kind of thing might happen. It was, after all, the reason why so many friends of his had returned to America exhausted, but with their college loans paid off.

So Covington spent the next hour telling a bemused Mr. Agatsuno how to pour drinks in English, since that was about all they were doing anyway.

He was just about to say, "May I go now," when in swept an entirely new group of some twenty men, women, and children and one particularly old, large, and fiercely impressive matron who sat slightly to one side as everyone waited on her hand and foot. Mr. Hirano, Weasel Umezawa, and his brother Kazuaki all went over and made nearly prostrate obeisances.

Covington was sure there would soon be kneeling boys with hot towels like in the club at Mishima. But, no, he was asked to go up there, too, bow politely, and receive a blessing.

"It's my great aunt," explained Ronnie. "She's the head of our family."

So this was a family reunion? There was more food and more drinks. And another trip to the bath, this time insanely crowded with the younger men climbing up the rocks to see if they could peek into the ladies' bath and falling over themselves in glee. Soon there were so many people that it was more like a gel or a stew, but nobody seemed to mind. Least of all Covington, who was now delirious.

As they carried him off to beddy-bye, he was entering the huggy-kissy stage, assuring Kazuaki that they would be pals forever. Kazuaki came into the room with him, laid out two futons together, then got up to a knock on the door, which turned out to be his wife and another woman, and said, "I must go now other room." Covington whimpered to himself, but quickly slipped into dreamland.

Which didn't seem to last long. All night, there was a sort of rustling back and forth in the corridors, and occasionally a wave of TV or music would rush over him. Then a door would slam and all would be quiet again, only for the cycle to repeat itself. Where were the *beppin*, Covington wondered.

At 7 A.M., Kazuaki came in, fixed him up and hauled him off to breakfast with twenty-six other very sleepy looking yukata. Covington insisted that all he wanted was an egg and a few pieces of seaweed, but ended up like a pate goose, stuffed with several bowls of rice with *natto*, multicolored pickles, fried fish, something slippery and oozy that seemed half-alive, and a hard gummy object that had to be dug out of an artsy-fartsy looking shell.

Kazuaki was looking dreamy and half slouching against him as they finished off the last epicurean delight. "Now we go another party."

Mr. Hirano explained that Sunday would begin with a group of social workers from Kazuaki's church who had just returned from America and wanted to get to know Covington. Covington obliged with a grin, especially since Kazuaki said he would join him. And even more especially because Ronnie was going home first.

The six of them were waiting in a small room around a kotatsu. It turned out they would spend the morning arranging and exchanging photos from their trip with interludes of conversation directed at Covington, with particular reference to book B of the Jack and Betty series.

All of them were young members of Sokagakkai. Like all the younger Japanese Covington had met, they had such mature and beautiful eyes, yet acted so moronic that Covington could not see them as adults at all. One woman, from Hakone, slightly older and uglier than the others, seemed to dominate the conversation.

Kazuaki was clearly getting as bored as Covington was, and Covington suggested they slip out. "Let's go to the beach or something." It might be fun talking to sea anemones and starfish for a switch. Kazuaki was ready but said, "First let me say goodbye to everyone."

In a minute, he was back. Covington asked him if he could leave his things there and pick them up later. He replied that no, we wouldn't be coming back. Then he seemed to just stand there like a statue. Finally, Covington turned to the woman from Hakone and asked her what was going on. She replied with just a trace of irony, "He's trying to see if anyone wants to join you so nobody will feel left out." But she added menacingly, "You know this is our only opportunity to exchange pictures."

Finally, Covington turned to Kazuaki and asked, "Well, do you want to go or not?"

"No, you looked bored. I just do for you."

So, of course, they stayed.

It dawned on Covington that everybody in Japan yielded their wills to the group. Except that in every group there was one little thug or bitch.

Hours later, as they filed out of the room, the woman from Hakone asked, "Do you have any suggestions as to how we should spend our reunion next Sunday?"

How very sweet, thought Covington. How about pearl diving?

[1994]

Dreaming of Glory

JOHN BRYSON

The restaurant was once a golf-house. Trophy cases in the hallway still displayed the chromium shapes of putting irons and golf balls and a wood that was once the instrument of a hole-in-one by a member of the Imperial Family. The names of winners of Japanese tournaments were celebrated on rosewood panels high on the wall. The titles were all in English. Old photographs of uncomfortable golfers in plus-fours and cloth caps were mounted on both sides of the doorway. Humphrey had not seen them when he came in. He was surprised to find a date as early as 1919.

He found Butcher and the four Japanese delegates already on the terrace. They were not waiting for him. Butcher struggled into the flaccid burden of his overcoat and his gasps fumed into the cold afternoon as if he were puffing at a cigar. He turned his back for Humphrey to lift the coat by its collar and held out his arms in the half-mast gesture of a heavy knight readied for the fray. Higher, he grunted, higher.

Their limousines had waited through lunch under trees at the edge of a driveway that touched the building only for a moment before curling back to the road. The guard box had a despondent air as if it were empty. The chauffeurs opened the car doors wide. Three hours of slow rain had speckled the gun-metal panels with the sunset red and amber of autumn maples and the windows had fogged with condensation from motors running to keep the drivers warm. Butcher wrapped the flaps of his overcoat about his thighs and took the last space in the rear of the first car. He took time to settle himself. Humphrey stooped to climb into the front. No, Butcher called to him, you ride with the others. He waved to the driver to close the doors and Humphrey turned away.

Humphrey rode in the front of the second car. Though conversation at lunch had been brisk, and often jolly, the two Japanese sitting behind him fell silent and only occasionally pointed out places that might be of interest to a foreigner. The traffic into Tokyo was heavy and slow in the wet. They crossed the river Sumida by a stone bridge Humphrey was told was famous for its age, and swung into the river-side boulevard. The curb was lined with riot police.

For nearly two kilometers they picketed the sidewalk at intervals Humphrey judged to be ten paces. Every plane and articulation of their bodies was cased in black cladding and the carapaces gleamed with the intensity of wet paint although the light was dull. Their scaled fists held staves upright in unwavering enfilades for as far as Humphrey could see. There must be hundreds. Narrow shields hung from their forearms with no emblazonment of heraldry so that they seemed to be responsible to no identifiable authority. Each visor reflected an unyielding and malevolent gaze behind which Humphrey could find no flicker of life and sloped at an angle that recalled nothing so much as an iron mandible.

The cars turned off the boulevard at a roadblock that had not been there before lunch and Humphrey felt a relief he thought was very foolish. He turned to Hogara. Why, he asked, were there so many police?

Hogara shrugged. Today, I don't know, he said. Maybe the safe movement of some important people, he smiled, big shots.

The air of the conference room was still stale from the morning session. Its warmth was welcome. Humphrey sat on the same side of the long table as Butcher but left an empty chair between them. He expected to take no part in this final and summary session. He had taken no part in the earlier three. On the morning of the first meeting Butcher had tapped with his thick finger the brief and its twenty-eight appendices; he asked Humphrey if he was familiar with the figures. I am the author, Humphrey told him with a smile, of their every digit; if you have any trouble, just ask. I see, Butcher had said, your reward for diligence, I wondered why you were here. I will do the talking, he said, I'm going to pitch it to them.

Butcher began. His voice had the stock-in-trade confidence of a door-to-door salesman. He had, Humphrey knew something of it, joined Mincorp as a publicist for petroleum extracts after a year with Lancia in Turin, he had spent two years as advertising manager for one of the toolmakers of the Ruhr and had directed promotion for a breakfast cereal, a brand of low-tar cigarettes, and had an expanding line of executive games from California. He had less German and Italian than he claimed. I am a marketing man, he said, as if there were no higher credential.

Humphrey thought of Butcher as having the mannered bonhomie of an Anglican prelate. It seemed unmanly and unvirtuous to disagree with anything he said. His weight must have been over a hundred kilos but at parties he danced intricately and with a sureness in his own center of gravity that unnerved his partners and they clung petulantly to him. His headstrong driving had killed his first wife and Humphrey had met only his second, a singer he had married in Munich. He spoke as though misfortune had deprived her of leading roles in Marschner and Wagner but sometimes late at those parties her voice made the vulnerable and searching notes of the blues and her thighs worked the slits in her skirt. She was not often with him. If asked about it, Butcher told of their asthmatic daughter whose sickness stifled her frantic breath at unpredictable, he said, and inconvenient hours.

None of the four Japanese took notes while Butcher spoke. Their blue folders lay on the table. All were executives of the same company, a corporation of immense size and diversification, through the baking of plastics, the harvesting of foodstuffs, and the invention of pesticides. And all were from the plastics division; the plastic arm of your corporate body, Humphrey had said as they first met, but everyone seemed to be smiling already, and one after the other exchanged business cards with him, accepting Humphrey's always with the left hand then holding the card toward him at arm's length in the expectation of a motionless instant, beginning with the minute narrowing of an eye's aperture and ending in the sudden flash of a smile, so that card and face were together printed in a single frame of permanent cognition. They bowed him on with a grateful excitement which Humphrey found impossible not to parody a little in return.

Strangely, Butcher had become uncomfortable and sat behind his placecard at the table before he realized the introductions were incomplete. Perhaps he was nervous. I want you to show complete attention, he had whispered to Humphrey, do you realize how important this deal is to us? Yes, Humphrey said, I do indeed.

Humphrey opened his folder, slowly so as not to distract them and turned the pages of "What's On In Tokyo." He passed quickly over advertisements for orchestral concerts, Japanese traditional theater and movies. Massage parlors, skin flicks, escort agencies, and night clubs took up the last four pages. He marked "Charon, intimate, drinks from 600 yen small beer, English speaking hostesses, piano music with song." And on the last line: "stress." Oh, songstress.

He drew out another pamphlet. It had the rectangular shape of a travel guide but its pages were firm and glossy with a bulky presence. It was a public relations brochure for the Japanese corporation he had plucked from a display box in the foyer.

Although the text stood in inaccessible lines of characters with the teetering columnar quality of alphabet blocks, the pictures were captioned also in English. A frontispiece laid together a montage of ships at dock, against paddy fields and office blocks and textile looms, all to promote the variety of the corporation's enterprise. Although Humphrey had researched these painstakingly for his masters, he had found and dealt out merely figures, quantifications, and categories. Here the incidences of effort were displayed as if through an opening of windows in the page: these looms hummed with countless threads unraveling the warp and weft of the spectrum; mimicking rows of rice plants wore a fresh and humid green

from the flush of morning rains; painters in bosuns' chairs swung against
the iron side of a ship and painted over spreading ink stains that had wept
from her blundering deck on bitter southern nights as deck-bins over-
flowed the slime of squid dying in their thousands under a cold halogen
glare visible for as many miles as the far corona of a small city.

A chart gave the corporation's income over a decade. Its yearly
turnover ranked twelfth of the companies of the world and was exceeded
by the revenue of only fourteen national governments. A photograph
showed three chartkeepers marking a map of countries bordering the
Pacific Ocean with points of their company's conquest. Their mouths were
bunched from sucking rows of sharp pins like ageing seamstresses.
Humphrey looked up. That chart hung on the wall opposite him. The
seaboards glittered with colored pin-heads but its surface was surprisingly
faded and the clusters did not match those in the photograph.

On another page the executives of Plastics Division sat, as they did at
this meeting, behind nameplates in the manner of a press conference. Oku-
ra, Inter-Group Liaison, speaks English with a Cambridge accent; the tiny
Production Coordinator Hogara acts also as an interpreter for Kogo of
Finance, who will try no English at all and scratches marks into his agenda
margin but does not take them with him overnight; Shimizu, Marketing,
brown from much golf at his club where green fees of each game cost more,
he will tell you, than a laborer's monthly wage, and chatters only about sport
over lunch in his high tone of an excited spectator; and other faces from
other divisions and other places, all photographed in the foreground of fac-
tories so their capacity for industry is incontrovertible, or before attentive
groups of scribbling trainees, or behind busy desks and holding a calculator
or a pen warily still only for the interruption of the snapshot. None of them
had the appearance of being, even momentarily, at rest.

Butcher paused as Hogara's politely diffident port de bras and coffee
was served at a buffet table at the end of the room. The lacquered cups
were of paper lightness and painted with a small and modular emblem
reminding Humphrey of a pagoda: the mark of the company president,
Hogara told him as he faced Humphrey toward a portrait on the wall,
holding him by the elbow with a flattering courtesy as if introducing him
to an ancestor. The portrait was of an old man, perhaps in his seventies, and
of a sepia quality that may have been either of emulsion or of pigment. The
figure sat in an elaborately carved and high-backed chair. Yes, Humphrey
said, I noticed it earlier.

Butcher began to close his summary, the run home, he put it. He used
the shiny phrases of car yards and appliance showrooms directed across the
polished table to Shimizu. Shimizu is the opinion-maker of this group,

Butcher had said after the first session in his didactic voice of a business journal, every grouping has one. Shimizu is the power-broker.

Their case finished. Butcher asked for questions, for clarification, he put it, of our proposition. But it was the tiny Hogara who asked them while the others were silent, and who recorded with the quick strokes of a court reporter and with an interest only in the fulsomeness of the answers, as if their worth was a matter for some absent tribunal.

Humphrey found Hogara's president on the last page of the brochure. There were two pictures of him. In the first, he sat in a miniature of the sepia portrait on the wall. Underneath him were nine pillars of Japanese text and a photograph with the harsh shadows of a newspaper reproduction: a prayer offering, Humphrey thought at first, on the deck of a ship; a red-necked and awkward solemnity at a blessing of the fleet. But the faces have none of the compressed anticipation of waiting fishermen. Their posture is strict and their eyes are not on the sea but on the sky. They are airmen.

The president Shikoru is small for the chair carved with four hundred and seventy years of tumbling chrysanthemum petals but sits precisely in the center of them with a frail dignity, on the light bones of the carefully aged, his spectacled eyes the fading gray of incense drifting in the wake of solemn processions, his white shirt-collar stiffly hiding folds in his throat with the mute decorum of a Shinto cassock. He sits easily still. The gray pin-striped suit is exactly pressed. Slim hands lie gently folded in his lap. His fingers wear no ring.

Every morning he rises a half hour before dawn and, wrapped in the plain kimono of the bereaved, walks from his bare sleeping-room across a marbled courtyard. His wooden sandals make always four slow beats over the narrow timbers of the bridge, above the ancient carp whose silken tails lazed, as his son had said in childhood, to hold their sleeping in midstream; through a low doorway and into the consecrated cell to wait before its stone shrine, his wisping head bowed during the perceptible bleaching of walls, until first light darkens the frame of a photograph fastened above the altar and he can again begin to make out the raised eyes of the boy-pilot and his ghosted reflection in the curved cowling of a fighter plane already trembling with the deafening heat of the last long thunder. Twenty-eight tilted wings in a herringbone pattern across the flight deck in hard crosses behind one and a half rows of tomorrow's faces, fourteen, again he counts them, rigidly to attention; and standing alone facing the boy is the braided figure of a Flag Officer of the Imperial Forces, his rimless spectacles misting in the salt air, the silver imprimatur of the Emperor's own command heavy on his shoulders. His steady fingers hold a white scarf to the boy's neck, the banner of sacrifice fluttering in the photograph's instant. The Commander's thin throat is already too old for his prime, his hair is wisping and his eyes fade in the gray wake of five years' war.

When he can no longer see the detail of that day beyond his misting spectacles he leans forward and again kisses the chill over his son's glazed face and again draws back only far enough to whisper to him the soft syllables: Heiwa.

Peace.

Re-crossing the narrow bridge he feeds the carp.

Some illusions can assume the status of truth. Humphrey knew it no longer mattered that the details of his day-dreaming were invented and hallucinatory. He knew, in a way now indelible and complete, that this Japanese corporation is guided, not with the careful powers of delegation drawn from the teachings of London or Harvard, but in the manner of a kingdom, of old and familic loyalties and enmities, for which the tabular logic of immediate opportunity and risk are of incidental interest. Decisions will be taken only by this ageing ruler of those related to him through a lineology of belief in the nobility of ultimate conquest and the knowledge that time is not measured merely in terms of the accountant's year, or the historian's war.

Humphrey was suddenly aware he was the center of an expectant silence. He closed the folder. I'm sorry, he said, I didn't catch that. He looked along the table. They looked at him with the counterfeit enthusiasm of their subordinate authorities. None of them ranked as—he thought of Hogara's use of the words—big shots. I said, Butcher repeated while the others waited, that about wraps it up. Yes, Humphrey said, I'm sure it does.

On the stairs Butcher slowed him by the sleeve so they lagged behind. We are going great, Butcher said, Shimizu asked us for drinks and dinner. I said you fly out early in the morning; I want him alone, okay? He did not wait for a reply. On the ground floor his stride was long and his arms swung. Humphrey trailed to the position of an adjutant. Sure, Humphrey said, pitch it to him.

[1981]

Michiko's House

MEIRA CHAND

"Honey," Jack sighed as Michiko threw a towel from his morning shower over the rail of the balcony. "Of course, I leave it to you, laundry is not my department, but back home we don't do it like this. Not nowadays anyway."

Michiko shrugged. Jack turned, stepping from the narrow balcony into the room. He might say he left it to her but his tone was contentious. She had explained many times to him the difference between the hot air of the clothes dryer and the freshness given their towels by the sweet clear rays of the sun.

"Bullshit," he always answered.

She no longer offered an explanation but just got on with the job of airing the quilts, which she did twice a week, and pegging out the damp towels. In compromise she had moved the general clothes line from the balcony to a narrow space behind the house. Only on rainy days would she consider using the large American clothes dryer in the basement of the house. Michiko took up the bamboo beater and brought it down hard upon the eiderdowns hanging over the rail in the morning sun. Vlump. Vlump. Then she followed Jack into the bedroom where he sat on a chair pulling on his socks. As she entered the room he gave her a look that belied the soft curl of his words.

"I'm sure you know best, Honey. It's just that I feel there's no need to deck the house in bunting. It's not the kind of thing you see much in a neighborhood like ours. More foreigners in this area, I suppose." Jack stood up and looked into the mirror, giving his tie a last tug. "Well, I'm off to work now."

Michiko followed him down the stairs and presented him at the door with freshly polished shoes. Picking up the remote control for the garage she pressed it, listening to the creak of metal as the shutter wound up. She waited until Jack drove away from the house, then pressed the remote control once more. With a tortuous creak the shutter rolled down of its own volition. It stopped with the usual small, tinny thump. Michiko closed the front door and went back upstairs. In the children's room she collected the quilts off their beds and further damp towels flung down on the floor of their shower. Pushing open the large sliding windows of the room she struggled out onto the balcony with her bulky armful. The sun shone hotly onto the rail as she draped the quilts upon it. Since they all slept on beds and not Japanese style on the floor, there were no sleeping pallets to air, only the light fluffy eiderdowns.

There was no satisfaction like thumping the bedding, thwacking it hard with the beater. The dust flew up in a cloud. By afternoon the towels had dried hard and the quilts were filled by the sun. The maid who came each day could have done the job, but Michiko would not consider it. The ritual belonged to her. She stood back in satisfaction, hands on hips. Now the quilts were out airing her day could begin.

As a child she had helped her mother hang out the family's bedding. She had hated the chore, she remembered. Then, from that long ago balcony of her old home, she had looked out over rice fields, flooded and glassy in early summer, reflecting the movement of the sky. The view was velvet green through the hot months of high summer, alive with the croak of frogs and the sawing of cicadas. In autumn the brown of the cut rice stubble was caught by flaming globes of persimmon, hanging on bare trees. Snow blanketed everything in winter, deadening sound and filling the old house with an unearthly white light. In good weather the neighboring houses in the village were festooned through the day like her own, by a plethora of quilts.

Vlump. Vlump. Michiko's arm as it swung the bamboo beater had the muscle of a professional. Now, from her balcony she looked down on the city of Kobe. Michiko's house was built on a hill. It looked over the town to the port with its cranes and the smoking chimneys of a steel works. Beyond this jumble was the sea, unconcerned and vacant. Ships drifted slowly by. She was far from the rice fields of memory here.

Some distance away to the right she could make out the cobalt blue roof-tiles of Yoshiko Grant's house, and beyond it the gables of Emiko Wallace's home. To the left was the apartment block in which lived Megumi Smith and Tami Cooper. Its thrusting walls and gleaming windows almost hid the dilapidated residence of Fumiko Hall. It was an area of Kobe where many foreigners lived, for the American school was nearby. Michiko's two children and those of her friends who, like herself, were married to foreigners, all went to the school. Only Fumiko Hall sent her children to a Japanese school.

Michiko and her friends had been affronted by Fumiko's decision. She made it appear there was a choice in the matter. Their children were foreigners, like their fathers. By Japanese law they could no more take the nationality of their mothers than they could alter the structure of their bones. It was known they suffered taunts in Japanese schools because of their difference in an elitist system. And Jack would not hear of it. "They are Americans and have nothing to gain from an alien school system that anyway rejects them." The American school radiated a protective aura, sealed off in its own tiny world, unattached to the body of Japan. Michiko and her friends proudly observed their children as they merged with this elusive entity, absorbing its codes and ways of thought so different from their own. It did not seem fair of Fumiko to thrust such hardship upon her children, forcing them to identify with a culture that denied them. Why must she always try to be different? Neither Michiko or her friends saw much of Fumiko. She was a snob, they decided.

Vlump. Vlump. The quilts swelled beneath the beater. Each morning, surveying the town spreading away below her, Michiko was reminded that none of her friends had a home equal to hers. None had the money nor the prospect of permanence in Japan. Jack had his own company importing surgical instruments, and was doing well. He had been many years in Japan. Michiko had met him while she was working in a textile firm that had also then employed Jack. Against her parents' wishes Michiko had left the village and gone to live with a brother in Osaka. She soon found a job filling in documents, one of many girls in a large office. Jack, arriving as crew on a ship from America, had liked the look of Japan and stayed on. They never spoke much about those early years. Jack had done well for himself and nothing else mattered. He had made a life for himself in Japan.

Tami, Yoshiko, Emiko, and Megumi were all married to men who worked for multinational companies and could be transferred at any time. Only Fumiko Hall was different. She and her husband, Robert, were both enduring tenure at Kobe University. Michiko brought the beater down hard on the quilts. She did not know why she felt angry whenever she thought of Fumiko Hall. Although she did not like the woman, she was always curious to know more about her. Just the sight of Fumiko's old wooden house, its roof heavily tiled in an old fashioned way, and with white paper shoji at the windows, irritated her. The guttering needed redoing. Plaster-work peeled badly. The eaves sagged dangerously at one corner. Only the garden was immaculate, with clipped trees and several old stone lanterns. It seemed the Halls liked their lanterns. Recently, Michiko had observed an open truck arrive with a new acquisition. A small crane on the truck had lowered the heavy stone sections over the hedge into the Halls' garden. Michiko knew a good thing when she saw it. She had bought a brand new lantern of molded concrete, one of carved stone seemed an unnecessary expense; the effect was the same and that was what mattered. Lanterns like those the Halls collected did not come cheaply. Where would academics get such money? Michiko had told Tami about the lantern. But Tami already knew. She walked her dog in the grounds of a nearby shrine where Fumiko Hall also walked her dog.

"They get them off demolition sites, before the bulldozers scoop them up. The workmen are glad to be rid of them for free. Fumiko only had to arrange the price of a truck. She told me herself," Tami announced. A wave of relief filled Michiko, and she began to laugh with Tami. How absurd to admit to such a practice, instead of pretending to have spent much money.

Michiko gave the quilts a last whack and then left them to the sun. She had agreed to meet Tami, Emiko, Yoshiko, and Megumi at the club for lunch. At least once a week they met there for a meal or a drink in the bar after shopping, or in summer to sit by the pool. She dressed carefully in a smart new suit. There was a meeting of a group of ikebana enthusiasts at the club today. The dining room would be filled with them lunching before their meeting.

When at last Michiko reached her destination it was difficult to find a place to park for the crush of cars. Tall trees and the scent of seclusion engulfed her as she drove slowly up the drive. There was something secret about this enclave, cut off from the bustling world of Japan, catering only to the foreign community. On the street outside people passed but could not enter, unable to warrant distinction. Michiko never arrived at the club without a flutter of nerves, and a need to re-check her appearance before facing the scrutiny of the place.

They were waiting for her in the dining room. Emiko had phoned in advance for a table. As expected the room was crowded, mostly with foreign women. The only Japanese faces to be seen were a scattering of wives like herself, or the bartenders, waiters, and office staff. Michiko, Emiko, Tami, Megumi, and Yoshiko always went to the club together. They laughed a lot and ate a lot and enjoyed themselves immensely. Only once or twice had Michiko ventured there alone. Then, suddenly, the place had seemed daunting. Nobody stopped to speak to her other than in passing. She had left quickly, glad to regain the bustling street with its familiar knowledge and perceptions. With Jack beside her at the club everything seemed different. They were always part of a group and if nobody addressed her directly it did not seem to matter. There was so much laughter and conversation to which, even if she did not always follow, she could nod agreement. Yet, in whatever circumstances, once outside the gates of the place she was filled by relief. It was as if she were at last allowed to dismount an uncomfortable animal.

On the way to the dining room she passed the notice board and stopped short before it in surprise. It bore a large picture of Fumiko Hall. She was to lecture the following month at the club to the American Chamber of Commerce, on the novels of Junichiro Tanizaki. Michiko could not describe the emotion seeping slowly through her. Why should

Fumiko Hall be invited into the club in so elite a manner? Who could be interested in Tanizaki? Michiko had never read his books. Fumiko was not a member of the club and appeared singularly without ambition to penetrate the place. Once, when Tami had invited her to join them at lunch, she had replied, "Oh, I can't stand that place." They did not invite her again.

"They cannot afford the membership, that's all," Yoshiko decided, trying to plumb the mystery of Fumiko's aversion. "Don't forget, they are just teachers. Robert doesn't earn the same kind of money as our husbands. I feel sorry for Fumiko, don't you?" But somehow, once this explanation was before them, it was difficult to feel anything but pleased.

Michiko entered the crowded dining room. Several women waved from afar, or stopped her as she passed to offer her a word. At last she reached her friends and sat down gratefully amongst them. Even as they ordered from the menu the talk was all of Fumiko Hall and the forthcoming lecture.

"Did you know," said Tami suddenly, "that their house belongs to them; they own it. I'd always thought they rented it. Fumiko told me they have to get the roof redone and it is going to cost them plenty. They must be sitting on a gold mine. That house is almost on the main road and the plot is twice the size of yours." Tami looked at Michiko. "The house is apparently in Fumiko's name and inherited from her father. Did you know he was that famous writer who committed suicide with a mistress several years ago?"

Everyone looked at each other. No one knew quite what to say.

Michiko's first thought was, why should Fumiko Hall own a house at all, and one showered from Heaven so easily upon her? It had taken years before Michiko and Jack had been able to buy a plot and build a house of their own. Land prices were prohibitive, few people could afford their own home. Even now there remained a large mortgage.

There had been, Michiko remembered, a great argument between herself and Jack about the kind of house they should build. The whole thing could have been achieved at a fraction of the eventual cost had she agreed to a Japanese-style construction of thin plaster walls about a wooden frame and roof-tiles that blew off in typhoons. But the house of Michiko's dreams had been in ferro-concrete. Even as a child the heavy municipal buildings in the village, the town hall, the banks, the health care center, had seemed to her, passing them on her way to and from school, to represent superiority. In those buildings she was confronted by bureaucrats endowed with their fistful of power. There, the silent queues of village people, women in homely white aprons, old people bent from planting rice, rough farmers with weather-beaten faces, were diminished of any stature. Those buildings ended with the main street. Then again there was the jigsaw of rice fields and radish patches. Old farmhouses came into view with heavy roofs and wooden shutters and logs stacked up for heating the bath under the shelter of eaves; the houses of farmers, like her own family. The abrupt transition of that village road had even then impressed itself upon her as the difference between power and poverty. She had always vowed to leave the village.

"Did you know, Fumiko is making a name for herself as a journalist? My maid saw her on the television in some political program," Emiko informed them after they had ordered their food.

Michiko thought of the old lanterns in Fumiko's garden and the dilapidated house, still rooted in the past, that always reminded her of her own village. Suddenly, she wanted to hear no more about the woman. Anyone but Fumiko, owning so much land, would have pulled down the old house, borrowed money from the bank, and built an apartment block. Everyone was doing just that. Who wanted an old wooden house?

Yoshiko, Megumi, Tami, and Emiko had all been envious of Michiko's house when it was built, but in a nice way, with many ohs and ahs at the pink fitted carpet, the glossy furniture, and the modern chandeliers. The house imposed on the curve of a hill, roofless as a bunker upon its deep foundations. A concrete fin, extending from either side, elongated the structure upon the tiny square of land. This deception of size had been Michiko's idea. "Bigger," she demanded, "I want it to look bigger."

When the house was finished Jack had insisted on a house-warming party. He had invited all the people in the foreign community whom they knew, and also some they did not. Michiko had hesitated, but Jack had been insistent.

"I want everyone to see the house." His pride had overwhelmed her.

Jack had also invited some Japanese business associates who had come and gone quickly, ill at ease in the crowd of foreigners who towered above them physically and, not speaking their language, ignored them. The only other Japanese had been wives like Michiko.

Michiko had made sure she personally gave all their guests a tour of the house. If she missed them on arrival she had gone up to them later and said, "Now, shall I show you the house?" Some of them had seemed surprised and been inclined to stay with their drinks. Walking before them she chatted about the fixtures and furniture imported from Italy, the lace curtains flown in from Germany. The guests were full of congratulations. Only once did she see a group of American women standing in a corner with their glasses of wine, looking about in a way she did not like. They talked too fast for Michiko to understand, but their expressions remained with her long after they left. It made her wonder if she had got everything right.

The planning of the interior had been a great anxiety. The more magazines she opened, the more foreign homes she surreptitiously looked about, the more confused she became. The things that Westerners put in their homes were things she did not want. There were so often objects about that were battered and old. Antiques. They all had a craze for antiques. To Michiko's eye these things littered their homes bizarrely. She had grown up surrounded by dingy, iron-bound chests and rough hand-stenciled fabrics of indigo. Braziers, large and small, of wood and lacquer or porcelain were all they had had to warm themselves by. Yet now, in the homes of foreigners, she saw these things put to ludicrous uses. Potted plants stood in braziers. A weathered wooden door was turned into a table. An abacus became a lamp stand. An obi was slung across a wall. It made her want to laugh. In the village her mother had thrown out all the old chests and replaced them with tallboys of laminated veneer. Instead of chilblains and braziers there were now gas fires. Metal shutters and doors replaced warped, weathered wood. Michiko was in no doubt about how she wanted her house to look; it must be bright and new and shiny.

She wished she had not remembered the housewarming party. The memory never failed to rankle, even though the party had appeared a success. All the women who had greeted her in the dining room had come to that party. She had met them again in other foreign drawing rooms. Although she had never been rude to them, they spoke badly in front of her about Japan. This country, they said in exasperation. Or these people this or that. The words "they" and "we" were always being used, Michiko had noticed. Sometimes, she even found herself sitting between two Westerners who were conversing in this manner, as if she were invisible. Invisible. That was the word, she decided. She only came into focus for them beside Jack. She looked about the dining room at the sharp-featured, ample-hipped, animated women, their eyes trawling the room for grist. Suddenly, she knew why Fumiko Hall must hate this place.

"What's the matter," asked Megumi, peering at her in a worried manner.

"Headache," said Michiko, and she began to eat her meal.

She drove home after lunch without even the motivation to pass a dilatory car. Her thoughts pressed down upon her. The memory of the housewarming party still floated in her mind, like debris stirred up in a murky pond. She squinted at the sky. The sun had already lost its strength. The moment she arrived home she must bring in the quilts. A surge of comfort filled her at the thought of the job ahead. Why she should look forward to a chore she had hated so much as a child was difficult to determine. The car in front stopped at a traffic light and Michiko came to a halt behind it. A crowd of children from the American school ambled across the road. They pushed one another and fell about laughing. One grabbed a schoolbag from a friend and threw it in the air. They began to fight on the crossing. For the first time their unkempt appearance and blatant manners irritated Michiko. Why could they not behave in the orderly way of Japanese children? Yet, who was she to complain? Her own children, Carol and John, affected the same conduct and appearance. Now, as they got older, it was more and more apparent to Michiko that she had produced two foreigners. They seemed to have nothing to do with her. Some molding about the eyes was all she could lay claim to. At first, as they grew, she had looked at them in wonderment, proud of their light hair and insolence, their fluent English and long limbs. But as they reached the edge of their teens a distance had grown, almost imperceptibly, between herself and them. Sometimes she had the feeling when they were with her at the club, or on those occasions she visited their school, that they were embarrassed by her. They giggled, rolling their eyes if she pronounced a word wrongly. Or they corrected her English before their teachers, or the people at the club. They refused to speak to her in Japanese. They chattered in English, and she was forced to follow, stumbling over the difficult grammar, ineffectual with her syntax. When they conversed with Jack the gabble of voices raced ahead of her, until she sat silent on her chair, without any attempt to follow. If she spoke in Japanese, she was answered in English. Her voice faltered before her children's stern gaze, and the rejection of all she offered. It was as if her own offspring were denied her. Her eyes filled suddenly with tears. She watched the children from the American school reach the further curb and continue on their rowdy way. The traffic began to move again. Michiko drove on.

The tears ran freely now down her cheeks. She almost missed her own road when she came to it and turned sharply, unable to see clearly where she was going. The car mounted the pavement and crashed into a lamppost. Michiko was thrown suddenly forward over the wheel, and then back in the seat again. The shock of it made her gasp, her heart pumped in her throat. Slowly, she realized she was unhurt, and her tears welled up again. Her fingers trembled on the steering wheel, but she backed the car until it sat by the curb. Then she sank her head in her hands.

There was a knocking at the window. Startled, Michiko looked up into the face of Fumiko Hall, who had already pulled open the car door.

"Are you all right? I was walking the dog. I saw it happen."

"I'm all right. I'm going home now." Michiko attempted to shut the door while searching for a tissue with which to wipe her eyes.

"You are in no state to drive. Come along, get out. I'll give you a cup of coffee and then you'll feel better. See, you've stopped outside my house as it is." Fumiko silently observed Michiko's distressed and swollen face.

Michiko looked up to see the neat hedge of Fumiko's house and the top of a large stone lantern. She nodded and allowed Fumiko to help her out of the car. Fumiko opened a rickety door in the roofed wooden gate and Michiko followed her and the dog up a cobbled path. She had never been inside Fumiko's house before. As well as the lanterns, she could now see the garden held a small tea house on the point of disintegration. Fumiko followed her gaze.

"My father used this house at one time. He enjoyed the tea ceremony. His mistress lived here, and he wrote one of his best books in this place. But, as you can see, it is impossible to maintain it properly. I'm afraid we keep garden tools in the tea house now."

"What about your mother?" Michiko asked. She removed her shoes and stepped up into the house behind Fumiko. The familiar, dank smell of old homes surrounded her. Michiko took a breath of musty air, and caught a faint odor of drains. Fumiko took her into a tatami room and motioned to a cushion before a low lacquer table. Oranges in a blue ceramic bowl glowed in the room but, in spite of large windows overlooking the garden, the sun did not reach far.

"My mother died when I was small. Although my father remarried, my grandmother brought me up. My father never had time for me," Fumiko said. Soon she went to make the coffee.

Michiko followed Fumiko's directions to the bathroom and assessed her face there in the mirror. She dabbed her eyes with a tissue and pressed some powder on her nose, then made her way back down the passage. The house was on one level and she passed several closed sliding doors. Michiko looked about but there was no sign of Fumiko. Quickly, she pulled back a door a few inches and peered into the room behind. A double quilt was laid out on the floor under an indigo coverlet with a bold stenciled design. A brush painting hung upon the wall above an iron-bound chest. A globe of thick rice paper covered a hanging light. This must be Fumiko and Robert's bedroom Michiko thought, and hastily shut the door.

She sat back before the lacquer table to wait for Fumiko. The matting of the floor was frayed in one place. A fine scroll above a vase of peonies filled an alcove. Books were everywhere. It was nothing like her childhood home and yet, the same presence of dampness and drains assailed, the same dim shuttered atmosphere possessed the place. The patina of age touched everything. The tension eased suddenly in her body. It was a long time since she had been inside an old house. If she shut her eyes and ran her hand over the smooth, cool matting she could imagine herself back in the village, curled up long ago on a cushion, concentrating on her homework. She wished suddenly now she had put a tatami room in her own house and not listened to Jack's objections. On the one occasion her parents had visited, they had been uncomfortable and not known where to sit.

Her parents had come to see the house not long after Michiko and Jack moved in. It had been difficult to persuade them to leave the village and take first one train and then another. They were not used to journeys. Her mother had packed warm underwear and a large quantity of rice balls, as well as a bottle of home-made plum pickles. All these things and more had been tied up in squares of cloth. They were then retied in a larger square which Michiko's father hoisted upon his back. In this manner they had arrived at Michiko's house.

At first they had been afraid to step inside. Her father had lowered the bundle from his back and stood, diminished without it, in his only suit of ill-fitting navy serge, looking about with an open mouth.

"Otosan," Michiko's mother had warned, and he shut his mouth obediently.

Before sitting them down Michiko had taken them on a tour of the house. They had walked silently behind her as she chatted, telling them how much had been paid for each item. Now even her mother's mouth hung slightly open. The old people's heads constantly revolved, right then left, up then down.

"The ceilings are so high I can hardly see them," Michiko's mother whispered. "What do you do with all these rooms? Aren't you frightened by so much space?"

"Okaasan," Michiko laughed. "This is the way all foreigners live."

"Even so," her mother replied.

She knelt down as she spoke and began to untie her bundle of belongings upon the living room floor. Retrieving a rice ball from a plastic box, she handed it to Michiko's father.

"If he is hungry there are many things I can give him," Michiko was unable to hide her disapproval. "Tonight I will cook you Kobe steak."

Her father sat down cross-legged upon a flowered velvet couch and took a great bite of his rice ball. "Simple village fare is best. Nobody cooks like your mother."

"We do not need expensive foods," her mother admonished gently.

"But every day we eat steak and things like that," Michiko laughed.

"That is why all foreigners are big people," her father commented. "They eat so much. Cow meat, butter, cheese. It is not for nothing they used to say foreigners stank of butter. Now, even our own people have become so crazy for foreign things they also smell the same." A morsel of rice dropped onto the velvet. Michiko rushed forward to clear it up.

Her mother now unpacked a kimono from the bundle upon the living room floor. Michiko's father stood up and began to remove his uncomfortable suit. Michiko hurried them upstairs to the spare bedroom.

"I have never slept on a bed before," her father announced, stopping in the doorway. "I shall roll off and break my head. I have not come here to die."

Later, Jack returned home and in order to break the awkwardness of the occasion, had plied her father with whiskey. He did not refuse and drank down glass after glass with gusto. His face became a bright red and his manner increasingly animated. From sitting cross-legged upon the couch, he had sprawled upon the living room floor, his kimono agape. His legs, in thick pale woolen underwear, were unashamedly displayed. In the night he had rolled from his bed with a resounding thump and insisted on returning home the next morning. They had never come again.

"Coffee," said Fumiko, putting a tray on the table before them.

Michiko drank the hot, bitter liquid gratefully. Before her Fumiko's face, devoid of make-up, was intelligent and concerned.

"I must get home. Soon the dew will come down and the quilts will absorb the damp," Michiko announced. She stirred but did not stand up.

"I'm afraid I'm not nearly as house proud as you," Fumiko sighed. "I always feel guilty when I see you airing the quilts, just like our mothers taught us. An old house like this has so much dirt, I really should do more. I'm afraid I'm very lazy."

Michiko could not but agree. In a house like this she might be tempted to air the quilts everyday. Obviously, from what she had spied of Fumiko's sleeping arrangements, she did not even bother to roll up her bedding by day. How much dust a good beating might release from this slovenly house. Michiko tried to feel cross and could not.

There was a noise in the porch as the front door was pulled back and then the sound of children's voices.

"Makoto. Yumi. We're in here," called Fumiko.

A boy and a girl appeared before them and Michiko smiled a greeting. They were both dressed in the dark serge of Japanese school uniform, the girl's outfit broken by a white-edged sailor collar. They returned her greeting politely. Michiko thought of the scruffy blue jeans her own children insisted on wearing, and the cursory greeting they would have extended to Fumiko as they threw themselves down upon chairs, schoolbags dropped by the door. Once or twice in the past it had been suggested that the children play together, but the occasions had not been a success.

"There are snacks in the kitchen, then get on with your homework. And afterward you'd better pack your bag for that trip to your great-grandmother tomorrow," Fumiko ordered. She spoke in Japanese.

"Don't they speak English?" Michiko asked in surprise. It was difficult to believe these children had a foreign father.

"Of course," Fumiko replied. "Although their reading and writing is terrible. We've got to do something about it. I keep telling Robert to speak to them in English, but he rarely does. I suppose it's all right. They get enough of America one way or another. We go back each summer to Robert's parents. When they're older they'll probably get their higher education there. It would be so easy for them to lose Japan, and I don't want that to happen. They've a few days holiday from tomorrow. My grandmother is really too old to cope, but she insists they come. And they seem not to mind. Of course, she is not far away, only in Ashiya and it is just for a night."

It had been nearly two years since Michiko's children had seen their grandparents. She frowned in shock at the length of time, lost without an accounting. In the past Michiko had taken her family each New Year to the village, to participate in the traditional festivities. But Jack's grumbles got louder with each year. He refused to adapt to the uncongenial conditions of her old home.

"My legs are too long to sit upon the floor," he glowered.

He raged about the toilet which, like most in the village, was no more than a hole in a tiled floor over an open cesspool. Until his shocked rejection she had thought little about it. Now she felt ashamed. He complained that there was not a chair in the house until one was bought especially for him. The small, rush-matted rooms were always swollen for the New Year's festivities with returning relatives. Privacy to bathe or shave was unavailable. Everyone walked about in states of drunkenness and undress. Jack complained at the number of people who, by necessity, slept with them in their room, and the unbroken diet of Japanese food. The television was on all day. In the end it was easier to leave him at home.

She had returned then to the village each year with only the children. But they, remembering his grumbles, seemed little happier than their father. They refused to join their cousins and the rest of the village to see the yearly pounding of soft, cooked rice for the making of New Year delicacies.

"Who cares," complained Carol, returning to the sounds of her Walkman close about her ears.

"We see the same thing each year. It's boring," John said. "When can we go home?" They watched cartoons on the television.

Their grandparents viewed them from afar, affection tempered by hesitation over so many unbridgeable things. On both sides the rot of distance set in. Michiko cringed before the glaring eyes of her children and soon left them at home with Jack. For some years she had gone overnight alone to the village on the last day of New Year. And later not at all.

Yumi returned from the kitchen brushing the crumbs of a rice cracker from her mouth. She pushed open the door of her room across the corridor. Michiko was relieved to see a solid bed in Yumi's room, and an untidy heap of books, puzzles, and tattered dolls. She had expected quilts upon the floor again and immaculate shelves. On one wall were several framed pictures of nursery rhymes. There was one of a girl and a spider. Next to it was an old woman and a shoe house. Another was of a mouse and a clock, and the last of a cow and a moon. They were all pictures of rhymes Jack used to chant to Carol and John when they were small. Michiko had never been able to remember the nonsense words that were without meaning to her. When they were small, before they went to school, the children had spoken to her in Japanese, just like Fumiko's children. There was no reason Carol and John should not still speak in Japanese, they were as fluent in that language as in English.

> Hey diddle diddle,
> The cat and the fiddle,
> The cow jumped over the moon. . . .

Some words came back to her. Silly words. Why should a cow jump over the moon? Jack had never been able to explain the meanings. Just nonsense, he said, shrugging off her efforts to understand.

Michiko put down her empty coffee cup. The vision of damp quilts welled up again in her mind. "I must go," she said, and stood up abruptly.

Fumiko nodded and called Yumi to say goodbye. Of Makoto there was no sign. "Eating," sighed Fumiko. "All he wants to do is eat. It is as if he has hollow limbs. It is the age, I suppose."

"I know," Michiko nodded. "John is just the same."

"Come again whenever you want," Fumiko invited.

"Maybe I will," Michiko answered.

She passed under the old shingled roof of the gate, and Fumiko closed the door behind her. At the soft coupling of the lock she turned. An inexplicable feeling of desolation filled her. Above the green of the hedge the top of a lantern protruded. She could just make out the broken guttering under the old tiled roof. Everything else in Fumiko's world was now hidden from the busy road of speeding cars. The gate held fast on a secret place. It was as if Michiko were shut out forever from something she could not define.

She opened the door of the car. Up the hill she could see her own home, perched like a sentinel above the other houses. The glass and concrete were caught now by the setting sun, and quilts colored each balcony. For a moment she had no desire to return to the immaculate rooms of glossy furniture and the pink fitted carpets. Then again she remembered the dew that would, even now, be descending upon her quilts.

She hurried upstairs as soon as she got in. But, as she feared, the bedding had already absorbed a blanket of dew. Tears of frustration welled up again into her eyes. Now she would feel the dampness upon her all night. After replacing the quilts upon the beds, she went out onto the balcony to unpeg the towels. Below her the rooftops were now settling into the dusk, no longer sharply defined. A smell of frying onions and grilling fish drifted. Above the town the underbellies of darkening clouds were streaked gold by the last of the dying sun. Suddenly, she saw her children in the distance, walking together up the hill toward the house. They straggled one behind the other, laughing and kicking a stone between them. A cool breeze had got up and blew in her face. Sometimes now, when her eyes settled upon them in this unexpected way, she failed to recognize them as her offspring. She had to look twice to make sure. And sometimes, from this very balcony, she had seen them walk off down the hill with Jack on a weekend, arms entwined, a threesome. She had stared after them for a long time, the hill falling away precipitously below the house, her emotions trailing after them until they were lost from her sight. Now, already, their voices carried up to her from the road below. But even as they walked toward her they seemed to come no nearer in the evening shadows. Above the world on her narrow ledge she was adrift, and they unheeding of her presence. She did not remember always feeling like this. Something had slipped through her fingers. She felt hollowed out inside. She remembered again those nursery rhyme pictures on Yumi's wall, and Jack's voice long ago repeating the nonsensical babble to his tiny children.

> Hey diddle diddle
> The cat and the fiddle,
> The cow jumped over the moon.

She said the words to herself and it was as if for the first time they acquired some meaning. She saw the cow spring toward the sky, felt the icy rush of wind on her own face as she sailed up, higher and higher. And then there was the darkness as she landed, the other side of the moon. She stared out into the evening, and saw at last the barrenness of the strange terrain, stretching out endlessly before her without a single comforting landmark. There were now no voices from the road.

In the distance the lights came on in Emiko's house, and then there was a sudden fiery blossoming of Megumi and Tami and Yoshiko's windows. They appeared of little matter. Michiko fixed her eyes upon Fumiko's house but darkness still enveloped it. She waited and slowly, as she knew they must, first one dim light and then another appeared, far away as if at the end of a plumb line. She remembered again the bare rooms, the faint smell of drains, and the frayed matting. She shut her eyes and the images filled her, like an old scent released from a long closed cupboard.

Now her children's voices were behind her. They snapped on the many shiny bulbs, filling the rooms of the house with light. Michiko turned, her arms full of towels, and stepped off the narrow balcony. She made her way to the children's room. They looked up as she entered, suddenly wary at the new grimness of her expression. She marched into their bathroom to fold the towels over the rack.

"Why are you back so late? Was it basketball practice again tonight? And what is today's homework assignment?" She stood before them, hands on hips.

"Okaasan." They growled in the terrible, warning manner they always did whenever she spoke in Japanese. But she stood her ground and did not back off as usual when they rolled their eyes Heavenward, and sniggered together in the alien slang she always failed to grasp.

"I asked you what your homework assignments are. What happened to that project on wells that you were supposed to research? When I was a child we only had water from wells in the village. My uncle knew all about wells. If we give him a call he would help you. That was pure water, no chemicals in it at all." Nostalgia gripped her throat.

"Oh God. Oh Christ." They grimaced and growled anew. They flung their limbs about, looking at her strangely. She continued to speak, her tone growing firmer, her feet planted firmly on the pink carpet. They frowned and grew silent and exchanged long suffering glances. She took no notice of them.

And slowly, as she stood her ground, she felt them advance toward her. They replied in perfect Japanese, as effortless as that other tongue they forked so threateningly before her. And now a new feeling filled her. It was as if she drew them in on a string, and at last they followed where she led.

"You have holidays next week. I think we'll go to the village. How long is it since you saw your grandparents? How about packing your bag?"

"Okaasan." The grumbles were faint now. And slowly, first one and then the other, went to pull knapsacks from the cupboard.

[1979]

Enlightenment with Tea

Chloe trudged up the slope on her way from the bus stop when she noticed the Japanese girl she had met about a year prior.

Chloe had been wearing a stylish gray suit that day yet she didn't feel sure in it because she had worn it many times. The Japanese woman had introduced herself in such a polite and friendly way, Chloe could not mistake that she wanted to become friends, but Chloe felt intimidated by her polished British accent and fine aristocratic lines of the face with her hair pulled back in a manner which would have looked too severe on anyone else.

Hamada-san had studied in both France and England. She had come back to Japan because she was to inherit the title of Tea Master when her mother retired. She had two small children and spent all her free time reading to reach enlightenment. She had extended an invitation to Chloe to visit sometime, politely saying, "I've seen you many times and wanted to meet you. You live in the big Western house, don't you? I live just down the hill. Come and see me sometime." Chloe accepted, fully knowing that she would never drop in on her; Hamada-san was too high class for Chloe. Chloe was a plain country mouse.

She had grown up on a farm in Canada and with her scientist husband had come to Japan on an exchange program with a famous university.

So it was with some mortification that Chloe met the young woman again. Hamada-san was wearing funky Japanese clothes like peasants might wear, similar to those she had seen other housewives bundle up in to keep warm when they didn't have the space heater on. It was late spring but there was a nip in the air and the ground was overlaid with a pink blanket of cherry blossom petals like a blanket of snow. Chloe wondered if the woman would recognize her, or if she could just amble by.

The Japanese girl caught sight of Chloe and boldly reintroduced herself asking if Chloe remembered her. Even in her baggy clothes she looked stylish; she gave them style. Chloe no longer felt so intimidated because she had a new job as a copy reviser at an Osaka newspaper, so when Hamada-san said, "I'm on my way to my mother's house where I study tea. How would you like to join us today?" Chloe accepted. She thought she could learn more about Japanese culture. They dropped off Chloe's groceries at her house and rode the bus together to Hamada-san's mother's house. Hamada-san elucidated: "Before we have tea ceremony we must clean the tea house and garden. At the entrance of the hall, I sprinkle water so as to avoid the dusty air. In the main room, I burn incense which suits the season. The fragrance fills the room and helps to create an atmosphere far from everyday life. I arrange flowers in the tokonoma, that is, alcove. The flowers must be simple. Their fragrance shouldn't be too strong. Poisonous flowers and trees are avoided. Also thorny flowers and leaves are not to be used. I hang a scroll which signifies the season. Japanese cakes and Japanese sugar cookies, *rakugan*, are prepared and put in a big bowl. They are also put in lacquer ware. A variety of ware is used, porcelain, pottery, jade cups. Their pattern often signifies the season. Early spring, plum blossom, the Japanese nightingale, camellia, *ohinasama*. Mid-spring, peach tree. Late spring like today, cherry blossoms."

Hamada-san said she would have liked to have stayed in Paris but couldn't because she had to come back to Japan and marry and learn tea ceremony to carry on the name of the school. She said her husband was like a child and she had to look after him like one. She said it's the custom to begin the eldest child in the art of tea ceremony with the intent that they will carry on the name of the school. Her new friend had said, "Usually it's the eldest, but my eldest is not too smart, so I want the youngest to carry on. She is bright. The eldest is too quiet and reads too much."

She told Chloe that from the way she talked and acted she thought Chloe was something like a fairy, someone not real.

They went to the main house first where Hamada-san's mother could be espied through the glass doors, writing at her desk. Chloe and Hamada-san slipped off their shoes, and as Chloe was arranging her shoes so she could step into them easily when she left, she was awed by the light and flower-filled adjoining room. Hamada-san perceptively explained that they were flowers which her mother had received from friends after she appeared on TV to do a modern flower arrangement.

Hamada-san led Chloe upstairs and introduced her to the maid. "Nice to meet you, Kyomi-chan," Chloe said.

Hamada-san suddenly turned to Chloe and asked sharply, "Why did you call her 'chan'? Here, our maids are part of the family and we treat them with respect." "I'm sorry," Chloe said falteringly, "my landlady calls me Chloe-chan so I thought it was a friendly gesture from someone older to someone younger." "Oh," was all Hamada-san said and Chloe didn't persist.

Hamada-san told Chloe to undress and step into the white undergarment. Then Kyomi plunged into dressing her in a pink-flowered kimono. Hamada-san's mother appeared and roughly pulled at the kimono neck, rearranging what Kyomi had done, saying in Japanese what Chloe thought was "I don't know why you are doing this for her. Foreigners do not understand tea. It's a waste of time." Chloe listened, wondering what would make her give such a brisk jerk of the kimono which could only be interpreted as contempt. Was it because she didn't speak Japanese very well? Or that she didn't speak English eloquently enough? Chloe stood like a mannequin as if nothing had happened, allowing Kyomi to finish securing the obi, the long wide sash which is wound around the waist and secured in a bow at the back of the kimono. She wondered what Hamada-san's mother's experience had been like when she was abroad. Hamada-san said her mother often went abroad. Perhaps someone had been coarse to her and she was just extracting revenge.

They were soon dressed and Chloe followed Hamada-san out of the main house toward the tea house through a Japanese-style garden with bonsai trees. Down the walk Hamada-san ritualistically washed her hands, demonstrating the procedure by gently filling a bamboo cup with a long handle full of running water and letting the pure water run over both her hands in turn and finally sipping the clear water. Chloe clumsily washed her hands trying to emulate Hamada-san without success, and accidentally dipping the kimono sleeve in the water. Embarrassed, she wiped at it with her hand. Hamada-san saw and said, "Don't worry—it can be dry cleaned."

Hamada-san moved like a swan on a lake entering the hut, with Japanese picture book stylized motions, and Chloe walked in bowing slightly, feeling chagrined at her rigidity. Hamada-san took her to see the scroll and cherry blossoms which had been arranged. "This is a piece of calligraphy which is very old and has been in the family for generations. It's my mother's favorite. It came from China."

Hamada-san told her to take a seat telling her she needn't try to sit in the Japanese style with the knees bent but to sit however she felt comfortable. Chloe could see the tea pot on a tall white stove beside a wooden cabinet for dishes.

A few minutes later the room was filled by an assortment of women dressed in kimono. A short squat woman with a mouth full of gold fillings sat beside Chloe. Hamada-san approached them with two ties to be secured on top of the obi, one with glittering gold trim and the other plain red. "Which one do you want? Pick one. Take your choice," said Hamada-san. Chloe couldn't resist picking the gold trimmed one with gold specks, and as she picked it up she detected a slight furrow on Hamada-san's soft delicate brow and was immediately sorry she had picked the nicer one. She wished she could put it back, but it was too late. Everybody watched her choose the alluring one. She breathed again when two more women arrived, one a beautiful Japanese, the most stunning Chloe had ever seen, who was introduced as Hamada-san's aunt.

More ladies arrived and Hamada-san introduced them to Chloe. They
were all very plain looking housewives. After she was introduced she sat
back and listened to her name being said. The woman with the bright
sparkling eyes who had been introduced to her as Hamada-san's aunt was
talking to the woman with the mouth full of gold. And some silver. She
was saying she was studying Chinese because she was planning a trip to
China. That's all Chloe understood. Then Chloe heard her name again. The
aunt was saying, "A friend of mine said she took her to a flea market at a
temple in Kyoto. She wanted to buy a kimono. 'Well,' she said, 'you should
have seen her go wild at the flea market. She looked at everything with
desire and bought indiscriminately, just like a child. She threw away 10,000
yen on a cracked bowl because I said it was a famous Chinese design.' My
friend picked out a children's kimono for her knowing that she'd never
know the difference. Those kinds of things don't matter with foreigners.
They don't know about Japanese things." Chloe listened shocked that anyone would utter such things about her right in front of her. While she did
not know Japanese well, she was able to pick up the meaning. She was
struck by the ordinariness of their conversation, mundane. She thought the
hut was a sacred place where nobody would dare speak of anything but
lofty things. Mundane gossip and about her, she thought.

Hamada-san took her seat in the middle of the room sitting on her
knees and started to go through the ritual of preparing tea. Chloe was sitting on her hip. The conversation died out and Chloe fastened onto watching Hamada-san sitting before the tall chimney-like stove with her left
hand motionless on her lap, working with her right hand. She lit the stove
and then bowed in a sitting position with both hands touching the tatami.
Then she took out the necessary wares. They were small cups because
Hamada-san practiced *sencha*, not powder tea, where the tea is whisked
with a brush in big bowls. She was using leaves in the pot and setting cups
in front of the stove. Every motion was calculated yet looked natural and
smooth. She set each tiny cup with its own stand on wooden saucers.

Then Hamada-san set a cup in front of Chloe and Chloe bowed as she
had been instructed to do on the bus to show her gratitude. She then took
in the cup and saucer and put them in front of her after bowing again,
which signified "Let's enjoy a cup of tea together." She drank it up—it was
only a small quantity—enjoying the taste, saying, "This is wonderful," when
Hamada-san asked, "Is it good?" Hamada-san told her to have some sweets
and prepared another cup of tea. This time Chloe only bowed once as was
required. She spilled some drops of tea down the front of the kimono as
she drank the second cup of tea. Hamada-san seemed not to notice and
asked, "Do you like spring?" and went on talking about the ancient cups

they were drinking from. Then she began washing Chloe's cup and Chloe watched her silently.

Chloe was again intimidated by her graceful movements. How, she marveled, could she be the same person who had spoken earlier so cruelly about her own daughter on the bus. Chloe wondered how she could talk about enlightenment when she didn't understand the special uniqueness of her eldest daughter. Then it dawned upon her that Hamada-san knew her own mind. She knew what was best for her daughter. She knew her mind enough to make decisions. Chloe realized she had been thinking Hamada-san was all surface because of the way she had talked about her husband and kids. But now she looked at her face and brow. She thought it best described by the word *furyu*—elegance, taste, refinement.

She was intimidated by that face and she hadn't felt the proper gratitude that she might have been expected to feel. It was all too difficult to understand. Hamada-san had said she studied and read books and devoted herself to the search for enlightenment. Chloe had read that enlightenment is reached when someone knows their own heart, or was it mind? In Japan there seems to be confusion. *Kokoro* is for heart and mind and cannot be translated into English.

She would never comprehend her own mind like Hamada-san. If she had two daughters, she'd never know herself well enough to brutally decide which one should succeed her were she in Hamada-san's position.

Chloe departed feeling inferior. She hadn't been able to give her hostess all of her heart, spirit, and mind. She felt no honest thankfulness. It was a bad *ichigo ichie*, a one-time meeting that could never be repeated. She was further confused by her feelings and recollections of a quote she read in Yasunari Kawabata's Nobel acceptance speech, "If you meet a Buddha, kill him. If you met a patriarch of the law, kill him." She didn't understand this any more than she understood Hamada-san or anything else, but she wished she could fathom her mind like Hamada-san did. Why did Kawabata kill himself when he stated that he didn't respect people who did? She remembered Hamada-san saying she was like a fairy. Maybe she had meant that Chloe could not understand reality. She was confused in her life. She wanted to leave her husband when he left Japan but she didn't know how to look after herself. What would she do without his money? How could she live? She ambled on thinking about her cousin's prediction. Chloe had told her cousin she had been thinking about leaving her husband for years. "If you don't make up your mind, you'll drive yourself crazy," her cousin had told her. Chloe was more fearful of suicide.

[1993]

The Trouble with Angels

CHERYL CHOW

Living in a cheap apartment in Tokyo as I do where the entry hall is accessible to anyone walking in off the street, I've had to get used to having my mail box crammed with flyers and handbills. So I wasn't surprised—just slightly annoyed—when I checked my mail box to find it stuffed, not with personal letters, but advertisements: sushi and pizza delivery services, adult videos, dubious massage services and "telekura," a sleazy telephone dating club for the lonely and the horny—complete with full-color photographs of larger-than-life sushi, pizza, and trussed up women in varying stages of agony. I started to wad them all up and toss them into the plastic bucket I kept in the corner for just this purpose, when suddenly I caught a glimpse of angels circling around a blue-and-white earth.

The angels were hand-drawn illustrations on a coral-pink flyer.

"Workshop by JANICE LANUGA," read the flyer, "in Maui, Hawaii: At the Heart of the Secret; Listening to Messages from your Personal Angel. June 6–15. Cost: 600,000 yen, including plane fare from Tokyo and accommodations. Free to anyone able to teleport to Hawaii. (Verification required.)"

I stared at the flyer. Janice Lanuga. I thought I'd heard the last of her when she came to Japan two years ago in spring.

Janice is a self-proclaimed healer and intergalactic warrior from Hawaii. She travels around the world spreading messages about angels and healing UFO abductees by removing implants placed in their astral bodies by hostile aliens. Janice considers herself a living bridge between earthlings and the Rainbow Nation (not to be confused with the Rainbow Coalition), a nation consisting of sentient beings of many vibrations, such as the Nature Kingdoms, the cetaceans—that includes dolphins and whales—the universal magicians, multi-universal beings, and the Angelic Kingdom.

Yes, name a New Age fad and Janice is probably involved with it. Frankly, I'd had more than my share of her and had no desire to see her ever again. I've never known anyone like Janice who could come up with the most implausible explanations and rattle them off in the most matter-of-fact way. Nor could I understand why she repeatedly came back to Japan, four or five times in a span of three years.

I first heard about Janice through Sara, a demure Australian free-lance business writer living in Tokyo. When I ran into her at a seminar, "Saving Up For Retirement," I was surprised to find the normally taciturn Sara raving to a group of rapt listeners about Janice, "a light worker." (Not to be confused with an electrician. A light worker is a healer who works with energies.) Apparently, Sara had been cooped up in the hospital for nearly six months with pneumonia. Then along came Janice and instantly healed her. But that wasn't all. Janice could actually talk to angels. In fact, you might say that she's on a first-name basis with all the archangels. Sara was astounded when, at their first meeting, Janice told her that the Archangel Gabriel had something to tell her: just a few days ago, Sara had had an uncanny dream about the Archangel Gabriel!

The finale to all this was the announcement of an "Angel Workshop" by Janice near scenic Lake Biwa. And an addendum: Janice was available for private healing sessions. The weekend workshop was a bargain at thirty-five thousand yen—or roughly four hundred U.S. dollars at the current exchange rate. My financial condition being in less than celestial shape, I decided to pass, but a friend of mine went, so I asked her about it. She started to giggle like a ten-year-old.

"I'm sprouting wings," Marla squealed. She said the workshop was strange, and Janice even stranger. They spent most of the workshop dancing in circles, and in the evening, howling at the moon. I could picture Marla's long and bony arms flung over her head, fluttering like wind-blown butterflies. "Janice has really weird ideas, some of the weirdest I've heard," she added. This, coming from Marla who assures me that since psychics are predicting that the world will end in another forty years or so, I shouldn't worry about saving up for retirement.

So why on the Star of Sirius did I go for a private healing session with Janice?

Because, for one thing, I'm a sucker for get-well-quick schemes. Besides, I was in pain.

Ever since my move to Tokyo from Los Angeles (the city of fallen angels) four years ago, I've been suffering from pain that radiated from the left side of my neck down to the tip of my left index finger. I'm sure it's from the stress of living in a city that's been likened to a desert for the soul, and, for foreign women, a sexual Siberia. The minute I set foot on Japanese soil, it's as if I'd been rendered sexless. A porcupine with a bad case of halitosis would've fared better in the dating game. I admit that I've never been a homecoming queen (in fact, I couldn't get dates for either the junior *or* the senior prom). But once I looked old enough to drink, I never again had to face a Saturday night alone. So I naively thought that ethnically half-Korean and half-Japanese, I would have an easier time in Japan than my Caucasian compatriots. But in fact, it was worse. I'm not sure why. Maybe it's racism. Or maybe it's just my age. In Japan a woman over the age of twenty-five is a *kurisumasu keiki*—as desirable as a Christmas cake after the 25th of December. And I am, after all, pushing the Big Three-Oh. A few more years, and my odds for being taken hostage by terrorists would be higher than for getting married. No, my situation is probably bleaker: I'd stand a better chance of being kidnapped by space aliens than of finding a meaningful relationship with a male earthling. (It now seems, however, that alien abductions are far more common than I'd believed—so there might yet be hope for my love life.)

Be that as it may, I tried to find a healing, for the physical pain at least. I tried various remedies (except exercise, of course, that would be too sensible) but none worked. I even went to a Japanese acupuncturist, touted as a renowned healer. She'd cured someone of edema instantaneously and worked wonders on Aikido-injured knees. Alas, her treatments didn't do a whole lot for my condition. She complained that she found it difficult working on me because of my garlic breath and kimchee-permeated body. (The truth is, I detest and abhor kimchee and I rarely, if ever, eat garlic.) And she proclaimed that I'd regain my health and be in tip-top shape if I'd make it a daily ritual to imbibe my morning urine. I confess that I wasn't able to stomach her suggestion, but it didn't matter anyway, since she cut me off after only three visits. She refused to treat me any further unless I could follow her dictum completely: give up reading books, quit my job as a technical writer, and make my livelihood washing dishes.

So I went to see Janice. The session was held in Sara's apartment where Janice was staying at the time, a modern, one-bedroom apartment with a baby piano in the center, and a chirpy parakeet in the corner.

"What now, what now?" he queried in his tinny bird's voice, flapping his yellow wings inside the bamboo cage. "*Irasshaimase*, my darling," he added as if in afterthought.

"Have a seat," Janice said, pointing at a low couch covered with a brilliant orange Indian sari. She was sitting on a stool across from it, crunching on a raw carrot.

Janice was a healthy, wiry looking woman with short-cropped brown hair peppered with gray. Although she was forty years plus, the word "middle-aged" just didn't seem to apply to her. Her angular body and the well-muscled arms beneath the still-quite-new-blue-T-shirt with dolphins splashing across made her look as if she might be a professional swimmer. Her eyes were pale blue, as if she'd been gazing out into the sea for a long, long time. Janice, as I came to find out, is very self-possessed, and she always has an air about her that reminds me of my best friend in grade school, a spunky redhead who claimed to be from Venus. The friend told me that she was also a witch and had magical powers. I guess what the two have in common is that they both seem to absolutely believe in what they are saying.

I plunked myself down on the sofa and looked around. The apartment was well-lighted, with windows all around one side of the room. A sleek black Sony stereo set perched incongruously on a lacquered Japanese *tansu*.

Janice came over and sat down next to me, so close that the one red feather earring she was wearing tickled my cheek. She put her arm around me. "Close your eyes," she said in an even tone, "just relax yourself and breathe."

"Breathe?" I thought. "I didn't come here to breathe." No, not at the equivalent of three hundred U.S. dollars that I was paying. But I did as I was told. Placing the notebook and pen that I'd brought with me on my lap (as always, I was prepared to take notes), I started breathing in and out as I listened to her voice guiding me through a visualization involving angels and dolphins. Perhaps five minutes into the meditation, my body, quite without warning, started flailing around, my pelvis gyrating as if I were having an orgasm—without the thrill. It lasted maybe twenty minutes or so. I was fully conscious and lucid, yet I had no control over my body. When the convulsions finally stopped, I immediately dived for the pen and notebook that had fallen to the floor. To hide my embarrassment about having lost control, I adopted an air of alert nonchalance that I generally reserved for job interviews.

"So what just happened?" I asked, my pen poised to take notes. I felt light-headed.

"Have you heard of a walk-in?" Janice answered, by way of reply.

"Like when you walk in somewhere without an appointment?" I said.

"No, what I'm talking about is another soul walking into a body."

I stared at her uncomprehending.

"You see," she said, giving the last bite of carrot an uncompromising crunch. "Sometimes some souls find that they've made a mess of their lives and can't take it much longer. So, they decide to leave their bodies—you know, to die. And at that point, a different, more advanced soul walks in."

I continued to stare at her.

"Think about it, sweetheart." She stood up abruptly. "It's not an entirely unreasonable thing to do, considering the options. And mind you, it's only done by agreement. These are generally very advanced souls, and they wouldn't just take over a body without consent. This different soul then literally 'walks in' to the newly vacated body. What the new soul is doing is taking on the challenges that defeated the original occupant. This way the identity of the 'deceased' person can be maintained."

(As I always say, never waste a good body.)

"Your case, however," she said with a flourish of her hand, "is not quite like that of the classic walk-in."

I heaved a sigh of relief.

Janice sat down again, and cradling her face with her hands, proceeded to explain that I had originally had two souls controlling my body, one dark, one light. The dark one, which had heavy (and I'm talking heavy) karmic debt to pay, was finally freed—thanks to her—and departed. The light soul—the sole (no pun intended) resident of my body now—had never before been incarnated on earth, and had no karma to pay off. So I was free! I could fully come into my power, things would only get better and better. Not to mention that with only one soul controlling the body, it should be a lot easier to navigate.

I pointed out to her that what I had come to see her for—the pain in my arm and shoulder—remained unchanged. Give your body some time to adjust, Janice replied, and the pain should go away. It never did. As it turned out—I would find this out later at one of Janice's workshops—I had implants. Which, naturally, were put there by hostile space aliens.

Janice has a fair-sized group of ardent believers, mostly expats, but also a handful of Japanese, including one psychiatrist. They claim that Janice has changed their lives completely. Janice, they say, is a genius. For one thing, she has a masters in mathematics, and before she began her mission of healing work, she was a computer programmer. She is a member of MENSA, the club open only to people with IQs of 150 or above. (I've always wondered about the kinds of people that would join an organization like MENSA. Now I know.) All I can say is, Janice definitely belongs in a different stratosphere than the rest of us mortals. As does Linda, who was hosting Janice on her visit this time.

Linda lives in a world apart from the rest of us non-Japanese who struggle to get by as free-lance writers or English teachers. Her apartment is in ritzy Aoyama, where the rent goes for three thousand dollars or more for a modest-sized apartment, in a tree-shaded building with expensive Chinese brush paintings in the lobby.

I felt slightly intimidated when I walked into the lobby of Linda's apartment and announced my arrival through the intercom. A matronly looking woman, one of the participants in today's event, opened the door for me.

Linda's house would be considered spacious in North America; here in Tokyo it seemed absolutely huge. My entire apartment, the seven-and-a-half mat studio the size of a closet that I pay almost eight hundred U.S. dollars for the privilege of living in, could comfortably fit into the foyer. There were four bedrooms, an American-style kitchen (a real luxury here in

Japan), a dining room, and at the far end of the foyer I caught a glimpse of the living room that could have popped right out of the pages of *Abitaire*. A black-and-gold lacquered Chinese screen inlaid with white jade spanned the entire length of the room.

Half a dozen women were already seated on the sofa in the living room. A couple of them seemed to be around thirty, but the rest, I'm sure, were past their fortieth birthday—overshot it by quite a bit, I'd say. I felt better already. There were only two men, one with a receding hairline, and a Buddha-like smile; the other wore a pony tail and a nicotine-stained grimace. I was the only Asian.

Sara, the once staid business writer who had introduced me to Julia, was missing. Someone told me that Sara was busy giving her own Janice-inspired workshops, having already made her personal connection with the Space Commands, and been "activated" by Janice.

I entered the living room and sat down on the sofa next to a woman in a chocolate-colored suit. I noticed then the coffee table with crystals spread out like the Milky Way on its glass surface. The crystals sparkled as the soft sun streamed in from the French windows. Outside them was a strip of fence-enclosed garden, a lush oasis in the heart of Tokyo. Kitaro's "Silk Road" music enveloped the room, relaxing nerves jangled by the Tokyo traffic.

I found Janice sitting on the sofa seat to my right. When I walked over to greet her, she stood up and gave me a hug that must have lasted at least five minutes. While hugging me, Janice exhaled as if pumping out air, as if she were cleansing me of everything that was wrong with me. The hug was nice, though I had a kink in my neck after the first minute.

Suddenly, I felt something tap at my ankle. I looked down. A black cat with a short, forked tail was batting me with its paw.

"Anwangonnrrr," the cat said, looking up at me with what seemed to me a manic glint in its eyes.

I bent down to examine its tail, the kind that the Japanese call *kagi-shippo*, or "key tail," for its shape. It's a common flaw found in the genetic makeup of many Japanese cats. Only, this one was even weirder: the tail looked as if it had a split end; one half curved outward at a sharp angle, the other ended in a stubby knob.

"Oooh, how niiice, she liiikes you," a voice cooed behind me.

I turned to find Linda, the hostess for today's event, grinning as if to show off her dimples. She bent over to stroke the cat and I was reminded again of yet another reason we lived in such different worlds: Linda is a platinum blonde with the physique of a *Playboy* centerfold.

"That's my angel Sakiko," Linda gushed. "Isn't she adorable?"

I stammered what I hoped sounded like an agreement, but I needn't have bothered. Linda's attention was diverted by newcomers who bustled in just then. At last everyone was here, and the workshop could proceed.

"I've finished healing all my lifetimes on Mars," Janice began.

I wished I'd stayed home.

"A lot of people have been healing their lifetimes on Mars." Janice continued. (According to Janice, many of us have spent several incarnations on Mars. During these lifetimes Mars was engaged in some type of inter-galactic warfare. But now it was time for us to heal the wounds inflicted during these battles of eons ago.) She also said something about how it was now all right for people to remember the good memories of Mars. She explained that she'd been "activated"—one of Janice's favorite words—by the Ashtar Space Commands. Ashtar, according to a book written about him by a believer, is what is known as an "etheric being," a Christ-like fig-ure from outer space with a higher vibratory level than earthly beings. He is the commander of intergalactic fleets and the head of an interplanetary fellowship whose mission is peace. Janice is a charter member of this fel-lowship, and she's been called upon to heal numerous pockets of unrest on earth.

Then one of the participants-cum-assistants, a plump, bubbly woman with honey-blond hair, made her introduction.

"Hi, I'm Penny and I'm so happy to be here," she said. "This is soooo wonderful. It just doesn't feel like I'm in Japan." (Of course not. Linda's apartment is *not* Japan.) Penny went on to tell us how the dolphins made the initial contact with her. "I kept hearing this high-pitched voice that seemed to come from nowhere," she said, shaking her blond locks and cupping her hands to her ears. At first she thought she was having prob-lems with her ears. But it turned out to be just the dolphins contacting her telepathically.

The next topic on the agenda was angels. Janice outlined in brief her relationship with the angels, and told us to listen to their messages. And now, we were ready for the highlight of the event: everyone was to "chan-nel" their personal angels. One by one each person stood up with her eyes closed and made a waving motion in front of her body, as if brushing off a cobweb. With eyes still closed, the person said, "I am . . ." and then would give the name of their personal angel. It was generally a fairly long but lyri-cal sounding name, none of which I remember, but which all sounded something like "Shaniharaelirahami." The "angel" also explained its pur-pose for coming to earth. She'd say something like: "I've come to bring peace and love." Or, "I've come to give the galaxy to the earth," "We've come to serve humanity." Each person took at least three minutes, general-ly longer. The man with the Buddha smile went through the motions but couldn't speak. He said he felt an angelic presence, but he couldn't hear the words yet. Penny said that sometimes they tell you syllable by syllable, as it happened with her. Like this:"Mmmmmmmmm, eeeeeeee, rrrrrrrrr, lllllll-llll, iiiiiiiiiiiii, nnnnnnnnnnn, Mmm-eeee-rrrr-llll-iiii-nnnn, M-e-r-l-i-n."

I could tell this was going to take a lot longer than I'd counted on. I thought of the 200-page computer manual I had to rewrite by the end of the week. Whatever possessed me to come here? If I missed the deadline, could I plead temporary insanity? It didn't seem as if anyone else shared my sentiment, however. In fact, one woman was so moved, she wept. As for me, I feigned a headache and declined.

When we'd finished giving our angelic introductions, that was it. No more scheduled activities. Apparently, it was more of a get-together than a real workshop. People broke off into little groups and chatted with each other. Everyone seemed to know everyone else. I felt a little left out, but immediately Janice and one or two other women came over to "heal" me. They heaped a pile of crystals on my lap and gave me a large, translucent crystal to hold in my palm. Janice kept breathing. When the "healing" was finished, I fully expected her to claim that she'd removed an implant from me, as she had in the past. As Janice says, many people have these implants. They are placed there by extraterrestrials to prevent a person—generally, someone quite powerful—from fully expressing his or her power. Once, during one of Janice's earlier visits, I'd sat in for about an hour on her workshop. I had a cold that dragged on like a bad relationship, and Sara had suggested that Janice could cure it instantly. When I arrived there I found everyone sitting around in a circle playing drums, triangles, and bells.

After an interval, Janice stood up to begin a short discourse. "As many of you are aware, intelligent beings from other parts of the universe have been visiting the earth," she explained. "And throughout the history of humankind these extraterrestrials have been abducting chosen members of the human race. In recent years especially, the pace has been accelerating." She said that in Japan Mount Fuji serves as the gateway for UFOs. Which is why so many Japanese—though unaware of the fact—are UFO abductees. (When I mentioned this to a friend, she jumped up and exclaimed, "That's it! That explains everything!")

Throughout the speech, I sat on the floor rubbing my shoulder, yawning, and half-listening to her words when suddenly, Janice announced to the group that I—and several other people present—had been abducted many times by extraterrestrials. During one of the kidnappings, the aliens had placed implants in me. Not that I was able to see them. They're invisible, of course. So far, Janice has removed at least two from me. No, make that three. She removed one from my heart once while we were talking on the phone.

What could have induced these aliens to come all the way from another galaxy to abduct me, a mere child at the time, whose main interests in life at the time were Barbie dolls and Marvel comics? I must be pretty darn important, much more so than I ever realized. The only hitch is, I'd never had the slightest inkling that such a thing could have happened to me. I've never even entertained such a possibility, nor do I have the remotest trace of such a memory. I've never suffered from amnesia, black-outs, memory lapses, migraine headaches, multiple personalities. Nor do I have any large blocks of time that're unaccounted for (although that's apparently no problem—these aliens work in a different time system).

I felt no different when I left the workshop, except that my wallet was now lighter by ten thousand yen. My goal of saving up for my retirement seemed further away than ever. And I still didn't know when, if ever, I'd have sex again.

I was musing about all this when there was a slight commotion at the far end of the coffee table. Apparently, the cat had spilled a silver tray filled with cards.

"This is a sign," Linda announced. "Everyone, pick a card. There's a message for each of you." As I found out, these were called angel cards, and each one had a word or phrase written on its back.

"C'mon," Linda encouraged. "Take a card, any card." In her enthusiasm to have me choose, she nearly hit my nostrils with the tray. I was strongly drawn to one card, and though it kept slipping out of my fingers, I persisted in chasing it and managed finally to grab it. I turned it over for the message. It said: "Trust."

Whale songs were now spewing out of the stereo. I slipped over to the other side of the room, and sat on the floor on the pale gray carpet where half a dozen people were congregated. I was curious to find out who they were, what they did for a living. After talking to everyone, I discovered that many were wives of expats whose perks alone were fatter than my month-ly income. Others claimed to be rewriters, proofreaders, copywriters. Except for the man with the Buddha smile, who readily confessed to teaching at an English conversation school, the rest would sooner have admitted to being raped by extraterrestrials than to teaching English.

Penny, the assistant, was now sitting alone on the long sofa, the Chinese screen acting as a dramatic backdrop. She called for our attention, and then gave an impromptu talk about her work with dolphins. Janice had taken her on her first dolphin swim about a year ago.

"Dolphins are wonderful healers," she asserted. They are able to appraise humans instantly, and can often cure them of whatever is ailing them, not just physical problems, but psychological ones too. She cited one example where a mother and her children came together to swim with the dolphins. The family was not, in fact, related by blood, as both generations had been adopted; consequently, both mother and children had unresolved fears of abandonment.

"Yes," said Janice, who came to join us. "These dolphins worked magic with them," she added, with a flourish of her hand, then related the rest of the story. The dolphins swam toward the family as soon as they entered the pool, then looped around them in circles, around and around, healing them, dissolving their abandonment fears, strengthening their ties as a family.

But of course. What else would dolphins be interested in other than to heal humans of their all too numerous problems? And unlike humans, a dolphin would be doing this all for free too, without charging twenty or thirty or even forty thousand yen per session like its human counterparts. Yes, the next time my friends have a marital crisis, I'll just send them out for a swim with the dolphins. It's cheaper than marriage counseling.

For those who'd rather not get wet, there are nonaquatic healing sessions too—as I've already discovered—unassisted by dolphins, whales, sea lions, or sharks. "How some of that works," Penny spoke up on behalf of Janice, "is by changing a person's cellular structure at the level of the DNA. This makes it much easier for your body to go up to the higher dimensions."

"Waawoogangunraaarrrrngggrrrr!!" Linda's black cat suddenly let out an ear-rending shriek and streaked past the sofa and over the coffee table, knocking a few angel-shaped crystals onto the floor.

I think I knew just how the cat felt. The tide had turned; it was high time I left. I didn't know why I'd even stayed as long as I had. I gathered up my belongings to make my getaway—though not before inquiring as to where in Japan one could swim with dolphins (in case there's ever scientific evidence that dolphins can heal arm-and-shoulder pains instantly).

At that point, several other women decided to leave too, and followed me to the foyer. Linda caught up with us and asked us somewhat breathlessly to not forget our donations. I wadded up a few bills and put them into the envelope that Linda had prepared. Suddenly, I found Janice standing next to me. Smiling benevolently, Janice informed us that she won't be seeing us for a while—she'd been called by the Space Commands to assist in intense healing work in another part of the planet.

"I won't be back in Japan for a long, long time," she said, a little wistfully, and asked for a group hug. All the women present shuffled around to get into a circle. I complied with the same show of enthusiasm I display toward group shots. I ended up having to stand there with my arms stretched out as far as I could.

For a long time afterward my arms were sore.

[1995]

Hair Nudes

DAVID LAZARUS

I remember reading somewhere how half of all Japanese lack this like enzyme in their bodies. I suppose I got it from the health and science page, although I can't believe we were actually running something interesting in the paper. But this enzyme, what it did was help the body process alcohol, and because most Japanese don't have it, that's why their faces turn red when they drink, and why they're always dropping from heart attacks, and why they become absolutely spud-eyed from just a whiskey or two. You'd think they wouldn't drink so much, seeing as how, scientifically, they can't hold their liquor. But they drink like fish. All of them. I mean sometimes I think everyone here is a drunk, which wouldn't be so bad if they were nice, cool, Humphrey Bogart–style drunks. But Japanese, they go out, get totally pickled, and then come straight to my subway line so they can puke all over the platform just before I'm on my way home. I mean like every night. It makes me sick.

So I was standing with Shin, my boyfriend, at this kiosk at Tokyo Station. It was about eight o'clock in the morning, and Shin was picking out a couple of foul-looking bento boxes for our breakfast. Then he told the woman at the counter to add a couple of those little sakes to the meal, the "one cup" kind that you always see ratty homeless guys clutching in train stations.

"What are you doing?"

Shin didn't seem to understand what I was asking. He laid his money on the counter.

"I don't want any sake," I said.

"Okay," he replied. "I'll have it."

"But it's still morning."

He gave me a puzzled look, like how he looks whenever I betray my amazing ignorance about "his" culture. Shin doesn't even like to discuss this kind of thing. He thinks, because I'm living in Japan, I should be this like huge expert on everything Japanese. I've been here a couple of years and I can still barely speak the language. For Shin, this is like a major tragedy, this incredible disappointment. We had a big fight after I stopped taking lessons. Shin acted like it was personal. He wanted to know how I could do this to him, when I'd been wondering just the reverse, sitting there in class trying to remember the "stroke order" of thousands of these impossible little kanji. I mean, right. If I wanted to learn a million Chinese characters, I'd have moved to Beijing.

Shin handed me the plastic bag with our bentos and the sakes, and he picked up the suitcase we'd packed with our stuff. We were going down to Kobe for a few days, to see his family. He'd wanted to go for New Year's, but I absolutely refused to go anywhere during the holiday. Like I really wanted to set foot on a bullet train when every day there were stories in the paper about how the Shinkansen were at two-hundred-percent capacity. It was bad enough commuting forty-five minutes to the office every morning. The last thing I wanted was to have my atoms smashed for four or five hours.

I followed Shin through the station. He'd been weird since we got up, and when I asked what was the matter, he just shook his head and said nothing was wrong. But Shin's a really terrible liar, which I guess is nice, seeing as how he's a reporter and all. So I was tempted to say that if he was freaked about introducing me to his family, why were we going down there? I mean, I wasn't exactly looking forward to playing the humble *gaijin* for three days. But I didn't say anything. He'd just keep insisting that everything was fine, so what was the point?

We went up to the platform and right onto the train. As usual, Shin had timed our movements down to the second, which you can do in a place as anal as Japan, if you want. So just as we settled into our seats a little Minnie Mouse voice was announcing that we were about to get underway. Then it was repeated in English in this very proper British accent. That's another reason I stopped taking language lessons. Everything you need to know is repeated in English anyway.

We pulled out of the station and Shin wasted no time popping the top on his sake. My tongue curled.

"It's not even eight-thirty," I said.

Shin ignored me, like I was peeing all over his culture again. And I suppose I was, considering how I could hear beer cans and sake bottles being opened all around us. What is it about the Japanese that travel and getting shit-faced always go hand in hand?

We stared out the window for a bit watching the buildings go by. Both of us were looking for the newspaper office, which isn't far from the tracks. It slid past and I tried to think who from the features section was working this weekend. We get most of our pages done in advance, but someone has to be around just to make sure that the paste-up guys don't suddenly decide to rearrange all the paragraphs, or that a caption hasn't fallen off. It's not so bad working weekends. You can kick your feet up, or go over to the news section and chat with whichever reporters are on.

That was something I liked doing with Shin, working weekends together. He was always more relaxed in the newsroom, more in his element. He'd come over to features and sit beside me and watch CNN, never failing to shake his head over whatever proof was being offered about the degenerate state of American society. If a Japanese person got shot or robbed in L.A., which seemed to happen at least once a week, Shin would complain that American "morals" and "ethics" had disappeared. He takes it really seriously, like we're really letting Japan down. Like I'm sorry.

The train picked up speed as we got out of Tokyo and began zipping through Yokohama. Shin took out a magazine. It was one of those weekly "news" magazines, although from what I could tell, news was never that much of a priority. The fact that they ran color photos of naked women was one indication. It used to be that Japanese magazines weren't allowed to show pubic hair. They could show just about anything else, like S&M or schoolgirls in their underwear, but pubic hair apparently was too much for local sensibilities. Then the police changed the law, and suddenly a bunch of art books appeared with sulky, pouty nude models, pubic hair and all. Next the weekly magazines started featuring pubic hair in their photos, all in the name or "art" and "free speech." They called them "hair nudes." Real arty.

I watched out of the corner of my eye as Shin flipped through the pages of his magazine. He went right past the hair nudes, which I knew he was doing for my benefit and which I appreciated. Shin can be pretty considerate, I'll give him that. He'd check them out later, of course, when I was in the bathroom or something, but it was nice of him to at least pretend he wasn't interested.

We'd gone through it before anyway. I'd started in on how Japanese men are all sexist scum, which they are, and how it's offensive in the extreme to be sitting on the subway beside some middle-aged lecher who's staring at nude photos of young girls in come-and-get-me poses. Like that's not offensive? Could you imagine someone in America taking out a *Playboy* on a train and drooling over the pictures, right there in public?

Shin tells me I've got it all wrong. He says Japan has different cultural values, and I have no right to judge society by my "Western, Judeo-Christian value system." Oh sure, like it's a cultural thing to treat women like sex muffins, like this goes back to the Edo period or whatever so it must be okay.

Maybe I do have it wrong. I don't know. It's getting so every little thing is driving me nuts. I used to think Japan was so fascinating, so Asian. Now all I ever feel is frustrated. I read somewhere that this is natural, that all foreigners go through this endless love-hate thing with the country. Lately, I think I've been stuck in the hate part.

I'd brought a book to read, and I held it in my lap, but I wasn't in the mood. This trip to Kobe, I wanted to tell Shin about the thoughts I'd been having, how I was thinking more and more about moving back to the States. We'd talked about it before, sort of, how maybe we could move together back to New York and he could go to journalism school and I could find some kind of magazine work. My roommate Leigh-Ann had already returned home to Seattle, and I hadn't found anyone to replace her. (It was nice, I had to admit, having the whole apartment to myself, although I could hardly afford it.) I'd asked Shin how he thought about living together, but he said it was too early to discuss this. I suppose fear of commitment is a cultural thing too.

It wasn't until we were all the way to Osaka that Shin suddenly felt like talking.

"You'll like my parents," he said, although he'd already told me this at least a dozen times before.

"I'm sure," I replied.

"They're really looking forward to meeting you."

"Me too."

Shin's dad was a manager or something at some little company that made headlights for Toyota or Nissan or one of those guys. He was getting near retirement age, and apparently the big issue at Shin's home was what Dad would do after giving his entire adult life to his company. I didn't see what the big deal was. Now he could play golf or pachinko or whatever it was that he liked to do. But Shin seemed to think that all this free time was going to be real traumatic. He also worried that there could be friction between his parents. His mom had grown used to having the house to herself. Apparently she wasn't exactly thrilled by the thought of having her husband underfoot all day.

We got off the Shinkansen at the next stop and transferred to another line that took us into central Kobe. Shin's family's place was then about a fifteen-minute walk from the station, which I didn't really mind but which seemed to be a bit much for Shin. He kept passing the suitcase from hand to hand and giving me dark looks, like he was going to start in again on how I wouldn't need my hair dryer, like it was even up to him what I would and wouldn't want on a trip. Shin's kind of a control freak, but that's okay because so am I. We cancel each other out, I figure.

His folks' home was on a narrow street in a residential neighborhood. Lots of little toy houses with those great blue-tile roofs, which I think would look so beautiful on a real house, like in Vermont or somewhere like that.

"Well, here we are," Shin announced.

I nodded and wondered why we weren't just going in. What was he waiting for, a big welcome-home ceremony? Shin gave me a long look.

"What?" I asked.

"Nothing."

He went up and rang the bell. The door opened and Shin's mom and dad appeared. I could see right away that Shin got his looks from his mom. They both had these little noses and great cheekbones. Shin's dad looked about like any other guy I'd see on the train, with his gray hair glued firmly in place with some kind of goop.

I heard Shin introducing me and I muttered the correct excuse-me-for-being-so-impolite words, which you have to say even when you're on your best behavior. I even bowed a little and Shin's mom bowed lower in return. Shin's dad wanted to shake hands so I shook his hand, and he stared at me with an uncertain expression, like how Shin looks whenever I say something that he isn't sure is an insult or a joke.

"Nice to meet you," I answered, and everyone laughed. That, I figured, was the extent of all conversation for the coming three days.

We went inside—they had guest slippers waiting in the hall for Shin and me—and I followed everyone into the living room. It was dominated by a huge TV and stereo setup, and the shelves had trophies that Shin's dad had won in golf tournaments, and plaques his mom had won playing *go*, which I knew was like Othello but a lot harder. She was apparently some kind of *go* champion, and Shin had suggested that perhaps I could learn how to play so she and I would have something to do together. He even bought me a book of *go* strategies. I left it in Tokyo.

Immediately Shin's mom was forcing food and drink on us, and I noticed that I was being referred to as "Grace-chan," which I thought was kind of informal of them. "Chan" is like "san," except it's cuter and cuddlier, and mostly people use it when they're talking to small children and animals. But since they were calling Shin "Shin-chan," I figured they were just trying to make me feel at home.

The two of us went upstairs to unpack. The only thing that said we were in Shin's old room was a bookcase full of school textbooks. Other than that, there was no evidence that anyone had ever lived in there. Not like my room back home, which my parents were preserving like some kind of shrine to their Long Lost Daughter.

"So what are we going to do for three days?" I asked.

"Anything we want."

I already knew this; he'd said as much when I'd asked the same question back in Tokyo. But now that we were here I still didn't know how we'd fill the time. Probably take long walks. I was hoping Shin would loosen up so we could maybe talk a little about the future.

We went back downstairs, and by this time Shin's mom had laid the table with a ton of food, most of which I had no problem with. I really sympathized with Shin as we ate. His parents were making a big effort to be friendly to me, and poor Shin was stuck in the middle trying to translate everything. I only made things harder by cracking a few jokes, which are impossible to translate, and watched as Shin struggled to explain at length why what I'd said was funny.

I wondered why Shin's dad kept giving me these little looks. I mean the *gaijin*-in-the-house thing was old news. He could give it a rest.

It was a Sunday evening and I wouldn't have minded going out. Instead we all sat on the sofa and watched TV, mostly those incredibly lame quiz shows where the same old celebrities sit around competing for goodies that they couldn't possibly want anyway. From time to time Shin's mom would ask if I was all right. I told her I was fine.

What the hell, I thought. Three days. Two nights. Wouldn't kill me.

By the next afternoon I was bored out of my mind. I kept waiting for Shin to take some action, to get us out of the house and doing something. But all he wanted was to sit around chatting with his mom. Or rather, sit around listening to his mom chat away, because that woman could talk. It was like this running monologue. Most Japanese, they let others get a word in every now and then, just to maintain a feeling of consensus. Not Shin's mom. Whatever consensus there was, it was her consensus. Shin and Shin's dad, who was taking the day off from work, could only nod their heads and make little grunting sounds every so often to show they were awake.

I tried to keep up at first. I sat at the table with the rest of them, and I smiled and did my best to decipher words here and there, so that maybe I could at least understand the gist of the conversation. But after a half-hour or so, I was so mentally exhausted I had to move over to the sofa and lie down.

"*Daijobu?*" Shin's mom immediately asked in this tone like I'd coughed up blood.

"*Hai,*" I answered. I'm fine.

I thought that by my going over to the sofa, Shin would've understood that some of us weren't getting as much attention as we'd like. But he let me just park there and turned his attention back to his mom, who started up again at full throttle.

Finally I turned on the TV and started watching a samurai drama—there's always a samurai drama on Japanese TV—and I heard Shin's mom's voice drop to an almost-whisper and I heard my name tossed around. Then Shin, who hadn't had enough sense to figure it out himself, came over and asked if I wanted to do anything.

"How about a walk," I suggested.

"Okay. Where do you want to go?"

Sometimes guys are so thick you wonder how they make it past childhood.

"Anywhere is fine," I said.

"Okay."

He went back and talked to his mom a bit more, like he was asking permission to go out and play. I went upstairs and got my coat. It was January but winter had been pretty mild so far, not like some years when Japan turns into the world's biggest meat locker. Or maybe it's just that none of the houses or apartments have insulation, which of course is cultural, seeing how no one had insulation back in Edo times.

Shin and I said our goodbyes, and Shin's mom told us to be careful. Yeah, okay, we won't play in the road. Then we started walking to Shin's old high school, which he wanted to show me because he said it would help me understand who he is, like I don't already know.

"So what do you think?" he asked.

"About what?"

"My family."

"They're great."

"Yes?"

"Sure."

What else was I going to say? Your mom's a self-centered, motor-mouthed old hen, and I keep catching your dad staring at my chest?

"I'm glad you think so," Shin said. "I really wanted you to meet them."

"Well, I've met them."

"Yes."

Japanese guys have a lot going for them over Americans. They're sweeter by and large, and usually more thoughtful. They're nice in bed. But at least Americans don't feel this need to inflict their families on you. Not once did I have a boyfriend in the States who wanted me to meet his mom and dad. Like I'd show my folks to an outsider? Please.

So we reached Shin's old school and stood at the fence watching a bunch of boys in their black, military-style uniforms running around with soccer balls. What fun.

"Shall we go back?" Shin asked after a few minutes.

"How about if we walk a little further," I said. "Maybe we could go visit a temple or something."

Shin shook his head. "I think we should be heading back. My parents really want to see us."

"They're seeing us. But it's nice to be outside for a bit."

"I think we should go back."

"You go back. I want to walk a little more."

Shin got a pained look on his face, like he didn't know what to do with me. Then he said, "All right. Can you find your way?"

"I'll manage."

He turned and walked off.

I knew I should have been making more of an effort to do the family thing. I mean I could see how important it was to him. But we'd just finally gotten out of the house, and would it have been so bad just to spend an hour together, just the two of us?

I memorized how we had come and continued walking. Kobe seemed nice enough, a little slower than Tokyo, a little less crowded, but the same basic gray buildings everywhere. Eventually I came across a small shrine, one of the ones with the two little fox statues out front, and I sat down on a bench. It's nice the way Japan has all these little shrines and temples tucked away all over the place. Kind of compensates for the sameness of everything else.

I don't know how long I stayed there, maybe twenty minutes, maybe a half-hour. Not that long. Then I got up and made my way through the little streets back to Shin's place. I thought I might get lost, but I didn't. I've got a pretty good sense of direction, and you can always use the convenience stores on every corner as markers.

I rang the bell when I arrived. It took like almost a minute and then Shin's mom opened the door.

"*Konnichiwa*," I said.

She didn't reply. Just stood aside so I could enter. Now what?

I put on my guest slippers and went back into the living room, where Shin and his dad were sitting quietly at the table looking like someone had just died. Fine. I didn't want to get into whatever it was they were hashing out. So I turned around and went upstairs. Let Shin do his own thing.

I was just settling onto the futon when Shin appeared in the doorway. Still had that gloom-and-doom look on his face.

"What's going on?" I asked.

He didn't answer.

"What?" I said.

"How could you do this?"

"What?"

He stepped into the room and handed me a large book, which naturally I recognized, having one just like it in my apartment.

Visions of Venus.

I glanced at the cover, the coy Japanese model playing peekaboo in a steaming hot spring. Her name, I'd been told, was Suki. It killed me. Suki. How come models never have ugly names?

I set the book down and looked up at Shin. He was staring at me like I was supposed to burst out in tears or something.

"Well?" he asked.

"Well what?"

It was priceless, the bewildered little look on his face.

He practically fell onto the futon beside me and snatched up the book. He flipped through the pages.

"Page eighty-seven," I said, trying to be helpful.

Shin stared at me a moment and then quickly turned to page eighty-seven. Yup, there I was, perched sweet as can be on my couch with the newspaper. You couldn't tell from the photo, but it was turned to the health and science page. My own little joke.

It was a pretty good photo, actually. Normally I don't photograph well. I think I always look fat. But this one, the photographer got the afternoon shadows in this really cool way. I looked nice.

Shin gazed at the photo, then back at me.

"What's the matter?" he repeated.

"Yeah. It's a nice photo."

"You're naked."

"Uh-huh."

Shin frowned, at a loss for further observations.

"Everyone in there is," I pointed out.

In fact, my picture was one of the tamest. The one that would have pissed me off, if I was Japanese, would have been the blonde they had nestled in the lap of the giant Buddha in Kamakura. Surely that's some kind of major insult to the religion.

"Naked," Shin said again.

"Yeah. So?"

"So?"

"So what?"

"You're . . . " He struggled for the words. "You're a hair nude!"

"Not really. It's just a little. You can barely see it."

Shin examined the picture more closely. Technically speaking, he was right. I mean there was some hair. But the newspaper mostly covered it up.

He looked at me again and I could see it was time to offer a little assistance.

"It's no big deal," I said. "A friend told me about this book they were putting together, a collection of Asian and Western models. She introduced me to one of the photographers. It only took like an hour."

"But why?"

"Three hundred thousand yen, that's why."

And it was the easiest three thousand bucks I'd ever made. Nearly two months' rent. But I was saving it. For the move home.

I could see Shin's mind working.

"But this is pornography," he said. "You told me that this is violence against women."

"This isn't porn. It's an art book. It's nothing."

Shin wrestled with that. I reached over and took the book from his hands and closed it. I set it on the floor between us.

"Where did you get it?" I asked.

"It's my father's."

His father's? That explained a thing or two.

"What, may I ask, is your father doing with a book of naked women?"

Shin stared down at the book like the question hadn't even occurred to him until now. He shook his head.

"That's not the point."

"Why isn't that the point? Why is it okay for your dad to keep a book like this around the house, but it isn't okay for me to pose for one of the photos?"

This was almost fun. Poor Shin.

"It's completely different," he insisted, although I could tell from his expression that he wasn't sure why.

Shin was quiet for a moment and then lay on his back and stared up at the white stucco ceiling.

"This screws up everything," he said.

"How's that?" I asked, lying down next to him.

"Now how can we get married?"

I had to laugh. "Who said anything about getting married?"

He popped back up into a sitting position.

"Why do you think we're here?"

"To visit your parents?"

"So they can meet you."

"And we've met."

"So we can get married!"

"Hang on, kiddo," I said, sitting up. "Just because I came down here with you to meet your folks, that doesn't mean we're engaged or anything."

"That would come next."

He was getting way ahead of me.

"Look Shin," I said. "I'm not ready to get married. Okay?"

"But . . . " His objection didn't go anywhere.

"What about what we talked about," I said. "About moving together to New York?"

"New York?"

"Like we discussed."

He turned his gaze to the window. The sun was going down. It'd be dark soon.

"I don't want to go to New York," he said.

"I do. I think it's time for me to go home."

Shin didn't know what to say to that. I was a little surprised myself by how firm my voice sounded. I hadn't realized until just that moment that I'd already made up my mind.

"I want to go home," I said.

Shin was lost. I put my arm around his shoulder but he shrugged it off and stood quickly. He picked up his dad's book and left the room. I heard his footsteps going down the stairs.

So what was I supposed to do, go after him? Tell him everything would be all right? To be honest, I was more interested in all the plans I'd now have to make.

I stayed up in the bedroom for another half-hour or so, until Shin called me down for dinner. When I got downstairs I thought I'd walked into the Twilight Zone. I mean everyone was acting like nothing was the matter. Shin's mom performed her usual monologue throughout the meal, and Shin's dad kept stealing peeks at me. And Shin—he was smiling and laughing at his mom's little quips, translating for me like I was part of the happy family. Only once did I get a sense of reality. That was when Shin went into the kitchen to get another beer, and I caught his mom gazing in my direction. It was a real Charles Manson kind of look. Then Shin returned and his mom went back into her patter and everything was fine.

In bed that night, Shin said he didn't feel like talking. He said we could talk when we got back to Tokyo. I said okay, fine, if that's how you want it. He could act like such a little boy sometimes.

Neither of us slept well. We both tossed and turned for hours. I pulled back a curtain and stared out the window. There was this really intense orange moon.

I must have finally fallen asleep, because the next thing I knew I was awake and the room was falling all over me.

I'd been in plenty of earthquakes in Tokyo—more than I'd care to count—but nothing like this. I mean the whole room was bouncing. Shin's old schoolbooks came tumbling off the shelves, the closet doors swung open, the dresser skittered on the floor. I ducked under the futon and it still kept going. Like almost a minute. I heard a cracking sound from some-where deep in the house.

Then, like always, it let up gradually. Everything slowly came to a halt.

"Jesus," I said, emerging from the futon.

"Are you all right?" Shin asked.

"I think so. You?"

"Yes."

He climbed to his feet and looked out the window. It was still dark out. The room looked like a tornado had just swept through.

Then Shin went running downstairs calling for his parents.

I sat up feeling jittery and shaky and totally spooked. I could hear glass breaking.

"Grace," Shin called.

"What?"

"Come down. Hurry."

I slid into my jeans and grabbed a sweater. The house still felt like it was moving, like we were floating at sea. I made my way carefully down the stairs. There weren't any lights. The power must have been knocked out.

Downstairs was a mess. All the trophies and doodads from the shelves had been knocked to the floor, and the big TV had fallen over. But that was nothing compared to what I saw in the kitchen. Or what I didn't see. The entire kitchen wall had collapsed. You could walk right out to the street.

Shin and his parents were running around throwing things into suitcases. I almost went back upstairs to get my stuff, but then I figured this was no time to be greedy. Not if the house was about to come down. So I grabbed my jacket from the closet and my shoes from the entryway. I put them on and walked right through the living room, violating like a dozen Japanese cultural taboos. I stepped through the hole where the kitchen wall used to be and out into the cool morning air.

Shin's mom was behind me, wrapped in a blanket. She stared open-mouthed at the remains of her kitchen and then shot me a nasty look like it was all my fault. I mean, what, because of a nude photo?

Shin and Shin's dad came out a few minutes later carrying a bunch of suitcases. They set them down right there on the road.

I looked up the street. People were slowly spilling out of their homes. It looked like all the houses had been pretty badly damaged. None of them had completely collapsed, at least none yet, but walls were cracked and broken, and windows were smashed.

"Come on," Shin said to me.

"Where?"

"I don't know. Around. We've got to find a phone."

"What, you want to go cover the story?"

"Of course."

"Are you crazy?"

"No, come on. This is important."

"I'm not going anywhere. I'm going to wait here for help."

"But this is a disaster."

"No shit."

Shin wasn't going to waste time arguing. He said something to his folks and went running down the road. His mom flashed another helter-skelter look in my direction and went chasing after him, calling, "Shin-chan! Shin-chan!"

Then it was just me and Shin's dad. He reached inside the kitchen and handed out a couple of chairs. We set them in the middle of the road.

I could smell smoke. There was a fire burning somewhere.

We sat quietly for a few minutes, just listening to all the activity, the sirens starting up all over the city. It would be light soon.

Shin's dad was gazing up at the sky. He had a calm, not-quite-all-there expression on his face.

"I'm sorry about your house," I said.

Shin's dad got up again and poked through the remains of his kitchen. He returned with a bottle of whiskey, unscrewed the cap and took a swig. He offered it to me. I held it to my lips and took a little sip, then a bigger swallow. I could feel the chill easing inside me.

The smell of smoke was heavier now. You could practically taste it in your nostrils.

Shin's dad and I sat there for I don't know how long, passing the bottle back and forth, not saying a word. People walked by with dazed looks on their faces. They couldn't seem to comprehend what was happening.

What was the problem? This was Japan. It you're going to live here, you might as well get used to the idea that earthquakes happen. I mean they've been hitting the country for like centuries, right?

I took another pull from the bottle, feeling a whole lot better now. I started thinking about how I'd be returning home soon. I'd go to New York, find a job, an apartment. Get serious about my life. My parents would be glad. They'd been asking when I was finally going to settle, stop running away from things. Like that's even what I do.

The whiskey was nice. It went down smooth. I handed the bottle back to Shin's dad and stared up at the sky.

Or maybe I'd move to Italy.

[1995]

The Circuit

MICHAEL FESSLER

"They said he was using those . . . what do you call them? . . . Little bitty . . . Bonsai, no, uh . . . those poems the Japanese like to write. . . . "

"Haiku."

"Yeah. Haikoo. He fooled everybody. They thought—what was his name? Killer, Kimble, Kaizer, something—"

"Kendall."

"But it was a funny first name—"

The FASTEN YOUR SEATBELT sign came on. We were making our descent. Both of us buckled in. I finished the last of my wine, and said, "Otto John Kendall."

"That's it. Funny name. They said he was one of those types that went bamboo. Real character, but underneath, well, nobody knew." The man chuckled. "Just between the two of us and that cloud out there, I always admire . . . but that's off the record."

For an instant something flickered in his eyes. A misgiving. Never know who you're talking to on these Pacific flights.

"Off the record," I said.

The plane banked smoothly, descended gradually, and before we knew it, we had touched down and were taxiing toward the terminal. We deplaned, passed through immigration, claimed our baggage, and then moved through customs.

"Say-o-nara," the man said, once we were outside. "Don't let the geisha bite!"

"Sayonara."

I headed for the limousine stand. When the bus arrived, I took a seat in the back. As we started off for Tokyo, I opened my old leather bag and removed a book: *Otto John Kendall*. Underneath that, *Volume III: The Life*. And then came the name of the editor: *Henry Stark*. Who happens to be none other than myself.

Otto John's secret is now a matter of record. When I first met him, though, no revelation could have strained credulity more. It had been my job at that time to interview Otto John Kendall for *Ganbaro* magazine. He was the premier haikuist in English of our era. The dossier that my editor had given me ran as follows:

Kendall, Otto John. 1931–. b. California. Ed: Cal. system.
Terminal degree: Ph.D. Foreign languages: Spanish, French,
Japanese, some Chinese. Residence abroad: London, Paris,
Mexico City, Tokyo (current). Teacher & scholar. Widely
published. Specialty: haiku and haiku criticism. Founder/editor
of *smalletters*.

It was common knowledge that Otto John had created many enemies
along the way. He was an independent scholar whose opinions were both
strongly held and frequently divergent, and there had been many clashes
with the academic community. It was rumored that he had indeed *gone
bamboo*, as the man on the plane had said. I spoke with several Americans
and Brits who had had contact with Otto John and arrived at this profile:
he was completely abstracted, and a little batty.

I caught up with Otto John in the lobby of the Marunouchi Building
in the spring of 1991. He was a slight man with graying reddish hair, and a
triangular-shaped face. He wore a wisp of a goatee. One was reminded of
Ho Chi Minh. He was smoking; his clothes (a brown suit) were dirty; a
slight must emanated from his person.

"Otto John Kendall," I said.

"Does this hallway go this way?"

"If you turn around, it goes the other way," I said, feeling as if I had
scored a point.

He coughed, shifted his shoulders, and kept on walking.

"Mr. Kendall, I'm Henry Stark. From *Ganbaro*. I wonder if you might
have some time. . . . "

His eyes looked dry, the sockets sweated out.

"Perhaps you're a bit tired at the moment—"

"I wouldn't know."

"You mean, you wouldn't know if you were tired? If you wouldn't,
who would?"

He said nothing. I mentioned a restaurant at which we might discuss
the matter of the interview. By then we had reached the end of the hallway,
and he took a quick right; we were descending a staircase into Tokyo Station. Finally, he said gnomically, "There are numerous circuits."

I acknowledged the truth of it.

"Good day," he said, and walked off into a maze of pillars that had
conveniently materialized. I let him go.

Well, that's that, I thought. I won't be interviewing Otto John Kendall,
and thank goodness. The next day, however, I received a phone call from
my editor. "Kendall wants to talk to you."

I expressed my doubts about it.

"You interrupted his thoughts. That's all. Tea shop called The Grape. Friday. At one."

To my surprise, Otto John Kendall was actually there. He was sitting at a table in the corner and a woman with a gray pixie haircut was massaging his shoulders.

"*Katakori*," she said in explanation.

While the illustrious haikuist's shoulder-ache was being tended to, I took a seat, though no one had asked me to.

"You don't object?" I asked, taking out a tape recorder.

"I object to many things."

"Bad writing, for example?"

This led to a discussion of the internecine haiku-wars, which reminded me of ant-fights. The most recent had originated over the use of a phrase—Otto John referred to one of the combatants as "the woman who wanted to copyright two o'clock." Amusing as this was, I tried to steer Otto John onto some personal topics and matters concerning his writing. I quoted one of his early poems:

> In a warlike voice
> a man shouts
> Peace!
> War,
> a man says
> in a peaceful voice

"This poem is a little unusual in your canon. I'm not sure that it could be called a haiku. It contains no *kigo*, season word, for example. But I've often thought of it as a kind of double haiku in the shape of an hourglass. . . . "

The notion seemed to travel directly to Otto John's shoulders. The woman grasped them and kneaded away.

"Moreover," I heard myself saying, "it has a political dimension that is lacking in your work. Perhaps—"

Otto John's eyes glazed over, and he seemed to have fallen into a trance. Well, no need to press.

"I've heard," I said, attempting another angle, "that you run seminars at some of the Japanese and international hi-tech companies in the area. Has this had any influence on your writing? The haiku as microchip, so to speak. . . . "

Otto John, however, had already stood, and the two of them started for the door. Marched toward it would be more precise.

"*Ichi ni ichi ni,*" the woman counted.
"Next Friday," Otto John said.
Did this hallway go this way?

Over the next six months of Fridays I got my interview. Otto John was always at The Grape with the woman, and she was always massaging his shoulders to relieve his *katakori.* There were times as he sat with his green tea in front of him, hardly taking a sip, when his body took on the appearance of a vertical haiku, slight and wispy. Along with the mystery, however, there gradually came clear and direct answers to questions I put to him about the journal he had founded, *smalletters,* and his haiku life in general. Moreover, as I became accustomed to the format and venue, I ventured more, though not always with success. Once I mentioned that there was a sayonara party for a poet whom he undoubtedly knew and surprisingly had never attacked. He dismissed the idea of attending with a curt shake of his head.
"You'll be missed," I said.
"I'm not leaving. He's not staying."
It was an odd way of putting it, but it gives the flavor.

In the summer of 1991 Otto John Kendall, crossing the street absent-mindedly, was hit by a car and died. He was sixty at the time. Thus did this slight other-worldly poet, whom I had gradually been getting to know, pass from the interviewer's net. Naturally, it was quite a shock. My editor phoned in a panic, asking that I get the "deathbed" (no less) interview to him immediately. Fortunately, the bulk of the work was ready, so I rounded it off and faxed it. Otto John had died on a Sunday and the obits came out on Monday. On Tuesday *Ganbaro* brought out its cover story on Otto John. My interview was the featured piece. On that Friday, not knowing just what to do, I went to The Grape as usual. There sat the woman, with no one to massage. She had two boxes, and she handed me a letter. I opened it and read:

To: Henry Stark

I would like you to be my editor. *Kendall Zenshu,* if you will.

Otto John Kendall
3.16.91

I looked up.
"I am Koko. Otto John was my husband. In these boxes are the haiku. If you wish sexual gratification, I can provide it. My late husband felt that a

spiritual transfer might result, and aid you in this, his life's work," she recited, as from a script.

"I'm honored," I said goofily. "But no."

No sex, that is. I agreed, however, to edit Otto John's works. It seemed the fitting thing to do. She informed me that money was available, and that I would receive expenses and payment.

"Six months," she said. "This place."

I looked down and coughed.

She was gone.

The boxes were surprisingly in perfect order. I had anticipated a mad mess. The title page read:

/Haiku/Otto John Kendall/The theory is in the writing./

What followed on A4 sheets, with a good many penciled-in revisions, were the haiku. In the first box were haiku categorized as *Juvenilia and Transitional;* in the second, *Mature.* The haiku were arranged seasonally by *kigo.* They started with haiku from January 1958 and proceeded down the years to the summer of 1991 when Otto John had died. Pagination was continuous.

In my spare time from Tozai University, I did the necessary bibliographical work. My tasks were indeed formidable. Not a few times I reflected on the dry methodical process of recording, aligning, etc., and contrasted it to the mysterious and wispy life of OJK. (He had become his initials by now.) On the other hand, I was well aware that behind every chromatic poet was the plodding scholar who kept him alive and before the public year by year.

Within the allotted six months, I had all the poems on floppy disks. They were prefaced, chronologized, footnoted, and indexed. I noted in the preface that Kendall Koko had been the source of the manuscripts and that I had worked from the materials that she had provided. I omitted any mention of the "spiritual transfer."

I returned to The Grape on the appointed day, and there sat Koko-san. I presented her with the disks and a statement of my costs. She handed me my fee (a nominal one), checked my statements cursorily, and reimbursed me for my expenses right there in cash. Then she picked up two more boxes from under the table.

I think I must have slumped back in my chair.

"You want sex?"

I declined again.

She stood, bowed, said, "*Ichi ni ichi ni,*" and marched out.

One two one two. Odd way of doing scholarship. On the other hand, better than being interfered with.

Boxes three and four were more like the man I had known, so I had my work cut out for me. Since Otto John had requested a *Zenshu,* or Collected Works, all of this needed sorting out and ordering. In the meantime, *The Haiku* came out. It was a hardback, handsomely produced, and had been designated Volume I. Included were off-sets of various holographs with Otto John's calligraphic Zen circle, or *enso.* I felt that my scholarly judgments in the preface sounded right. The success of the edition was gratifying and I derived energy from it, which I needed. Boxes Three and Four contained mainly prose, about half of it typed. The typed pieces were, however, replete with corrections and marginalia. Those essays that were in long hand were occasionally very hard to read, and I had to purchase a magnifying glass to decipher them. Again, the work of scholarship, the work of detection. I divided the prose writings into two volumes: *The Criticism* (II) and *The Life* (III).

Volume II, *The Criticism,* included Otto John's columns from *smalletters,* various essays published in periodicals and anthologies, attacks, objections, etc. Much of this was already part of the public record. Nonetheless, I dutifully gathered the work together, bringing up a few new things in the process.

The writings that came to make up Volume III, *The Life,* were another matter. The first thing that differentiated them from the other works was that none of them had been previously published. Secondly, a large proportion of the writings was fragmentary. Unfinished essays. Lacunae. Truncated passages. One of the first essays I encountered concerned his father. According to this essay, his father had been an herbalist and an amateur magician. As to the latter activity, OJK wrote:

> The audience believes it is observing the magician. This is
> the magician's art.
> It is he who is observing them.

The elder Kendall had been an outsider and in spite of his skills had died in penury in San Francisco's Tenderloin. Otto John had interpreted this as a rejection of "the superior individual by corporate dominated society." The essay in general was a little bitter, and clearly unfinished. I put it in the most readable shape I could.

★ ★ ★

It was about halfway through Volume III that something began to feel wrong. One Sunday I sat down at my desk and pulled out a manuscript from the box. The subject was the university in the '60's: sit-ins, rallies, agit-prop, bullhorns, rapping. Otto John made the point that this was all child's play:

> Upper middle-class kids had a party, their protest-habit
> supported by their fathers.

He drew this lugubrious contrast:

> In the mornings their fathers left for corporate HQ: my father
> went off to gather camomile that dogs had sullied.

In the margin was the hour-glass haiku that I had queried him about at our first meeting, but which he had been reluctant to discuss: militant doves, pacific hawks—Otto John's somewhat detached view of means vs. ends.

A lot of the scenes had to do with the undergrad angst and politics of that period, but by this time Otto John was in his thirties, hanging around the old U. long after he had graduated. He seemed to be trying to learn something about computers. There was a confusing section about work in which he stated that everyone wanted recognition for his accomplishments, but that this for some reason would be denied him. "Big Biz will subsidize the Arts!" he wrote unexpectedly. Then followed some oddly conflated identifications: *na no hana* = Hibiya, *ajisai* = Machida. . . . It was a strange jumble: California in the '60s and flowers and place names in Tokyo. I turned the page and noted the penciled marginalia: kiku, Tuesday, cash.

I read on and began to see what the haiku circuit was about.

The following Friday I went to The Grape.

"You want sex?" Kendall Koko asked.

I coughed humbly.

"Come," she said. We walked along as if we hardly knew one another. Finally, we arrived at a stairway, and went up. There was the faint, oily voice of someone singing *enka* at a karaoke bar. Once we were inside the apartment, I put my briefcase on the table.

"Sex now," she said.

The life of the scholar. I held up my hand, removed some pages I had printed out, passed them over, and asked if she approved of them. She studied them for about ten minutes and said, "Good."

"Your husband was quite a writer. This is very fine."

She agreed.

"Did your husband ever ask you to help him in his work?"

"I give him massage. *Katakori* . . . " Otto John must have had the sorest shoulders of any man who had ever lived. By now I had a good idea what had been making him tense.

"How did you feel about his training programs at hi-tech companies?"

"*Katakori*," was all she said.

I thanked her and stood.

"You want sex?"

I declined again. I had played a dirty trick on her, but the failed reading test might keep her out of prison. "*Mata ne*," I said, and put the printed sheets from Humphrey Todd's *Adversarial Biography* (London, 1958) into my briefcase. Then I left.

The bibliographical ethics of the situation were ticklish. I decided to follow through with Volumes II and III. The former had no direct bearing on the issue. As to *The Life*, I would simply let the evidence speak for itself. For the next three months, accordingly I labored over the essays in Volume III, photocopying, inputting, producing a clean, readable text. Order from disorder. When I had completed the work, I returned to The Grape and presented the disks to Koko-san. She bowed, paid my fee in cash, looked over my statement of costs, and reimbursed me for them in cash also.

The Criticism and *The Life* were published within two months by a small arts press in Kanda. I had, as before, corrected the proofs. It was obvious that neither the printers nor Koko-san understood much of what was in the texts. Subsequently, all three volumes (*The Haiku; The Criticism; The Life*) were reissued in a gilt case. A very elegant publication. *Otto John Kendall Zenshu*. Edited by Henry Stark, M.A.

For some time there was no reaction. Then, as I had expected, when readers and editors began to look again, the impact of the text was felt. The drama, you might say, was in the footnotes. There were two types of interviews. The first were from journalists. I played down the matter, which naturally persuaded them to sensationalize it. The second were official. I told it exactly as I knew it. Not a few companies and individuals had been stung.

At Tozai, I teach a course in contemporary East-West intellectual history in which I include the works of Otto John Kendall. The inclusion is controversial. OJK was involved in industrial espionage. He was, you might say, a major poet but a minor spy. Incredibly, and perhaps preposterously (in part, his cover—Otto John was hardly absent-minded), he was sending messages over the haiku circuit. The season words of a number of his haiku designated drop-off points. To be sure, scientific developments in the hi-tech industry move very swiftly, but certain strategic concerns do not. These OJK monitored and passed on to people interested in them (occasionally out-and-out rivals). It must have pleased him to have worked the back streets of the information highway. Psychologically, I think OJK was avenging his father's treatment by society, which he blamed on big business. ("Big Biz will subsidize the Arts!" he had written.) OJK was also a proud man and therefore wanted his secret divulged: he had spied without getting caught. No doubt this was the reason for his titillating hints about "the circuit" and his retention of compromising but exulting details in the manuscripts.

Questions remain, however. Throughout literary history one often finds writers whose work is unassailable but who were otherwise blackguards. In OJK's case the work itself (artistically right, ethically wrong) was tainted. Tainted but beautiful. Therein lay the terrible tension. Initially duped myself, I tried to right things. I footnoted these conflicts in Volume III and adverted to them in the Preface, making known that the questionable poems had served a double purpose. I was performing a trick within a trick. I "bugged" the *Collected Works,* you might say. Such literary sabotage verges on casuistry, however, and cannot explain away the fact that the elegant three-volume edition was almost certainly subsidized by OJK's spying activities. It has left me not without a certain tightening in the shoulders.

[1995]

Shades

ALEX SHISHIN

You might say I was a total failure in life until the day I found the shades on the subway train on the Midosuji Line in Osaka and transformed myself like Clark Kent when he goes into a phone booth and comes out Superman.

I was shy as a boy. I was so shy that I don't have a really clear recollection of how my teachers and classmates looked in school because I was always looking down at the ground. I can tell you a lot about floors and pavements, though. Because I was so shy I was bullied a lot. In junior high school my teachers beat on me worse than the worst school bullies. I remember once how Mr. Etoh my math teacher and also (my luck) my homeroom teacher, beat me over the head with a ruler because I couldn't do a problem correctly. Like a lot of others, he thought my shyness was really insolence. Once Mr. Etoh and several other teachers took me into an empty classroom and hit and kicked me for an hour. I was out for a week. My father and mother were outraged but they too were shy and so they did nothing about it. After Mr. Etoh cut my hair I stopped going to school.

He said my hair was too long and made me stand up in front of the class. He brought out some scissors and grabbed a clump of my hair in his fist and cut. He was no professional barber; he just yanked and cut, yanked and cut until I had no hair left and was bleeding from scissor wounds all over my scalp. I just stopped going to school afterward and that was the end of school for me, though Mr. Etoh took to calling me at home all the time to accuse me of disgracing him on purpose and all these school officials made a lot of noises to my mother and father. But by the time the system got around to begin dealing with me, I was old enough to quit school if I wanted to.

I eventually started looking for work and I got the sort of jobs you'd expect a total failure to get. I washed dishes in a noodle shop. I handed out packets of tissues advertising a loan shark company. I loaded boxes of scrap metal onto trucks. And I was a janitor at a movie theater where they showed pornographic movies.

I lost every job, except the last one, in less than a month. It's not that I wasn't a good worker. It's just that I'd end up not going to work and that would be that. The truth is that I hated all those jobs except the one at the porno theater. I really liked that one and I held onto it for over a year—and

I only lost it because the place closed down. You know, I would have stayed home and probably done nothing if my family was rich. My mother and father were kind people and they would've let me. Unfortunately we weren't rich. Father was an office worker in a small car parts company and Mother was just a housewife. I had to work if I wanted things besides food and clothing.

That porno theater job was really nice because I got to see all the porno movies I wanted for free. I really thought those porno movies were interesting. But not just for the reasons you might think. Sure, I liked to see naked gals having sex as much as any guy. But there was something more important after awhile. I got curious.

I couldn't quite figure out just what kind of gal would risk her reputation by doing a porno film. You see, I thought of all the punishment I'd gotten mostly for just being shy. But with these gals, surely there were people looking down on them and maybe even bullying them for what they did, I figured. What kind of gal is a porn gal? I asked myself. The question really bugged me. I ended up watching the same movies over and over just to see the gal's expressions and the way they moved their bodies and listen to the tones of their voices just so that I might get at least a clue. After the theater shut down, I started renting porno videos and watching them in my room. I'd play back certain scenes maybe a hundred times in a day. Still I couldn't reach any conclusions.

I know this sounds really stupid. But look—back then I'd been so used to being put down that I never had time to wonder about the world around me.

One day at dinner time, I asked my parents what they thought made a regular gal become a porno gal. My father mumbled that he didn't like porno. My mother began to cry. She cried a lot after my dropping out of high school.

I'd given up working for a while when I found the shades on the Midosuji Line. They were French and expensive. I put them on and liked the way things looked, so I left them on. By coincidence, I guess, a guy with shades got on and sat down in the seat across from me. His hair was permed and he was wearing really bright clothes, like this red checkered sports jacket, an orange shirt and green trousers. I usually didn't pay attention to people, but I noticed him. I then noticed that people weren't sitting down next to him. That seemed pretty reasonable to me because this man was probably a yakuza or something. Then I saw that people weren't sitting next to me either. When the man was getting off, he turned to me, smiled, and gave me a friendly hello: "*Osu!*"

Bells and firecrackers went off in my head. Have you ever had that sudden rush of pure ecstasy when you suddenly understand everything? Well, it had never happened to me before that moment.

I got off at the next stop and searched out a barber shop and had my hair permed. It cost me 6,000 yen, all the money I had with me. I mean down to the last bit of change, so I couldn't even take the subway. Fortunately, I was close enough to home that I only had to walk a couple of hours. My parents didn't like my perm at all, but being shy, they didn't say much about it. My mother cried all night and my father sat in front of the TV until some time past midnight without moving from his place and not saying a single word.

The next day I took out the 100,000 I'd been saving in the bank and bought a lot of bright clothes with it. I got a red checkered jacket and an orange shirt just like the man I had seen the other day. But instead of green trousers, I got a few pairs of designer jeans. I remembered a video in which the hero, who kills his enemy with a blow torch in the end, wore designer jeans. I also bought a pair of cowboy boots.

Just like Clark Kent, I became a new man with a change of clothes. I had walked into the department store wearing my old windbreaker, one of the cheap striped shirts from the bargain bins that my mother had bought me and rubber shoes. I left looking like a yakuza. People actually got out of the way as I walked down the aisles. With my shades on, I found it easier to look at people. I noticed some of the gals looking at me and some of them reminded me of how the gals look at the men they do it with in the porno movies.

I had only a thousand yen left after shopping. I put my shopping bags into a coin locker in the subway and then I went to a pachinko parlor and played pachinko like I never played pachinko before, and would you believe I had 10,000 yen when I decided to finish. Next, I went to the video store to get a fresh supply of porno movies. You know, something incredible happened. Usually when I went into a video store, the clerks took their time serving me and then kind of just tossed stuff at me. This time they were fast and polite. Nervously polite, but polite. I went to a coffee shop and, wow!, there too everyone was polite to me. Nervously polite, but polite. I tried an experiment. I went to another coffee shop. Same thing. I went to eat lunch in Umeda in a classy-looking Italian restaurant. The head waiter got this frightened look when he saw me. After I was seated, he hovered around me and would come to my table every few minutes and ask if everything was all right. I wouldn't have enough money for the subway if I paid the entire bill, so at the cashier's I mumbled that I didn't want to pay the service charge. I didn't have to, the nervous clerk said, no doubt thinking my shyness was my way of being tough. I'd thought that out, by the way. I know I didn't even graduate from junior high school but I'm not exactly stupid.

Did it go to my head, all this? It went to my head. It was winter and Osaka was so gray and so cold. But it seemed like spring to me. For the first time, people were treating me with respect. That night I was so happy that I wore my shades to bed.

Once I had a teacher of Japanese who asked us to write a composition about whether we preferred to be feared or to be loved. I don't remember what I wrote. But his question returned to me as I lay in bed looking at a porno video through my shades. I preferred being feared, I decided. Being loved was nice but love takes too long to develop. The respect you got from fear was instantaneous like an instinct.

The next morning I woke up realizing I was dead broke. I knew that if I was going to pull off my yakuza act I'd need money and that meant I'd have to get a job. But I was so happy from the other day that even this couldn't depress me. My parents were still recovering that morning from the clothes I'd bought and I guess I shocked my mother some more by coming to breakfast smiling, which I'd never done before, and announcing that I was going to look for a job and not come home until I found one. I was wearing pajamas and my shades and my mother cried over breakfast. She cried again after I'd changed into my checkered jacket, orange shirt and designer jeans but she gave me money for subway fare without saying a word. I impressed this pachinko parlor manager in Nanba so much that he hired me right away as a janitor.

Soon I had money again, but cleaning up in that pachinko parlor after it closed, amid the smell of machinery and lingering smell of tobacco, I had a chance to think about things. I realized that if I wasn't cool, if I pulled stunts like I had in that Italian restaurant, my shyness would eventually expose me; maybe a real yakuza would come along and beat me up. I figured just getting respect in video stores and coffee shops and from my pachinko boss was enough.

That was in February that I got that job. I stayed on until June, when I decided I didn't want to work any more and stopped coming. It was getting hot, and I figured that if you have to be hot, you might as well stay home.

I didn't start looking for work again until autumn. But I wasn't entirely idle in the mean time. I watched a lot of porno videos. I also studied men's fashions by checking out what yakuza-looking guys were wearing, and imitated them. Of course I wore my shades day and night. The other thing I did was to go to Nanba and watch gals. I played a little game with myself, trying to figure out which of the gals I saw would make good porno stars. There were lots of bare legs and breasts walking around Nanba that summer, which made this game kind of hard to play.

Oh yes, I also got a motor bike license. That was so I could drive my mother's motor scooter to do shopping and stuff. You see, my mother kind of went crazy and refused to go out of the house. So my father insisted that I get the license to take over my mother's chores. (We lived in a rather isolated part of Osaka where the public transportation was poor and you needed a scooter or something if you were going to carry a lot of things.) My mother sat in front of the TV all day without turning it on and sang little songs to herself. I think they were popular songs when she was my age. I tried talking to her once—asking if she wanted to watch some of my porno videos—and she just looked at me and laughed hysterically. I left her alone after that.

Anyway, in autumn I thought I'd better go job hunting after looking in the mirror one morning and seeing that my perm needed some tending to. It was starting to grow into a great Afro, which really made me look cool, but I knew it would soon be pouring down my neck, over my ears and over my shades. I'd look like those dumb punks who handed out tissues downtown. Really ratty kids in dirty jeans and with tinted hair. Looking in the mirror reminded me I was nearly broke again. I was getting picky though. No more sweeping up chewing gum wrappers for me. No thank you. It so happened that in Nanba I met another guy wearing shades and he asked me if I wanted a job. Okay, I said. He led me to his boss who had an office over a bar. The boss took one look at me and asked if I had a motor bike. Yeah, I said. He said, good, I'd need one for the job.

You know those stickers and cards for telephone dating clubs that you see covering the outsides and insides of telephone booths? Ever wonder who sticks them there? Well, it's guys like me. I worked at night when there weren't so many people using the booths and it was harder for cops to spot me. See, it was illegal to do it but it was okay if you didn't get caught because the cops didn't hassle our company. The boss told me not to stick them anywhere except telephone booths, but one night, as a joke, I put a sticker on the gate of my old junior high school.

It was pretty steady work, because people were always taking our cards and scratching off our stickers. And also the boss had all kinds of new names and numbers coming out that needed to be put up. It was fun work. It got to where I'd not only cover the windows but also the telephone receiver with stickers. I did it so that when you picked it up my sticker would be right there under your nose.

One night I was having coffee and a snack in an all-night donut shop when I saw my old homeroom teacher, Mr. Etoh, come in, buy a donut and coffee and sit down by himself at a table. He sat there looking around nervously, like he was expecting someone. He didn't notice me or, anyway, recognize me. The person he was waiting for came in a few minutes after he sat down. It was a gal—a really young gal—with red hair and very pale make-up and big earrings with fake rubies and diamonds. She was wearing an imitation leather coat and a mini-skirt and mesh stockings. No need to tell me what her line of work was. She sat down next to old Mr. Etoh but didn't order anything. She sat silently with a blank look on her face while Mr. Etoh finished his donut and coffee. Then, still not speaking, they went out together.

The bells and firecrackers went off in my head for the second time in my life. I thought it would be neat if I could get some pictures of Mr. Etoh with this teen-aged whore and send copies out to his principal and his wife and maybe a few newspapers. But I didn't like cameras—not since the school photographer kicked me when I was in sixth grade. Then I thought: What if that gal was from one of our dating clubs? Maybe Mr. Etoh even found her through the sticker I put on the gate of my old junior high school. I could mess things up for our company by exposing him. I didn't care! I wanted to catch him at it again. I wanted him to know that I knew. I wanted him to see me in my shades.

Mr. Etoh had pretty regular habits. Exactly two weeks later he was at the donut shop at exactly the same time I saw him there before, and he sat down in exactly the same place. The same teen-aged whore came in looking for him. When they went out, I followed.

They caught a taxi. My motor scooter was parked on the sidewalk right outside the donut shop, so it was no problem to follow them. The taxi drove them to a love hotel just a few blocks away. It drove right into the parking lot, which, typically, had a stringy curtain hiding it from the street.

It was a cold windy night. I soon began to shiver after I parked my machine and started waiting for Mr. Etoh to come out. He was taking a long time, which I thought was natural. He had been very energetic when he beat up pupils and I figured he must be very energetic when he was having sex with a teen-aged gal. I thought about going to the vending machine down the block for hot coffee, but decided not to. What if Mr. Etoh left before I got back?

After two hours, the gal came out. She tugged at the end of her mini-skirt and went straight to the main road and caught a taxi. I wondered if she had parents worrying about where she was. I wondered if she did porno films. If I were her, I'd surely rather do porno films than have Mr. Etoh climbing on top of me. . . .

Mr. Etoh slapped back the stringy curtains and came out on to the street.

"*Oi!*" I cried and stepped out of the shadows.

He turned. His face under the love hotel's neon lights seemed to change from blue to orange to green as he stared at me. Before he could say a word, I lifted up my shades so he could see who I was.

You know, this was the first time I'd ever gotten a close look at Mr. Etoh's face. It was long like a Japanese potato. His lips were like a tuna's. His whole face began to quiver when he saw me and he turned and ran into a side street. I followed.

I will always remember my pursuit of Mr. Etoh in terms of cartoons. Here is this funny man, really a little man with short legs, fleeing from a gigantic pair of shades. He was actually a fast runner, despite those short legs. We ran past I don't know how many store fronts with their steel shutters down and how many stand bars with their windows glowing softly in the windy night. All the time, neither of us spoke. He was probably too scared to say anything. I, as usual, was at a loss for words when dealing with a teacher. Never being a good runner, I could hardly keep up with him. My legs are pretty short too.

Then suddenly Mr. Etoh halted. With one hand he grasped a utility pole. With the other he clutched his chest. Then he just kind of crumpled up into a squatting position. When I came up to him he didn't budge. His eyes were bulging out and his tongue was drooping from his mouth. I was breathing hard after running, but he wasn't breathing at all.

My body was sweating all over inside my heavy clothes, my feet were frozen to the ground and my eyes were glancing about with panic. What if someone had seen us? What if I couldn't remember where my motor scooter was? The narrow street was totally dark and deserted. A dog barked in the distance. Far away there echoed the roar of a hot rodder's car. A kind of fuzzy numb feeling spread over me, like when the dentist gives you pain killers. My breathing became regular and all my muscles seemed to relax at once. I took off my shades and put them over Mr. Etoh's bulging dead eyes. It seemed to me like a symbolic thing to do, like something someone would do in a movie, though to this day I don't know why I did it.

Back home I thought it was a really stupid thing to have done. I worried that maybe the police could trace the shades back to me if they wanted to. But worse than that, I really missed them. I really, really wanted my shades back!

The next morning the local Osaka TV news program had a flash about Mr. Etoh being found dead from an apparent heart attack in one of the city's red light districts. Then there was no news at all. Only years later, when I ran into someone from my old homeroom, did I learn that there had been gossip about Mr. Etoh and prostitutes, and our junior high school principal had apparently gone to the police to plead that they hush everything up about Mr. Etoh's death.

I bought a pair of shades exactly like my old ones. Let me tell you, they were super expensive and on my salary buying them was no small thing. But life without them was hell. My eyes burned, I was short of breath like I was suffocating, and my head hurt and hurt. But it all stopped the moment I put my new shades on! It did, it really did! My life returned to normal like nothing had ever happened. I went back to putting stickers on telephone booths, and I even started going again to that donut shop where Mr. Etoh had picked up his teen-aged whore.

Actually, life got better after all that. Miraculously my mother recovered. She started going out again and shopping and washing our clothes and fixing our meals. She still sang those songs to herself but now her voice sounded happy. My father got into singing them along with her. He bought her a karaoke set for Christmas.

And can you believe it? I got my dream job right after New Year's. It's a job for which I needed a lot of training. For six months or so I apprenticed with a pro with no pay. Then I got so good that I got hired full time and have worked solo ever since.

I'm a talent scout for a porno movie company! I really am! What I do all day is hang out at train stations and coffee shops and spot gals who I think would make good porno stars. When I see a likely one, I walk up to her and in my own shy but deliberate way start talking to her. Me! The kid who spent most of his life looking at the floor at school! Me—actually having the courage to tell a complete stranger that she would look great naked in a porno movie! I don't come out and say that at first, but I do get to it quickly if I believe I'm talking to a winner.

To this day—and I've been on the job for ten years—I get letters from many of my old porno stars thanking me for discovering them. (I get letters of the other kind too, but I throw them away.) I might as well tell you the secret of my success. What I finally realized after watching thousands of hours of porno videos and checking out thousands of gals in Nanba was something so utterly simple: that gals hide their hurts, their fears, and their angers under make-up and sexy clothes the way I hide mine to this day under a pair of shades. I'm sure I have a winner when I see a gal who somehow reminds me of myself. Most of the time I can at least get such a gal to consider doing porno.

I've got my own apartment now, and a car too. I get all sorts of neat video movies with the young stars I've discovered for free and I watch them on a fantastic wide-screen TV. Funny thing is, though, I'm still a virgin. I could've lost it long ago—my boss has offered to set me up a number of times—but I'm not interested. When I think about doing it, the idea of taking my clothes and shades off kind of makes me feel sick. Then I worry that if I lose it my magic touch with gals might go away. Where would I be if that happened?

My boss has sex with a lot of the gals I find and knowing that makes me glad. He's the pro who taught me all I know. He's the man who gave me my self-confidence. I owe him my life. Would you believe he's the guy who said, "*Osu!*" to me that day on the subway when I first found the shades. No kidding!

[1993]

Angels of the Unknown

LAUREL OSTROW

The first time she saw the figure was right after the accident on a busy Japanese street. Clara was walking from the train station on her way to teach English. She heard car brakes squeal and a thud; the white car stopped in the middle of the street and a man in a brown suit jumped out. She felt her own increased heart rate vibrate in her ears, and she turned around.

A man in a blue work shirt lay face down on the street, his hands above his head. Though Clara stood completely still, she imagined herself with her hands up, like ballet. People scurried about and spoke Japanese she couldn't understand, loudly and quickly. The woman who kneeled by the man looked small. Clara waited a moment, thinking how to help. Then she saw the figure. Standing next to the fallen man, then sitting on the hood of the car, the man was dressed in loose, black trousers and a purple beret. She thought he must be a man because of his length and his lean appearance. His face was powdered white and his eyes were outlined in black.

Clara's body felt weighty and slow, but she moved toward the figure, toward the accident. The woman kneeling by the injured man was now crying. The palms of her hands on either side of his face protected him from the rough pavement. A security guard from an office building wanted to move him.

"No, no, *abunaiyo, abunaiyo*," Clara put her hand up. She told a woman standing nearby to call an ambulance. With help, she carefully turned the man over, checked for breath. His light shirt made his breaths easy to see. Blood was running down his forehead and onto his eyelids. An old man with thick glasses gave Clara a white handkerchief. The cloth was crisp, as if it had been starched. The ambulance came. The woman and her man were taken away. Gone now, too, was the figure she had seen. Clara's white stocking was smeared with blood at the ankle, covering a raised flower in the hose.

Trembling as she walked away, her thoughts turned to David and Jonah. How flesh runs and tears, she thought. Her man, her baby the same. She felt a pressure in the center of her chest, and she couldn't stop it until she entered the office building, and focused on her teaching for the day.

Sawada waited for her in the classroom. "I'm sorry I'm late," she said. "I saw a man hit by a car," she tried to tell him in Japanese. He gazed at her blankly. "A car, a man, boom, boom," she made crashing gestures with her two hands.

"Oh, I see. They drive too fast in this town," Sawada interjected. "There are many accidents." He looked down, rolling his silver pen between two fingers.

Her student Sawada was bulky, and smelled of aftershave lotion. He had shared his medical history with her, which included problems with his stomach and pancreas. He loved to drink and play pachinko. He talked to Clara about strawberries grown in his home town; how proud his people were of their strawberry fields. Clara told him of the song about strawberry fields written by the Beatles but he hadn't heard it. He was only twenty-eight.

This day he asked her, "Do you believe in God?"

"Why do you ask that?"

"I just wondered, with the New Year beginning. Americans believe in God, don't they?"

"Some of them do. I do, I guess," her voice sounded hollow. "And do you?"

There was a knock on the classroom door. "Just want to clean up," the voice said in halting English. This was the man she'd seen at the accident, the white face. His clothes were the same, except that he wore a denim apron over them.

Sawada said, "Sure, come on in," also in English. Sawada looked back at the vocabulary they were studying, as if the man looked quite normal.

He emptied ashtrays and swept. She thought it was reasonable for him to be here, so close to the accident scene. But it was odd that he looked Japanese and spoke broken English to Sawada.

After he left, Clara asked, "Don't you think that he was a little different looking for a janitor?"

"Don't know. I have never seen him before. I suppose he is one of those hippies. Of your time period. When you were young."

They always laughed that Clara was nearly forty, and so much older than Sawada. They called each other by last names in affection. She was attracted to him, she thought, because he was outspoken and the skin on his hands looked very smooth. Now, they laughed and she forgot about the white-faced man.

Riding the train back to her home in Okayama, she watched the other passengers. Many people slept, packages on their laps. School boys in short pants prodded each other, squeezing together on the long seat. Small children sat quietly and looked at her. Another child pulled on her father's shirt as if she wanted to breastfeed from him. This made Clara smile, and the man smiled back at her. She thought of the figure again; she almost expected to see him here.

After arriving home, she visited her best friend, Hiroko. Rare were moments when she could be alone with a woman because children were always present here.

Hiroko had a small face, with a mouth that didn't open wide. Yet, when she talked, her speech was clear. Hiroko only wore loose-fitting dresses; her hair was pulled back. She wore only the slightest amount of face powder. Clara wished she could paint a watercolor of her. Hiroko taught traditional calligraphy. Her walls were full of her own work. Hiroko translated the elegant black strokes and red markings for her, but she loved the peaceful sense about them more than their literal meaning.

They ate mashed sweet potatoes out of star-shaped individual baking tins. Their steam smelled strongly of nutmeg and butter.

"This is good," Clara said. Hiroko often gave her food to try.

"So glad you like it," Hiroko said, and rubbed her eyes as if they itched.

"There is much in my heart that is difficult to say in English. About my life. About yours. Family matters." Her eyes were penitent for a moment, perhaps wanting the lightness of their earlier conversation back, Clara thought. Clara reached out her hand, which Hiroko held for a moment before pulling away.

There was a knock on the door. The man who came and sat with them was white face. He sat at the third seat where there was a Chinese New Year's placemat, and Clara noticed his hands on the table were small like a woman's hands, the empty palms faced up. Clara saw thick hair beneath the beret, long strands of gold and black hair. There were no wrinkles on his face, and his straight lips were pale. He was trying to sell Hiroko filters for her stove fan, and spoke fluently in Japanese.

Hiroko noticed her staring. "What is it?"

"Oh, nothing." Clara wondered at seeing this man again. She couldn't understand why Hiroko didn't see how weird he was.

After he'd gone, Clara said, "He was very odd, don't you think?"

"Oh, well not all businessmen wear suits in Japan."

"Well, of course, but . . . there's a lot I don't understand about your culture, I guess."

"And if I were in your home, I would feel this way."

She walked down the three flights to her apartment home. The lights were out. Jonah was still napping. David had spent the day with him and didn't try to keep a schedule. He was loose, like his stride and his way with money and time. He was sentimental. "That one was my father's," he would say about an old, stained tie. She understood him well after their ten years together. She understood him more than she had ever understood anyone.

That night Jonah had a few angry outbursts and many demands. Clara and David were in bed before they had a chance to talk.

"How was your day, dear? I barely talked to you today."

"You wanted to visit Hiroko so it was your choice not to come home early and be with me." His back was to her.

"Are you angry?" She couldn't remember him sounding so hurt before or turning away from her in bed.

"This morning the company reviewed my ad campaign and called me about it. It was a big deal."

"I'm sorry. I didn't think about it as I should have."

"Just want you to know I need you. Sometimes it's hard trying to understand the staff and the business. I'm not as good at figuring things out as you are."

Clara rubbed his back, pushing at tight knotted places under the skin. He fell asleep, and the room was very quiet when she saw the white-faced figure again. He was at the door. Like an angel, she thought. She was frightened at seeing the apparition, and closed her eyes to avoid him. She felt empty, gutted, without the sense of knowing that comforted her. She mentally rummaged through her thoughts, looking for something that seemed solid and familiar.

She opened her eyes and reached toward the figure in anger, with one arm. Her hand slipped through the air, landed on David's soft hair, which smelled of American cream rinse. "Explain yourself," she said to the figure. "Who are you?"

The man turned his hands palms upward and held out his arms as if to receive her within them. Then he left the entryway, stepping around Jonah's Sesame Street stool.

"David." She pushed his arm gently to slip hers around him.

"What?" He looked at her from under a long shock of hair. "Why aren't you sleeping?"

"I had a dream," she said, "about falling slowly into a space in the earth. I'm heavy, then light. . . . "

"Scary," he answered in his sleep. He would remember nothing of their conversation the next day. He turned over and put his hand under her leg. Completely asleep again, she knew.

She, too, finally slept and envisioned the figure stroking her on the head. Her mind filled with images of blood rushing, then the single organ notes which also pumped out of her heart, tremulous and continuous. She was a child in dreaming, back bones pressed against a church pew, the wood cold on the backs of her knees as she sat. Jesus was dying again. Clara, in her ribboned hat, smelled his sweat as she touched his toes, then played with them as Christ became her baby Jonah, who giggled as he fed at her breast. She'd become the Madonna and then, the white-faced man approached with a large, wrapped box. An iridescent, fluffy bird flew from it, showering the air with glittery specks of light.

White face smiled in her dream, as he had never in life, coming closer and closer until the face was all she could see, until it exploded into brightness and was gone.

When Clara awoke, there was an ache in her stomach, as if she hadn't eaten enough the night before. David had left without kissing her. She felt alone and sad for a few moments as she stared out the window at the Japanese children in uniforms, walking to school noisily hitting each other with their backpacks and chasing each other. One of the older girls was walking alone. She wore only ankle socks and the knee length blue skirt and short-sleeved uniform shirt. Japan was cold in December. "*Samui,*" Clara said to herself. The girl looked up, seeing Clara in the window. Her pale face was in full sunlight, yet she didn't squint or shield her eyes. She smiled and waved to Clara. The girl had the face of the man in her dream, of the salesman, the janitor, and the figure at the accident. By the time Clara raised her hand, the girl had turned to continue up the hill.

Through the sound of traffic and children, she heard the high babble of Jonah, awake and playing in his crib. She didn't know what he was saying and she was happy not to know. When she picked him up, the sight and smell of him was enough, his small body pressed close to her warmed her well.

[1994]

from One Hundred Views of Raoul

RALPH McCARTHY

ALIEN

As I walked past the police box at Roppongi crossing I noticed one of the officers watching me. It was Sunday evening, and I had about an hour before I must be at a studio down the road.

I'm an assistant professor in German language and literature at a university on the outskirts of Tokyo, but I live in Nogizaka and often do narration work. I have a beautiful voice. That's the only beautiful thing about me, though.

There is, I fear, some truth to the stereotype of Germans as lonely, gloomy people, and I am lonely and gloomy even by German standards. I first came here three years ago with a Japanese woman I'd been teaching at my university in Tubingen. I was madly in love with Emi; we planned to wed, and she helped me find employment here. I started to study Japanese even before we left Germany, thinking it would help me blend into the society, and learned to read and write 2,000 kanji in less than a year.

Emi changed after she got back to Japan. She moved in with her parents and took a part-time position teaching at a junior college. At first we met at least three or four times a week, but she gradually started inventing more and more excuses for not being able to see me. Just a year after I moved here, she told me it was over. A few months later she wed a Japanese man.

I was devastated. I probably should have gone back to Germany, but didn't like to waste the knowledge I'd acquired about Japan. Wait. That is not exactly true. The truth is that depression had robbed me of the energy to make any major decisions. I've remained at my university, going through the motions, but I must admit to being even less motivated than most of my students.

The longer I'm here, the less I understand these people.

This is what I was thinking as I walked around Roppongi with over an hour to kill and no one to talk to. When I approached the intersection, the WALK sign began blinking and a herd of loud young Americans ran across. I was in no hurry and stopped at the curb to wait. A moment later, someone shouted in my ear.

"Hi!"

My nerves were on edge anyway, and I nearly jumped out of my skin. I spun around to see the little police officer who'd eyed me as I walked by.

"Understand Japanese?" he shouted up at me.

"To a certain extent," I said.

"Oh! You're good! Show me your alien registration card!"

"What?"

"Are you carrying an alien registration card?"

"Why?"

"Because, if not, you're breaking the law! You don't have one, do you!"

"I have one."

"Show it to me! No, wait! Come inside the police box!"

He took a firm hold of my arm and steered me inside. I was livid with rage. Another policeman was sitting at the desk, doing paperwork. He glanced up at me indifferently while I showed my card to the little officer, who seemed impressed that I was a university professor. "OK, you can go now," he said.

"Why did you stop me?" I growled. "Did I do something bad?"

"Don't let it bother you!" he said. "We ask everybody!"

"Ha," I said, and gestured outside, where a group of foreign models were laughing and shouting as they waited for the light to change. "You mean you ask everyone who looks suspicious to you."

"No, no! Today's Sunday, right?"

"So what?"

"It's Sunday, and you're all alone! Everybody else is walking around with friends, but you're alone! That's unusual, right? Just checking! It's my job!"

I didn't know whether to burst into tears or strangle him. Fortunately I did neither, but stormed outside and marched straight to a bar around the corner. There was one other customer in the place—an American named Raoul, whom I knew slightly. He was drunk. I don't believe I'd ever seen him when he wasn't.

I bought two large beers, plunked one down in front of him, and began to relate what had just happened to me. I was so distraught that my knees, my hands, and my voice were shaking.

"Ha!" he interrupted me. "You think you've got problems. I've just been stood up again. Third time this month. . . . "

I spent the rest of the evening buying this dimwit beers and listening to his woman problems. I never made it to the narration job. I did, however, decide to return to Germany.

RHINOCEROS

At Charlie Congo's the head of a rhinoceros protrudes from the mirrored wall behind the bar. A real rhinoceros. The eyes aren't real, of course, but very realistic. Amazing how gentle-looking those eyes are.

"What am I doing here?" they seem to say. "The last I remember, I was romping through the savannah with my mate and child . . . then a sound like thunder . . . a searing pain in my heart. . . . "

It's one of the saddest things I've ever seen.

Not as sad as the character sitting a few stools down from me, however. He is surely European—perhaps German—but he is studiously ignoring me, staring now at his beer, now at the muted variety show on the television. On the sound system, Jimi Hendrix demolishes and recreates the cosmos, but this person is wallowing in misery and doesn't even seem to notice.

I want to help him, to offer some words of encouragement, if not a moral sermon on the evils of negative thinking. Or, then again, maybe I just want to talk. I do like to talk.

I pull out my cigarettes and ask if he has a light. He smiles shyly—look, he can smile!—and slides a white disposable lighter toward me. I've got him now.

"I feel sorry for this rhinoceros," I say, and he looks up at it as if noticing it for the first time.

"I know what you mean," he says. He sighs and shakes his head. "Human beings are disgusting creatures," he mumbles. Ah, we come straight to the crux of the matter.

"You are German?" I say.

"No, American."

He doesn't sound American.

"You were born there?"

"Yeah."

Perhaps he is lying.

"New York?"

"No, no. The Midwest."

Where is the Midwest, I wonder? Texas, perhaps? Impossible. No, he must be lying. But never mind. Probably he has his reasons.

"And you?" he says.

"Me? I am Parisian, of course."

I have a beret, a goatee, and a thick and unashamed French accent, and I chain-smoke Gauloises. Even the Japanese can usually guess where I'm from.

"Oh? I love Paris," he says.

"You have been there?"

"Well, just once. But I couldn't believe how beautiful it was. And the women! Why would anyone ever leave?"

I stub out my cigarette and give him a stern look.

"It is true," I explain to him, "that Paris is the most civilized and cultured city in the Western world. But one must spread one's wings. I am quite happy in Tokyo. And I like very much the women here."

"Oh," he says. "Ah."

"What is more," I add, "they like very much me." And I proceed to tell him about Mitsuko. At the moment I have three women, but Mitsuko, ah, Mitsuko. . . .

We met at a small reggae bar in Aoyama called maze. I knew she liked me right away, and I explain to this Texas German named (he claims) Raoul that the reason she liked me was that I was obviously not only intelligent, but sensuous as well. It is not enough to be merely intelligent.

"Perhaps," I tell him, striking a somewhat personal note, "that is your problem. You are too much in your mind."

He squints at me and smiles again. "I'm not in my mind," he says. "I'm in *your* mind. Who says I've got a problem?"

"It is Friday night. You sit there alone, sighing into your beer. You do not look happy."

He thinks about this for a minute. "And you are?" he says at last.

"Yes. I am happy because I believe that someday I will be happy."

"Say that again?"

"Happiness," I pronounce, "is believing that one day you will be happy."

His eyes go out of focus for a moment, and then he comes back. "I'm not sure I know what that means," he says, "but it sounds good. I'd better write it down." And he takes a little notebook from his pocket and begins scribbling in it.

He scribbles for some time. I fire up another cigarette with his lighter and try to steal a glance at what he's writing. But all I can see, at the top of the page, is the word RHINOCEROS.

HELLO KITTY

Mutsumiko got on the train at Ikejiri-Ohashi, as usual, and of course I was saving a spot for her. Our school's in Kanagawa, so there are always plenty of seats in the morning.

"He isn't here!" she whispered as she plopped into the seat, craning her neck to peer up and down the car.

"Maybe he's sick," I said, and she gave me a wounded look.

Mutsumiko has a crush on a foreigner who rides in the same car on our train almost every Tuesday. It's the silliest thing—he's at least as old as her father, and I really don't see anything all that wonderful about him. He's handsome enough, I guess, in an ancient, wrinkled sort of way, but nothing like some of the tall young foreigners you always see in Omote-sando, for example, which is where this aged person gets on the train.

But Mutsumiko says it isn't a questions of looks.

"He's so mysterious," she said one time. "What kind of work do you think he does?"

"Teacher. Businessman. Bartender. What else could he be?"

"No," she said. "His hair's too long, and he doesn't wear a tie, and why would a bartender be up so early in the morning? No, he's not just your average foreigner. I think he's a spy."

"A spy?"

"A spy, or, I don't know . . . a detective . . . something like that."

I had to laugh. Mutsumiko's strange. We're friends, but it's really only because we're in the same class and ride the same train to school and, besides, neither of us is smart or pretty or funny or athletic or talented enough to be very popular, and you've got to have someone to talk to, right? We don't really have much in common otherwise, though.

She wears cute little ribbons in her hair, for example, and has little plastic cartoon characters—Garfield, Donald Duck, Snoopy, Hello Kitty—dangling from her schoolbag, and she squeals "How darling!" about seven hundred times every day. Personally, I think that once you've reached the third year of junior high school, it's time to put away childish things.

It's only natural that you start thinking pretty seriously about men when you're our age. But middle-aged foreigners? Please. Why can't she fantasize about some of the senior boys in our high school, like everybody else? It's perverse.

Maybe that's what happens when your parents brand you with a name like Mutsumiko. My name's Aya—not very original, I admit, but at least it's not Mutsumiko. I'd kill my parents if they gave me a name like that. All the girls in our class have nicknames—mine's "Petchan," thank you—but "Mutsumiko" is already funny enough, so that's what everyone calls her.

I do like her, though. She's grown on me over the past couple of years. I was thinking about that lately, and I decided the reason I like her is because she doesn't really fit in, and I don't either. The difference is that Mutsumiko doesn't even seem to realize that she doesn't fit in. It's kind of sad, but kind of endearing, too. Most of the other girls think she's a total geek, but it's as if she's not even aware of that.

I know everyone thinks of me as gloomy, but it doesn't bother me, because I know I'm not. If I don't run around squawking like a chicken and bursting into uncontrollable giggles every time a chopstick rolls over, it's only because I have a little dignity. I'm what they call a late bloomer, anyway. One of these days, I'm really going to blossom.

"Raoul," said Mutsumiko, as we reached Mizonokuchi.

"What?" I said.

"Raoul. That's his name."

"Whose name?"

"That foreigner. Last week, when you were absent? I talked to him."

"You're lying."

She swears it's true, though. She says that last Tuesday, when she saw I wasn't on the train, she sat down next to him and said, "Good morning," and asked if she could practice her English with him. She wanted to find out what his job was, but she didn't know how to ask that in English. All she found out was that his name was Raoul, that he was twenty-nine (Ha!), that he lived in Harajuku, that he was from South Africa, and that he was tired and didn't really want to talk.

We reached our station and stepped out on the platform as she was telling me all this. I still didn't believe she'd actually talked to the foreigner, until the train started pulling away and I saw him. He was sitting three or four cars down from the usual place, and when he noticed me gawking at him, he hid behind his newspaper. Poor Mutsumiko.

WRONG

I couldn't believe it when he called me. We'd only had one date, and that was more than three months ago.

We first met in a bookstore. He was looking at Ryu's latest book—glancing through it and actually reading parts of it. I'm mad about Ryu, and I was curious about what a foreigner would think of his work. So I just went up to him and said, "This book is really interesting."

I don't know what got into me. It's not like me to talk to people I don't know, let alone a foreigner. Maybe it seemed all right because he was a foreigner. I don't know. I wouldn't have thought I could ever do something like that.

We ended up going for a cup of coffee and talking, mostly about Ryu. I offered to lend him the book he'd been looking at, and we agreed to meet for dinner the following night.

That was our one and only date, and it was quite a disaster. We met in Shibuya, near Hachiko, and he took me to this little Indonesian restaurant he knew. The food wasn't very good, but the conversation was even worse. I'm too shy to be much of a conversationalist, and I think he's kind of shy, too. Or maybe he just didn't like me. It was hard to tell. He certainly wasn't trying to charm me off my feet, at any rate.

After about fifteen minutes of small talk, it was as if there was nothing left to say. He looked very uncomfortable. He kept wiping his face with the moistened hand towel, and he drank a beer in nothing flat and then ordered another one. About halfway through his second beer, his Japanese started to get a lot cruder, and he started complaining about his life in Tokyo.

I didn't know what to say to most of that. It made me feel embarrassed, and defensive, and sad, and guilty, and angry, and, I don't know, confused. I always thought Americans were supposed to be cheerful and positive, always joking, but he certainly wasn't like that. Mostly, I guess, I felt sorry for him. Here he's been in Tokyo all these years and speaks Japanese pretty well and everything, but he doesn't really fit in, and he probably wouldn't fit in if he went back to America, either.

After dinner, I told him I wasn't feeling very good (I wasn't) and said I had to go home but that I hoped he'd call me again. He seemed relieved that it was over, and I wasn't really expecting him to call, and in fact he didn't, until a few nights ago. The funny thing is that I'd been thinking about him a lot, wanting to see him. It was weird—as if I was falling in love with the person I imagined him to be.

"Mariko-san? This is Raoul, do you remember me?" I have to admit I was kind of excited when he called me up and asked me that. And when he invited me to dinner again, I said sure, I'd be delighted. I thought it couldn't possibly be as big a disaster as the first time. Wrong.

I was supposed to meet him just outside Shimokitazawa station, and I got there a little early. Picture this.

I'm standing in front of the coffee shop, with a fine rain settling on the patchwork of umbrellas all around me—people waiting to meet other people—and I'm watching the crowds pouring out of the station in waves, when finally, a little after seven, I see him hurrying down the steps. He's looking all around, and I wave to him, but he doesn't see me, and finally he goes and stands by the curb across the square.

So I trot over and tap him on the arm, and he turns and looks at me in a very strange way, as if he doesn't recognize me at first. Then he says, "Oh! How are you?"

"Fine. And you?"

"Fine, fine. Long time."

"Yes."

So I'm waiting for him to say, "Hungry?" or "Shall we go?" or something, but he doesn't say anything. He just stands there, still looking around. I think, maybe someone else is coming to join us, so like a dummy I just stand there too. Then, finally, he turns to me and says, "Waiting for someone?"

I don't know what to make of this. A joke? A mistake in his Japanese? Or does he think I've invited someone else? At last I just say, "I'm waiting for you."

Well, he furrows his brow and looks at me as if I'm crazy. "Look," he says, "I'm sorry, but I'm meeting someone here. Let's make it some other time. I'll call you."

I went home in sort of a state of shock. When I got back, there were two messages from him on my answering machine. The first was, "Mariko, I'm waiting." The second was, "Mariko, it's eight o'clock and I'm giving up. Maybe I'll see you again in Hotown next weekend."

I've heard about Hotown. It's a bar in Roppongi where foreigners go to pick up girls. I've never been there in my life.

[1994]

Mr. Robert

VIKI RADDEN

"Mr. Robert! We are so surprised! You do not look like the picture you sent. We thought you were a fat Mexican!"

A fat Mexican? Me? I'm 5'9", weigh 155 on a full stomach. Mexican? OK, I had a tan in the picture I sent in for this "Teach English in the Japanese countryside" job, I admit it. My hair's dark brown and my mother's Italian, but that's as far as I can stretch it. My name's Robert Rhys, and they thought I was Mexican? I didn't want to disappoint them; they seemed so set on having their fat Mexican English teacher.

I have to admit that I was caught off guard by Mr. Uno, the school principal's, greeting. I guess it was the 900-degree August heat and the tropical rain forest humidity. Or maybe it was the seventeen-hour plane trip from New Orleans, and the six-hour train ride out of Tokyo station. Usually I could come up with some witty barb, but my shock at the audacity of his comment left me unable to do more than weakly extend my hand for the upcoming introduction.

"My name is Seiichi Uno," he said, with a smile that covered half his face. "I am principal of Ube Nishi High School, and this," he added, turning to face the painfully thin young woman who stood next to him, "is Miss Yamagishi, our new English teacher."

I shook both their hands, wondering if I should follow their lead and bow. Miss Yamagishi couldn't seem to stop bowing, up and down she went, like an oiled buoy in deep water. I wondered why she seemed to turn her eyes demurely away from me when I looked at her, and why she always put her wiry hand over her mouth when she talked or laughed. I chalked her strange behavior up to a cultural quirk, a topic on which I already felt like an expert, even though I'd been in Japan less than twelve hours.

So there I was, dazed and sweating on the platform, wishing for a moment that I'd stayed in New Orleans. I mean, how bad could it be, working for a school district so bankrupt they couldn't guarantee my job for more than one month into the school year? "If this is Japan," I thought, wiping a torrent of sweat from my forehead. . . . Little did I know at the time that the evening would only get curiouser and curiouser, stranger even than the introduction.

Mr. Uno, who I guessed to be in his late fifties, wore a frumpled plaid jacket at least two sizes too big for his bulky frame. Both his wrinkled shirt and his jacket were soaked through in the stifling, muggy air. His smile was no vision of beauty either: crooked, decaying teeth seemed to gape out of his mouth. It didn't bother him though; he was always ready with a smile as we headed out of the train station turnstile. Miss Yamagishi, in her pale pink skirt which hung emptily over her nonexistent hips, scurried alongside us, giggling at every possible opportunity.

"Mr. Robert," said Mr. Uno as he lifted my bags into the trunk of the gray Toyota sedan, "we hope you will like the apartment we choose for you."

"I'm sure it will be fine."

"Maybe it is not so big as your American apartment. Japan is small country. You will have VIP seat, Mr. Robert," he said, opening the door of the passenger seat.

"Thank you," I told him, wincing as the scorching car seat warmed the back of my thighs as I sat down. "It certainly is hot in Japan," I said feebly, to no one in particular.

"Yes, Japan is very hot in summer months." Mr. Uno adjusted the rearview mirror and cautiously backed out onto the street. "I think Japan is more hot than America, isn't it, Mr. Robert?"

Japan hotter than America? I didn't know what to say. What part of America? I didn't know whether he meant Juneau or Jackson, Phoenix or Boston. I hesitated. Mr. Uno turned to wait for my answer. "Yes," I replied vaguely, "Japan is hotter than America."

My answer seemed to satisfy him. He nodded his head and drove on.

The Toyota, air conditioning blasting out cool bursts of relief, plodded through the countryside: endless green fields of rice on one side, stands of new bamboo bracing themselves against the firm green hills on the right. A white heron, ignoring the scarecrow flapping its arms in the early evening breeze, landed proudly and stood erect in the center of a ripening paddy. Sensing a sign of life from Miss Yamagishi, I turned to face her. "What's that smell?" I asked, wondering about the smoke billowing up from a roadside paddy.

Miss Yamagishi cleared her throat quietly. "The farmers," she said in a near whisper. "They are burning trash for their farms."

This burst of English speaking gave her the courage to go on. Leaning forward in the seat, she inched closer to me and spoke again.

"Mr. Robert-san, I have once been to America."

"Is that so? Where did you go?"

She began counting on her fingers. "In 1987."

"Isn't that nice," I crooned. "How long were you there?"

"By airplane. Package tour."

"Oh?" I replied, stretching the vowel sound as far as it would go, sensing I'd better slow my speaking down a bit. Enunciating clearly, at a snail's pace, I asked, "And which cities did you see?"

Mission accomplished. "San Francisco, Los Angeles, Las Vegas, the Grand Canyon, New York, Niagara Falls, and Hawaii."

"Oh, my," I said, raising my eyebrows, truly impressed. How did a hardworking Japanese schoolteacher take enough time off for a vacation like that? I'd heard the Japanese felt lucky if they got a week off each year. "Did you do a homestay on a summer holiday?"

"Eh?" Her head was tilted to one side, while her hand rose almost instinctively to cover her mouth. She hadn't understood my question and was becoming nervous. I'd slipped back into my natural speaking speed.

"Homestay?" I repeated.

She shook her head. "Vacation. Vacation only."

I was thoroughly impressed: all those cities, all those cultural interchanges. . . .

"Eight days," Miss Yamagishi added finally.

"Eight days!" I said. "You saw the west coast, the east coast, Las Vegas, the Grand Canyon, and Hawaii, all in eight days?"

"Yes," she said. "Very busy. We Japanese must work hard, even on holiday. We have not much time to travel, so we must see many things in only a few days."

"Yes, I understand." One thing I did not understand, I realized after we'd been on the road a few minutes, was where we were going. I thought it would be rude to ask, so I didn't. We were on a small two-lane freeway; finally Mr. Uno turned the car and headed down a narrow road.

"Mr. Robert," he began, "we will have welcoming party, small welcome party at our school. After that we will go to my home for eating dinner."

"Thank you." I couldn't help being disappointed about the evening's schedule. The last thing I wanted to do was go to a school reception where chances were I'd feel even more self-conscious than I felt then; I just wanted to go to my new apartment, take a bath, and go to sleep, that is if I could actually sleep, in the heat. I wondered how the other teachers were going to react to me. Did they all expect me to be this "fat Mexican"? "Is the school near here?" I asked.

"Yes, very near."

"Mr. Robert?" he began again, turning his head at an angle so that the last rays of sunlight flashed wildly on his protruding gold tooth, "You are thirty-four years old?"

"Yes."

"And you are from New Orleans, in Louisiana state?"

"Yes, that's right."

"New Orleans is the home of American jazz."

"Yes. You're right."

"And are there many Mexicans in New Orleans?"

I sensed trouble. "Uh . . . no, not so many, I don't think."

"Do you have the, what do you call it, discrimination? Discrimination of Mexican?"

"Well, yes, I suppose. I mean . . . I guess. I-I don't know exactly, since I'm not Mexican."

A shriek of disbelief from both of them, in unison. "You are not Mexican, Mr. Robert?"

"No, I'm not. I mean, well, my mother's Italian, so that makes me one-half Italian, and sometimes they have dark hair, but no. I'm not Mexican."

Mr. Uno turned to face the startled Miss Yamagishi. They mumbled something quickly in Japanese. Then Miss Yamagishi giggled again and said, "Oh, Mr. Robert-san, when we receive your picture about the English teacher, almost all of the teachers said, So, Mr. Robert Riley-san is fat. He has dark skin, with moustache. We think you are Mexican man. They have moustache. And we think you are very fat. In your picture your face looks very big. But Mr. Robert-san is not fat," she finished, suppressing a giggle. "You are very thin. Oh, Mr. Robert-san, teachers will be very surprised. They think you are fat Mexican with long moustache."

"Yes, Mr. Robert, we Japanese think American man is tall and big, like Cary Grant," said Mr. Uno, turning to regard me intently. "You are small like Japanese man."

"Yes," I replied. I felt deflated; my heat-logged, humidity-riddled, jet-lagged brain failed to come up with any other polite way to respond. "I'm not very big."

With one turn of the steering wheel we headed through the massive iron gates into the schoolyard and parked close to the door. I glanced in the window and saw three pairs of eyes gazing out at me. I stepped from the car, wondering what was going to happen next.

"So, so, so," Mr. Uno said, chuckling as he opened the front doors of the school. "A fat Mexican."

I stepped into the teacher's room as Mr. Uno and Miss Yamagishi held the doors wide for me. I suppose, in light of the day's events up to that point, I should have been prepared for the sight that greeted my astonished eyes.

The teacher's room wasn't too large: there were about twenty desks arranged in rows, and four of the teachers stood at a desk in the center, bowing at me. What made me return their gap-mouthed stare was the decorations shouting at me from every corner of the room.

The room was done in a Mexican motif. It was Grade A tacky. A flag of Mexico hung on the center wall; red, white, and green streamers adorned every corner. In the center of the room, hanging from a string, was a huge *piñata,* a yellow donkey with twinkling red eyes. The three teachers at the desk were all wearing black velveteen *sombreros* and *serapes.* "*Buenos dias, Señor Robert,*" they all said in unison, bowing again.

"Thank you," I said, wiping a fresh stream of sweat from my brow. Not wanting to appear completely ungrateful, I turned to Mr. Uno for support, some hint of what to do. They had gone to a lot of trouble and expense to set up the whole show. . . .

The same toothy grin covered his face as he approached to do the introductions: There was Mrs. Ebisu, a short, round-faced woman in her fifties, in a red plaid straight skirt with white slippers. This woman *had* to be someone's grandmother. From the look on her face, I thought what she wanted to do was hug me, but she bowed deeply instead. "Mrs. Ebisu is our school servant," Mr. Uno explained. Next was Mr. Abe, a tall lanky fellow wearing blue Adidas sweat pants and a T-shirt with Japanese writing. His eyes focused on me only for a moment; they seemed to be everywhere in the room at once. He did everything quickly, the blink of his eyes, the short crisp bows. He said, "I am English teacher and Physical Education teacher." Last was Mr. Ikeda, an English teacher whose cool relentless gaze left me wondering if he would be friend or foe during the coming school year. "Pleased to meet you," he said with an almost imperceptible nod.

I went over their names in my head: Mr. Abe, Mrs. Ebisu, Mr. Ikeda, Mr. Uno, and Miss Yamagishi.

An awkward silence descended on the room, though only for a moment, after the introductions. Mr. Uno looked across to Mrs. Ebisu, said a few sentences to her in Japanese. She and Miss Yamagishi said in unison, "*Hai!*" They both excused themselves and scurried off in their white plastic slippers, with Mrs. Abe leading the way.

I was left alone with the men. I cast a quick glance at the garish decorations, wondering what was waiting for me, hoping it was innocuous.

Mr. Ikeda, so smooth in his blue pin-striped suit, lit a Marlboro and directed a few sentences to Mr. Uno, in Japanese.

"Yes," Mr. Uno soon replied. He turned to me. "Mr. Ikeda says you do not resemble your picture."

Mr. Ikeda, directing his gaze toward his boss, once again fired off an even longer string of unintelligible sentences. At first, I thought he was shy about speaking English to me, but Mr. Abe, the P.E. teacher whose eyes roved so quickly around the room, set me straight after several exchanges in Japanese between the surly Mr. Ikeda and the principal. He showed not a speck of shame as he announced, "Mr. Ikeda does not like Americans. And," he went on, smiling like he was about to let us in on a juicy secret, "Mr. Ikeda wanted a girl teacher." He laughed and directed a few words in Japanese to Mr. Uno.

Mr. Uno laughed. "That is right, Mr. Robert." He moved a little closer to me and said in a quieter voice, so the women wouldn't hear, "Mr. Ikeda is very happy about English teacher program from America. He told me, 'get a beauty'—he wants beautiful, young girl English teacher. Blond hair. Blue eyes. Long legs. Tall. So maybe he is disappointed."

Great, I thought, looking at the man who refused to direct any comments to me. I had an urge to punch him, or better yet, take the *piñata* and break it over his head.

Soon I heard the scuffling of slippers on the ancient gray tiled floor. Mrs. Ebisu and Miss Yamagishi, her skinny legs protruding like toothpicks from beneath her pink skirt, had come back, carrying trays with snacks. Miss Yamagishi set the trays of drinks, short glasses filled with ice and cold brown rice tea, on the table in front of us. Mrs. Ebisu cut the tiny chocolate cake and gave us all a piece. The cake was good, in an ultimately unsatisfying kind of way. Just so. It was sweet. It was also chocolate, and so beautifully adorned, wearing its white chocolate shavings like a diamond tiara. But it had no substance. Like eating tiny bites of chocolate-flavored air.

After she served the cake, Mrs. Ebisu pulled out a small 35mm camera, and shot a roll of film. I'm serious. Not five or six shots. An entire roll of film. Me in the *sombrero*. Me without the *sombrero*. Me with the *sombrero* and the *serape*. Me holding the *piñata*. Me with the women teachers. Me with the men teachers.

Seemingly on cue, as soon as the cake was eaten and the tea drunk, the two women leapt up, stacked the dirty dishes neatly on their trays and took off. The three men stood talking to each other for a while, leaving me free to explore the room, look at the chalkboards, with their cryptic messages scrawled in Japanese hand, the little kitchen just off the teachers' room, where Mrs. Ebisu and Miss Yamagishi were drying the last few glasses. It was an old country school, with no modern amenities: no carpet, no air conditioning. I wandered the room slowly, taking in my new office for the coming year. It looked almost like the teachers' room back home, I couldn't help thinking—books stacked too high on overcrowded desks, leaning dangerously, like the Tower of Pisa, cups overflowing with pens, a saucer on one teacher's desk, dotted with a few bread crumbs. The collective din of the cicadas was almost deafening when I passed by the large open window. The sight of me startled one resting on the windowsill; it flew into the room, heading for the light, crashing into it time and again.

Miss Yamagishi and Mrs. Ebisu were back, tidying the room. Mr. Abe ambled over and said to me, "Do you have cicadas in America, Mr. Robert?"

I smiled at him. "Yes, we do. I used to play with them when I was a boy."

"I also did that," he told me.

Mr. Uno's staff instinctively gathered around him as he said to me, "We will go now, Mr. Robert. We will go now to my home for eating dinner. Mr. Ikeda is busy tonight, and he cannot eat with us. Are you OK?" he asked me.

I gathered he meant, "Are you ready?"

"Yes, I'm ready." At least there was one thing to be thankful for. Mr. Ikeda would not be joining us.

"Oh, Mr. Robert," said the P.E. teacher, as he bounded away, "do not forget your *piñata*."

"Thank you," I called after him. I wondered if any of them knew that a *piñata* was supposed to be broken, by someone wearing a blindfold. I cradled the yellow donkey in my arms after he lifted it from its perch. The papier-mâché covering scratched my arms, but I held it tight, looking into its red eyes. It seemed almost animate to me, and I felt a pang of pity, thinking of the poor *piñata,* trapped in a box on its long trip across the Pacific, then locked in a dark room of a musty old schoolhouse, waiting. Waiting. And finally on its big day, its coming out party, to be carried home in the arms of a foreigner, an American in Japan, a foreigner carrying a foreigner, the metaphors of Mexico still locked tight inside its muzzle. Metaphors of Mexico trapped in yellow papier-mâché.

"Let's go now," Mr. Uno said, as the teachers began walking to the door. Mr. Abe with his long legs was the first outside. I followed him; the sun was going down; the darkness of my first night in Japan was descending. The cicadas hummed, more quietly now, in the oleander.

"Mr. Robert," said Mr. Abe, looking at me with the wide eyes of a young man just out of college. "Do you have fish in America?"

I smiled, more to myself than to him, then looked again into the donkey's shining red eyes. I ran my fingers lightly over its rough skin. "Yes," I answered him. "We do have fish in America."

Mr. Uno unlocked the doors and we climbed into the car, with me once again in the seat of honor. He eased the car onto a road lit by the flashing neon of a pachinko parlor, and we drove off into the night.

[1993]

Ghost Stories

LEZA LOWITZ

All of her foreign women friends were witches. That's what Yukihiro, her Japanese lover, said. She could hardly argue with him.

Was she a witch too? He wondered. He was a writer who lived alone in an old wooden house near the fish markets on a twisted street, and she was his first lover. He wrote love stories, but every time he tried to write about her the page stayed blank.

The street had once been filled with such houses but was now lined with shining white mansions, huge lighthouses in the quiet neighborhood pond. She wondered what the street had looked like when all the houses had been like his, but when she watched the fishmongers in their thick rubber boots fill their tubs with water she could no more imagine the lives of the past than she could envision the deaths of the future.

She had never been with a Japanese before. Everything seemed new, mysterious, otherworldly. Except the fishmongers.

She watched the men catch the slick brown fish in their fists and hammer sharp nails through their heads and slice their bodies with thin steel knives, slicing them so quickly there was no time even for regret. She wanted to live like that, but then she had met Yukihiro.

"Little sister!" the men called out to her sweetly in the morning when she passed. "Where are you going?"

They knew. They knew because they talked to her softly as if she were a mermaid with delicate ears, and when she answered, "Here and there" they nodded their heads deeply, not looking up from their work until she had entered the gate to her lover's home.

Yukihiro was from a small village in the Ryukyu Islands and wore his hair in a ponytail and dressed in old silk kimonos and went out at night to collect bones from the fishmongers to put on his veranda. Bones for the stray cats who came seeking shelter, came every night to his apartment while he wrote love stories.

The old man who'd lived in the house before him had been a taxidermist, and when he had died there was no one to inherit the two-hundred-year-old family house, no one to sweep the tatami mats and change the white paper in the shoji screens or get rid of the animals, their bellies sewn in perfect stitch. And then there were the stories. He never finished them, never finished anything he wrote.

Yukihiro loved the cold blue eyes of the stuffed animals, their skin soft

but not warm, like a fish so expertly sliced into sushi that its heart still beat
on the cut flesh: alive but not living. She had come to this country with
nothing, and they had met in Ueno where she had gone to see the lotus
flowers of Shinobazu pond in full bloom. Two months ago, he had stood
beside her for a very long time taking pictures of the flowers. She could
feel the eye of his camera on her but she looked at the white flowers in the
still water and did not turn to him. Finally she began to walk away and he
followed her, asking her what she thought the pond might look like when
the flowers disappeared in the cold winter air. All she said was *hai-iro*,
which sounded to him like "hero" in painstaking English, but what she had
really wanted to say was *gray*.

That day, Yukihiro had taken her to the noodle shop on the edge of
the park where Mori Ogai had written *Wild Geese* a hundred years before.
There was a bicycle leaning against the shopfront, and in the middle of
their meal it had fallen over with a clamor. She had jumped slightly but he
pushed her back down with his hand. Then he invited her home.

The first thing she saw at his house were the birds high on the shelves
with the books, looking down on the ripped white paper of the old shoji
screens that wore their sharp tears like scars. Fox and eagle and sharp-
toothed viper. Animals of prey, bewitching things. He always took them
down.

The books in his room: English, Japanese, Russian, Czech.

She saw him all through the spring when the lotuses were in bloom,
but they did not sleep together until a month after they had met. His confession: he had masturbated to the pictures taken of her in Ueno Park, and
the first time he had her legs tangled in his he feared he could not love the
real her. Her confession: she knew he could, and would.

She wanted him to make love to her and not the image he had cap-
tured of her. *Without fail*, he said in the way Japanese sometimes do, *without
fail. I will learn to love you*, he said. But when she stayed at his house he slept
all day and apologized. She took the books down from the shelf. He had
written down famous phrases in the margins of the complicated philo-
sophical novels and moral quandaries that made up his thoughts but not his
dilemmas. She did not know if he understood the other languages, or if the
books were dear to him too, and she almost gave up hope.

Virtue is its own reward and *We can no more guarantee the continuance of our
passions than that of our lives*, he had scribbled. She did not know if he
understood the words and she stared at them for a long time while he slept.
Perhaps she didn't understand them either. When he awoke, she closed the
books and could not help but think that the words he had scribbled were
meant for her. But then again, Yukihiro was a modern man and a supersti-

tious one at that, so he had left the animals where the old man had placed them, and she made sure to put the books back in the shelves the same way she found them.

He could read English perfectly but could not speak it at all, his tongue having been meant for better sport. When they kissed, his body impressed itself upon her with its human needs, like the cats that had come to the veranda. To be needed! To cry for milk and say feed me!

She wondered what kind of life of the mind a man like that could have when he bit her nipples rapaciously and ate her diamond earrings as if the very spirit of the abandoned cat purred inside him and called out to be taken care of each time his lips met hers. Still, he could not love her, and this made her desire him all the more.

He told her his friends said all he ever wrote about was love, but she was to learn that he had no greater chance of writing about love than one of the stuffed animals had of suddenly springing to life.

He liked the fact that she lived on faith and had a certain nostalgia for the old days neither of them had known. *Natsukashii*, he said. Nostalgia. Longing. But he didn't really know her, and she knew even less of him.

She liked the fact that some day he wanted to live in her country, and that he was afraid of the water but slept with a full glass by his bed just the same. It was not often she fell in love at all but soon she could think of no one but him, this man who lived among dead animals and old words like some bridled and beautiful aesthete.

He, who said he had never known a woman, had held her with such passion she could not believe him and wondered why there was so much to be said and no way to say any of it, not a word. And yet she thought he understood each muscle speaking its own tongue silently in the night between them.

But he had not.

Finally, he was able to make love to her. He was insatiable and ferocious, and she thought he might break her. But she could not be broken by love.

From that point on, whenever she called him he was not at home. He did not call her for many weeks, and then, late one night he called her, telling her a strange cat with a haunted face came to him like a refugee.

He named it after the god of drunken revelry. Dionysus. Drunk, was he, when he named it thus? Or did the stray cat who had crept onto his veranda and into his room represent some inimitable recklessness inside him clawing to be let out, or in.

Perhaps it was a modern incarnation of the *preta* in Buddhist hell, destined to wander at the gates of its fiery inferno for a scrap of food, drink, love. No, it was just a stray cat, she decided. He was the one in hell and he would draw her down into it and she would go, willingly. Still he would not see her. He said he could not see her anymore, so she crept into his house and took the books out, one by one, when he went out on his daily walks to photograph the small crooked streets.

She discovered that he put a green stuffed toy beside the cat, a soft round figure, a Japanese comic-book character, a senseless thing. She imagined that the cat loved the toy and had returned to it every night, meeting its false warmth with true affection.

Then one day he noticed his books had disappeared and he put Dionysus in the whoosh and whirl of his washing machine, turning and spinning underwater while he sat on his bed and held the blue sheets in a ball in his fist and laughed at his perfect cruelty. Then he placed Dionysus on the shelf with the others, a still life, *memento mori* of all he had failed in.

Then he sat and waited for her to steal into his house. When she did, he grabbed her and slammed her up against the books and made love to her fiercely, holding her up against the bookshelves, her legs wrapped around his slender waist. When they were both satisfied she sat next to him and asked him to hold her, but he would not. Instead, he told her what he had done to the cat, pointing up to its lifeless figure on the shelf.

She yelled at him: Had the cat known the rounded soft features of its lover to be inhuman? Was it wrong to love something that could not return your love? No, she said, its crime was to have given witness to a love the man himself did not have—even if that love were no more real than the women he imagined making love to in the videos he carried home in silver aluminum bags at night, after work.

He said he could not believe that such beautiful women would act in pornographic films. She said she could not believe such a beautiful man would watch them, and she asked him to watch them with her and let her see what he saw. But he did not.

She supposed that in his school days he had studied the animal world: genus, species, etc. As for her, she and her classmates had pinned animals alive to small corkboards and cut open their flesh and peered inside the small yellow veins at the thin sacs of muscle and heart to see what made them work.

Forgive me, said the man who had once loved the cruel blue eyes of the stuffed animals. *Please*, he said softly, you are foreign, and I am Japanese, as if the differences were greater than that of books and animals, and we cannot be together.

Did you not know that before? she demanded, did you think I would become Japanese?

Shiyo ga nai. It can't be helped. For him, that was enough.

She went swimming in cold blue water to wash him from her skin. She felt herself disappearing in the water, but then she heard his moans like music in her ears and suddenly the waves she made pulled her deeper and deeper into the knowledge that he had lured her to him only to abandon her on this strange island, like Theseus leaving Ariadne on Naxos. Surfacing, she noticed for the first time the three bruised finger marks on her thigh like a paw print where he had picked her up from the couch and carried her to the wrinkled blue sheets of the bed where they would stay all night but would not sleep.

She tried to forget about him, but she could not.

One night she dreamt that Dionysus came to her door, his fur wet and matted like muddy hay. She dreamt that she poured him some milk and when he drank it his tongue scraped against the bowl like sandpaper, and she was surprised to find that she had quickly grown to love him. She, who hated cats. She took him in, and from then on, he became hers in her dreams.

Soon it was December and the winds blew in, sweeping up sand and the stench of the fish from the market and drawing her back to the park where the lotus flowers were dying and the impossibly thick leaves had turned into themselves, turned gray.

She gathered some in her hands and walked to Yukihiro's house, her feet burning into the ground like an arsonist's torch to dry wood. All of the stray cats in the city seemed to follow her through the twisted streets in search of a scrap of food, drink, love. But like her, they found none.

When she got to the old wooden gate she knocked, then pounded on the door but he did not answer. She knocked and knocked but there was no sound of life, so she broke into the house which was empty. There on the shelf were the photographs he had taken of her. She held them in her hands as if they were images of a dead girl and let them fall to the ground.

Yukihiro had been right, she was a witch, and now she would return to that element, to the water from which she had been born, no time even for regret.

Leaving, she passed the fishmongers'. She waited until their backs were turned to step one foot after the other into the tub of water, looking into the sharp light of the gray blade that would soon be held above her in the fishmonger's steady hand. She turned into an eel and the blade fell upon her as sharp as Yukihiro's stabbing into her, and then she disappeared.

Yukihiro came home to find the photographs on the floor. He went to the lotus pond to find her, but all he could see was the still, murky water. He stayed at the park until nightfall wondering what it felt like to be needed! Cry for milk and feed me! He knew he had lost her forever, so he stopped by the fishmongers' on the way home and picked up some bones for the cats. When he got home he tried to write a story on the piece of newspaper the day's scraps had been wrapped in. But he could not. He knew the pictures were looking at him. He knew she would go back to the country she had come from and he already missed her, thinking only of her flesh against his and wanting her more than he had ever wanted anything in his life.

He walked out into the night and looked out for passage in the light of the huge white mansions that lined the street like lighthouses in the quiet neighborhood pond. There was nowhere to go after all. Soon after that, he returned to the Ryukyus and married his childhood sweetheart, but when they made love he thought of the American. When he was with his wife, he had to pull away from her and run to his study to write.

From then on, he only wrote ghost stories. And he wished he could tell the American; he finished them all.

As for her, she would return his unborn child to the earth and tie a red apron around a small stone statue in its memory. Over time, the apron would fade like all the others.

[1994]

Casualties

ALEX KERR

In Sanda Yoshio's neighborhood in Kobe, there is a large pub-restaurant that survived the earthquake. It stands alone in the middle of an empty block that used to be crowded with shops and houses, and since it is the only cheap drinking spot in the area, it is very popular with students and salarymen relaxing after work. Recently it is the setting for Yoshio's stories.

Yoshio has been telling me stories since I first met him when he was eighteen. I have never seen him in Kobe or with his family, so I don't know if any of what he tells me is true. It seems improbable that one youth should have so many adventures, when the chance of adventure in well-behaved modern Japan is relatively slight.

On the other hand, Yoshio is a complete outsider. His family owns large plots of choice Kobe real estate, making him extremely rich. So his life will not follow the typical career path of most of his fellow students—university, salaryman, retirement. In addition he has lived abroad, speaks English and French fluently, and likes foreigners—all of which sets him up to have adventures.

Yoshio looks ordinary enough. He's short, round bodied, dark skinned, and wears his hair cut short to his round head. On his flat face, heavy lids swell over his eyes, reducing them to half moons from which the black irises look out, half-obscured. The eyes of a spy.

His most recent story concerns job interviews.

The other day Yoshio met his old friend Higashida in the corridor of their college library. Higashida, tall and lanky, was looking his usual slightly shabby self, dressed in T-shirt and jeans. The fourth class hour had just finished; it was the end of the day. "Let's go out somewhere for dinner. Tell me all about your job interviews," said Higashida. So they set out to find a place to eat. For no particular reason they walked toward Yoshio's apartment, and there being no alternative, found themselves in the pub-restaurant in the empty block.

They took a table in the crowded smoky room, but the atmosphere between them was strained. Higashida seemed distracted. "Sure. Anything's OK. Fine," Higashida murmured, while Yoshio ordered. In the end, Yoshio chose the entire dinner; Higashida ordered nothing of his own. Yoshio could see Higashida had something on his mind. He waited.

"So how are your job interviews coming?" blurted out Higashida.

"Just fine at the moment," Yoshio replied cheerfully. After putting in a few years at some company to gain experience, Yoshio is going to take over his father's business, so he hardly cares about his interviews.

"I hear you make a better impression if you look the interviewers in the eye," said Higashida. "But I just can't do it."

"It's easy," said Yoshio. "When I had my interview with Sanwa Bank, I looked at those tired old salarymen, and I thought, 'Your bank would be declared bankrupt if the government allowed the truth to be known.' These bankers have more to be afraid of than I have," he laughed. But Higashida wasn't laughing. It struck Yoshio that Higashida's interviews must be going very badly.

"I've been rejected at several places," began Higashida. "Come on, don't cry," thought Yoshio, looking at Higashida's stricken eyes. Higashida turned his face down. He seemed to be staring between his legs. Then he coughed, and brought his hand up to wipe his mouth.

"Ah! . . ." Yoshio could say nothing more.

Around Higashida's mouth was a ring of something red and squishy. "I'm sorry, I'm sorry. . . ." burbled Higashida, as blood oozed out of his lips.

Yoshio shouted for a waiter, and they called an ambulance. Yoshio rode with Higashida to the hospital. As he lay on the cot in the ambulance, Higashida kept crying and repeating, "I'm a failure, I'm a failure."

After about an hour in the hospital, an orderly dressed in white came up to Yoshio. "What's your relationship with the patient?" he asked.

"Just an acquaintance," answered Yoshio. Which was true. He hardly knew Higashida. He didn't even know his first name. But even as he said it, he regretted it. "Is this all Higashida ever meant to me?" he thought with a pang.

"What is wrong with Higashida?" Yoshio asked. The orderly replied, "It seems to be an ulcer. He'll have to stay in the hospital a few days until his condition stabilizes. Let me take you to his room." Higashida was lying tranquilized on the bed. Even asleep, his features looked drawn and strained.

There were four beds, and only Higashida's was occupied. "Why not spend the night here?" suggested a friendly nurse. So Yoshio spent the night at the hospital.

The next morning he had to get up early to go to class. Walking away from the hospital in the early morning, his feet dragged and his head ached. He had not slept well. Somehow he survived his classes, and then in the evening he had to go to the station to pick up two friends with whom he had promised to have dinner.

Toyama and Kimura were waiting at the exit. Toyama, the plump one with glasses, always takes the role of leader of their little group. Kimura is good looking, with an angular face, and he dresses well, in expensive blacks and whites, but otherwise he doesn't have much personality, and tends to hang around Toyama. "Where shall we go?" someone said, and there was only one option: the same pub-restaurant Yoshio had been to the previous night. As they entered, the waiter gave Yoshio a curious look. As the other two sought out a table, the waiter asked, "What happened to your friend from last night?"

"They took him to the Municipal Hospital," said Yoshio, but he didn't want to go into the details. He noticed Toyama and Kimura already seated and made his escape to their table. He was exhausted from lack of sleep, and Higashida's problem still preyed on his mind. "At last I can sit down and relax," he thought. They began to order. Yoshio glanced at the hand-written menu and recognized two spots of blood from the night before. It was the same table. He tried to suggest changing tables, but his friends were already into their first two beers and were not listening.

Yoshio sat through the rest of the evening in a daze, hardly eating, while his friends drank beer after beer. The plan was for them all to talk about their job interviews, but conversation lagged. Prospects were not good. Large companies are downsizing by cutting back on the number of new hirees.

"I talked with my older brother, and he says it was completely different when he had his job interviews five years ago," complained Kimura.

"It's just a bad period right now. It'll get better in a few years. We were unlucky when we graduated, that's all," said Toyama.

"I think it's going to get worse," said Kimura. "That's what my father says." Kimura's father is a carpenter in downtown Osaka. "My father says the bureaucrats have ruined the country, and it's never going to be the same again!" Yoshio thought, "Count on the one from Osaka to come directly to the point."

Kimura had accepted a job at a local firm that builds high-rise parking garages. The pay was lower than he had hoped, and the job was anything but the elite track, but the job should be enough to afford black and white designer clothes for a few more years. Toyama set his sights higher, inter-viewing at several big trading companies and clothing manufacturers. But he had not been called back a second time by any of them. It was too depressing to talk about job interviews, so instead of talking, they drank. To Yoshio, the friends on the other side of the table, one wearing glasses, one without glasses, looked disembodied, like people in a movie.

Suddenly Yoshio broke into their conversation. "Have either of you heard anything of Higashida lately?" he asked. "No, why?" answered the one not wearing glasses. "We're in different years, so we never see him. Anyway, Higashida has no friends."

Yoshio thought back to the hospital. He had gone through Higashida's wallet, searching for his mother's number, so he could call her and inform her about his illness. He dimly remembered that Higashida came from a house with no father. A divorce maybe? As he was looking, a photo fell out of the wallet. It showed a little boy with his mother and father—but where the father's face should be there was a black smear.

He called Higashida's mother in Hiroshima, and luckily she was in. Yoshio had heard that she usually worked at nights. She seemed distracted and unable to focus on the situation. Should she come to Kobe? She would rather not, since it would be an expensive trip, and she had to work the next day. But she would come, if her son needed her. In the background could be heard the sound of a train going by. A cheap apartment by the train tracks. "He seems to be all right," said Yoshio. "The doctor says it's because he's too anxious about his interviews. He'll be out of the hospital in a week. I don't think you need to come just now. Tomorrow you can talk with him on the telephone."

Yoshio's mind was jerked back to the present. Toyama was saying, "Sanda, what's wrong with you?" "Oh, nothing. Just a lot on my mind. Job interviews. . . ," Yoshio answered. "I'm bored. Let's go to my apartment." Although his friends wanted to stay and drink more, Yoshio dragged them out onto the street.

Back at the apartment, they turned on the TV. It was showing the Thai-Japan soccer match. Yoshio's friends were soon fervently caught up in the game. "We should be able to walk all over a country like Thailand," said Toyama derisively. Yoshio began to argue. "What do you mean, 'a country like Thailand'? Don't you see what is happening to Japan? While we're going through a depression, this year China surpassed our GNP. Pretty soon people will be sneering at us and saying, 'A country like Japan.' Anyway, why get so involved in this game? Soccer is just soccer."

That comment threw a wet blanket over the rest of the evening. His friends stayed to see the end of the match—score 1 to 0, which was uncomfortably close for "a country like Thailand." Then it was time to go. "Please give me a ride on your motorbike as far as the station," said Kimura to Toyama. "I don't think either of you should be riding a motorbike," said Yoshio. "You've been drinking. Stay here tonight."

But everyone was in a fairly bad mood. There was unspoken resentment over the fact that Yoshio, heir to a real estate fortune, did not really care about his job interviews.

Yoshio had to admit that he felt somewhat superior to his friends in that their drab ambitions were not his. But, it also made him feel lonely, cut off from them. As he said to me on the telephone later, "For us Japanese, what else is there to life besides drab ambitions? If you don't share them, you're an alien." Yoshio has his own hidden agenda, which is how to avoid taking over the family business and become a writer. He dreams of writing novels and short stories. But there is a cloud on the horizon: His father has been diagnosed with colon cancer. He never voiced any of these concerns to Toyama or Kimura. But they could sense his distance.

Toyama and Kimura left. Yoshio found himself alone in the apartment. It was his first moment with time to think since the meeting with Higashida the day before. He went into the bathroom and turned on the spigot to fill the bath, and then called me.

It was an inconvenient time. I had guests. I could hear agitation in Yoshio's voice, but I was in no position to talk to him. I told him, "Eat something. Take your bath. I'll call you back in a little while."

Yoshio hung up the phone, and made himself something to eat. He had hardly taken a bite at the restaurant. The phone rang, and he picked it up, thinking it was me. But it was the police. "Hello. Is this Sanda Yoshio? Your friend Toyama has been in an accident. He mentioned your name before he passed out. Was he drinking at your place tonight?"

Instantly on guard against the police, Yoshio answered, "That's a private matter between Toyama and me. Tell me where he is. I'll come over right away." "The Municipal Hospital," said the policeman.

So Yoshio found himself back at the Municipal Hospital. Toyama was in emergency surgery. It seems that he had got as far as the station and let Kimura off safely, but only a few blocks later ran into a telephone pole. Again Yoshio had to go through his friend's things in order to find his parents' number. This time the phone call was to Okayama.

Yoshio had visited Toyama's parents earlier in the summer when he and his friends had made an excursion to see the town of Kurashiki. The Toyamas live in a large house just outside of Okayama city in an area which was once rice paddies, but is now basically a suburb. The father works at a company that sells plastic packing nets to mandarin orange farmers. The mother stays home all day keeping the house spic-and-span, and the younger sister, also plump and wearing glasses, is finishing her last year in high school.

"Hello. Thank you for everything you did for me last summer," began Yoshio innocuously. But a late night call in suburban Okayama is a momentous event. Toyama's mother instantly sensed trouble. She asked, "Has something happened to my son?" All Yoshio could tell her was that Toyama was in surgery, and the doctor said he would be OK. "We'll drive over immediately," said Toyama's mother in a fluster, but Yoshio warned her, "Don't drive yourself! Then we'll have another accident. Come by train or taxi. It's already midnight, so why don't you wait until the first train in the morning?"

She agreed. Standing in the pale greenish light of the hospital lobby, Yoshio thought about his two friends in the hospital. For poor Higashida, with his dreary family background, becoming an average salaryman was his one avenue of escape. In gray post-bubble Japan, that avenue was looking increasingly remote.

Unlike Higashida, plump, pimply Toyama seemed so normal. He had no obvious family problems. He was the sort of person who would slide through life without a hitch, practically born to be a happy beer-drinking salaryman. But Toyama was just as much a victim of his job interviews as Higashida. If he had been in a better mood, he would have agreed to spend the night at Yoshio's apartment, and the accident wouldn't have happened.

Yoshio thought of spending the night at the hospital again, but the same nurse he had seen the night before urged him not to. "Bringing friends here twice in two nights is already too much," she said. "There is nothing you can do for Toyama before his parents arrive in the morning. Go home. And don't let me see you here with somebody else tomorrow night!"

Yoshio had a little money left on his telephone card, so he called home to ask about his father's recovery from an exploratory operation. "You're father is doing very well," his mother told him, "But they found malignancies. We'll talk about it when you come home on the weekend." Yoshio hung up the phone. The worst had happened. His father's illness meant that he would have to take up his position at the family real estate company much earlier than anyone expected. The curtain had just fallen on his writing career.

Yoshio left the hospital, head reeling. This time he was too tired to walk. He took a taxi, and tried to avoid thinking of his father and himself. The taxi stopped at a light, and through the window, he could see the pub-restaurant standing in the empty block. Kobe real estate.

He saw his future: "Sanda Real Estate Co. may be worth billions of yen, but I will never see any of that money. My responsibility will be to preserve the business for the next generation. It will be much harder for me than it was for my father. Kobe is losing its importance as a commercial city, and what will happen to real estate in the process? On the surface I will be a *shacho*, 'company president,' but the reality of my life will be working long hours in a smoky office. Just like Toyama, Kimura, and Higashida." Suddenly he felt not so much an alien.

Opening the door to his apartment, he heard the rush of water. He had left the bath water on, and it was running an inch deep on the carpet! He dashed in to turn off the faucet, and began mopping the floor. Then the phone rang. It was me. And Yoshio began telling me his story.

[1995]

Is There a God in Your Heart?

MORGAN GIBSON

He was of that generation that had come to Japan seeking enlightenment rather than wealth; but the more he meditated, the more he wanted to fall in love. "Desire," he noted when he felt it, all too often; "Desire for a woman," he noted, as his meditation master had taught him to do back in Ohio. But the desire would not pass by. His mind would not stand still. The longer he sat in the lotus position alone in the little house provided by his university, near Toyota, the warmer the lust. It spread through loins, belly, chest, into his head, until his mind bubbled with fantasies. He would jump up, rush outside, and hurry through crowds of salarymen, shoppers, and students on their way to the station, trying to work off the passion; but every beautiful face turned his eyes, filling his mind with delusions. "I'm lost in samsara," he thought, staring at long black hair, "clinging to the floating world."

In calmer moments, he reminded himself that he was a sexist pig for having such desires, a hypocrite for teaching in a system in which young women were relegated to serving tea to male professors. But what could be done? He could not quit or change the system; he could not switch off his desires; and *zazen* intensified them until they were unbearable. Reading the tantras, he was convinced that the passions could become avenues to enlightenment, if only he could find a shakti with whom to unite, and a guru to show him the way. But his individualism bristled at the notion of a guru; and where would he find a tantric master near Toyota? His Japanese colleagues who taught English, all thoroughly modernized, smiled when he asked them about Buddhism. "For funerals," one said, others laughed, and that was that. On the other hand, more than once they offered to find him a wife. No thanks. He had no desire for the kind of ideal Japanese housemaid that they had in mind. He was resigned to suffering heroically in his quest for enlightenment, or for a woman, or best yet for an enlightened woman, the perfection of wisdom who would rescue him from drowning in a river of light.

Sometimes he laughed at himself, but more often he moaned. Sometimes, wretchedly lonely, he had regretted divorcing his wife in America, though her feminist harangues had become unbearable. He could not disagree with her principles: of course women should be as free as men, enjoy equal rights, and all that. But her daily nagging and his outbursts demoralized both of them, until she finally spent days and nights with her "womyn" friends, leaving him with plenty of free time to meditate. He could not possibly return to her, or enjoy life with other American women, much as he agreed with them in principle. He couldn't make love to a principle, could he? No, he had made the right decision, to come to Japan where there were, at least, Buddhist monks and nuns, temples, reminders of nirvana, though the few women, Japanese and American, who came his way scoffed at all that: "For tourists," they said.

Nevertheless, he prevailed on one of the secretaries at the university to take him on a tour of Kyoto. She dutifully complied, but knew no more about Toji or Ryoanji than could be gleaned from the tour brochure that she consulted every few minutes on the way. The atmosphere of the temples and gardens, however, intoxicated him so much that he paid little mind to the not-so-young woman, older than he, who tried her best to keep up with him as he raced from one site to the next like a hungry ghost. Entering each gate, contemplating each Buddha, staring at the stones, he felt, over and over, "This is it!" But invariably, it wasn't. He moved on, and on, up and down, with Miss Hama puffing beside him, guidebook in hand.

Sitting beside her on the train returning to Toyota, he felt a sudden let-down, a shudder of embarrassment as he glimpsed her fatigue. He had used her without any concern for her at all. In fact, he had scarcely noticed her blank face, eyes that looked as if she were always about to fall asleep, short straight hair, plain and practical clothes. Hours before, they had exhausted all topics of conversation—how she lived with her ageing parents, how she had studied Bret Harte in college, it seemed only Bret Harte, and only one of Bret Harte's short stories, which he had never heard of, how she had been taking English conversation classes at the Y for years, but had almost nothing to say. He had explained how he had come to Japan to teach, how he had been divorced in America—but he did not go into the gory details. She had periodically yawned all day, covering her lips politely as she hissed, "*Shitsurei shimasu*"; and now, beside him on the train, when the conversation flagged, she fell asleep, her head bumping his shoulder without waking her till the train stopped in Toyota.

He had never been so anxious to get away from a woman in his life. Near the exit of the station he thanked her more profusely than he felt or she deserved; and she kept bowing and thanking him so mechanically that he thought they would never separate. "See you Monday at the university," he said at last, waving to her as he walked into a men's room.

"Thank you very much for taking me to Kyoto," she was saying even when out of sight. Sitting on the toilet, he was disgusted with himself; he strained to remember her name. "Hama" at last came to him. "Miss Hama.

I must give her a box of chocolates," he thought. But he decided against it, for fear it would lead her on.

When he did in fact see Miss Hama in the English office on Monday morning, just after his first class, she was talking to a luscious young secretary whom he had not seen before. He had to brush past her to fetch his mail from the box on the wall. Her hair was curled in perfumed ringlets, pale violet eye-shadow circled her eyes, her short chic dress rustled on her thighs. "Good morning, Professor Baron," Miss Hama said, still looking fatigued from her tour of Kyoto. "Have you met Miss Yukiya?"

He dropped his mail on the floor. Stooping with the women to pick it up, he jabbered apologies, trying not to rub against Miss Yukiya as his body was tempted to do. He dropped his mail again, not entirely by accident. They stooped again, blood rushed to his head, he swooned from Miss Yukiya's perfume and seductive presence. Standing up straight at last, he clutched his mail, apologized to them, thanked Miss Hama for helping him collect his mail, thanked her for the fascinating tour, thanked her for introducing him to Miss Yukiya, thanked Miss Yukiya for helping him, thanked them again as they, bowing, thanked him for what he could not know. Backing through the door, still thankful, he bumped into the chairman of the department. They apologized to each other, dancing around each other until Baron was free enough to hurry to his next class, through which he daydreamed of Miss Yukiya as he conducted grammar drills.

After class, he returned to the English office for more mail, but Miss Yukiya was not there, and he was too embarrassed to ask Miss Hama where she might be. So he went searching for her, peering in every office, exploring the second floor, looking everywhere that was decent until at last, in an office at the end of the corridor he found Miss Yukiya at a small desk nearly obscured by a bouquet of wisteria, beside which her distinctive hairstyle, though not her face, was just barely visible.

"Miss Yukiya?" he ventured. "Excuse me. . . . "

"Professor Baron," she said, jumping up to bow at him beside the sprays of wisteria. "Excuse me."

"Excuse me," he said. "I'm sorry to intrude."

"Not at all," she said. "I am sorry not to see you come in. Please sit down. Tea?" She was already pouring it as he sat on a small chair beside her desk, trying to think of something to say. He remained tongue-tied, drinking tea, while Miss Yukiya sat demurely behind the wisteria, the sweet odor of which mixed with her sharp perfume and the odor-taste of Darjeeling. Sipping, he had the opportunity for a closer look at her lovely face. On either side of her wispy bangs her hair rippled to her shoulders, backlighted from the window.

When she whispered, "Excuse me," he was so startled that his teacup clattered the saucer.

"I'm sorry," he said.

"Not at all," she said. "Excuse me, Miss Hama was saying that you are from America."

"Yes, I taught in Ohio. Have you been to America?"

"Not yet, but I have read *On the Road*. I hope to hitchhike there someday."

"You had better be careful," he said. "You had better let someone show you around. Like me."

"Thank you very much," she said. "Do you know any Beatniks?"

"Yes, but that was some time ago."

"May I ask, were you a Beatnik?"

"Not exactly. Actually, no one likes to be called a Beatnik."

"Please excuse my poor English."

"Your English is excellent. It's just that Beatniks are a stereotype, but Jack Kerouac, Allen Ginsberg, and Gary Snyder are really unique." His throat was too dry to go on.

"It is confusing," she said, gazing at the floor. "By the way, Miss Hama was saying that you are interested in the Buddha."

"Yes, very much. Miss Hama was kind enough to show me some temples in Kyoto."

"Miss Hama is very kind," she said.

"Yes, very kind. Are you a Buddhist?"

"I know almost nothing of Buddhism," she said, blinking, as if her scent, or that of the flowers, had tickled her eyes. "I read about it in *On the Road*. I went to a Christian college, but I am not a Christian. I do not know what I am."

"You are as much the Buddha as anyone," he said hoarsely, but immediately felt utterly phony.

"Oh no," she said. "I do not know anything about it. I read the Bible in college, but I did not understand it. I sang hymns and heard lectures on Paul Tillich's theology. I did not understand it, but I hope to be reconciled to people and to god."

"You seem to be," he said. "But trying to believe in god makes many people unhappy, guilty, and maybe less loving than if they had not tried at all."

"Oh." She looked so forlorn that tears came to his eyes. "May I ask you," she said softly, "is there a god in your heart?"

"That's a wonderful question," he mumbled. "I'm really moved by the question, by you. . . . "

She glanced at his eyes, then looked down again, as if searching the carpet for an answer.

"I don't know," he said, placing the cup and saucer on the table, beside the wisteria, wishing that he had never read Henry James. He was beginning to feel like a parody. "I believed in the Christian god when I was a child, then later could not. I came to Japan to understand the Buddha."

"Is the Buddha in your heart?" she asked, looking into his eyes again with such intensity that he wanted to touch her. But he was not so foolish, in Japan.

"When I feel . . . compassion . . . perhaps you could say . . . I don't know," he muttered. "Perhaps you could say the Buddha is in my heart, but not as a god. I am sorry, I am not very clear about it. Why do you ask?"

"Sometimes, in trouble, I have been helped," she said, the look in her eyes softening. "And the person helping me remains in my heart as a god."

"How marvelous," he said, "for you to feel that, and to say it so splendidly." At that moment the eye shadow made her look more sorrowful than glamorous. He thought that if she wept, so would he. "I will always remember what you have just said, and how it has helped me," he added, feeling most sincere at last. "Yes," he went on, "you have really helped me."

"Helped you?"

"You will always remain in my heart."

"Thank you for saying that, but I must admit, right now no one is in my heart."

"No one?" He was disappointed that he had not yet entered.

"Yes, no one."

"Is your heart empty?" he asked.

"Empty of help," she said.

"I wish I could help you," he said. "I wish I could be in your heart."

"You have helped," she said. "Thank you very much. You have helped me, but are not quite a god in my heart, I am sorry to say. Do you think Beatniks have gods in their hearts?"

He was stunned. No one had spoken to him like this before. He wanted to go on, exploring, but he had to go to another class. "Gods or Buddhas or just desires, I don't know," he blurted. "I'm late. I'm sorry. I must go to class. Let us help each other. Would you care to visit my home for a longer talk?"

"You are too kind," she said.

"Please come after work. I live in the faculty house near the cemetery."

"I know."

"This afternoon, after five?"

"I am sorry, I must go home right after work today."

"What about tomorrow? Saturday: aren't you finished at noon?"

"Yes."

"Then tomorrow, for lunch at my place. OK.?"

"You are too kind. After lunch."

"Whatever you say. One o'clock?"

"One o'clock. OK."

She had not smiled during the entire conversation, but he was so encouraged that he jumped up as if to cheer, and excused himself, not mentioning that he had to run to the toilet. There, he felt that he had sunk into hell, leaving an angel floating among wisteria.

The next day she arrived at his home, but unfortunately not alone. With her was Miss Hama, looking as plain and as glum as ever. He was astonished to see that Miss Yukiya has slicked down her ringlets and ripples, even the fluffy bangs, with glossy gel, and tied a pony tail with a pink ribbon. Her checked shirt and blue jeans completed the imitation of someone she must have seen in an advertisement. Though he was repelled by the looks of both women, he ushered them in with cheery welcomes and sat them on his sofa, while he perched on a straight-backed chair, too embarrassed to look straight at them. When he glimpsed at them, they were casting their eyes down.

"Are your jeans from America?" he asked Miss Yukiya.

"They say Levi Strauss on this label," Miss Yukiya replied.

"Neat," he said. "In America, you know, they would be torn and faded. Often," he added.

"Is that so?" Miss Yukiya said, looking as melancholy as she had behind the wisteria. Miss Hama stared at the coffee table.

"Your hair's different, too," he lamented. When Miss Hama glanced up, he said, "Your hair is the same, Miss Hama. Lovely as ever. I meant that Miss Yukiya has changed hers."

"I thought this would be more American," Miss Yukiya said, smoothing her bangs back.

"They're quite smooth," he said, nostalgic for her perfumed ringlets. "But still beautiful, of course."

"I'm thinking of cutting it very short, like a boy's," she said.

"Why would you want to do that?" he shouted. The women quivered. "I mean," he added softly, restraining himself, "why destroy your crowning glory?"

"I saw a photograph of a model with a crude cut," Miss Yukiya said.

"A crew cut?"

"Forgive me, a crew cut, like a soldier's. She was a girl with almost no hair. I was touched."

Miss Hama's mouth twitched. Miss Yukiya went on, "I want to purify myself, like a nun."

"To find a god in your heart?"

"You are making fun of me," she whispered.

"Oh no, I meant nothing but respect," he said. "Sympathy. I would help you if I could. But I don't seem to be getting anywhere, in my quest. I don't even know what I am looking for. I don't know how to help, except to say that your hair is too beautiful to cut. I liked it yesterday."

"Curled? But it is such trouble. Even with a perm I must set it to make it just so, the way it was yesterday. Such bother."

"But it was amazing. I fell . . . " He caught his words.

"You fell and dropped your mail," Miss Yukiya said.

"Yes," Miss Hama added. "It fell on the floor."

"I am sorry," he said, so annoyed that Miss Hama had come along that he thought he had better compliment her to mask his wish to show her to the door. "You were so helpful, Miss Hama," he said.

"Oh no," she said, covering her mouth and looking at Miss Yukiya.

"Helping me pick up my mail," he went on, "and every day helping me understand the rules of the university, and showing me the temples. What would I have done without you?"

"Oh no," she said, hanging her head.

"Oh yes," he added, masking his annoyance as he spoke, "you have been just indispensable. Much more helpful than the faculty."

"Oh please," Miss Hama gasped.

"Oh yes, you deserve a promotion. You should be on the faculty."

"Oh no, I am just a secretary and always will be. I am lucky."

"You are very . . . " he said, lowering his voice as he leaned toward her, "special!"

She was breathing heavily, as if he were taking off her clothes. Stroking her ego, had he gone too far? Letting her recover, he turned his gaze on Miss Yukiya, whose severely slicked hair and clothing could not diminish her natural beauty. "You are both very beautiful," he added.

"Oh no," they said in unison. "Please."

"Oh yes," he said, nodding his head emphatically. "The two most beautiful women at the university."

"Oh no," Miss Yukiya said. "My brother is much more beautiful. He plays in a rock band. He wears silver eye-shadow and blue lipstick. His hair hangs down to his waist. He spends every Saturday morning in a beauty saloon. He is the most beautiful Japanese person I know."

"I can't believe it."

"I will bring him to see you."

"Don't go to all that trouble," he replied sharply. "I believe you. I just want you to appreciate your own beauty, to let it shine. Please don't cut your hair."

"Thank you for your advice," Miss Yukiya said, looking more down-hearted than ever. "No one has spoken of my beauty before."

"Not your family?"

"Girls are not so welcomed in Japan," Miss Hama interjected.

"Is that so?" he said.

"Boys are preferred," Miss Hama went on. "Have you seen paper fish?"

"Yes."

"They are for boys."

"Prejudice," he declared, frowning. "We call it sexism."

"Sexism?" Miss Yukiya said.

"Discrimination based on sex. Japanese women do not seem to realize how beautiful they are. Otherwise there would not be American mannequins in department store windows, all over Japan. Absurd."

"Mannequins?" Miss Hama asked.

"Big dolls wearing clothes, in the windows."

They nodded. "Some look American, some French," Miss Yukiya said.

"But not Japanese."

"We like their looks. Their clothes," Miss Yukiya said.

"Why do you buy foreign fashions?"

"We change. We are modern," Miss Yukiya said.

"Do those foreign fashions make you happy?" he pursued.

The women conferred with each other in Japanese for a few minutes before Miss Yukiya said, "Fashions must change to be fashions, but true happiness never changes. It is from gods or Buddhas in your heart."

He was struck dumb. From samsara to nirvana in a flash. He stared at Miss Yukiya, dumbfounded, as if his quest had ended. There was the strangest silence he had ever known, as if he had been struck deaf as well as dumb. Nobody moved.

Then again the women were whispering to each other in Japanese. Opening a shopping bag, Miss Hama pulled out a box which, being opened, disclosed a chocolate cake. Miss Yukiya jumped up to run to the kitchen, and before he could stop her she was filling the kettle with water. They would not let him enter his own kitchen. Miss Hama found small plates and forks, and a knife to cut the cake. Soon the trio were eating, and drinking tea, without a word.

Sipping his second cup, he watched them, wondering what they were up to, but they sipped and nibbled as if aware of nothing but tea and cake.

Had they come just to be friendly? Had Miss Yukiya imagined that he might find a god for her heart, or that he might become a god for her heart? Or teach her how to be a Beatnik? Had she worn blue jeans to turn him on, or to chill his ardor while she searched his mind? Had Miss Yukiya brought Miss Hama as a chaperon, or was Miss Hama pursuing him, with Miss Yukiya's protection? Had he gone overboard, complimenting Plain Jane Hama? Was he acting like a gentleman, or a sexist pig in pursuit of Miss Yukiya's body? Or both? He had always hated Henry James, yet here he was, ruminating in a Jamesian muddle.

"God is love," Miss Yukiya said softly, so suddenly that his cup rattled on the saucer. "I learned it in college," she added.

"Do you love?" he asked.

"Not yet eternally," she said. "Are you still seeking god?"

"I gave up seeking the Christian god in college, then sought the Buddhas, and now seek . . . I don't know . . . love, I think."

"Love is god," Miss Hama ventured. He waited for more, but she sat still as a sculpture. In avoiding her looks, had he missed out on her wisdom? She was transfixed, like one of those preserved Zen masters who had died in satori. Unable to take his eyes off of her, he was strangely aroused, certainly not with desire but with wonder, fascination, as if in the presence of . . .

Suddenly the women rose together, swept the dishes off the coffee table, washed them, dried them, put them away. Staring at the space they had occupied on the sofa, he did not even try to prevent them. They remained there, hovering over the sofa as well as in the kitchen and in his heart, simultaneously.

"Thank you for a nice talk," Miss Yukiya said, bowing with Miss Hama.

"My pleasure," he said, standing up, sleepy. "I have been very lonely. You have helped me understand a little of the mystery of Japan."

"It is a mystery for us too," Miss Yukiya said. "I have been trying to understand it through tea ceremony."

"That must be very beautiful," he said, stifling a yawn. "I have never seen the tea ceremony."

"Really? Would you like to come to my lesson tomorrow?"

"I would love to."

"Can you meet me at 2 P.M.? I will draw you a map."

He watched, enchanted, as she drew, and listened as she explained how he could meet her. Miss Hama looked on in silence. "Thank you," he said. "Now I will walk with you to the station."

"Oh no," they said.

"Oh yes."

The dusk was cold. The three walked quietly past walls, homes, gardens. The women were slightly behind him, but he could think of nothing to say to bring them alongside. Would he have felt differently, alone with Miss Yukiya? Would he have whispered sweet nothings? Touched her? Or simply wandered near her as he was doing? Alone with his thoughts he felt far from them. He looked up at the first stars. Searching for the Big Dipper, he fell into a ditch.

The women screamed and held each other, not him, as he climbed out, shaken.

"Are you hurt?" Miss Hama said.

"Not a bit," he said, so shaken that he was suddenly tired of company. They brushed him off, but their touch meant nothing to him. "That's all right, that's all right," he kept saying.

"Thank you very much for the conversation," Miss Yukiya said.

"Thank you for coming over," he said, shaking his jacket.

"Thank you very much," Miss Hama said.

"There's the station. I had better go back now," he said.

Everyone said, "Goodnight."

In the cold air, trembling from his fall, he wept on his way home, past the cemetery, ready to die. A poem came to him,

> Is there a god in your heart?
> Only one love.
> A cloud passed over the moon.

★ ★ ★

He could not sleep that night, lying on the futon, staring through a window at the cloudy sky, imagining each breeze on his cheek to be her cool fingers' caress. Questions obsessed him. Did he truly love Miss Yukiya? Who was she, really? What could he say to her? Or do? If he did, would he be fired? Could she care for him at all? And if she did, the problems would be insurmountable. "Insurmountable" echoed in his head like a mantra.

What did Miss Hama know? She was older, deeper. Did he need her more than Miss Yukiya's body? He turned both women over and over in his mind, unable to sleep. Both were insurmountable.

The next morning, depressed, he found his way to the station on Miss Yukiya's map. He looked up a flight of stairs, crowded with passengers, to the gate where she had promised to meet him. "Insurmountable," he said aloud. He just stood there, too tired to place his foot on the first step. Then he saw her, up there, looking down at him like a Bodhisattva in the Western Paradise. Energized by the apparition of her face in the crowd, he raced up the steps, two at a time, dodging the people coming down.

"Wonderful to see you!" he panted. She was in a green kimono, carrying a little brocaded bag. Her hair was gracefully coiled on the back of her head. Looking as if she had stepped out of an ancient painting, she bowed. Stunned, he bowed.

"When I told my teacher you were coming, she asked us to arrive a little later," she said.

"I hope she doesn't go to any trouble."

"Don't worry. Shall we go in here?"

She pointed to a bakery and coffee shop called La Vie de France, where they were soon sitting at a glass table among stunning young women sipping coffee and nibbling cakes. Miss Yukiya sat stiffly, with her eyes cast down, as if in meditation. He was careful not to disturb her. But after they ordered, he said softly, gasping a little, "I have never been with anyone like you. You are like someone from *The Tale of Genji*, someone the Shining Prince loved madly."

"Oh no," she said. "I am just a secretary."

"Do you always dress like this for your class?"

"Oh no," she said. "Today is a special tea ceremony. Because of you."

"I have not stopped thinking of you," he said. "I could not sleep after being with you. Now I am not quite awake, as if I am dreaming of you, the most beautiful woman in Japan, certainly the most beautiful woman I have ever seen, anywhere."

"Oh no," she said, turning her head away.

The waitress brought small cups of coffee and napkins marked "First Romance," in red.

Pointing to the words, he asked, "Have you had one?"

"Thank you," she said, picking up the napkin to dab her lips.

"I meant the meaning," he said, embarrassed but insistent.

"'First Romance,'" she read slowly.

"Have you had one?" he repeated, forcing the words out.

"I cannot say," she said, staring at the words.

As they drank in silence, he wondered what to say next. She looked so low, he wondered whether she regretted inviting him. Or was she waiting for him to make the next move?

"I wish that I deserved your first romance," he said at last, as frightened as if climbing a mountain.

"Please do not speak of it," she said.

"Excuse me, I am just confused and want . . . "

"We do not speak of it," she said, tears in her eyes.

"I am sorry," he said. "I did not know . . . your feelings . . . customs. I meant only . . . I care . . . How can I help?"

"My fault," she said. "So weak." She dabbed her eyes with a tiny violet handkerchief.

"You are wonderful, most wonderful."

"No, please," she said, looking at her empty cup, stained by a few grounds. Customers were looking at them. They must think he was a brute. Suddenly, he felt like one.

"I am sorry to trouble you," he said, wanting to escape. "Shall I go?"

"With me," she said, looking at a tiny silver watch. "Almost time for Tea."

"I would love to go with you."

"I do not know what love is," she said. "How can I find a god for my heart? To stay in my heart forever?"

"I am sure one is there."

"I have searched and searched."

"You may be searching too hard. The harder you search, the farther away your god seems to be."

"So it is hopeless."

"You might let yourself be loved," he said.

"Please," she said, getting up.

They said nothing as they walked to a small old-fashioned house where her teacher, an old woman in a plain gray kimono, opened the door, bowed them in, and ushered them into a tatami room, where they sat on the floor. His legs ached, but he resolved not to move until the end, remembering the Buddha's vow not to budge till enlightened. Then he would leave her alone. He had better leave everyone alone. He didn't belong here. He wanted up, to stretch his legs; he wanted out, to run free. Why had he presumed to live in Japan, much less become enlightened? What a fool. He had better go back to America. But he couldn't budge. His eyes stung from the pain.

The teacher whisked green tea in the bowl and passed it to Miss Yukiya, who turned the bowl, sipped, wiped it, and returned it to the teacher. Love for Miss Yukiya and from her was hopelessly unspeakable, he thought: their separateness was insurmountable. "Love" was a misnomer for madness. His thoughts clouded his vision.

When Miss Yukiya's turn came to make tea, her arms and fingers moved like those of a puppet, and her face was lifeless. He sank into despair as the bowl passed to him. The tea was so bitter that, shuddering, he dropped the bowl, which cracked on the edge of the table. "No!" he gasped, picking up the pieces of what may well have been an heirloom; but the women were imperturbable, continuing the ceremony with another bowl as if nothing unforeseen had happened as he hung his head in abject emptiness.

[1994]

Summertime

KAREN HILL ANTON

Before the real heat of summer, the rainy season came. A month of rain when all life seemed to take place underwater. Infrequently, the sun came out and the sky turned blue; a cruel reminder. As summer approached, the warmth turned the dampness into mold, a fine blue film covering everything. The tatami straw mats became unpleasant, and the futon, soaked with the mixed moisture of the air and our bodies, were as soggy as sponges.

Then the entire area would begin to crawl with bugs. And I fought them, trying to turn the old farmhouse, with its cracks and crevices, into an air-tight bug-free bunker. An impossibility. Poisonous centipedes that I feared would bite the children (the old woman had told me a grown man she knew had to go to bed for a day after being bitten) crawled out of the most unlikely places. One came from the back of a *tansu*, an old bureau we hadn't moved from the place it'd stood when we moved there; the thing was black and orange with dust clinging to each of its one hundred legs.

Summers were unpleasant. Days started out hot, and all my energy was taken up with keeping Mai and Luca cool. And dry. I hadn't known about the dry part when Mai was an infant, and had seen the skin on her neck slit neatly, and just as neatly, bleed. When I took off her kimono, the armholes of the soft white cotton were stained with baby blood. The old woman gave me a stack of cotton-gauze handkerchiefs and told me to pat Mai dry whenever she became damp with sweat; one cloth as large as a bath towel was to dry her after the bath. "Put this on her," the old woman said, handing me a tissue paper with some white powder in it. I thought it might be the root of some wild plant ground to fine powder. It was talc.

The morning was hot and I was grateful to be finished with all the house chores earlier than usual. Mai sat at her table with pencil and paper doing her "studies," in imitation of her big sister, deeply occupied. I wouldn't even peer over her shoulder for fear of attracting her attention and distracting her. I could easily curb my curiosity for the higher goal of having time to myself. Luca lay on his *zabuton*; the large cushions we sat on were just the right size to be a small futon for him. He'd been well dusted with powder and was comfortable, entertained just by Mai's presence. He was an easy baby; if he wasn't hungry or wet he didn't seem to need anything, and smiled more than he did anything else.

It was going to be a stifling hot day but the room was a sanctuary, dark and cooled by a breeze that passed through from the bamboo grove on the west side of the house.

Hardly spontaneously, but rather after looking around the room like a surveyor, I decided nothing else required my attention and that I could use the time to practice calligraphy. I'd all but given it up after Luca was born, but Kobayashi-san, Akira's mother, had encouraged me to continue. She couldn't have cared less about calligraphy herself, but she said, "Whatever brings you satisfaction, guard as precious." She'd come up to the house for the first time about a month after Luca was born, bringing fruit and a bottle of wine. She seemed surprised I wouldn't drink the wine because I was nursing, and after only a brief glance at Luca, looked through all the calligraphy papers I had lying on the desk. "Don't bother trying to get a ranking," she'd said, "You'll put too much pressure on yourself and then give up." I wasn't even thinking about rankings though I realized it would be a way to measure my progress. Especially since my teacher never talked; his way appeared to be silent instruction and I found it frustrating. In five years I could count the times I'd heard him speak. Akira's mother didn't drive and I knew he'd had to put things on hold to bring her up to the house, but after only an hour's visit, she slid her very small feet into a pair of Italian shoes and was already at the door when she said, "You don't have to nurse them forever, you know. I nursed Akira and his sister Yuriko for exactly three months; I checked the calendar. They're fine." Akira had told me his mother was a "spoiled selfish woman" who only did what was absolutely required of her; he said she'd been neglectful of him and his sister and her duties as a wife, though his father never complained. She seemed all right to me, especially when she said, "Continue your calligraphy. The children will survive. Keep something for yourself."

I'd kept calligraphy and enjoyed this moment now as I settled myself at the low desk. My inkstone was a simple but good one and I watched the slow disappearance of the characters, written in gold on the inkstick, as I ground it with water, and ink, the consistency of blood, filled the well. Applying the thick, ink-soaked brush to the delicacy of the rice paper always seemed incongruous; the black ink indelible, the paper white, light, even flimsy, had to be held down with a paperweight. Though I longed to write characters in the bold manner I admired, more often than not my resolve did not come out at the tip of my brush, and the weak strokes gave the characters a scraggly line. Sal had given me a *zafu*; this small bamboo leg-rest could be placed under the folded knees to take the weight off the legs, allowing you to sit in the traditional *seiza* position for hours. But Mai couldn't sit at her little table for hours, and no sooner had I settled myself at my writing table than it was time for lunch, nursing, and naps.

While Luca continued to sleep, Mai and I went out to the garden. Far from stalking around in shorts as I once had, I now covered myself completely; the only skin showing was my face, and that was shaded by a wide brim hat. The vegetables I'd planted, a few requisite tomatoes, cucumbers, squashes, were choked with weeds and stunted with neglect. Only my flowers smiled brightly in gratitude of the care I gave them. When we first came to the farmhouse I spent months filling successive wheelbarrow loads with rocks as large as babies.

"Mama, let's visit Aki-chan." Mai stopped playing and stood in front of me empty-handed as though she had not until that moment been busily occupied with her own pursuits, amassing the small rocks I'd piled up next to the weeds, lining them up along the thick hedge that fronted the house.

"Yes, maybe we'll go down there later," I'd said, turning to look around at her, "but Mai, please stay in the shade." She refused to wear a sun hat because she said it made her curls flat (and surely the sun hats had been designed for people with flat hair) and I could see her face heating up. As was her custom to become immediately insistent, Mai issued a "let's go now."

I took an intentional breath and tried to offer Mai an alternative to her hard-head stance. "Would you like me to fill your pail with water so you can pour it over the rocks?"

"I want to go to Aki-chan's now!" She'd gotten loud, and I knew Luca had woken up. He wouldn't cry but simply open his eyes and roll his big round head from side to side.

Mai, who had insisted she needed to have my cotton work gloves, now easily grabbed the finger ends of the gloves that dangled over her own fingers, pulled them off, and said, "Let's go."

Luca was ready to go too; his bright eyes had no sleep remaining in them. As I got him ready I remembered Esther had asked for photos in her last letter and I had answered, laughing to myself as I wrote, "Who do you think is standing around taking his picture?" The baby pictures of Arwen and Mai had piled up to the point where getting them into an album would become a project. Sal and I spent the first few months after their births with camera in hand tying to catch them in a smile. Luca smiled all the time; even when he cried his face seemed to hate to give it up. It was too bad we had almost no photos of him.

Normally I would have carried him on my back, but it was much too hot and humid to think of skin touching skin and I put him in the stroller. The Ishikawas' house was just a few minutes walk downhill from ours, but by the time we got there we were all in a sweat.

The old woman's mother, the real old woman, sat on the *engawa*, the veranda bordering the house. Her knobby hands were all knuckles. She held a large sharp knife and carefully sliced something I couldn't identify. At their house food was always in some stage of transformation, moving from its present stage into some other manifestation, usually pickled, sometimes dried. In the late fall it'd be *fuki*, and nothing about the long thin strips draped over a pole in the yard hinted at the fact that they were edible. Often dried shiitake mushrooms, browned and shriveled, were spread out on a mat looking like a hundred ugly toads.

"*Dozo*," she said, nodding for us to enter. Old and soon to die, she had dispensed with all the other unnecessary words.

We stepped into the entranceway of the kitchen, and as the earthen floor and dark wood interior enveloped us in a welcome coolness, the very idea of bright sunlit rooms seemed alien and foolish.

The daughter-in law came out to say Aki-chan would be back soon. He ran from house to house in the village on his own, and most of the places he went were the homes of relatives.

"I'll just wait here for a minute," I said, declining an invitation that hadn't been offered. The daughter-in-law smiled at Luca and said a few words, but he was already fretting, and the smile that was usually embedded in his fat cheeks disappeared. Now he was crying. I lifted him out of the stroller and patted and talked to him but I could already tell he was not going to accept comfort. I hadn't seen her move, but the daughter-in-law was no longer in the entranceway and had no doubt passed into or out of the house to do some chore. The great-grandmother's shadow had gone by, and I knew she was no longer on the *engawa*.

"Mai, hand me one of those handkerchiefs from the back of the stroller." I felt more like saying "Go for help." Luca, now a deep rose and howling, squirmed uncontrollably in my arms.

"When is Aki-chan coming back?" Mai asked, as though the moment were hers.

I sat down on the wooded step that led into the inner house and tried to nurse him; it was too late, he wouldn't take my breast and stretched his legs and arms their full length in an effort to be free of me. Totally distressed, he would not be soothed and the dark foyer was now a hell filled with the energy of his cries.

I'd never seen him like this, had not known he had the passion for these tears. I stretched him out on the wooden step and changed his diaper though it was dry. Angrier now, indeed outraged, he cried louder. Now his distress was mine and the tears rolled down my cheeks in quiet uncontrol.

"Come," the old woman said as she bent over me. She'd come into the foyer, her feet as silent as cat paws in her soft-soled working shoes. Quickly

unfastening the hooks at the back of the canvas tops, she slipped them off
and led us into the cool darkness of the front room. She left and soon
returned with a frosted glass of plum juice and honey. "This will make you
feel better. Drink it."

Luca, now sucking and calm, was falling asleep in my arms.

"He was too hot," the old woman said.

Mai sipped the cool drink served to her in a pink plastic cup and ran
outside when she heard Aki-chan come in the yard.

I sat with the old woman for awhile. She made herself a cup of green
tea and now seemingly completely refreshed, prepared to go back in the
field.

"Take your time," she said, indicating I could sit there.

Less than half her age, I was being told to rest while she went to do
heavy physical labor. I'd fallen apart at a baby's tears and now drained, was
ready for a nap.

"Oh, I should be getting back," I said, gathering my things together
and making a point to stand straight.

[1995]

The Podiatrist

DANIEL ROSENBLUM

Susan rises before dawn to make breakfast for her daughter. The autumn air is cool and sweet and not yet tinged with the smells of the city. Susan dresses in the dark and goes down to the kitchen on slippered feet. On some mornings, if the wind is blowing off the bay toward the east, she can smell the sea. This morning Susan is lucky. She closes her eyes and breathes in deeply the smell of seaweed and salt water. It is always comforting to her, this smell, a reminder of the ocean's soft and lolling presence somewhere beyond the hard geometry of Tokyo.

Plumes of fire fan out below a pot of water, enclosing the kitchen in a scrim of shadows. Eggs, milk, plates, cups—Susan moves gracefully around the small kitchen like a blind person who has grown comfortable with the dark.

She has lived with Koji in this house for nearly fifteen years. But Koji is not here. He is away, gone on a business trip. São Paulo, Los Angeles, Bangkok, New York. He could be sleeping on an airplane or drinking at a hotel bar. Koji is gone so often that Susan sometimes forgets he exists, and only his slippers waiting in the entryway remind her that he is real.

Eriko emerges dressed in her school uniform: pleated skirt, blue blazer, ironed white shirt buttoned primly to the neck. Her chestnut hair is braided and damp from last night's bath. Head bowed, she picks at her breakfast in silence. Eriko is fourteen.

Watching her daughter, Susan feels familiar pangs of guilt. Putting Eriko in a public Japanese school had been a mistake, but what could she do? A private school was beyond their means, and anyway, Koji wouldn't approve. Maybe Susan should leave Koji, take Eriko back to the States. Would Koji even notice they had gone? Susan wonders. She pours herself another coffee, her fingers gripping the cup for warmth.

"See you tonight," Eriko says, rising from the table. Her black school bag waits in the entryway next to Koji's slippers. There is no smile, no animation as Eriko kisses her mother. To Susan, her daughter's face is as white and expressionless as a winter moon.

Standing in the doorway, Susan clutches her bathrobe as she watches Eriko move down the short driveway. The sun reflects dully off the asphalt road. As on many mornings, Susan's heart pounds furiously. She is sure she will never see her daughter again: She is certain Eriko will be swallowed up by the vastness of Tokyo, never to return.

★ ★ ★

An elderly woman in a gray blouse and brown wool skirt arrives a little before nine. She is Susan's first patient. The woman carefully removes her shoes and lowers herself into one of the chairs in the narrow hallway.

Susan is a podiatrist, a doctor of feet. Corns, plantar warts, athlete's foot, muscle injuries, fractures, sprains, aches, bruises, ingrown toenails—these are her foes.

Susan practices from home. Her office is beyond the living room, down a hallway cramped with India ink drawings and Japanese pottery. There is a writing desk and a large diagram on the wall depicting the foot's anatomy. Next to the examination chair is a table with a tray of cotton swabs and a bottle of alcohol for cleansing wounds. A fish tank burbles in one corner; an ancient goldfish, the tank's sole inhabitant, rummages lazily along the bottom for scraps of food.

Through glass doors, the office opens out onto a veranda and a small Japanese garden where luminous carp haunt the green shadows of a tiny pond. In the spring and summer, Susan opens the doors and works to the gentle rhythms of the Sozu: the sound of water rushing to fill an empty bamboo vessel, and the hollow tock-tocking of wood against stone as the water rushes free.

And then there is Lunaire, the cockatoo Koji brought from Australia. Lunaire sits in his cage on the veranda overlooking the garden, intoning an occasional comment on the general state of things. Susan had picked the name Lunaire simply because she had liked it. Koji had wanted to name the bird Koro.

"But that sounds like a dog's name, not a name for a bird," Susan had protested.

"Yeah, but who ever heard of naming a bird after the moon?"

Susan had prevailed in the end. Koji had sulked for a week afterward, then he was gone, off on another business trip, his slippers arranged neatly in the entryway awaiting his return.

It was around this time that Susan had realized something was wrong. Koji was traveling more than ever. When he wasn't abroad he was leaving for the office early in the morning and working until late at night. At home he ate his meals by himself, retreating afterward to the back room that served as his study. Susan thought: It is Koji who has changed, not me. "Has something happened? Is something wrong?" she would ask. A look of contempt would cross his face like the fleeting shadows of clouds on a windy day. "Of course not," he would answer. "Don't be silly."

Koji went away, came back, and was gone again. Each time he

returned it was as if he had left a small but elemental part of himself behind in the places he visited. These were the parts of Koji that Susan had known. Numb and tongue-tied, she watched her husband become a stranger.

"How are you feeling today, Sugiyama-san?"

"As well as can be expected considering," says the woman in the gray blouse.

After seventeen years in Japan Susan's Japanese is as close to fluent as it will ever be. Mrs. Sugiyama tries to smile, but the lips twist into a grimace as she lifts herself into the examination chair. The chair is raised off the floor so that Susan can sit as she works, her feet tucked in beneath her Japanese style. Kneeling, she takes Mrs. Sugiyama's foot in one hand and peels back a thick protective sock with the other. Peering into the lines that loop and swirl around the sole of the old woman's foot, Susan tries to recall the last time she talked to Koji.

She remembers the night he returned from a long and difficult trip to Malaysia. That was the night he had pointed at himself and declared: "We Japanese are at home anywhere in the world."

Susan had bristled at the words We Japanese. They were words that seemed calculated to widen the gulf between them. Koji seemed to be saying to her: You are a foreigner, an outsider, you will never belong to my world. Susan had felt hurt and confused. Koji was not rejecting her because of something she had said or done, but because of one immutable fact: she was not Japanese. It was this impersonal quality that pained her most. And what about Eriko, Koji's half-American daughter? Did his rejection of Susan extend to her? Circumstantial evidence, it seemed to Susan, said yes.

About the same time Susan had begun dreaming about the foot. In the dream, she would be working in her office or walking in the garden when the foot would appear before her. Sometimes the foot would climb into her arms and caress her breasts with long, crooked toes. When this happened, a feeling of great tenderness would wash over her, and Susan would stroke the foot and talk to it lovingly. Taking pleasure from her affection, the foot would make cooing sounds, quivering like a dove in her hands. Sometimes the foot was her foot, solidly attached to her leg. But at other times the appendage seemed to have a mind of its own, coming and going, detaching and reattaching itself from her as it wished. Invariably, however, the foot would vanish before she woke, leaving her with a feeling of loss.

Now Susan remembers: The last time she spoke with Koji they had had a fight.

"You should be spending more time with your daughter," Koji had said. "What kind of mother are you, spending your days fiddling around with strangers' feet?"

"I'm a doctor," Susan had retorted, "a podiatrist."

"You're not a real doctor," Koji had snapped back. "A real doctor doesn't waste his time stooped over the feet of old women."

Susan is kneeling over Mrs. Sugiyama's foot. Mrs. Sugiyama is talking to her, has been for some time, but Susan hasn't heard a word.

The mail arrives at a little past noon. In among the bills and carry out menus is a postcard from Koji. Dated some weeks ago, the card features a blurry color photograph of a marketplace in Thailand. "Sun very hot here. I am fine. Working hard. Mitsui contract is almost ready for signing. Hope Eriko is doing well in school." The card is unsigned. Susan turns it over several times as if looking for clues. She holds the card to her nose, half expecting to smell dust, spices, and sun-ripened vegetables, but there is only the faint odor of paper and ink.

Susan eats lunch at her desk. She eats quickly, not tasting her food. There is paperwork to be done before the afternoon patients arrive but she can't concentrate.

Looking around the room, Susan feels a tremendous sadness. How ordered her office is, with everything in its place. She knows this orderliness should comfort her, but instead she finds it depressing. Scissors, shears, knives, razors—the tools of her trade are in their proper places, tucked away in locked drawers and behind latched cabinets. They are the dangerous things that Susan knows must be hidden but not forgotten: They are the things that cause pain.

Susan feels the sudden urge to find Eriko at school and bring her home. "I know it's been difficult for you," she will tell her daughter. "I know."

A few oblique remarks had been made by the occasional ill-mannered child. Perhaps there also had been some overt cruelty—taunting and teasing by some of the children—but whose childhood didn't include some of that?

On bad days Eriko comes home in tears. "Everyone hates me," she cries. At night Susan can sometimes hear her pounding her fists against the walls of her room.

But it is the silences that bother Susan most—the long quiet periods that stretch out for days when her daughter will haunt the house like a mute ghost.

At the breakfast table one morning, Eriko said, "Can Dad come to school with me sometime?"

"Why?" Susan had asked.

"To prove my father really is Japanese."

Will Koji call tonight? This is the question Susan asks herself as she washes her hands. Once he telephoned from Italy. He'd been drinking, and his slurred words came careening through the crackle of the long distance line like the body of a dead man tumbling down a hill. Sometimes the telephone rings in the middle of the night. Susan lifts the receiver and listens in the darkness to the sound of someone listening back at her on the other end. "Hello, who's there?" she'll ask but no one replies. She is sure it's Koji calling to make sure she hasn't betrayed him, that she is home where she should be, fulfilling her duties as mother and wife.

The afternoon appointments trickle in. Mr. Shimada, a small man in his early sixties, wears a dark blue pin-striped suit, his company pin with its stern corporate logo clamped tightly onto a lapel. His socks shine out like bleached lightning from beneath his somber blue trousers as he limps over to the examination chair. Even after seventeen years in Japan, Susan is still amazed when Japanese men wear white socks with dark business suits. The little man gingerly lifts himself into the chair and begins to take off his socks. His feet don't reach the floor, leaving his legs to dangle awkwardly as they search for anchor.

"How can I help you?" Susan asks. She'd like to close early today; she is tired and emotional, and suddenly feeling annoyed that this man is demanding her attention.

"I have warts," Mr. Shimada says.

This is Mr. Shimada's first visit. He gazes out at the garden, detached and imperious as he answers Susan's questions.

"Do you have warts on both feet or just one?"

"Just the left one."

"Mind if I take a look?"

Eyes still fixed on the garden, Mr. Shimada issues a terse grunt which Susan takes to mean yes.

"When did you first notice these?" Susan asks, bending down to inspect a cluster of tiny lumps just below the big toe. It takes her just a quick glance to confirm that Mr. Shimada is suffering from a bad infestation.

"I've had problems with my feet for many years," Mr. Shimada says, looking at Susan for the first time. "I know I should have gone to a doctor sooner, but what could I do? You speak Japanese very well, just like a native."

"That is very kind of you, but nothing could be further from the truth," Susan says.

"Nonsense. You speak Japanese just like one of us."

This is familiar dialogue, and although Susan finds it wearisome, she has learned to play along, always giving the same self-deprecating reply. If she really spoke Japanese fluently, she knows there would be no need to flatter her. In Japan, she has learned that silence equals respect, and the truth of one thing or another is rarely relevant.

Mr. Shimada clears his throat. "Recently I have had to miss my regular golf game, the pain has become so unpleasant. That is why I decided to see you, Doctor."

Standing, Susan removes a pair of surgical gloves from the cabinet. When she received Mr. Shimada in the waiting room and he passed her his calling card, Susan had recognized the red diamond emblem on the card right away as belonging to the rival trading company that Koji so often talked about. Mr. Shimada is the Fukushacho, the Vice-President—a very important man.

No doubt there is a Mrs. Shimada somewhere, Susan is thinking. She wonders if Mr. and Mrs. Shimada are still in love, or indeed if they ever have been in love. They might be estranged but still living together, going through the motions of married life for the sake of appearances. Susan has known many Japanese couples who live that way, couples of *omiai*, arranged marriages, where social rank and family pedigree matter more than love.

Years ago, when she first came to Japan, Susan remembers thinking how Japanese women had seemed like ciphers, unreadable masks. Their smiling faces, like the faces of painted dolls, had seemed to parody true emotion. Over the years Susan has learned to read these masks, to see beyond their bright exteriors. Slowly she has learned these women's languages, and slowly she has discovered that she is just like them.

Susan slips on the surgical gloves and faces Mr. Shimada. He is a slender man, thin almost to the point of being frail. Sitting there in the examination chair he seems more like someone's kindly grandfather than a mighty executive. For a moment she marvels at how such a small man can hold so much power. And then anger rises inside her—anger at Koji for abandoning her, anger at herself for passively standing by. Susan wants to scream until her lungs burst, but she can't utter a sound. Rage surges from her stomach and lodges like a stone in her throat, filling her mouth with all the sourness of hatred and self-pity.

When Susan speaks, the words sound to her as if they are coming from far away.

"Shimada-san, I'm afraid the treatment I have in mind will be rather painful."

Mr. Shimada shifts uncomfortably in the big chair. For a moment it looks as if he may say nothing, but then his mouth begins to move.

"You're the doctor," he says.

Susan fixes a fresh blade on the tool she uses for excising warts.

The fact is that she can either burn Mr. Shimada's warts out with silver nitrate and cut away what remains with a razor, or she can use painless but time-consuming method of applying medication that will dissolve the warts away.

Susan takes Mr. Shimada's foot in her hand and examines its many lines and creases closely. It is a well-worn, well-traveled foot, with sandpaper calluses and deep crevasses. She has never before felt pleasure at the prospect of hurting a patient. Inflicting pain has always been part of her profession, an unwanted companion she has tried to keep at a safe distance. But now a strange excitement runs through her body as she tries to steady her trembling hands.

The knife goes in deeper than it has to.

Later, Susan knows, she will feel ashamed.

A fine mist gathers on the old man's brow; his eyes stare out at the garden, as if searching for something in the foliage.

The silver nitrate eats the flesh of the wart, exposing the raw skin below. Susan breaks this last barrier easily with her knife.

Mr. Shimada bleeds surprisingly little.

After ten minutes of cutting to make sure all visible traces of the virus are gone, Susan applies more silver nitrate.

"This is to make sure I didn't miss anything," she says.

Mr. Shimada doesn't seem to hear her, though. He is taking the pain stoically like an old Japanese soldier, never flinching, never speaking a word, his eyes fixed on the garden.

Half an hour later, his left foot swaddled in bandage, Mr. Shimada leans heavily on his chauffeur as he hobbles to the black Toyota that will take him back to his office.

At five o'clock a loud speaker in the park calls the neighborhood children home for supper with the first few notes of an unfinished melody. It is a song for the faithful, an invitation to prayer. There is the wail of the sweet potato vendor wending his way along the narrow side streets. Housewives appear from doorways to make a last few purchases from a man selling vegetables out of a truck.

It is night when the last patient leaves and the waiting room is empty.

Exhausted, Susan turns the lights off in her office and closes the door. Out in the hallway, she wearily lowers herself into one of the chairs. It had been a bewildering day, and she is unable to think about making dinner or the myriad other tasks she must perform. It only now occurs to her that Eriko is late, that her daughter should have been home from school an hour ago. Somehow Susan does not find this fact alarming. She is too tired to feel much of anything.

Maybe Koji will call tonight, Susan thinks, resting her head on the chair and looking up at the darkened ceiling. If he does, she knows what she will say: She will tell him she is leaving to go back to her country.

Susan closes her eyes. The darkness feels so good. She knows that tomorrow morning, if she is lucky, there will be the smell of the sea.

[1993]

Wakanomiya

CHRISTOPHER BLASDEL

A gravel path led up the mountain from Nara to the door of a wooden hut surrounded by trees. The last rays of the setting sun filtered through the structure's walls, faintly illuminating a solitary profile poised deep in contemplation.

He knew from the activities in the village below that they were preparing to come get him. After all, it was that time of year; the harvests had been gathered, the firewood was cut and stored, and the frost line was slowly inching its way down the mountain. Soon the nights would grow very cold, and he had already noticed that his visitors—the few that came his way—were dressing more warmly and were moving more briskly through the forest. He also knew their numbers would increase over the next days, until the night when they all arrived with their torches and the official summons.

Although he went down the mountain only once a year, it seemed he had been doing it for a very long time. Right now, however, he couldn't recall exactly why. Each year, before his journey began, he recognized the sounds and smells which wafted up the mountainside from the village. The villagers were working on the feasts and entertainment. This part he remembered very well; it was meant for him.

During the days of waiting he often recalled what the previous feasts had been like: table after table of the best the village could offer, fish brought in from faraway coasts, nuts and mushrooms from the forest, bales of the finest rice, fresh winter fruits, brightly colored cakes, and great barrels of local sake. The food was always tasty, and the villagers took great effort to arrange each serving on individual trays of fresh cedar carefully festooned with red, white, and golden bands. Then with great ceremony and fanfare they carried and set it before him. He had been told by the old ones, long ago, that it was the food of his ancestors, made for him each year with a specially kindled fire of pine shavings set smoldering by the friction of a string and crossbow.

The space they provided for his village sojourn was always the same; a small grassy area, half-way between the mountain and the village, surrounded by the old pines and new, hastily constructed tents. His vantage point faced south, and from it he could see the sun rise over his mountain home and set on the village below. From here he could also get a good look at the villagers who came up to greet him. There were the children who regarded him with a fear-tinged awe, the ruddy faced boys and girls who were too busy looking at each other to notice anything else, the village merchants trying to appear pious, and the wizened elders who were the only ones who seemed to see him. He loved gazing and being with these people, though he long ago stopped trying to recognize any faces; he was given only a short time—a day and a night—to be among them.

Through the years, however, he noticed gradual changes in the villagers; changes which made him happy but also worried him. Certainly they seemed more content than before. They were well fed, and no one looked hungrily at his food as they had so often in the past. The villagers' clothing had also become richer. He was amazed at the many woven textures of soft, colorful materials with intricate designs. Before, only the wealthiest priests or land barons could afford such attire, but now it seemed even the laborers enjoyed sumptuous garments.

He also admired their increasingly handsome faces; elongated noses, fine lips, and brows arched in an expression which seemed through the years to have gained in worldly intelligence and happiness. In spite of their laughter and merriment, however, he sensed in many a deep and dark discontent. He wanted to think about this some more—did they themselves realize it? He longed to look into their hearts to see if he could discover some clues, but he had lost that ability long ago. Or perhaps it was they who had lost the ability to become transparent to his gaze.

His thoughts turned to the ancient orchestral music which would be performed for him on the grassy arena. Suddenly his heart quickened to imagine the soothing sounds of the *hichiriki* and *sho* flutes which would accompany his trek down the mountain. The tones of the flutes, drums, and the shrill reeds always thrilled him as they pierced the still mountain night and reached deep into the forest. Listening carefully, he thought he could detect several melodies going on at once, but it was actually the same tune played slightly differently on each instrument. The collusion of melodies sometimes had the effect of sending him reeling back in time, reminding him of occasions, years ago, where several poets would gather and all recite the same poem, simultaneously but minutely out of sync. The result was that each word echoed and emphasized its counterpart, confusing the sense of linear time.

But lately he had been hearing new sounds which didn't make sense and disoriented him in a different way. These sounds didn't come from musicians playing his songs but seemed to emanate from metal containers or from poles set along the pathway. The sounds were sharp, and the rhythm, though executed very quickly and efficiently, induced a sense of leaded dullness which carried no respect for the dignity of his world or for the people who listened. Yet, he thought, these people appeared to worship these sounds as they had once worshiped his music. The tones of his music resounded in his memory long after he returned to his mountain home, the other was quickly forgotten.

After his music would be the dances, another of his beloved memories. Four young men, dressed in the finest costumes, solemnly queued in front of him on the grass and took their place on stage. With slow, concentrated movements, they danced in choreographed symmetry, re-living battles and stories from faraway lands, so ancient and remote that even the old ones could not remember them.

He remembers however, each year the same dance, the same music, and the same pathos. The dances used to be performed in firelight, but now powerful white, electric torches illumine the stage. These lights were made for easier watching, but nowadays fewer people seemed to take the time to watch, except for the omnipresent troupes of scribes who recorded the events with devices which were held and pointed at the dancers like small cannons. These scribes, however, had an extremely short span of attention and always left soon after the dances began. Nonetheless, he wondered if the dancers were not dancing for their sake rather than for his.

After the night dances had finished and the dawn had broken, he could look forward to the theater. He imagined actors and musicians slowly taking their place on the grassy stage in front of the great pine next to him. With great deliberation they began chanting, their words a simultaneous combination of narration and song. The stillness of their voices calmed him, yet there emanated a vital energy from the actor's highly measured movements. Through their masks the players seemed to speak directly to him; they spoke his language, and they knew its secrets. Their acting and dancing nourished him more than any of the choice foods. He decided that although the villagers might have become opaque in their speech and action, the actors had remained perfectly transparent behind their delicate, wooden masks.

The sounds of wood being chopped awoke him from his recollections. Yes, they were cutting the fragrant pines to make torches for the procession, he thought. This means that they will come tonight, at the stroke of midnight. He was glad for the clear weather and the half moon which would illuminate the path for the villagers. But right now it was almost dark, and he realized he must soon begin his own preparations, though he couldn't quite remember what it was he was supposed to do. He loved the music, food, and the chance to mingle with the villagers, but it was invariably confusing for him to be removed from his familiar surroundings and carried down the hill, and there were surely some new changes waiting for him again this time. He still had so much to think about, and there seemed so much expected of him.

Midnight approached. The sound of the torch-bearing procession on the gravel leading to his home grew louder, their flames brighter. Suddenly, everything became completely dark—no fires, no lanterns—and the villagers gathered quietly, solemnly in front of his doorway. There was a hush, and the men in front, dressed in white robes, began to intone a chant that recalled from somewhere deep inside him a vague longing. It was the summons, the call to life. The pine torches were again set aflame and the censers lit. He could hear the doors of his home being opened, and the sounds of the flutes and drums becoming louder, mingling with the smells of incense and pine.

Then he remembers. It is for this moment he yearns and waits; it is the moment he is rejoining the world of the living and his loved ones.

As the deity Wakanomiya is removed from his mountain shrine and carried down in the arms of the chief priest, the villagers rejoice. They know this year's festival will be successful and next year's harvest bountiful, and they know that if they become chilled from the crisp winter air, they can retire to the warmth of their living rooms and watch the rest of the yearly festival on television.

[1994]

Bloodlines

HOLLY THOMPSON

Akiko set down the iron and watched with a shudder as Carl bit deep into the peach, fuzz and all. The thought of chewing on that fuzz, like the hide of a rodent, made her wince, but Carl sat back with satisfaction and gazed into the crater left from his large bite; he always gazed into peaches as he ate them, as if he were reading them, divining even, searching for sudden revelations in the ridged inner pits. Not fond of them herself, Akiko had suggested he peel them, and in the evenings when he sat at his crowded desk correcting papers, she served them to him on a square plate in neat peeled slices, toothpicks protruding, for which he always seemed grateful. But he clearly relished a peach most like this, just reaching into a bowl on impulse and biting in. He chewed slowly, ruminating.

"We don't have these back in Ohio," he'd said once when she'd asked how he continued to get such pleasure from a white peach. He spoke Japanese well, but often used English.

"What kind do you have?" she'd asked.

"Just those little yellow ones, too much flavor," he'd said. And he was right. The summer before, several days prior to their wedding in Cleveland, he'd shown her, offered her a bite into a whole fuzzy lobed fruit, then at her hesitation pulled out a pocketknife to peel a section of skin and cut a crescent, handing it to her stabbed onto the blade tip. The taste was strong and dense. His mother had baked them into something they called cobbler, pans and pans of it, for the reception out on Carl's parents' stretch of back lawn, and later, after their honeymoon in Chicago, sliced them thin over biscuits and smothered them with whipped cream—shortcake, she'd called it. A month later, back in Japan, in their hot, dusty Kagoshima house with their furniture forever filmed with volcanic ash, Akiko, thinking of Ohio lawns and the coolness under tall shade trees, had asked Carl if she should make a shortcake like his mother's. To her surprise he protested: "Suffocate strawberries, not these."

Her own father had called him Momotaro—Peach Boy—and laughed at his infatuation with the fruit, joking that peaches would give him a long life. He'd even put up some peach liqueur and presented it to Carl, an enormous wide-mouthed jarful, the winter before they'd announced their engagement. Of course, that was before her father's forbiddance of the marriage, back when Carl was still apprenticing to her father's potter friend down the road, back when they were just dating once in a while, back when she still lived at home. Now her father refused to see Akiko or Carl, refused Akiko entrance to the family home, and forbade the family from communicating with her. Her mother insisted that this old-fashioned Satsuma streak would eventually fade, that he'd simply backed himself into a corner having once said that his ancestors wouldn't tolerate the impurity of a marriage to a foreigner or the mixed blood of the children they'd bear. "*But they'd still be your grandchildren! My children!*" Akiko could recall protesting. "*How could you disapprove of my blood?*" But her father had bellowed back, "*Who the child's mother is, is of no importance!*"

Her mother consoled her: "*Be patient. He's just nervous about a foreigner in the family. A foreigner for his youngest daughter. Don't fret; it's just a matter of time before you'll be welcomed home again.*" But after more than a year enduring her father's cold silence, Carl having even quit pottery except on weekends and taken up a respectable teaching post at the university, Akiko had her doubts.

She ran the iron a few final passes over the gores of the skirt and matching short-sleeved jacket, then carried the outfit down the hall to the bedroom. She dressed directly before the low mirror, noting by the strain on the skirt's waist-hook that she'd need to start sewing maternity clothes soon. She tilted the glass for a better angle; she liked seeing that soft bulging of her stomach, liked to turn sideways, rub it, warm it. She'd last met her mother in secret two weeks before, when she'd spilled the news, and it seemed in that short time she'd truly begun to show. She knew her mother would notice—with the slightest of glances, her mother caught everything.

Dressed and made up, Akiko carefully placed the box of sweets she'd purchased at a neighborhood specialty shop into the bottom of her large bag, and on top of the sweets two boxes of handkerchiefs. The handkerchiefs for her mother had dragonflies poised above a pattern of just-blooming water lilies; those for her father—green the shade of young bamboo, with a trunk curving up and leaves draping from the top—she'd spent a week searching for. She'd wanted bamboo, safe, a plausible gift from her mother's "friend," but indicative of her resilience should her father realize they were from his ostracized daughter; the bamboo would tell him she was bending, but hardly broken.

She hooked the bag over her shoulder and surveyed the kitchen for anything else to take to her mother, but seeing there was only a gift set of tea, one of which she'd brought the last time they'd met, she poked her head into the living room where Carl was reading an English-language newspaper: "*Itte kimasu,*"—I'm off—she called out. But instead of the quick ritual reply, Carl jumped up, rinsed and wiped his hands at the sink, then walked her to the entryway with his arm about her waist. He spoke alternately in Japanese and English. "*You're bearing up well.* I'm really proud of you, remember that. *But please, stay calm and take it easy for the baby*—our little pea pod." He placed his hand over her belly; he had a different nickname each week, reflecting roughly the size of the growing fetus. "*Give your mother my regards,*" he continued, "*and tell her to come here sometime—you needn't always hide in coffee shops.*"

Akiko blushed. He kissed her softly on the cheek, and she could smell the peach on his breath. It was a tender kiss, stirring, but because of her makeup, because of the heat already beading her upper lip, and because of her preoccupation with meeting her mother, conversations already floating through her mind, the touch felt obtrusive, and she flinched. "*Itte irasshai,*" he said. "*Itte kimasu,*" she said again, and she stepped into her summer dress shoes, and went out the door.

She was grateful for Carl's calm acceptance of their difficult situation with her parents. Though his initial reaction to her father's dictum had been quiet, tooth-grinding rage, he now talked like her mother—"He'll come around in good time"—and could even joke—"He'll miss me too much. I make him laugh." Sometimes she wondered how Carl could stand it, living in this country that was often so cold and unkind to him.

Recently he'd suggested she write a letter to her father, telling him she was pregnant, thinking that such news might move him to relent, but she'd reminded Carl that all the letters they'd sent months before, pleading for reconciliation, had been returned unopened, unread. Once in the early spring, Akiko had even ventured out to the section of river where her father frequently fished, but upon seeing her on the bank behind him where she'd been perched quietly for a full half hour, he'd pulled in his line, packed up his basket, and left, walking past her without a word. There seemed to be little hope, and Akiko couldn't help but wonder when and if all this nonsense would make Carl want to move his new family back to the States, back to easier relations.

From near the apartment, Akiko took a bus and tram into the center of the city, glad to have seats the whole way. The day before, traveling to the culture center where she taught *sumi-e*, she'd had to stand the half hour into town, dizzy and weak-kneed, nearly retching, but too shy to ask for a seat with her condition not yet obvious.

From the tram stop, she went straight to the Cafe New Rose without pausing at shop windows, partly to keep her shoes from becoming too dusty with volcanic ash, and partly because she was running a few minutes late. Her mother would already be there, she knew, waiting anxiously, and indeed, when she stepped inside and peered hard into the darkness, she found her at a rear table, several large bundles and shopping bags at her feet. "*Sorry to be late*," Akiko said. Her mother brushed the apology aside, insisting she'd only just arrived, but Akiko could tell by the empty water glass, by the unfurled washcloth, and by her mother's dry brow—long since air-conditioner cooled, that she'd been there for some time already. Akiko noted her mother's quick glance downward and instinctively put a protective hand on her abdomen. Then she tried not to sink too heavily into the chair, not wanting to alarm her mother, who, as it was, had stood with urgency to call the waitress to fetch a glass of barley tea.

"*I'm okay*," Akiko said, though the odor of something from the kitchen, cooking egg perhaps, was turning her stomach. She forced the nausea back, and her mother finally, almost reluctantly, sat down in her chair again.

"*Look, I brought you some things*," her mother said, reaching down to the bags at her feet. "*Sachiko sent these the day after she heard the news. Of course, she sent them to Teruhiko—I told him the day you told me, and he called Sachiko that night*." Sachiko was Akiko's older sister, married with two children in Kyoto, and Teruhiko her older brother, who with his wife had bought the house next door to their parents.

Her mother was breathless, opening her bags and producing samples of the contents for Akiko to see—tiny outfits, booties, blankets, and bibs from one bag, and ballooning shifts and maternity blouses from another. Akiko nodded graciously at each item but glanced around the cafe, embarrassed, glad they were at a rear corner table, and she finally persuaded her mother to replace the clothing and have a look at the menu so the waitress could take their order.

"*Oh, I'll just have the daily set*," her mother said, and when Akiko had indicated she'd have the same and the waitress had turned away, her mother leaned forward and whispered, "*Your father knows*."

Akiko nearly spat out her tea. "*You told him?*"

"*No, no, never*," her mother said laughing, though they both knew that he was now well aware that they met regularly. For whenever her mother planned to meet Akiko, she used the excuse of visiting an ailing friend Haruko. Yet after several such clandestine visits, before which her mother always prepared some gift ostensibly to take to Haruko, Akiko's father had begun making suggestions. "*Why don't you take your friend some of your shiso-eggplant pickles?*" he'd say, or "*How about some Oolong tea today?*" or "*I bet she'd like those chestnut sweets*," or, handing her a bagful, "*Some persimmons from our tree*." Her mother would agree, nervously pack up the goods, and pretend to go off to visit Haruko. But instead of meeting her friend, she would appear at a designated coffee shop or cafe and present Akiko with the sweets, teas, pickles, and fruits her father had selected—all her child-hood favorites. Akiko would take them home and open the fancy packag-ing or *furoshiki*, sometimes tasting with tears the morsels that were all she now had of her father, other times, bitter, throwing them straight into the trash.

"*You see I called Teruhiko before your father returned from gateball*," her mother was saying, "*and of course he called Sachiko. But then Saturday, I guess it was, Teruhiko came over to help move that old sofa out to make room for a new one, and when they'd finished the moving and were sitting down eating some watermel-on, Teruhiko just brought up rather casually—he's a clever one, that Teruhiko—that he'd heard from your old friend Megumi that you were several months pregnant.*"

Akiko smiled at her brother's guile. "*Well, and what did Father say?*" she asked.

"*Well, I was in the kitchen, mixing Calpis drinks, so I couldn't see his face. I had to act surprised, of course, so I brought the Calpis in and sat down, excited, as if this were the first time I'd heard, too, and I asked questions, you know, if you were well, if he knew if you'd had morning sickness, when the due date was—and when your father heard the winter date, he said, 'February. Is that so? Boy or girl?' And Teruhiko and I laughed and said no one knew that yet. Then your father grunted and changed the subject. But he didn't get angry. And lately several times I've seen him staring at nothing, just staring, then he'll look hard at me, and I'll ask what, but he shakes his head. Oh, I just hope he stops his foolishness so you can return home in peace for the birth.*" The waitress came back with bowls of miso soup, and Akiko's mother took a hot, airy gulp, then caught her breath.

Akiko hadn't really pondered those details yet, under the circum-stances, the complexity of receiving her mother's care before and after the birth in the comfort of the family home. She sipped her soup and stirred the cubes of tofu up from the bottom. She'd just assumed she'd be able to return, assumed that all would be normal by then, always pictured herself recuperating in her old room, under her quilt with her favorite cotton cov-er and with the branches of that old pruned pine tree just outside her win-dow sweeping against the outer wall of the house, just scratching, on a light breeze. Carl claimed to want to be present at the birth—insisting that the sharing of this beginning was of the utmost importance to a couple—and he also claimed to be willing to nurse her back to health, but Akiko knew that in February he'd be into his full teaching schedule, and that none of his colleagues would look with favor upon his taking time off to tend his post-partum wife; moreover they would frown upon her mother for neglecting her maternal duties to her daughter and grandchild.

Yet Akiko couldn't imagine this issue resolving itself in time for her to recuperate anywhere but in their apartment. For there was no grand or easy gesture with which to apologize; she couldn't very well back out of her marriage, she wouldn't reject Carl for her father's sake, and no gift would suffice, no word. And her father would never apologize either; he'd never imply that he was in the wrong. She knew that his initial outburst at the news of their engagement had been in the name of the household; he was the eldest after all, the family altar was in their house, and she was breaking with tradition. And she knew now that it wasn't so much her having married Carl that irked her father, but rather that she'd flagrantly disobeyed him; instead of waiting patiently, however many months it took, for him to agree to the marriage, she'd waited only five turbulent weeks, then defiantly gone off to the States with Carl for an American wedding. There'd been no ceremonious joining of households, no exchange of betrothal gifts, no trousseau. She could see now that she'd rushed, hurled herself blindly forward, but ever since spending a summer in a California homestay program her first year of college, and especially since meeting Carl eight years later through her father's friend and then in one of the *sumi-e* courses she taught, she'd lost her Japanese sense of timing. She felt forever out of tempo, always off just a beat.

In those weeks before she'd left home, her father had ranted about the purity of Japanese blood and the importance of ancestral bloodlines. "*Your children would have no ancestral home! And what about the bloodline? There won't be a Japanese bloodline!*" he'd shouted. But she didn't see the importance of bloodlines and pointed instead to the richness of duality, the fact that her children would have Japanese *and* American ancestors. Teruhiko was the eldest son anyway, married and likely to have children, true Yamashita heirs, and Sachiko already had children, now part of her husband's bloodline. If Akiko married a Japanese, her children would be of a different household, and she would have to pray for the comfort of another household's dead. Akiko was the youngest, a girl. What did it matter the blood of her children? The only bloodline of any import to her was the one coursing in her womb, twisting from the placenta, delivering oxygen to the little being forming in her belly.

But Akiko realized with a sadness that nearly choked her that her child might be born virtually without grandparents, with Carl's parents thousands of miles away, and her own stuck in some feudal conflict. She bit her lips to still their trembling, but she could not still the worries for her baby, who would struggle for acceptance as it was being of mixed blood in this rigid society, but who, Akiko felt, shouldn't also have to struggle for acceptance by his or her grandparents. She felt a tear well over, slide down her cheek, and couldn't help the sob that followed.

"*Ara . . .*" her mother said, promptly presenting her with a handkerchief. "*Now don't you worry. If your father's still being stone-headed when the baby's due, I'll come stay at your apartment. Or you'll come home anyway, and if your father doesn't like it, he can leave. But he'll want you to be home though, just wait and see. He'll change. Bear up, now.*"

Akiko nodded, though she knew women never told their husbands to leave. She knew it was her father's decision whether she entered the house again. But her mother was probably right: he would soften, he would want the birth to be at the clinic near their house, and he'd want Akiko to be cared for by her mother. She recalled that her sister had come home for her two births, mostly at her father's insistence; Sachiko had felt it was too far to travel, too long to be away from her husband in Kyoto, but each time she'd ultimately relented.

The waitress brought their lunches on two trays—pork cutlets, pickles, cabbage salad, and rice. Akiko nibbled, but only the rice and pickles agreed with her. Her mother prodded her to eat more of the pork, and she complied for several bites, then pushed the tray aside and sipped at her barley tea. Her mother frowned, then reached into another bag and withdrew two packets of tiny dried fish. "*Put a spoonful of these on your rice each day—lots of calcium.*"

Akiko nodded, but she didn't want to think about food.

"*Are you eating carefully?*" her mother persisted.

"*Now I am. Carl's on vacation—he's doing the cooking.*"

"*Ahhh,*" her mother said, with genuine envy in her voice. "*You found a good husband. What your father thinks doesn't matter. You're really very lucky, despite the trouble.*"

Akiko concurred, though she didn't feel lucky, just worn. And she knew that they were both well aware that what her father thought mattered completely. The waitress brought some hot tea and Akiko drank, hoping it might keep her awake until she got home. These visits had always been hard, but now with the baby growing inside her, they seemed to pain and tire her more. She felt heavy with sleep, and knew that this afternoon she'd need a nap. Some days she felt energized; on others she had to drag herself through the most basic of daily tasks—putting rice on, setting shoes out to sun, sweeping ash from the terrace, selecting fish, rubbing *sumi* ink, hanging clothes to dry.

Her mother paid the check and they left the cafe with bundles and bags dangling from their arms. They walked slowly to the tram stop and boarded together, pleased to find space enough to sit side by side. "*Are you all right?*" her mother asked repeatedly—as they approached the stop, as they stepped aboard, as they set the bundles overhead and on the floor.

"*Yes, fine,*" Akiko continued to say, though she felt weak and shaky. She wished she could lie down on the seat.

"We'll get you a taxi. You look too tired to take a bus," her mother said, and Akiko detected alarm in the quaver of her voice. She closed her eyes, not wanting to panic herself, trying to stop the blood draining from her face; her ears felt cold suddenly, her head was listing, and she was short of breath. Beside her, she could feel her mother sit up erect.

Moments later they reached the station, the last stop, and as Akiko started to disembark, she swooned. She felt the gritty wood on her knees, wanted desperately to lie down, to nap on the floor of the tram, the boards looked inviting. But her mother was lifting her up, and she felt the arms of another woman, a stranger. She saw them as if from a loft high above—struggling to collect and carry all the bundles, leading her to a bench, and then the taxi stand. Her legs could barely hold her.

But the outside air seemed to help, and by the time they were seated in the cab, Akiko was breathing more evenly. Her mother mopped her brow for her and gave the driver directions to the apartment. "*Now I'm all right, Mother,*" Akiko said. "*Really. I don't know what happened back there,*" but her mother's face remained drawn with worry.

"*Stay quiet,*" she said, and Akiko obeyed, closing her eyes, feeling for, and dreading, a wetness between her legs. She drifted into a shallow sleep until the taxi jerked to a stop.

They climbed out of the cab, and Akiko could walk on her own now, though her mother kept a supporting arm about her waist. The driver followed them up the stairs with the bags and parcels, and Akiko opened the door. "*Tadaima,*"—I'm back—she called out feebly, and she beckoned her mother to follow her inside. Carl was sprawled on the tatami of the inner room, reading, Akiko could tell at a glance, one of his university textbooks, and at the sight of her followed by her mother, he jumped up with a welcoming smile. But Akiko must have looked a wreck, and her mother's words soon twisted that smile into a grimace of concern: "She needs to lie down. She fainted on the tram."

Akiko could hear him gasp. Then he was in the other room, pulling futons from the closet, setting out pillows, drawing a glass of water, turning up the air conditioner, laying out pajamas, and with her mother, leading her to bed.

"*I'm fine,*" Akiko told them both, ushering them back to the kitchen. "*Just let me change.*" She closed the door and partition, and then, standing in the middle of the room, alone, took a deep breath. She unbuttoned her short jacket and undid the skirt-waist, fumbling to get out of her clothes. Then she pulled down her sweat-drenched pantyhose, terrified, not quite wanting to see, checking for blood; there was none. With relief, she ran her hand over her belly. From the other room, she could hear her mother and Carl talking in low undertones, and she felt like shouting to allay their fears, but she contained herself, dressed in the pajamas and put on a summer robe. Then she opened the door with decorum.

Both Carl and her mother looked up abruptly from the kitchen table. "*I'm okay,*" Akiko said. "*I just need to take a nap.*"

Her mother was studying her face. "*Nothing hurts? Nothing feels strange?*"

"*No, I'm fine, really.*"

"*Well then,*" her mother said, rising, "*I must be going. Your father will begin to wonder. Oh, I almost forgot.*" She reached into a shopping bag and pulled out a *furoshiki* bundle. "*He packed this up this morning, for Haruko,*" she said with a wry smile. "*Tomatoes perhaps. He's been talking about tomatoes all week. I was rushing so much to get the bags from Sachiko at Teruhiko's that I never peeked inside.*" Carl set the bundle on the table and began to untie it.

"*Oh, and I nearly forgot, too,*" Akiko said, and she found her bag by the entryway and pulled out her gifts—the specialty sweets and the handkerchiefs. She handed them to her mother, but her mother wasn't looking, didn't even reach out to accept them; instead she had a hand to her mouth, and a croak of surprise sounded in her throat as she watched Carl peeling back the corners of the *furoshiki*. Akiko turned to see what was inside.

Then she dropped into a chair, the faintness having returned. "*Bring me the water,*" she said, and Carl ran for the glass he'd set beside the futon. She gulped, and then he wrapped his arms around her, and she wept, the tears rolling onto his forearms. Her mother looked away, and they could hear her weeping, too. And then she was laughing. And Carl was laughing, too. For sitting inside the square of silk, in protective foam netting, were three enormous white peaches.

Carl reached around Akiko and removed some netting, and she could see it coming—that enormous bite, deep to the pit, dry fuzz and all.

[1995]

Tokyo Tremors

ALAN BROWN

What my mother did predict: The 1989 eruption of Mount Unzen in Kyushu. The big Hokkaido quake in January '93. Almost every seismic shock above a 3.5 on the Richter Scale that's occurred beneath Tokyo in the past five years.

What my mother didn't predict: That my father would walk out on us. That my sister would wake up one morning and speak to us only in Pig Latin.

Although my mother's predictions are confined to changes that take place below the earth's surface, she has, since we arrived here five years ago from California, become quite the celebrity—not just in Tokyo, but all over Japan. Last week, for instance, she and a seismologist from Waseda University taped an interview for FEN, the American Armed Forces radio station. So now we tune in on the radio, and while my mother-of-the-present is taking a casserole dish out of the microwave, my mother-of-a-week-ago's voice floats through the kitchen.

"Twentieth-century Japan is no stranger to natural disasters," she reminds listeners.

Neither is our family, I think.

Mount Unzen: For weeks beforehand, my mother had headaches and bone aches. Dizzy spells. The morning of the eruption, she burnt everything she laid her hands on: The toast. The eggs. The real American sausage patties my father's friend at the Embassy gave us for Christmas. My sister and I sat at the table and watched little volcanic plumes rise up all over the kitchen. My mother held out her hands and we watched them tremble.

"It's going to be a big one," she said.

It was. And a week later, my father left.

"I've had enough," is all he said to us one night after dinner. And then he went upstairs and packed a duffel bag.

My mother was doing the dishes. I was sitting at the kitchen table helping my sister with her kanji homework. She was two years ahead of me at St. Ann's International School, but I was light years ahead of her in Japanese.

"Enough of what?" I asked, racing up the stairs after him, hoping to make him retrace his steps, to take back his words.

Now my father lives in this two-hundred-year-old farmhouse full of macrobiotic people, out in the middle of the rice paddies in Saitama Prefecture. Everybody's Japanese except for him and two old German ladies, and they all live just like people here did back in the Edo Era, with no electricity or indoor plumbing. The kitchen has a dirt floor. It's not a religion but a philosophy, he explained to me the one and only time I visited him there. It took an hour by train from Ikebukuro, that's how nowhere it is. We went for a walk in the fields and played frisbee like we always used to. And then we talked while I helped him weed the vegetable and herb garden out back. Everybody in the house has these assigned chores for each day of the week. Although I do miss my father a lot, I will now only meet him somewhere, like at Shinjuku Gyoen on a Sunday afternoon, or in Shibuya for Thai food. But I won't go back to that house again. It was too depressing: All of these grown men and women living like nothing good has happened in the world in the past two hundred years.

And my sister. After we came to Japan so that my father could teach Early Music at Sophia University, and before she moved out, Sheila and I would whisper to each other at night when we were supposed to be asleep. We'd whisper through the thin wall that separated our bedrooms in our little house here in Meguro. We'd play word games, like "Geography" and "I Went To My Grandmother's House." Now Sheila is married to a Japanese policeman. I don't know if she speaks to him only in Pig Latin or not. The only way we even knew she was married was that she sent us a postcard from her honeymoon in Guam. My sister still writes in English.

Me. At the moment, I am between motor scooters and girlfriends. So I spend a lot of time sitting at the kitchen table with my mother, dreaming up ways to make money, which is her favorite topic. Unfortunately, predicting earthquakes and volcanoes doesn't pay the rent and my mother can't tune into the stuff that does: The stock market. Death.

Now my mother tells me what she thinks: That when I graduate high school in the spring, we should pack up everything and move back to America, but this time to Hollywood.

"Can't we go back home? My friends are still there."

"I know that, Honey. But Hollywood's where the big bucks are in the fortune-telling business." She turns off the radio. The interview is over.

Home, Foster City, is where all of our family's troubles started, where my mother first discovered she could read fault lines like some people read palms. So I could understand why she might not want to go back. But I read the American occult magazines she subscribes to, and I point out that the field is all sewn up in Hollywood.

"Stars like Goldie Hawn and Cher already have their personal psychics," I say. "They're not going to switch."

She passes me the Cranapple juice chicken and I scrape what's left onto my plate. Cranapple juice chicken is my favorite and she always cooks it for me on special occasions, even though she has to go all the way to Aoyama to buy the juice and it's more than ten dollars a bottle here in Japan.

"Besides," I remind her, "Dad wants me to go to college. He said he'd help pay."

"Sure. Your dad's a bigshot," she says. "I could give them a free reading. You know, the first one for free so they'll try me out."

"Mom, no offense, but Cher's not going to try you." I watch her slide a cake box off the top of the refrigerator. I pretend that I don't know what's up. "Anyway, what are we talking about? You don't do past lives."

"You're right," she sighs.

According to her magazines, past life readings are very big right now in Hollywood. And my mother, she can't even read the life we're in right now. She even forgot my sister's birthday, which was last month.

My birthday, though: It's tonight, and suddenly there's this big yellow cake covered with eighteen burning candles on the kitchen table. "Happy Birthday, Jeff" is engraved with blue frosting in my mother's handwriting and the flames light up her face as she sings to me. When she's finished, she hands me a small, heavy box wrapped in yesterday's *Japan Times*.

"Here's your present," she says.

I open it. A crystal ball.

"Mom?" I pick it up. The candles on the cake are still burning and the flames dance inside of the crystal ball as I roll it back and forth, and weigh it in my hands. "This is for me?"

She shrugs. "Sure. Why not? Maybe you can see something in it that I can't. Maybe it's the ticket."

"I don't think so." I put the crystal ball down.

She's waiting for me to blow out the candles and so I bend forward, huff, puff, and out they go. I make a silent wish for things that I know it is just too late to wish for.

"I read that these things are often inherited," she says. "Come on. We'll have some cake and then we'll give it the old college try."

I cut the cake and my mother gets beers from the refrigerator. It's a cool, rainy Friday night. I have no school tomorrow and nowhere in particular to go, so we take our time. We talk about what we call our "financial picture."

My mother has the Debi Dawn Cosmetics franchise in Japan, and she sells door-to-door here in Meguro Ward. Because she's a blonde American, and because the Japanese housewives she visits don't understand anything she's saying and are too polite to say no, she's amazingly successful. Her most popular item is the Alo Vera Anti-Wrinkle Formula, which Debi

Dawn promises will make your face look ten to fifteen years younger in just thirty days. When she has more than one beer, my mother likes to practice her sales pitch on me, which she does now.

"Throw your clocks and calendars right out the window. You'll scoff at time when you're looking and feeling like a young woman again," she says, holding up her beer bottle like it's a jar of skin cream.

"Sounds great. I'll take a case," I say, but she ignores me. She's on a roll.

"Debi Dawn's Anti-Wrinkle Formula contains a miracle of modern science, the 'moisture magnet,'" she says. "It's powerful enough to draw water right out of the air. And that's just what it does for your face, while you walk, eat, or even while you sleep. Plump with moisture, your damaged, ageing skin will become as smooth as a baby's you-know-what."

"I'll take ten cases," I say.

"Your husband or boyfriend will thank you for this." She puts down her beer bottle and sighs. I think she needs cheering up so I take the crystal ball out of its box and say, "Ready?"

"Ready as rain," she says.

I get up and walk toward the front door.

The doorbell rings.

"See?" she says. "I just knew it."

I open the door and a gust of wind and rain blows in my face. My sister, Sheila, is standing outside under the orange entrance light, and she doesn't move as the rain swirls around her like a tiny tornado.

"Hi," I say. We haven't seen my sister in at least a year.

"Ap-hay y-pay irth-bay ay-day, eff-Jay," my sister says. Or something like that. She's no better at Pig Latin than she is at Japanese.

We're all sitting at the kitchen table now, drinking beer and polishing off the cake. The crystal ball, still untried, is on the counter. My sister's wearing one of my mother's bathrobes and her wet hair is wrapped in a towel. She looks just like she did when she lived here, which makes me feel happy. For a while, I considered going out and leaving them alone to talk. I thought I might go to Roppongi and hang out, just to see what was up, see if my fake I.D. would get me into one of the discos. I might have run into one of my old girlfriends there, or maybe even found a new one. But now I think I'll stay home.

My sister has left her husband, the policeman. This much my mother and I figure out.

"Ight-fay," my sister says.

"That's 'fight,'" my mother says. She squeezes my sister's hand. "Poor baby."

My sister sneezes and then starts to cry.

"It-hay," she says.

"That's 'hit,'" I say. "Right?"

My sister nods and I clap my hands. This is like a game show. We're good at those in this household.

"He hit you? Cop or no cop, he shows his face over here, I'll kill him with my bare hands." My mother moves her chair over and hugs my sister tight. "You tell him in Japanese that I said that, you hear me?"

My sister sneezes again.

"You caught a cold." My mother feels her forehead.

"Maybe you should try healing her," I say, and my sister and I both laugh. My mother shakes her head and tries, unsuccessfully, not to smile.

Right after we came here my mother read in one of the English-language newspapers that healing was a very big business in Tokyo. So she got on this kick, using us as her guinea pigs. Because there was nothing really wrong with either of us, she worked on clearing up my complexion and on the dry skin between my sister's fingers. One look at my face now and you'll know that it didn't work.

My mother gets up to put water on to make my sister a hot drink. "Your mom's a failure," she tells us.

She doesn't ever talk like this. What's going on? My sister and I both look at her as she shuffles around the kitchen, gathering up the honey jar, a lemon, the bottle of plum wine.

"Not true," I say to her.

"O-nay," my sister says.

"Yes I am," my mother says. "It's this crazy power I have. What good is it? It drove your father away." She looks at my sister. "It drove you crazy. And now here we are, the three of us, stuck in some strange country in the rain, with TV shows we can't understand. What can I say, kids? I'm sorry, okay?"

Poor Mom. "You didn't do anything wrong. It's not your fault. We like living in Japan. It's fun. And you're a great mom," I say, and at exactly the same time my sister and I both get up and go over to her and hug her. The three of us sort of dance around in a circle with our arms around each other. The kettle whistles on the stove but nobody does anything about it.

"God knows, I didn't ask for any of this," she says.

I can't fall asleep, and I toss and turn. In my right ear, I can hear the wind and the rain, and the last train of the night pull in and out of Toritsu Daigaku Station. In my left ear, on the other side of the wall, I can hear my sister cough and sneeze in her old bedroom.

Just as I am getting comfortable—I am thinking about getting up tomorrow and going to Ueno to look for yet another used motor scooter—I feel my bed move slightly.

Did I imagine it? I wait and now I realize that the rain has stopped and that everything is quiet.

Then my bed moves again: a small hop and a tilt. On the other side of the wall, I hear my sister sit up in bed.

"Eff-Jay?" she shouts.

Somewhere, a dog howls.

Oops. Another sharp tilt, and then I hear all of the open doors in the house slam shut in sequence: The bathroom. The hall closet. My mother's bedroom.

An earthquake.

Downstairs, our empty beer bottles fall like dominos, roll off the kitchen table onto the floor.

"Jeffrey? Sheila?" my mother yells from her bedroom. "Don't get up. Stay put."

"I'm fine," I shout back. "Sheila?"

"Ine-fay," Sheila yells through the wall.

Boy. I wish she'd cut that out.

And then I hear something fall off of the kitchen counter and bounce across the linoleum. It's the crystal ball. I can hear it roll out of the kitchen door and down the hallway, until it reaches our Japanese-style room and disappears onto the tatami. That's when it occurs to me: Hey, my mother didn't predict this one. We sat at the kitchen table all night long and there wasn't even a sign. I can hardly believe it. This earthquake rolled right past her.

The house hops one last time, like a hiccup, and then everything is still. It's over, all except for the crystal ball, which rolls right through the paper shoji screen and bangs into the glass terrace door.

"Whoa!" I say, and I jump out of bed, ready to head downstairs to rescue it. But then I think, So what? Who cares? I sit down and I start to laugh.

"Jeffrey?" my mother yells, and I hear her coming down the hall. "Are you all right?"

Who needs the crystal ball? I don't want to know the future. The future isn't the ticket. My mother comes into my room, and I am still laughing, and she looks at me like I am crazy. I bang on the wall.

"What?" my sister says.

"I knew it. I knew it," I say to my mother.

"Knew what?" she asks me.

"Everything. Everything that I already know," I say, barely making sense even to myself.

My sister comes into my room and sits down on the bed next to me. My mother squeezes in between us, and she puts her arms around us. Outside the window, the bright globe of the street lamp looks just like a glowing crystal ball.

And then we are moving again, only it's not the earthquake this time. I can feel the three of us traveling backward—me, my sister, and my mother, enclosed in the bubble of that crystal ball, rolling across the tatami, heading back, fast into the past, to our past life in America. Time swirls around us like a tornado.

"Jeffrey?" my mother says.

"Jeff?" my sister says. "Are you okay?"

"Fine," I say. And I look out the bedroom window and I wait. I wait for the morning light and for my father to come home.

[1994]

The Screen Man

ELIZABETH BALESTRIERI

It's that kind of day. Frozen clouds, dead center of winter, weak hint of spring from the jaded sun. A retrospective day, all that photographable snow on the roped pines, the red-blooming *sazanka*. Flowers in the snow? Karen is still not used to them.

A bird is caroling outside her office window.

The mountains beyond the tile roofs shiver with blue light.

Her fingers dangle over the keyboard as she stares at the black screen, trying to get into the life of Lafcadio Hearn. What brilliant ideas can she work up today when she'd really like to crawl back under the futon?

As she has grown older, writing has become a more dubious, less scandalous act, now that there's nothing to rebel against and all the unmentionable subjects have been mentioned.

She's sitting in the relative dark while her Japanese colleagues squander electricity to make up for past deprivations. Everything old, shabby and out-of-fashion reminds them of the starvation and frugalities of the War and/or Occupation. Few want to live in "historic" houses or collect antique furniture the way Westerners do. Every day walking home she sees bulldozers leveling beautiful old wooden homes, beautiful to her eyes. New houses and apartments springing up everywhere with solar collectors on roofs—in a country of rain? Architectural absurdities in sometimes eye-stabbing colors identify Japan's growing pains.

Her friends' latest food fad is sushi wrapped in thin gold leaf, washed down with gold-flaked sake. Or even more desirable, "longevity noodles" and gold flakes in Korean ginseng soup—eating gold is supposed to be good for your health. Karen is reminded of the '60s when people used to entertain with jumbo shrimp, Maine lobster, and imported French cognac V.S.O.P., before taxes escalated in America and so—

Such lavishness seems criminal to Karen, when in downtown L.A. more and more people are taking up residence in cardboard boxes. In Japan, though, the poor are well hidden (if they exist at all?), making all this *nouveau-riche* craving a forgivable sin, a chasing after tinsel dreams, for who is deprived?

So what does she want to write about Lafcadio Hearn, a man who remained money-poor, but never gave up dreaming the impossible spiritual dream? Why did he come to Japan, and when—

She steals another look at the mountains, otherworldly and stunning

in their snow-covered immensity. Why was she always longing for something else, more—

Her husband Sam told her she needs to live three lives to end her
restlessness.

She thinks she needs seven.

She turns on the power, calls up the file "Hearn":

"Picture books so beautiful as to exercise a magical effect on the
beholder," Hishigawa Moronobu writes in the latter part of the seventeenth century, a founder of the Ukiyoe school of illustration, Hearn says.

Is Hearn intrigued with art history or the magic of art? Why does he
always go after the unfamiliar and mystical, at the same time denying it
exists? Exasperating! Trying to catch the translator of Flaubert's *The Temptation of St. Anthony* and fix him in a biographical sketch is like trying to cage
a cricket.

Exiting that file, she pulls up an old Japanese folktale, one of Hearn's
favorites. It's soothing to read, stops the Ache—

A young scholar of Kyoto was walking home after visiting friends
when he happened to pass a second-hand shop. In the window was a
single-panel screen covered with paper. The woman painted on the screen
was incomparably beautiful. Tokkei went in and bought it for almost
nothing.

Looking at the screen in his lonely room, he found the woman as
lovely as a lotus blossom. "I'd give my life to embrace her!" he said, feeling
something he'd never felt before. Was she a portrait of a living person, or
one who died long ago?

His hopeless passion grew until he began to neglect his studies, sitting
for hours gazing at her.

Soon he fell sick from desire and thought he would die.

An old, wise scholar heard of Tokkei, wasting away over the screen
maiden. He came to see if he could be of some help.

"That picture was painted by Hishigawa. That woman is no longer
with us, but her spirit lives in the screen."

Tokkei stirred in his bed.

"You must give her a name, then call her gently every day until she
answers you."

"Are you serious?"

"Prepare a cup of sake made from one hundred drops of one hundred
different sakes. Then she will come out of the screen."

The old scholar left. Desperate, Tokkei decided to try the old man's
remedy. He called the woman "Yoshiko" (meaning "good"), his voice quavering like music from a reed flute in the hands of an unskilled player.

For days, nothing; yet he kept faith in the old scholar's advice and continued to sit in front of the screen, breathing the name, "Yoshiko, Yoshiko."

From the Kyoto wine shops he gradually collected one hundred different sakes.

One evening he took an eyedropper and extracted one drop from
each of the bottles, thinking his behavior was ridiculous. At once, he decided to abandon his pursuit. Yet he'd come this far, why not continue? And
what was life for but to perform one great act of love?

He knelt on the straw matting with the cup of precious sake in his
hand, and again called out in a love-choked voice, "Yoshiko, Yoshiko."

"*Hai*," the woman answered, stepping out of the screen. Her feet were
like pearls, hips all silver motion, breasts golden goblets, and lips formed for
kissing.

Quickly he reached for the cup of sake and offered it to her.

She knelt before him to take it from his trembling hands. "How could
you love me so much?" she asked. "Won't you get tired of me?"

"Never," he said. "I pledge myself to you for seven existences," he said,
squeezing her soft hand.

"If you're ever unkind to me, I'll go back in the screen," she said.

Karen imagined Hearn's longing to be like the screen maiden. To be able
to reincarnate at will, according to the presence of selfless love, and to fade
into non-life when scorned or abused, what a double dream of happiness!

She's seduced by this story as well. Only in this strange alpine region
where she now lives, with its ghostly mountains, its wild beauty, its never-
stable atmosphere, could she think, could she give into an irrational wrin-
kling of her mind.

Outside the window beyond the university grounds, the lowest slopes
are masked with mist and high peaks drift foundationless. A curtain of
gray silk falls over her eyes, obliterating her usual empirical way of seeing
finally—

She no longer wants to write the essay on Hearn. Her mood changes
with the dimpling of the sun, a smear of rose-pink light on the mountains,
a vision so breathstopping she feels the atoms of her heart collide—

She wants to write about her own desires which give her no peace.

She wants to explore them to kill them off.

She switches to a blank screen and types the letter "I." Then, her fingers freeze. Her peculiar reticence, a fear of revealing the murkiness of her
deepest thoughts, even to herself, has paralyzed her. Like the rabbi who lost
his faith and couldn't speak beyond the first letter of the Hebrew alphabet,
she has no confidence to continue—

Slipping out the word-processing disk and inserting "Hanako Graphics" delays real work time. The colors in the program are rich, illuminative, giving her a playful freedom beyond words. She draws a man's face, trying to make him look racially unidentifiable. Hazel eyes with violet centers, pale walnut skin, black hair streaked with red and gray. Neither Asian nor Western. The screen man appears as though dozing in the depth of wakefulness.

Karen puts her mouth against his and kisses plastic.

A sudden knock on the door shocks her back to reality. "*Hai, dozo,*" she says, exercising her feeble Japanese and—

Her friend Chao Wong enters. Karen's heart sinks, a stone in a pond. Chao, lonely and expatriated, can't deal with her present crisis. And Karen, who prides herself on helping others help themselves, can't either.

Chao's face looks like it's been stretched on a clothesline, ready to rip in the wind. Karen imagines it's the Chinese ambassador, his handing down of "new rules," giving Chao grief again and if—

Chao's student visa and her husband's are about to expire. They've finished their master's degrees in literature and physics, but Pu wants to stay on in Japan and get a doctor's. He's afraid if he goes back to China, he'll never be permitted out again.

Chao is tangled in the tormentous need to be with their four-year-old son who lives with her mother in China, and her longing to stay with her husband in Japan against government orders. If Pu starts a Ph.D., she will work to support him, sacrificing her own goals. But this doesn't bother her as much as facing a prolonged separation from her child. That makes her feel mutilated.

Chao accepts a cup of green tea and talks about Pu's latest scheme to foil government regulations.

"He thinks he should go back to China so he'll be recorded as returned, but stay only one week. He can't see our son. Too risky. He'll slip back into Japan by ship before the visa expires."

"Why ship?" Karen asks, adding more hot water to the bitter tea.

"If he gets into trouble, he has a better chance to bribe the officials."

Karen remembers the humiliating body check she had to endure via Korean Air after the Christmas break. No one under four was frisked though. She imagines an unscrupulous mother could sneak in baby sticks of dynamite under the ruffled skirts of a sweet-faced child. Which leads her to further thoughts of intrigue.

"Why don't I go to China, bring your son out as an orphan I'm adopting?" Karen realizes how naive she sounds. Chao's desperation has left its mark. "But, I suppose your mother would be in danger when they find out."

"Of course not. That isn't done anymore." But Chao's face reveals she isn't sure what's being done these days. "It's obvious they wouldn't let me bring my son to Japan so they could hold power over my husband. He's valuable to China because we have so few advanced scientists." Chao shakily puts down her cup. "I'm going to buy you some oolong tea. This green stuff is dreadful!"

Karen likes green tea. It's good for the complexion and fights off colds. Chao is in that mood of hating Japan for being too comfortable for Pu and pounding China for being too repressive.

"I love my country, but I hate its government" is her line.

Karen can relate only obliquely. Her own children, tucked away in various colleges, have it so good they can "stop out" for a semester of skiing. It's these terrible global inequities that bring nausea, the Ache back. She feels a small typhoon of anxiety rising in her chest, as if—

She scolds herself for being unhappy with the least discomfort in her life, the squat toilets, the chilly rooms.

"We could use a savior here," she says, looking at the computer to make sure it's not self-exiting. "I think Pu should stay in Japan, start the Ph.D., lay low. Maybe the rules will change again."

"If we're caught, we'll be ordered back and they'll take his passport. If we stay, and he can finish the degree before he's caught, he'll have more power in China." Chao weighs these positives and negatives the way she cooks, virtually tasting the words as she goes. "But if he loses his freedom, it'll be like death. I think he doesn't even care about our son. Only his bloody research!" Chao dabs at her cheek. A tear is slipping down her face. Another one. She cries so quietly you would never know it, if you weren't looking at her.

"I've got an idea. You have a valid working visa. Let's get you hooked up with an international trading firm that sends you to the U.S. on a buying trip. But before you go, Pu gets you pregnant. You make sure the baby's born in America. Pu could get permission to visit you. They can't say no to that, can they? Once he's in America, something can be worked out. He's a genius, after all. . . ."

"You have the craziest ideas, Karen!" The tears have stopped. "First, my government doesn't allow me to have second child. Second, that doesn't get my son out of China. There I'll be, marooned in Dizzyland with another baby—maybe no husband, and . . . you're so unreal!"

"Dizzyland, I like that!"

"Don't be offended. You understand Shakespeare, but you don't . . . skip it. Your zaniness makes me feel better, at least."

"It's not like we can weigh all the factors and come up with a compromise. We need help." Her microcomputer chooses to go. "Bleep, bleep." Its memory is warning her like—

She gets up to turn off the machine. Just as she's about to push the button, the man in the screen moves his lips. "Shush, shush," he says.

"Did you hear that?" Karen startled, turns to Chao.

"What?" Chao absently bites into a tea cake, then puts it down with distaste.

"Oh, nothing." Why reveal her tendency to "hear voices"?

The sun, lower in the sky, is leaking lavender through the mountain peaks.

"I've got some library work to do. I'll come by next week and let you know if there's any new development."

Karen hugs her. "Why don't you and Pu come for supper on Saturday. Sam might have some ideas."

"Pu loves talking to Sam. Why not? Thanks," Chao responds, listlessly as ever.

After Chao leaves, Karen feels drained of everything she wanted to accomplish. She goes to the computer again to shut it down, staring at the screen man.

His lips part. "Don't despair, she'll find the way. Those who suffer the most, find the way. . . ."

"Under a strain," she whispers, punching out the power.

Oddly, an afterimage of the screen man remains in her head, his words echo in her ears and not—

She decides to go home and watch the birds in the pond—that never freezes—in front of the house. That always calms her after a day of teaching. Perhaps Sam could be induced to fix dinner, often his way of relaxing after a day of painting in his studio.

As she walks home, the purple-falling night hides the mountains. The *sugi* trees turn black and feathery in the wintry wind. "Those who suffer . . . ," the screen man keeps sending stray words between her ears. She shivers in the damp February air.

A brown hawk rides the pale night sky, searching—

Of course, she doesn't mention the screen man to Sam. First, because he thinks computer graphics are ruining the fine art of oil painting. "We're going to go the way of the epic poets. No one will appreciate, let alone buy us."

Karen has nothing to say when he turns so pessimistic, partially because she suspects he's right. And she doesn't want to confess her growing imbalance from too-close an identification with Chao. She has always had an unreasonable empathy for people in trouble, but never before did this feeling cause her to burn out her own switches.

Sam has a smudge of vermilion paint on his chin. She smells his special spaghetti sauce. "What a good guy. How did you know I'd be too tired to cook tonight?" Karen rubs the paint, holds him close.

"Because Chao phoned asking when you'd be in your office, that she wanted to see you."

"Well, she did. I'm exhausted from it. What are we going to do?"

"It's not our responsibility to help them, Karen."

"But it's too horrible. I think she's going to off herself."

"Well, I haven't been idle. Today I wrote to Gucci at Berkeley. He has a lot of pull in international physics. Maybe he can do something for Pu."

She envies Sam's ability to take an action, then put trouble out of mind. But she has no faith that Gucci or any other big-gun physicist can alter the deeply-rooted cruelty of the Wongs' split existence.

After dinner, Karen sits on the floor with her legs stretched out under the *kotatsu*. The little heater under the table keeps her lower body warm, but above the waist she's so cold even her heart shivers. She tries to read a biography of Lafcadio Hearn, but behind the cover of the book she weaves a fantasy of bringing the screen man to life.

We think we know so much. Now it's hadrons, tachyons, quarks, and gluons, yet we still love so imperfectly. Why can't this Superforce, this World-Consciousness that the new physicists have been writing about incarnate itself in us? Why are we always at war with ourselves, or each other? Karen makes a mental note to get Wong's opinion on this. Is conflict encoded at the sub-atomic, atomic, or molecular level?

She can't wait to get to the computer, spills morning coffee on her dress, yells at Sam not to forget the clothes in the dryer in between brush strokes, grabs her briefcase and umbrella, throws a kiss in his general direction.

"Slow down before you fall down," he says, just like her mother.

The snow is falling in huge flakes, sopping-wet flower petals. When she gets to her office, she is soaked clear through her coat. She locks her office door from the inside, takes off her dress and turns on the supplementary heat source, a smelly kerosene stove, to dry off.

Sitting in front of the computer screen in her white lace-trimmed slip, little flecks of burnt fuel flying around her head and landing on her shoulders, she calls up the screen man, deciding to re-form his mouth. As she moves the mouse, he starts speaking something that sounds like old Anglo-Norman:

"oure soule bi vertewe of this reforming grace, is mad sufficient at the fulle to comprehende al him by loue, the which is incomprehensible to all create knowable might, as is aungel & mans soule. . . ."

Not fond of this sexist blurb, Karen lays on the delete key. It jams. An error message flashes on the screen. His face disappears but his voice goes on speaking out of crackling blackness:

"of the workes of God self-may a man thorou grace have fulheed of knowing, & wel to kon think on hem; bot of God him-self can no man think. & therfore I wole leue al that thing that I can think. . . ."

Words, the power of mountains. She feels like the throbbing of a giant pulse. She has a sudden desire to see his face, slips her dress on again, straightening her shoulders, pushes a couple of buttons.

His face appears.

She wants to hold him in her arms.

A knock on the door registers as a blow to her body.

"*Dozo, dozo*," she says. A young Japanese woman steps inside.

"Sorry to interrupt, but do you have time? Your chair suggested I ask for help, but I'll come back, if not free now. . . ."

It's best to cut the long string of Japanese apologies short, or you can use up an hour finding out what they really want. To Karen's trained teacherly eye, this woman appeared mildly desperate.

"Of course I have time. What may I do for you?" Karen turns reluctantly away from the computer, which oddly has silenced itself at the woman's entrance.

"My name is Keiko Makihashi. I've won a Rotary scholarship to study in the U.S., for M.A. in linguistics. I'm the first woman in this prefecture to be allowed a leave-of-absence from my teaching job for study." Keiko is wearing a Scottish plaid skirt, a cameo at her buttoned-up throat, standard dress code for young woman professionals in Japan, but her boastfulness separates her from her sister-pros. A refreshing lack of humility she'll need to survive in America.

"Well, congratulations."

"Yes, if you would please look my statement of purpose? Make sure it's right for graduate school in U.S."

"Where do you plan to go?"

"I want University of Michigan, but they returned my application. They're stopping Department of Linguistics."

"Disbanding."

"What?"

"Disbanding, not stopping. I'm surprised to hear that."

Keiko chuckles, holding her hand to her face. "It's ironic. It seems car industry is suffering so much in Detroit due to Japanese imports, money has to go to welfare and not to university. So they cut. And I, Japanese woman, cannot go there because of my country's success."

"Yes, it's ironic," Karen says without laughing.

The entire world has become a contracting village.

A new economic melting pot, but most of us are getting screwed.

"I have a class now, but if you leave your paper, I'll go over it this evening. You can pick it up tomorrow, okay?"

"Oh, yes, yes, thank you, thank you. I'm so happy. If there's anything I can do you, please let me know. I have a car, if you need to go somewhere."

Karen holds back. Once she admired a very expensive Kutani vase in a Japanese home, and the host made a present of it, despite her protests. If she wasn't careful, Keiko would give her the car when she went to the States.

"Yes, I will. See you tomorrow, Makihashi-san. *Dewa matta.*"

She swivels back to the computer. The screen man is imploring her with his eyes.

"What do you want from me?"

"*Ask not what your country can do for you, but what you can do for your country,*" he quips.

"You're out-of-date. This is the age of internationalization. We can't think in terms of 'country' anymore, that old nationalism. We've all got to pull together."

He seems to be mulling this over, then answers with romantic intonation: "*. . . his very soul Listened intensely; and his countenance soon Brightened with joy; for from within were heard Murmurings, whereby the monitor expressed Mysterious union with its native sea.*"

"What?" She recognizes this line. Not Shakespeare, but—

"*Come into the monitor,*" he continues, in prosaic English this time. "*I'm cold. Keep me warm.*"

"What? You're kidding!" she says, taking him seriously.

"*All you have to do is press the 'HOME CLR' button three times, and you'll be inside, with me.*"

Karen's mouth hangs open, catching air.

Time passes without her noticing.

She stares into the eyes of the screen man.

"*Uchi e kimasen ka?*" he asks softly, trying another language.

"You're not serious, not serious."

Suddenly, he is speaking in many tongues, his eyes growing larger, a deeper violet. "*Una esperanza—aiiiii—kokoro—ee—so desu ne—donde va—te amor—corazon—l'amour que vous me portez—una poema fidelidad—shinko—aisuru—inamorado—anshin—*"

Her fingers hover over the home-clear button. She is tempted beyond belief. Tempted? "You're really a new kind of devil, trying to seduce me with the highest of human desires. Not greed, not ambition, wealth, power, no. The promise of lasting love and world peace. A kind of devil."

"I'm not in the least a devil. Come inside and you'll see."

Wasn't there a price for everything? Shouldn't she exact a price from him? "If I do, will you fix it so Chao's son can leave China?"

The screen man is absolutely silent.

"Okay, okay. I understand, *wakarimasu*, everything. I come inside the monitor without any demands, without any knowledge of whether I can get out again. Completely on faith."

"On love."

"Yeah, love. Give me a minute, will you? This isn't easy."

Karen turns away from the screen, not wanting to be influenced by his alarming sensuality. Letting her make the decision, he remains silent.

She looks out the window, the mountains at twilight. So beautiful. She sits watching the moon float over the crest of the highest peak. Strange, as the sun has not yet set.

In another minute, she will have to choose.

[1994]

A Roasted Potato at Dusk

PHYLLIS BIRNBAUM

They always talked too loud. My relatives seemed to believe that Shiro would understand their English better if they spoke at double their normal volume and added extravagant hand gestures for key words. During that week, I had turned around on several occasions, only to catch an aunt actually shouting at Shiro in the course of relating a family anecdote he couldn't possibly comprehend.

Once, Uncle Joseph cornered my husband on the sofa at the opposite end of the living room and told him about the time his ship had docked in Yokohama. That was about sixty years ago, during his refugee journey over from the Old Country to New York. If I had not married a Japanese, I would never have realized how many people have stopped in or near Japan on their way somewhere. The postman wouldn't give me my mail until he reviewed his experiences during the Occupation; the taxi driver described his spiritual awakening as a Zen novice in Nara. Then there were the one-time Yokohama tourists like Uncle Joseph who had reached Japan on his way from Eastern Europe to America. The rest of his Polish village had taken the shorter route, and so they only had stories of the miserable conditions on the Atlantic crossing. By contrast, Uncle Joseph's journey over the Pacific provided him with endless refugee tales about Kandy, Bangkok, Hong Kong, and, of course, Yokohama. He felt proud that the hardships he had endured smelled of more mysterious spices than those of most other Jewish immigrants.

"I was only there for two days," Uncle Joseph said, speaking English very loud and foisting two emphatic fingers in front of Shiro's nose. "But I remember walking around Yokohama waiting for the ship to leave. Everything tasted like fish. Even the tea. Finally, I decided to eat a bowl of noodles. Almost went into a shop, but on the street I met one of your people, and he invited me to his home. To his own home! His house was about as big as a closet. You had to take your shoes off. Bend down so you didn't knock your head into the ceiling. But me, a total stranger—he invited me to his home! I always tell that story when people complain about you Japanese."

Next Uncle Joseph raised his eyebrows and bobbed them significantly in Shiro's direction. "First the war. People didn't feel good about Pearl Harbor. Now this trade problem. I have a friend in the electrical business, and he curses your people for dumping color TVs on our market. But not me, I think Japanese people are the finest in the world."

When Shiro smiled, he could not match the nervous emotionalism of Uncle Joseph's outburst. I could tell from my husband's face—square, perplexed, and eager to please—that he understood only six or seven transitive verbs in Uncle Joseph's whole speech. The rest of the conversation was a blur of half-recognized vocabulary words ("very," "home," "street") from grade school English conversation drills that Shiro realized he should, though he did not, understand. This set the frustration and despair into his forehead. If asked, Shiro would have doubtless come forth with assurances about how it all made perfect sense to him. This lie would relieve Uncle Joseph, who was always being teased about talking too much, and also would allow Shiro to believe that his citizenry extended beyond Japan to a wider world.

Later, when we were alone, I quizzed Shiro carefully about what Uncle Joseph had told him. Not much had, apparently, got through. Shiro frowned at the memory and complained that he couldn't understand New York English since his teachers in Tokyo had all come from the Midwest. "And why can't they speak softly? It's frightening, like a big, noisy train coming out of a tunnel."

Shiro and I do not make our home in Westchester, New York, where the natives speak too loud in a strange language. We live in a suburb of Tokyo called Musashino, which has figured occasionally in classical Japanese verse. It is hard to believe that Musashino ever was a place that inspired any poetic sensibility since a hodgepodge of Japanese houses jam the streets now, and a housewives' brigade earnestly tends to the abundant litter on garbage days. Yet some larger homes, like ours, do ramble off onto small and tasteful private gardens. In such a retreat you can imagine composing a poem like the famous one from *The Tales of Ise* about not burning Musashino today, since a loving couple is hidden there.

I guess you could say that my husband and I are somewhat hidden in our home in Musashino, Tokyo, where we retire from the world each day behind a large plum tree and wooden front gate. We went on that January trip to New York, our first visit there since our marriage, to observe a mourning period after my mother's death. When my older brother telephoned to say she was dying, Shiro and I left as quickly as we could. Later, I realized that she died some time after we flew over Alaska, but before we had watched the airplane movie. I am relieved that she died then. A bedside scene would have not helped anyone, and what could I have said to make it easier? That I was sorry for wanting to run? Sorry for having run? Sorry for truly making the break?

Officially, my mother died of a heart attack, but every single person gathered in her Westchester living room knew that she had died from drinking too much. Drank too much? An alcoholic? The family didn't talk about this. In fact, I had never heard a word said about my mother's frequently muddled, frequently lugubrious condition, but everyone knew that my mother was a drunk. Alcoholism had never figured in family lore, which tended to center upon memories of pumpernickel in the villages of Galicia and Jewish life in the garment district. That was perhaps why no one would broach the topic. Overeating was the closest most of my relatives came to an authentic vice, and a person who was "from the drinkers"—as one of my aunts referred to anyone who drank more than ceremonial Passover wine—deserved no respect. "They're from the drinkers" was how my aunt dismissed the entire membership of a local golf club, which was short on Jewish members and long on those with double-digit Roman numerals after their names.

My mother had no Roman numeral in her signature. She was the original bearer of her own first and last names. Yet she drank in quantities that my aunt expected only of the patrician bankers who played golf at the nearby club. My mother's drinking was not elegant or cheerful. She could not drink socially, nor did she tell better jokes as the hour grew later, since no one drank with her. She drank alone and after midnight. Her goal was not to loosen up and become convivial, but to fall into a stupor. Later, she was denied even that pleasure because she developed stomach problems. Before she could get deliciously tipsy, her intestines would give out. At night, I sometimes used to hear her toilet flush for a long time.

My older brother, who came to the house for the week of mourning, also drinks. He drinks better liquor than my mother. He sniffs at his wines before he savors even a droplet and mentions vintages regularly in his conversation. He is particular about which glasses to use. My older brother doesn't turn red or get sick to his stomach. Still, he drinks too much. I hadn't seen him for four years, and so I noticed the change in him. His eyes were more bloodshot than before, his hands trembled, and he panted when climbing stairs. The relatives often spoke about how my brother resembled my mother, and such remarks probably gave him nightmares for months. They also made mocking remarks about his haughty Jewish wife who claimed intimate knowledge of British royalty and put butter on her corned beef sandwiches. Throughout the week, I could see how my brother longed to flee from the family gathering. Yet I could hardly consider a thirty-minute drive to the East Side of Manhattan enough of a distance from this old battleground.

My second brother drinks, but less than my mother and older brother. He becomes talkative and silly, especially when he is uncomfortable, as he was during those nights when all his siblings gathered together to mourn. Neither my mother nor my older brother ever acted as foolishly as my second brother does after too much drinking. This brother would probably drink more, but he is timid, and his wife watches his consumption of liquids, alcoholic or not. I think of her as a predatory beast once out of work, but now, in the drinking inspections, possessed of permanent employment.

In fact, that second brother's wife looks just like a fox. Whenever I see her, I'm struck by the resemblance. Skin tightly pulled back over her face, eyes sharp and focused, she has a long, pointy nose. She does not drink. Neither of my brothers' wives drink. They do not sip or merely shrug off their temperance. They could just say "No," when offered a cocktail, but both of them insist on answering with, "No, thank you, I never drink." They both uttered that same sentence many times in the days of our official mourning period. "No, thank you," the corned beef-and-butter sister-in-law and the fox said, "I never drink." My mother once talked to me sadly about how my brothers had drinking problems, yet they both married teetotaler wives.

I try not to drink, but when I do, I am far away from Westchester, in a place where no one cares to count the empty bottles. Tokyo people do not consider drinking a moral weakness, but a sensible way to relax. They, like my mother, also have weak stomachs, but they don't always flush their heavings down the toilet. The late night streets are sometimes their receptacles, and the cleaning squad hoses down the sidewalks at dawn. During the winter, Shiro and I drink only sake. As I said, I have tried to give up alcohol completely, but on chilly February evenings, I allow myself a few warm flasks. The truth is, I probably also drink too much. I used to get a headache when I drank sake, but determined nights have toughened me up. It's happened that I am still pouring sake for myself and the other patrons of our local bar long after Shiro has fallen asleep beside me. Women usually don't drink a lot in Tokyo, but no one minds if they do. When my mother-in-law, who lives just beside us, sees that I have a hangover, she smiles and consoles me with the same neutral Japanese sentence: "You're really a strong one! You really like to drink, don't you?"

During the summer, we sometimes sit around with friends in that bar, and, as the air-conditioning cools us, the men discuss the marketing of window glass. Shiro has inherited the family's window manufacturing business; Akagawa Glass K.K. supplies windows for all the high-speed bullet trains and for other lines on the National Railways. These days, window manufacturers like Shiro have to worry not only about glare and tints and earthquake-resistant materials, but they also need absolutely bullet-proof products in case of terrorist attacks. On a train from Tokyo to Kyoto, I rarely gaze outside at the scenery, but instead study the windows for defects. If the reports about Shiro's competitors make me gloomy, I can spend a summer evening emptying many beer mugs.

My brother called to tell me that my mother was dying on a cold winter evening, when Shiro and I were eating the hot fish stew my mother-in-law had prepared for us. We washed the tuna down with the last of the Kyushu sake we had received as a New Year's gift from a parts supplier in Beppu. Shiro prizes the slightly smoky flavor of this particular brand. When my brother called to tell me that my mother wouldn't last until February, I was thoroughly warm inside from all the hot rice wine. I speared a leaf of Chinese cabbage with my chopstick and nibbled while we talked. When my brother asked, in his thick New York accent, if I would come back to see my mother, I said yes, with the cabbage still in my throat. Later, I preferred to think that it was not emotion, but the sake that had made the room move.

"Our name means 'red river,'" I explained to my cousin three days after the New York funeral. "Many Japanese last names refer to a bit of scenery. 'Base of the pine,' 'This well.' I don't know, maybe there was a reddish river near the house of the first of Shiro's relatives, and that's how they got the name 'Akagawa.'"

"Who would have thought that you would have grown up to be a 'red river'?"

"It's no stranger than being a 'Greenberg/green mountain,' when you come to think of it. But I can write my name in Japanese characters, which I guess does make me more exotic."

My cousin Ella expected a few more personal revelations from me that evening, wanted me to bare my soul to her in the confessional style of true New Yorkers. On the one hand, she appreciated my daring and my Japanese earrings, but since she could pry no secrets out of me, she decided that I had become aloof, even cold. Yet she was thrilled to meet Shiro, who counted as her first Japanese experience, and he did manage to utter four very polite and grammatical English sentences when they were introduced.

"You know, I used to talk to your mother late at night all through last year," Cousin Ella continued. "I think I really got to know her. We would talk all night sometimes. I think by the end she had accepted what you had done. She used to talk of being proud of your courage. And she did like Shiro. You must have shown her a good time in Tokyo. She said it was the best city in the world."

"Well, not quite. But Shiro made sure she saw everything. And she was only there for five days."

"And the vase your mother-in-law gave her. She loved it. You can see she always kept it in a prominent place."

My mother-in-law's gift was a sake decanter, not a vase, but no one in Westchester could tell the difference. Actually, I always suspected that my mother-in-law had meant to convey some criticism when she gave my mother a drinking accessory as a farewell gift. Even so, the decanter did not lack for elegance, as befitted my mother-in-law's impeccable taste in Japanese works of art. The *tokkuri* had been decorated with drip glazes using the *nagashi-gusuri* technique, while the style of the short pouring neck dated from the seventeenth century. My mother-in-law had acquired the piece from a friend whose husband owned a huge pottery factory in Seto. He sold many of the best pieces in his private collection when the firm switched from producing plates, bowls, and bottles to Western-style porcelain dolls. If the gift of the sake decanter contained any hidden message, my mother never caught on and proudly used the Seto masterpiece as a vase for her fake Chinese flowers.

The vase-sake decanter sat on the display shelf beside a whole row of British mugs that bore the faces of famous historical personages. Next to the Seto decanter was Winston Churchill, then Henry VIII, and Marie Antoinette. The shelf above held a half-dozen Danish ashtrays, along with a modernistic Hebrew rendering of "Life" in wood and gold. On her tour through the Orient, my mother also purchased the giant teak Thai elephant with ivory tusks.

My mother liked collecting small objects. The house was full of knickknacks on coffee tables, hanging from walls, on the back of the toilet, and suspended from the lighting fixtures. Some things were even stuffed into spaces between the rubber-tree plants. Each object represented another of my mother's attempts to strengthen her will against sorrow. She vowed to buck up one summer and proved her new resolve by traveling off to Europe, where she bought the mugs. Her letters from Rome, Paris, and London were cheerful. She walked down the bright Roman streets during the summer and tried to get some light for herself. After she returned, the darkness caught up with her, and she promptly fell apart. The Israeli knickknacks and the Danish ashtrays likewise represented her struggles to shake herself into optimism. At her bravest, she undertook her Oriental Holiday, in order to meet Shiro and see me in my married state. I recall how she looked the night we went to eat skewers of chicken in a crowded Shibuya restaurant. The jolly and drunk office workers next to us were delighted to have two Americans beside them, and they kept offering to buy us drinks, but my mother refused to touch a drop. Staring at me as I eased the bits of chicken off the stick with my teeth, she looked puzzled. "Are you really my daughter?" she asked, curling and uncurling her hands on her lap. "How could you be my daughter?"

In Tokyo, Shiro's mother also spends a great deal of time collecting objects. Every month, a different family treasure is displayed in the alcove of the large Japanese-style room off the entrance hall. Last spring, my mother-in-law took out the hanging scroll she purchased years ago in Ueno. It dates back to the Edo Period and, in honor of the season, treats the whole theme of cherry blossoms scattering in the wind. During the rainy season, my mother-in-law unpacked her eight-sided lacquerware box, with hydrangeas and snails inlaid in mother-of-pearl. When she turned seventy, we bought her dolls costumed in ancient robes, and she showed them off last March. Just before we left, she took down her New Year's wall hanging, which she puts up in the tokonoma at the same time every year. This gorgeous New Year's painting, by a twentieth-century master, depicts a young woman wearing a bright red kimono with floating cloud designs at the border. Carrying a delicately-wrought fan in one hand, she seems about to begin a traditional dance.

The wall hanging of the charming young dancer is my mother-in-law's most cherished possession. Each December, when she removes it from the packing box, she exclaims, "The fan is beautiful." She really wants to speak about the passing of the year and the pleasure she takes in this occasion, but she would never say so directly. She only says, "The fan is particularly beautiful." Or, her voice will turn quiet in the autumn when the leaves are changing color, and she will sit outside our garden and say to me, "Autumn is better than spring," as if she had never seen the maples of the Japanese autumn before. "Autumn is better than spring," she says, year after year. At night, just after sunset, the vendor of roasted sweet potatoes rings his bell outside and calls out, "*Yaki-imo!*" For my mother-in-law, the bell and the vendor's cry signal the beginning of evening. She always will pause for a moment to exclaim, "Oh, I didn't know it was so late." Often, I can appreciate the wonder my mother-in-law feels for the dancer's fan or the splendor of autumn or the sweet potato vendor's bell. ("Oh, I didn't know it was so late.") I have learned much from her about the gift of a moment and the peace in small details. On some days, though, when my mood is grimmer, I feel unqualified for tranquility. On such a day, I run out of the room when the sweet potato vendor's bells ring out at dusk, before my mother-in-law can say a word.

I have also begun to collect Japanese art. Shiro appreciates fine pieces, and twice a year now I go with my mother-in-law to Kyoto on a shopping trip. I like to sit on the straw mat in a drafty shop, sipping tea, enjoying the odd softness of the Kyoto dialect, while my mother-in-law and I inspect the shop's calligraphy scrolls or lacquerware or ceramics. Usually, I can relax and enjoy the slow selection process and don't even mind answering the art dealer's questions about where I grew up or whether I can really eat with chopsticks. But in a shop sweet with the scents of old tatami mats and overflowing with magnificent tea utensils, I perhaps can be forgiven for remembering the living room back in Westchester, where, surrounded by her tasteless immigrant junk, my mother often told us that she felt old and ugly and alone.

That's why I don't always listen carefully to the dealer's talk about the originality of a woodblock print or how he happened to acquire a particular samurai sword. Clutching my latest acquisition, I endure the ride back to Tokyo and the return to our home, the annex of the main house. My mother-in-law, who helps me unwrap my new purchase, will point out each unusual feature to Shiro. See how the plum blossom sprigs give the antique robe a modern feeling, she will say. See how the formal crests balance the design. And notice how the shape of the sleeves is most unusual. Then we set our new purchase out on display in our Japanese-style room. "*Yoku atsumeta wa ne*," my mother-in-law always says, after we have the new piece in place. The phrase literally means, "You certainly have collected a lot of things," but actually she is expressing the joy she has taken in our trip to Kyoto and the preciousness of the hours we spent selecting our new treasure.

"You know," Cousin Ella continued that night in my late mother's apartment, "I want you to know that in her old age, your mother learned to be more understanding. She forgave you for so much."

Cousin Ella was not trying to be malicious. She had no real gift for the subtleties of spite. A crisis forces people to find ways to comfort, and this puts a great strain on all involved. Sensing that she had spoken unwisely, Cousin Ella changed the topic and was soon trying to comment on the snowflakes that had begun to fall outside. But her heart wasn't in the loveliness of the snowflakes, as my mother-in-law's surely would have been, and so Cousin Ella became silent. The snow covered the lawns, which, according to Shiro, had no "flavor" to them. As he rode around, he disdained the bland and grassy Westchester landscapes and made a case in his mind for the cultural poverty of America. He also disdained the filthy windows in my mother's apartment, which had not been cleaned on the outside for years.

"It's good that she died so quickly," my older brother said, when he caught me alone in my mother's kitchen. "I don't know how you feel about it, but I certainly didn't want to have to stay around her sickbed, nursing her for years."

He, too, spoke in a very loud voice, and his many enemies in the family must have overheard him. I could tell from the clarity of my brother's eyes that he was not drunk yet, but he faked inebriation as he heaved his shoulders over his whiskey glass. In his stylish Manhattan way, he would have said that speaking honestly about his dislike for his mother was his adult prerogative. After all, he'd doubtless claim, if he wasn't forthright, he'd get himself entangled in false and sentimental family emotions.

"You should come back and live here," my second brother told me the next night. "We have plenty of room. We could divide the place up for two families."

This brother, the fox's husband, had inherited all my mother's money. Perhaps my marrying into a window fortune had eliminated me from the division of the spoils, and my older brother's various financial catastrophes had gradually eaten away his share of my mother's estate. Even so, I never thought the money would go, like a Hollywood movie, to the son who curried favor with the old widow. Yet, I concede that this husband of the fox had earned his inheritance. This brother had a talent for service, which he put to use in fixing my mother's leaky faucets and taking her sheets out to the laundry every other week. It was he who knew when the brakes on her car needed tightening. I believe also that when she called him at midnight, with regrets about a dim light bulb or her whole life, he tried to offer words of sympathy.

"The sushi costs so much less here than in Tokyo. I just can't believe it. You can eat and eat for less than ten thousand yen."

Shiro told me this when we were alone in the guest bedroom the last night. Some of my relatives had taken him for a drive into New York City where they ate at a Japanese restaurant. My cousins finally had someone to order for them in Japanese—someone "who knows what's good." They ate quantities of raw *toro*, the best part of the tuna, and Shiro clearly appreciated the break from the heavy, meaty meals he had been eating.

"The *toro* here is fresh, the best quality," he told me. "But I feel strange eating sushi in New York City. Maybe the sushi is exactly the same as in Tokyo, but because the atmosphere is so different, you think the sushi tastes different, too."

This family ordeal would soon be over for him. A whole week of feeling shorter and slighter than everyone, laughing either at the wrong places or trying to comprehend loud exclamations of affection. Being kissed by total strangers in greeting whenever he turned around. At the end of that grueling day, he walked around the guest bedroom of my mother's apartment and talked more than usual, fluently, in his own language. He even peeked into the cupboards, amused by my second brother's collection of old *Playboy* magazines, which had once been locked up. Shiro paused by the Danish ashtray on the bureau and then studied the mass–market reproduction of the Polish rabbi. He came back to the bed carrying an artist's impression of the Wailing Wall in Jerusalem.

"She's certainly collected a lot of things," Shiro murmured as he sat down and began to speak at length about the small drawing.

[1995]

Season's Greetings

JOSEPH LAPENTA

Flowers. The headmaster reminded himself that he was supposed to be thinking about flowers. But from center stage, he could see a willow tree through the large plate-glass window. The bare branches were motionless, quiet, the long delicate lines—a willow, a silently weeping willow. Suddenly he felt the presence of the whispering crowd beyond the doors at the rear of the auditorium. Over three hundred teachers massed in the lobby, waiting for the first official school meeting of the year to begin.

He had been so easily distracted lately. Still, Kozo Nakamichi was confident he could give them what he had always given them: something just slightly beyond their expectations. He would use the traditional New Year's materials—pine, bamboo, plum—as he and six generations of headmasters before him had done. Always the same, but each time there had been a difference. Today he might hide the plum almost entirely in the pine, or treat some of the bleached leaves of bamboo as falling sleet. Everyone would appreciate the grace, the freshness, but above all, the clear sense of limits—the famous qualities of the ikebana of the Nakamichi School of Flower Arrangement.

Everyone, except perhaps the younger teachers. What did they think they were doing? Spraying plants with paint, chopping them up, sealing them in plastic, that sort of thing. His son Mikio, the assistant headmaster, who would someday succeed him, explained that they—"we"—were "exploring new possibilities." New possibilities indeed! Like that monstrosity he'd created for last year's spring exhibition. He had told his son what he thought of it—nature mummified, a horrible, unnatural thing. The argument had cast its shadow. I can't talk to my son anymore, he thought; we've become strangers.

Still the headmaster continued to gaze at the willow. Motionless, it seemed to be waiting for spring, waiting to put the old year aside. On New Year's Eve he had himself gone to sleep early, but had awakened in the middle of the night on the edge of panic.

Flowers. He looked down at the bronze vase, the scissors, the wire; he stepped back to peer under the long, low table that was covered in front by a thick length of green felt. The materials stood in blue plastic buckets half-filled with water—the pine boughs, the stalks of natural and bleached bamboo, and the thick plum branch with many twigs dotted with tiny, light-pink blossoms. Where was Mikio? he wondered.

Assistant Headmaster Mikio Nakamichi had been standing in the wings for a long time now, talking with one of his students. Soon his father would tell the ushers to open the doors. After everyone had entered and was seated, he would begin the New Year's greeting. Then the headmaster would introduce his son, and Mikio would walk out to applause, ready to assume his role.

The ushers had opened the doors and Mikio could hear the crowd beginning to file in, the low voices and rustle of kimono. They were all here, he thought, and they were looking to him for leadership, for new ideas. His father was getting old. He seemed tired these days, and irritable, especially since the spring exhibition and that argument they had had.

The Assistant Headmaster had worked so hard on his piece, and the idea was brilliant—a huge cone, four meters high, a primary structure. The top had been sliced off abruptly: a truncated cone, the image of Mount Fuji. Nothing new there. But what it was made of—that was the stroke of genius that made everyone gasp. He had been planning it for more than a year and had enlisted the cooperation of two large corporations eager to support new directions in the arts. There had been a discreet credit for them in the exhibition catalogue: "Thanks for the kind assistance of the New Japan Trucking Company and Tekno Central Refrigerated Warehouses."

During cherry blossom season the previous April, a team of students had been ordered to volunteer for the project. Hundreds of branches of cherry had been cut and kilograms of pink and white blossoms carefully picked at their prime had been hauled by New Japan to one of Tekno's giant refrigerated warehouses in Tokyo's waterfront district where the blossoms were freeze-dried. The company was proud of the process, which could instantly dehydrate any organic material while preserving the most delicate nuances of color and shape. A large conical plywood mold had been built. The dried blossoms, mixed with a transparent synthetic resin, had been poured into the mold. The plywood was then removed and the surface of the plastic cone polished to a sheen.

It represented a radical rethinking of basic concepts. The latest modern technology had been used to transform the traditional cliches, Mount Fuji and cherry blossoms, into a totally new work that fused material and container into a single, overwhelming presence. Critics, teachers, students had loved it. "Bold . . . forward-looking," they'd said. "The future of the Nakamichi School and the art of ikebana." But his father had only looked at it silently for a long time. Later, when they were alone, he'd become angry. "Horrible . . . unnatural . . . a monstrous thing. A thing, Mikio! A dead thing!"

Assistant Headmaster Mikio Nakamichi looked into the full-length mirror on a nearby wall, provided for those about to go on stage. He tightened the obi of his formal kimono and made sure his small artist's ponytail was neat. He had had his ear pierced but had decided against wearing even a small, modest earring. Not yet. He waited for his name to be called.

The headmaster was still staring at that willow. He had always seen willows, especially in winter when they were leafless, as brush-written Chinese characters. Not the bold, squared-off kind, but those written in the smoother, cursive style, flowing—a graceful abstract sign. But as he looked intently, he noticed that the willow outside the window seemed different. The trunk was oddly twisted. The thicker branches seemed frozen, the long, thin twigs that drooped almost to the ground were many strands of light, gray-green hair. It seemed visibly alive. Someone sneezed. He turned quickly to the audience. They were all looking up at him, waiting. He knew the lines—he had spoken them a hundred times—but he was frightened. He took a deep breath.

"Happy New Year everyone, and may you all—may we all—have another full, productive year. At this first meeting of the Nakamichi School of Flower Arrangement, I hope that together we can look back over the past year, a year of great accomplishments, and look forward to the coming year with all of its possibilities. As we do this together, let us never forget how privileged we are to hold in our hands this great art, this precious heritage which our forebears have bequeathed us. Of course, we must also look to the future, so before I continue, I would like to introduce to you, my son, Assistant Headmaster Mikio Nakamichi."

He raised his hand and beckoned for his son to join him. Mikio came out on stage to loud applause. The headmaster looked at the audience. Yes, he had been right. The loudest clapping came from the younger teachers. They were smiling. The older ones were just being polite, and some of them, the survivors, the ones of his generation, were barely clapping at all.

"Mikio will assist me as I create for you and for all those hundreds of teachers and thousands of students, here in Japan and abroad, a small token of my gratitude for the trust you have placed in me."

The headmaster motioned to Mikio, who reached down, lifted the large plum branch from the bucket, and held it before his father. The headmaster picked up his scissors and with smooth, automatic gestures, the product of decades of practice, began to clip the small branches of plum.

"The future, yes, the future," he continued. "Still we must never forget that we are also custodians. What shall we hand on to the future? What of real importance shall we give to those who follow us?" He clipped as he talked, and the confusion of tiny twigs cleared to reveal the strong main lines of the branch.

Habit, the headmaster thought. All those years of molding nature's plants to the established forms of the school. When he had finished, the branch was no longer anonymous. It had become terse—not just any plum branch but the essence of plum.

Mikio helped him secure the end of the branch in the mouth of the bronze vase. Sons had practiced for generations beside their fathers, arranging in front of a mirror. A master could arrange the materials from behind. The finished work would be perfect for the audience.

The headmaster looked down at the few plum blossoms that had fallen on the green felt. Perhaps it was the pink in the blossoms against the bright green that made their edges appear to flutter. Complementary color vibration, thought the headmaster. The cones and rods in the retina get confused. The edges of the blossoms, so crisp, such detail. Each of them unique, like a snowflake. But he was becoming distracted again.

"Custodians, yes. Well, as you all know, I've been thinking about this for some time, and writing about it in the school magazine. I have been doing research in the history of our art. We Japanese have been an agricultural people from ancient times. When we sacrificed to the gods, we offered them plants, not animals. In a way, ikebana continues that ancient practice. You all know that to this day prayers are said to supplicate the spirits of the plants we use. There are Buddhist and Shinto ceremonies that go back for centuries and centuries."

There he goes again, thought his son. All that old stuff about Buddhism and death and eternity. Young people are too busy these days to bother with all that. Anyway, ikebana's not really about religion and plants at all. That's just the outer traditional form. It's an art. The plants are already cut. Once you do that, they're just materials like wood, rocks, steel, and glass. Materials for the artist to mold, to change.

The headmaster was continuing: "Yes, all artists must consume their materials, destroy them, if you will. But our art presents this problem in a particularly dramatic form because we are not sculptors in stone; our materials are living plants. Aren't we thus justified in taking only what they give to us freely: seed pods, nuts, leaves, cones, beans, ripe fallen fruit? Isn't taking anything more a form of violence?"

What's he saying? Mikio wondered. Violence? This is New Year's! All the top people are here. He's supposed to be positive, optimistic. Mikio suddenly felt a sharp elbow in his ribs. He looked at his father, who motioned for the pine bough. Mikio reached down to get it as the headmaster continued.

"We all know, don't we, that the essence of our art is in the cutting—the killing, if you will. Yet really, plants are just like us, aren't they? Our ancestors knew that. Now even science tells us the same thing. All life, plants and animals, has exactly the same basic genetic code. We are all different sentences written with the very same letters. Do you see that? We have children, make permanent plans. We put down roots. But all of this is a looking away from the lives we really live, a denial of the death that will finally consume us. Plants do the same, don't they? They put down their roots and reach up toward the sun, trying to deny the downward pull of gravity. They spread their pollen on the wind. They hope. Don't you see that?"

He looked down at the pine bough that Mikio held before him. His son's hand trembled slightly, and it made the long, bright green needles tremble, too. The headmaster saw each point of each needle, almost too sharp to look at, pressing in against his eyes. He paused, took another deep breath, and let it out as a sigh that no one could hear except his son, who looked quizzically at his father. The headmaster pointed to a place near the base of the branch and motioned to him to cut it shorter.

"When we cut, arrange, and present our materials, we ask the viewer to look. Look at them! Look at us! No real roots! We can see this basic fact of our existence through the plants. And if we treat them with grace, skill, and love, they thank us by being so beautiful."

The branch was too thick for the scissors Mikio was using. He rested it against the table and reached down for a bigger pair. But even these couldn't make a clean job of it. He tried again and again, but finally had to resort to a small saw. It was slightly embarrassing, the young man in full formal kimono, down on his knees, hacking away.

The headmaster looked over at his son, smiled tightly, and continued. "Beauty. You know what that is? It's not just points on your examinations. It's . . . ," he paused. The sound of the saw, stuttering, rasping.

Again, he took a very deep breath. "Beauty is a miracle and a mystery. It's the only justification for cutting, for killing, for our art. Real beauty takes us out of time for a brief moment—away from all the competition, the struggle for more novelty, more stimulation, the denial of death. It reminds us of what is real, of eternity. It's a precious gift, and we must thank the plants for that gift. We must live in supplication, in gratitude for what we take."

Finally, the steel teeth of the saw bit through the tough pine bark and pierced the moist pulpy core. Someone in the audience softly applauded. There was a titter of laughter. Mikio stood up, bowed slightly, and handed the bough to his father. Small drops of black pine tar fell from the wounds

in the severed branch, staining the crisp silk folds of the headmaster's formal kimono. He put the bough on the table next to the vase, and stepping
back, he reached down to touch the stains. The tips of his fingers were
blackened by the tar. He tried again and again to rub it off. Mikio whispered, "Don't bother about that now. We'll take care of it later."

"No, not later, now," the old man raised his voice, almost shouting.
"Let's take care of it now. Right now where everyone can see and hear."
There was nervous coughing from the audience, a shifting of legs. The
headmaster turned to look at the faces. Polite masks. Silence.

"Have you all been listening to me? To my words? You have, haven't
you?" He was angry. Mikio became alarmed, and moved in closer.

"Just words. Old words, hardly original with me. But if you don't see
the truth behind these words, you'll just make stupid declarations. Worse!
Salads that no one eats. Waste and garbage!" He was shouting. "Then our
school becomes just a business. Money, filthy money! All our rules and regulations—words with no pity, no love, no heart!"

Mikio stared at his father as the old man secured the pine bough in
the mouth of the vase, making sure that some of the bright plum was nearly hidden within the green, like snow. He turned to his son and, looking
directly into the young man's eyes, he smiled gently. Then he turned back
to the audience.

"I'm afraid many of you, especially the younger ones, have not
thought deeply about what you—what we—are doing here. Some of you,
I fear, are making sculpture. That's fine in itself. I admire Michelangelo,
Bernini, Rodin. Most sculptors are strong men with great egos but they are
just like all other human beings. They deny their deaths. But the great ones,
the great artists, use that denial. They press it into the stone. Our art, our
frail ikebana, is of a totally different dimension. It teaches a different lesson.
There are no masterpieces of flowers that will survive us. Go make sculpture if you like!" he shouted. "Make things that will last forever. But don't
call them ikebana!"

He turned to his son. "Mikio," he said, "the bamboo, please."

Mikio was gasping. He hesitated. The members of the audience were
holding their breath.

"Please, Mikio, the bamboo," his father repeated very firmly.

Mikio raised the stalk and handed it to his father. As the headmaster
looked down at it, the image of a shimmering dragonfly darted into his
mind and seemed to hover somewhere between him and the object in his
hand. Yes, he thought, the paper-thin leaves of bamboo look very much like
fluttering wings. And yes, the twigs that emerged from the joints look like
the glossy legs of an insect. And the green skin itself looks like . . . looks like

nothing, really, like nothing else. As he continued to stare, the dragonfly darted off. And it—that green, unique, untranslatable thing he was holding—slowly disclosed itself to him.

Bamboo, the headmaster repeated the word to himself: bamboo, bam–boo, bam boo . . . over and over, a word, not the thing itself—a word, a sound, a habit of the lips and tongue, a noise that slowly faded into silence.

The headmaster carefully clipped some twigs and leaves from the base and gently fixed the bamboo at just the right place in the mouth of the container. As he finished, the willow outside caught his eye once again. Willow—just a word. A soft breeze stirred the living branches into sinuous, cascading gestures of grace. He paused a while to look, then walked around to the front of the table, and made a few final adjustments.

He looked out over the stunned expressions. "Well, what do you think?" he asked. "It's for you. Are you pleased with it?" He continued in a voice that was filled with a sense of relief and was very, very tired. "Please forgive my rudeness. I'm an old man. Too old, perhaps." He looked over at his son, then back to the audience. "Please forgive me."

He bowed deeply, then walked from the stage.

[1993]

Standing There Naked

⚡ ERIC MADEEN

Returning to Japan after eight years away. Over the low drone of jet engine he heard the grind of landing gear and watched Tokyo Narita emerge from darkness. The sight of runway and control tower lights triggered memories of his smuggling days. In India he'd dice up an ounce of hash, seal the pellets in packets of plastic wrap shrink-wrapped over lighter flame, then swallow the stash on top of several tablets of atropie sulfate, praying his bowels wouldn't open like a trap door at Immigration's crucial moment.

Now, though, he was smuggling something else.

Something that didn't need smuggling. But mere declaring, exceeding by two grand the ten-grand limit. Since declaration curbed the delicious feeling he now sensed all around his waist, where the goods encircled him like sharks' teeth gobbling at him, and deeper with that sharp tingle in the drop of his gut, he thus leaned toward the risk, the vibrancy of the risk. Helping him quadruple his investment, the yen had soared again and Japan's hip *uchujin* would see the goods—what would soon be contraband—as *smart-o*, snapping up all those gold and ruby high school rings he had bought for next to nothing off Border City's pawnbrokers. He had strung them, all fifty-eight rings, on a length of string he then tied off around his waist. If Japanese Immigration searched him, he'd merely tell them what he had told the inspector when the metal detector sounded at Border City International. "Just my belt." "Well," the black woman had said, "you gonna have to take your belt off and put it right in here." She handed him a plastic bowl. He untucked his shirt, untied the string, dropped the jingling goods into the proffered bowl while those behind him stared at the mound of high school rings jingling on a string. "Some belt," the black woman said, curious. "What you gonna to do with all them rings?" "Wear 'em," he said. "Wear 'em in good health then. You may go."

The wheels hit the runway, jarring the field of heads before him and jostling loose thoughts of seeing his father, after eight years of estrangement, at the naval base at Yokosuka. He had two things to do: sell the rings and see his old man. But a third thing was getting in there which had him unconsciously thinking in Japanese and tracing ideograms on a thigh. A Seishi Yamaguchi haiku that began with the katakana for *naita* then the hiragana *no*, then the second line, the more tricky ideogram *soko*, referring to the bottom of a bowl, the horizontal strokes then vertical, the near diagonal last, his father's stern face flashing to mind in his ordering (everything was an order with the old man) Jack to memorize ten ideograms a day, every regimented day, demanding him to scratch them out before dinner, until Jack had learned four thousand more than the standard two thousand. Through his finger now came the stunning ideogram for *gekai* (four squares making one square over a houselike structure that looked ready to take flight) then a particle in hiragana. His finger stopped halfway through the poem. Shuddering, he uttered the words in Japanese, "*Naita no / soko gekai* . . . The very bottom / of a night game. . . . " He repeated the phrase aloud and her face flashed behind his eyelids. Wing slats whacking at wind, the aircraft screaming, he squeezed his leg and told himself, *Dammit all I won't go see her.*

At Immigration ran deep lines of Filipinos and Thai, soon to be shivering in light tropical clothes, and Indonesian and Malaysian Muslims in flowing robes and head scarves, nudging along huge stacks of taped boxes somehow allowed as carry-ons. Like Cobb, miners in a rush for gold.

Taking his passport back from the Japanese official, he told himself again that he wouldn't see her, old Motoko Ogawa, not out of pride but from fear of rousing the nightmare memories of his dreaded time as captive . . . in his cubbyhole over her house . . . at her greedy mercy. Already just the thought of her, hair-triggered by the high gloss sheen of Narita terminal, this stepping foot again on Japanese soil, had busted loose in Jack Cobb that dread he felt a hundred times for not willing himself to resist her. He tightened his abdomen, shivering against the icicles of gold and ruby stabbing at him, trying to think of something—anything—to keep that time from coming loose in him and toppling him into nightmare depths that'd open up like diseased whores, leaving him armed with nothing to swing back at his demons.

Clanking over farmland on the Yokosuka-Sobu Line, Cobb watched dawn sunlight slash through a bamboo grove. Then strobe about the coach. Bamboo fell away to squares of frost-lacquered rice paddy pressing at the tracks. He was tired, ignoring two junior tourists, American girls new to the Asian trail, busying themselves with currency conversions on a calculator. One fingered a pig-tail and tried to hold Cobb's eye, "Can these seats be flipped around?"

Jet lag, and not being able to shoot, equalled a boxing glove wad of fatigue mashing his brains up against the top of his skull. His head hurt and felt icy cold. Untangling his beret from a coat pocket he knew the pain had something to do with his trick bag of memories of Japan. Having to see the old man. Having to resist the whirlpool current pulling opposite. Grabbing him back from that current was the memory of the falling out with his father. The wrestling match. Cobb's mother coming home in a drop of groceries, screaming at them to stop, trying to break holds of half nelsons and cradles as they rolled across the floor, breaking lamps and end tables.

"I'm not the conductor," the other girl said and winked at Cobb. "Don't ask me about these seats." Startled, Cobb peered across, reading a diary page. He read in big block letters, "THE LAST THREE DAYS IN HAWAII WE ATE EXCELLENT FOOD!!!"

Such simple-mindedness on the part of the tourists made him realize that he hated people, all people, for their inanity more than anything. He wondered whether his misanthropy was borne of envy of their innocence, since he could never delight in such childish conversation that went with living on the social surfaces of the self, nor could he generate such a clean, simple observation (then inscribe it diligently in a hardbound diary). He took refuge in watching Tokyo cropping up. A flare of sunlight struck a flock of pigeons, now diving below sun-splashed aluminum. Above warehouse roofs then flapped the flock, banking at the same time about six times before dancing, like ash, around an office tower. Then down over some houses and shops that looked more like big boxes sided with corrugated tin, then divided by easement gaps strung thick—the last cat's cradle—with shadow and electrical wire running every which way. At local stations passengers flooded trains. Cars and buses clogged streets. Tension prickled the air. *Stress City.*

Tokyo. Iron clatter roaring into tunnel darkness. Tourist girls antsy in the dark. They hit light and he realized that by helping them he'd be helping himself (he'd try anything to climb out of his funk), so he smiled to bring on the questions. He answered all: Where can we stay? Have you heard of a youth hostel in Okubo? Where can we change money? How much will we need? Tell us about Roppongi. When they finished taking notes he excused himself, stood, grabbed up his pack and headed into another car. There a few sailors drank beer and looked at him, hungry for another personality to explore. Encouraged by drink one of them, a red haired fellow with a slight scar on his chin, pointed to Cobb, "Nice coat, man. Like Eastwood in *High Plains Drifter.*"

A tall black sailor seconded, "I can see it. Don't know about the beret, though."

"Want a beer, man? Have a seat." They motioned for Cobb to sit.

The beer looked good—a bracer to take the edge off the reunion. As he quaffed one he thought that maybe these sailors could escort him through the gate, enabling him to take Captain Lloyd Cobb by surprise ("Dad!"). Another beer was proffered and he quaffed that, too, registering the cold glare from the Japanese whose homogeneity made them look all sewn together. Open drinking like this, on a train with seats that faced each other, was selfish and rude and threatened to make their country into something that wasn't their country. But they didn't say anything. Cobb finished another beer, still fretting the grilling from the Naval Intelligence Officer in the Office of Naval Intelligence (ONI), Division of Special Projects with a secret history of covert-overt, who in a minute would have son Jack's arm pinned behind his back, disarming him of his living. (*Peddling used rings to teenagers? Say what?*)

When Jack turned a rebellious thirteen, the family moved to Japan following Lloyd's transfer there. Jack fell in with a gang of base brats. Shore Patrol caught four of them once, including an admiral's daughter (Jack's girlfriend), spray painting obscenities on base buildings. At eighteen Jack had his last conversation with his father who came home snapping off the television and standing rigid: "Tell me it isn't true, son."

"It isn't true, Dad."

"Tell me you didn't jump the Peterson kid's motorcycle over a dry dock on a bet last week." Silence. "Jesus Christ, over a dry dock!? What, sixty feet wide, ninety feet deep, solid concrete—dry dock!?" His father exhaled, deflating. Exasperated, "You have a mental problem, son. Some sort of death wish. You're going to see the base psychologist."

"I'm not going to any shrink."

The order delivered with an officer's glare, "You will go."

"Why? Because I accepted Peterson's dare? Thomas wanted to do it and would have if I hadn't, and you know Thomas can't ride let alone jump. Just think of the mess then, Dad, the rear admiral's son scraped off a slab."

"Better him than you. Why did you do such a crazy thing?"

"To save Thomas's ass and win the bike. That was the deal. You know if you bought me one I wouldn't have to risk my life earning one."

"Earning one? I'll tell you what you earned." Lloyd yanked open a kitchen drawer and pulled out the old spanking paddle. Sitting down, he patted his thigh. "Come bend over my knee here, son."

"You're joking. You try to spank me and I'll take that paddle away from you, Dad. Swear I will."

He found temporary digs in Yokosuka with The Family, a religious cult founded in the sixties. Family members didn't work in the formal sense of the word but did *witnessings*. Cobb met more than his quota by bringing in sailors for witnessings but couldn't make that scene, crammed into a tiny apartment with five other adolescent American teens listening to the same Dire Straits tape every day. Instead, he found work as a host at a club in the Ginza after dropping out of school.

He impressed the Mama-san with his Japanese in an interview down in her little basement host club. She asked him if he knew how to dance. Then asked if he could drink. "Like a fish." She brightened. "Good. That's how we make our money. You start tonight. Remember this, though: No fraternizing with customers outside of work." Cobb used her as a guarantor to secure his working visa. He lived in a noisy youth hostel then moved to the Ogawa house. Then his luck changed.

Dropping their empties on the floor now, the sailors stomped the cans into hockey-pucks, which they kicked back and forth. Jefferson grabbed out four more full cans from a gym bag. The others raised their hands against the spray. "Don't you get me!" Jefferson laughed, ripping open a can, mist spraying everyone.

Hatred from the Japanese passengers became a stink in the air. Cobb remembered his base brat days, escaping the confines of the base for the larger surrounding culture of Japan only to find himself thrown back. Rejected by Japanese girlfriends under orders from parents or friends, rejected by roving teenage gangs of Japanese adolescents, rejected to the margins of a karate dojo whose instructor bullied him, in turn inciting his students to bully the gangly adolescent Jack Cobb, to make fun of his feet, his hair, his eyes, his big hands and long arms, his way of walking, talking, as a gorilla in parody, mockery that never failed to bring the group—always the group subtracting Cobb—to laughter at his expense, for what but having broken one of a thousand unwritten rules that kept all but the strongest from pushing through. Banished to that no-man's land between cultures, he had become, he realized, the barbarian they had seen in him. It was all wrong, he knew, that each of the sailors took up too much space, slouching, drinking beer, forearms and knees all over the place in complete indifference toward other passengers. But there was something incredibly right, something Generation-Xer real for him, in the brashness of being bulls in a china shop only half-assed open to them anyway. What did they have to lose? Clanking beer cans together then having a guzzling race, swilling beer. Spilling beer. Coughing. Dribbles wiped away with coat sleeves. Laughing bleary eyed drunk, Cobb turned to a fiftyish woman across the aisle. She was reading, or pretending to read, a small book in Japanese. "What are you reading?" he asked her in English.

Startled by a foreign voice breaking into her space, she glanced nervously at Cobb, jutting her face toward him in a move engendered to throw the confusion back at the interrogator. "*Hai!?*" (What!?")

Undeterred by the nasty glances of two businessmen, "I asked you what you're reading."

She held up the book and said in English, "This?"

He pointed. "Yes. That. What's it about?"

"I don't know," she said in faltering English, shaking her head nervously, looking down. "I don't know."

"You mean to tell me you don't know what you're reading?"

She jutted her face in his direction again. "*Hai!?*" But Cobb wasn't having any of it. In his experience those Japanese brave enough to sit beside a foreigner on a train, when plenty of other seats were available, craved an encounter. Looking at her skin, her make-up, realizing his assault on her, this stranger on a train, sprang from his Christian guilt and the anger generated from memories of what his old Japanese landlady and he had done (he remembered her now snorting away down in the trough of his youth), he suddenly felt thwarted from thinking the emotion through, feeling instead the grip of something cold around his waist. Unable to grasp anything other than rage to steer clear of the emptiness, he kept looking at the woman before him, figuring she had probably graduated from a woman's junior college thirty years ago, majoring in English literature and flirtation with her foreign professor that had her now wanting to step out of the clutches of her culture to sit among the *gaijin*—to draw from the outsiders a little bit of that free feeling again. But here she was trying to placate him by revealing big crooked teeth stained with flecks of brown before realizing that foreigners found such ivory unbecoming. She closed her smile down to a grimace. His goosing of this total mother and housewife bringing him out of himself, Cobb bent forward and held out a hand. "Here. Let me see your book."

She reluctantly handed him the slim paperback over with both hands, as if making a present of it (a small price to pay for getting him off her back).

"Oh, is this a present?" Cobb asked in English, ignoring her tilted head and mouth sucking air, meaning that she was terribly confused by his rudeness and that no, it wasn't a present. "Thank you very much." Making a show of accepting it with both hands, he bowed, then examined the cover, which he simultaneously translated into English and read aloud, "*The Asakusa Crimson Gang*, by Yasunari Kawabata. You like Kawabata? I prefer Endo myself, especially *Scandal* for its honesty, its liberation of repressed desires." He lowered his voice, "You have any repressed desires, madam?"

She tilted her head the other way, sucking air, "*Wakaranai.*"

"About this book: There's one scene in particular," he gestured, "where he's spying on a girl through a peephole" (Cobb knelt, twisting his neck as if to spy through a peephole, resting a hand on her leg to steady himself against the train's sway), "and he was certain, and I quote, 'as he had watched through the peephole, thanks to the magnifying lens, that he had seen lines of saliva, like slug trails, glistening on her body.' Isn't that stunning, her body glistening with slug trails of male desire? Almost as if his eyes were his tongue." His head tilted back, mouth cracked open, he gaped up at her.

"Mmmm," she said, nodding. "Mmm." Still nodding, seemingly captivated by his voice as evidenced in the loosening of her cheek muscles. She showed him her broken English. "You speak Japanese well." She pointed at the ideogram on the cover. "You know kanji. For Kawabata. Why you no speak Japanese?"

Cobb shrugged, handing her book back. "Why should I speak in Japanese?"

Confused, she crossed her arms, tilted her head, sucked air through her teeth. "*So, ne. Mmm, so ne.*"

Jefferson elbowed Cobb. "You read that scratch, man? I'll toast that." They bumped cans and the train stopped at Tokyo Station, Cobb chasing that third thing—the urge to see her—couldn't help himself from mumbling a farewell and getting off and heading for the Marunouchi Line when he knew he should have taken JR. The prick of the ticket in his palm set off thoughts of her. Going to her house (his house where he used to live in that jail cell of a second-floor room) he kept hearing her voice clattering on in his mind, like a heavy coin refusing to give up its flip on the floor. *Whenever you come back to Japan, Jack-san, promise me you'll visit.*

There he was barreling across Tokyo on the Marunouchi-sen resonating with the exuberance of the thousand times he had gone from her mansion in Ogikubo to Shinjuku and environs to work or play but now at Shinjuku he tried to put on the brakes again (give it up, Jack!), telling himself that she was evil and that he shouldn't venture any closer but bail here and now and cut through the station to catch the Yamanote on down to Shinagawa, then transfer to the Keihin-kyuko bound for Yokosuka and reunion and all that noise. The feeling, turning more novel and wicked the closer the train pulled him to Ogikubo, had hooked him so deeply that now he just sat there, leaning back against the curled chrome rails at the seat's end until the conductor called Ogikubo and he snapped to attention, grabbing his bags, piling out then stowing his stuff in a locker.

Big fluffy flakes of snow fell as he trekked down labyrinths of wall-lined streets. The farther from the station he trekked the narrower the streets became, looping off and back on themselves and around between grand old three-story palaces. He kept to that enchanting way he had devised by trial and error over countless treks. Down along the river and moss-covered concrete slopes, morning steam rising from clear water where mallards dove and bobbed with teal, marbles of water rolling off feathers. Through the vertical bars of railing he watched carp, color bleached by current, feed on bread an ancient Japanese woman rummaged from a plastic sack, downy flakes of snow catching on her hair and eyelids. She shook all over in delight at the snow, dropping a handful of bread crumbs to the water surface broken by carp, then nodded at Cobb, both savvy not to break the snow's spell.

He crossed the bridge then turned left, heading down another narrow street. High block walls on either side, autumn brown and fluted, were skirted by barbed wire along the summit. Every fifteen paces and under a protective snow-covered hood, a surveillance camera whirred silently, training itself on Cobb's advancement up this rich street. How money separated, he thought, brushing snow from his arms.

Money. He didn't want her, Motoko Ogawa's, money. He asked himself why he was there then, starting up her walkway then fumbling with her trick latch under the heavy temple-style covered gate. Her dog barked at him as it had always barked when she was home, but now the sharp woof, in the recollection it had set off, was like a quiver of arrows hitting a target one after another, cracking the protective coating around this part of his past.

"We spend much of our lives pursuing that magical first love feeling. We do anything, even chase the perverse, to get it back." A fellow host, another American, bestowed that wisdom on Cobb one evening as they set up their drink station, their customers middle-aged Japanese women, often frustrated wives of executives who spent wads of yen culled from family finances on favorite hosts. Cobb himself, along with an Australian surf boy, was in great demand. Just such perversity Cobb had felt burning between him and his landlady, a woman who had seen at least thirty more years.

At her living room table, English text open before him, he watched her ballroom dance around the room, one arm held high and the other wrapped around the waist of a ghost partner. The English lessons were her idea and to show her appreciation she had cut his rent in half. When he protested she countered, "You're just a teenager. Think of me as your Japanese mother." She motioned to him, "Come dance with me, Jack-san."

He patted the text before him, saying they'd better finish the lesson so he could get ready for work.

"Now come. Today I want charm, not English. Charm me as I imagine you charm your customers." She danced over and took his hand then pulled him over to the center of the large room. She smelled sweet, maybe too sweet, as they danced to some Brazilian tune, but he didn't like to dance—reminded him too much of work where a steady stream of horny, frustrated middle-aged Japanese women, "shy" by culture, had no inhibitions of getting right in there for some serious bumping and grinding.

Though Motoko-san led, he felt too self-conscious, nodding in the direction of the clock on the richly ornamented shelves. "It's almost four. I have to get to the public bath."

"Take your bath here." She stopped dancing. "Let me show you the bathroom."

He watched her kneel near the tub in her kimono. An anachronism, she always wore a kimono (her late husband had insisted she wear nothing but, and she honored his memory).

Kneeling primly, her knees swung to the side over tile and thus showed a glimpse of bare calf, above kimono socklets, separated at the big toe, and bath sandals. She rested a hand on a pink plastic bath stool while the other broke a stream of water gushing from the tap. "There's a problem with the water heater," she explained. "Water jumps from hot to cold."

Watching her there in unexplored, private regions of her palacious old house, fiddling with the tap, kneeling correctly in her kimono, he felt a rush of excitement—something he didn't feel with the women at the club. He began to strip. She didn't move, but he felt the corner of her eye on him and her head tilt to listen to the shucking of his jeans, as she sat there, in no hurry, one hand under the water gushing into smaller streams falling from her palm, the other making adjustments. He pulled off his pants and shirt and socks until he was standing there in the laundry room in only his underwear, which he took off now.

Standing there naked, watching her attention on the faucet waver, he felt he was playing with something huge, teasing her so. Leaving him excited as she continued the pretense of adjusting the tap. Finally she stood, walked past him. Doing nothing to cover himself, watching her eyes twitch down and around. She moved stiffly, aware of the nudity of this exotic white Western boy standing naked in her peripheral vision. Speech was a struggle. "*Dozo* . . . Go ahead. *Dozo*. Turn the knob. When the water gets too hot. If you need help. Call. . . . "

The next day they did the same dance, the rumba, then proceeded to the more intimate dance in the bath. She played with the knobs of the faucet as he stripped just outside the door. She walked past him, voicing her sweet offering of the bath, then she paused before him in the tight space of the threshold and looked down. She patted him there and his erection sprang into her hand. She marvelled, staring, "How it moves to me."

He sighed, incapable of saying or doing anything until she had turned the corner of the living room. When he finished his bath and opened the accordion-style door, there she stood. "*Dozo*. Please. Let me towel you off, Jack-san, then do a massage."

She led him to her bedroom, which smelled of her hair, her skin, her body oils: the odor of linen closets and cedar chests. Dead air charged now with something he couldn't bring himself to resist. She pulled back the covers and had him lie down. She raked long, light strokes over him. He couldn't bring himself to touch her. But he wanted to. Or wanted her to. Wanted something. "How your heart thumps, Jack-san." She rested a hand on his chest, feeding the monster. That he couldn't pull away from. Nor could he steer. Lying back. His skin prickling with a thousand sensations. Her pulling away a hand towel she had spread over the heat in his loins. Couldn't make any move to stop. Her. She. Untying her obi and letting big milky breasts spill out. Taking him in her mouth. He exploded in a few gentle bobs. She lay between his legs. Lifted her eyes to stare into his. From her mouth the dribble. Her matronly Japanese face framed by short cropped hair which, together with big front teeth, gave her the look of a beaver. Small nose. Narrowed, alert eyes. Milky white breasts hot on his thigh. "Jack-san. You taste. Sweet. The sweet sweet taste of a young boy." She lowered her head and licked down his scrotum, her little hands pushing up against his buttocks as she twisted around until he raised up to give her tongue total easement. In a childish voice she told him something then her tongue divulged ancient secrets across his flesh as he just lay there, fluttering under her as she'd have the both of them plowing around up on all fours so she could, lying on her back, burrow up against him, again, day after day, at the same hour of the afternoon before he went to work then again after work at midnight or so and earlier since he stopped going out with the other hosts for drinks and dinner, instead heading straight home, walking along the river, watching ducks on the water with their heads tucked back under wings in slumber until out in the world together they went for the first time, the old lady and he, she a good fifty paces ahead, short legs pumping to clear the neighbors and their surveillance on this jaunt of her seeing him to the hospital (his appendix had burst and he needed an appendectomy) and through the hoops there, telling receptionists, nurses, doctors, all the way down the clip-boarded line that Cobb-sensei was her English teacher. He was at one time, yes, but hadn't given her a lesson in months, telling her she couldn't have it both ways when she whined about his lapse in that area.

In bed he had become by turns bored and frightened and once even wondered, what with her age, if she were having a heart attack and not an orgasm the way she hissed and writhed under him when she soared with the gods, as she put it. Cobb began to feel repulsed at her drawing from their lovemaking an incredible energy that had her practically swinging from silk curtains and riding a unicycle across the ceiling while Cobb himself, drowned in guilt and self-hatred, wanted to yank the tablecloth out from under the china and her expensive steak dinners then pull down the drapes, clear off the shelves in a violent crash of precious Edo dolls and knickknacks. Instead, drawing from his reserve of self control, he went over to the window and looked out (because he wanted out), his back to her, trying his best to ignore her fluttering around like a butterfly, ballroom dancing the rumba with a ghost partner to the same cursed Brazilian tune she kept plunking the stylus on in mad jabs and scratches coursing through the speakers, day after day, all full of the life (his life!) he had given in bath and bed and which had caught the eye of an old Japanese dandy in her dance circle. On those days the old fellow's black Nissan President was parked out front Cobb actually felt a pang of jealousy, running by the door and up the rickety old staircase bolted to the side of the structure, grabbing at the railing and shaking it like playground equipment, jolting the house—*them*—with his wrath, before taking refuge in his little *roku-jo*, or six-mat.

In retaliation he picked up a little doll of an office girl in Roppongi who looked all of fourteen (perverse for him!) compared to her fifty-plus or was it sixty (who knew? who could tell?). Alerted by her watchdog's barking, she came out for a snoop, head craning around the corner, watching her Jack-san say goodbye to his new girlfriend at the gate. In the middle of that night he was visited by a ghost, waking to a tube-headed creature stomping across the ceiling scape of his room. Horror-stricken, he looked up from his futon, watching the creature, the ghost, framed by streetlight glow and ceiling, a towel wrapped around its head, her head, he realized, her face a towering white tube, a bath towel clipped closed with barrettes. Nudging him again with her foot, she proceeded to step like a tin soldier toward the door then turn and stomp back through. The worst possible nightmare to wake into, staring at this ghost marching around his apartment. Cackling, she unclipped the mask of towel, untied her kimono, then hunkered down, breasts swinging around, crawling under futon covers despite Cobb's protest voiced in English: "Just what do you think you're doing?"

She was trying to straddle him and he pushed her off. Got her to leave finally but couldn't get back to sleep, haunted by the image. He was haunted, yes. She was all around him, in the clothes and goodies she had bestowed, her presence (presents!) everywhere. Inside and out. She had become a part of him, that part of his self that he loathed. He was tempted to run downstairs and wrestle her key (his key?) from her to end it once and for all.

In early November the Siberian express blew down from Mongolia and Kamchatka. To escape from Ogawa-san Cobb now and then accepted the offers of the more winsome and glamorous customers of the host club. They'd go drinking, then to love hotels. He'd cab back home long after the trains had stopped, then tiptoe through the gate, hoping not to wake the dog. The damned dog. An insomniac, he drank heavily and read until morning, cringing at the sight of her letting herself in to deliver an armful of laundry, neatly folded then put away in his futon closet, his resentment growing in direct proportion to his dependence on her. His whole apartment, however, was not much bigger than a walk-in closet, and she did nothing in the way of improvements, a ploy to get him to spend more time with her in her glorious rooms downstairs.

His apartment depressed him. Its curtains hung ragged. No water heater or bath or exhaust vent for his gas-powered heater—of the variety that required an open window, which let in great gusts of cold air as he sat there and read, book held in gloved hands, his breath visible in steamy jags, cursing the racket from tenants flushing toilets through paper-thin walls on either side. Only the distraction of reading kept him from going home to make amends with the old man on the naval base at Yokosuka.

In his apartment that winter he read, in Japanese, novels by Mishima, Kawabata, Dazai, Oe, Endo, haiku and tanka by famous poets of past centuries, the literature a sublime distraction from her.

The next time he visited to pay his rent he was surprised to find her beau there, a short Japanese man in his late fifties who dressed to the nines and wore a gold Rolex. She introduced Cobb as her English teacher and sat between the two of them deep in the corner of the sectional sofa, keeping their beer glasses poured full. When they were feeling good she made jokes, lightening the mood, resting her hands on their knees as a bar hostess might, or slapping them in fun for an off-color joke. The more they drank the farther down his thigh her hand explored. She suddenly had Cobb hold out a hand, comparing his to her beau's smaller hand. The old beau made a joke, pointing to Jack-san's crotch, saying in terrible English, Beeg. Vedy big.

Cobb knew then where she, perhaps under the old beau's directive, wanted to go, either hand of hers now in either crotch, wanting to drive the three of them toward an old Japanese custom that'd have Jack-san lying in the middle giving it to her while being corn holed by him. Without saying a word, Cobb stood, then headed to the genkan, jumped into his shoes, then ran back up the rickety staircase bolted to the side of the house, giving extra action to his step, wanting them to feel his displeasure. The next day at noon (when he got up) she let herself in, carrying his breakfast on a tray, making no mention of the incident, instead asking if she could use his toilet in the mornings, since her toilet had just broke and the plumber couldn't come until Friday. Unable to stomach the image of her squatting and moving her bowels in his toilet, he refused, telling her to go over in the park.

"In the park!" she crowed. "You're going to make me go over in the park!?"

He didn't say anything, eating his breakfast, letting her wind down then head back downstairs.

At work things worsened. The women he had bedded had banded together in an angry pack, hounding him on his way to the station. The mama-san had her rules forbidding her hosts from fraternizing with customers outside work and special host club functions. All the hosts were the mama-san's property in that regard, and having an old woman's miserliness she wasn't one to give the store away.

On his way to the station, seven or eight women in their forties and fifties jumped out from a doorway, designer bags flopping from shoulders, diamonds and gold glinting off ears, necks, wrists, fingers. "Ya!" They scared him. He hurried on, straining to hear what they said just out of the range of his hearing. At work they passed Cobb notes while they danced or drank. A team effort, for each note said the same: that he was forbidden to continue with anyone but her or else mama-san would be informed.

At a stoplight, the pack caught up. Michiko (Cobb remembered her, the mole in the crease of her thigh) said, "Let's follow him all the way home."

Cobb could just imagine the old lady, tipped off by the dog's barking, opening her grand front door, neck craning, watching the *gaijin* groupies— as the hosts called them—tromping up after him. Annoyed, Cobb spoke in English. "This is the third night running you've hounded me, ladies. It's getting to be too fucking much!"

"*Eigo wakaranai*," one of them said. (I don't understand English.)

He didn't even bother going to work the next day or any day thereafter, not wanting to give the mama-san the pleasure of canning him. Women tightening the tension all around him, he made a decision to leave Japan.

Now he was back (*Tadaima!*—I'm back!), hearing her voice call to whomever was at the door. *Donata desu ka?* He wanted to reply, *Boku*, Jack *desu*. It's me, Jack. But he couldn't get the words out. He just stood there, realizing then that he hated the weakness in him that had driven him to see her, wanting to turn and flee and close off forever any emotional entryway permitting her back into his life but there he stood, listening to the apparatus of locks, the click and slide of metal, fighting an impulse to run, when the heavy hardwood door opened and there she stood, eight years of time exteriorized in a second on her chin's deeper recession, lip quivering, the looser folds of skin around her eye cracked deeper, the eyes themselves blazing with the image of him standing before her as if he were on fire, the way she jerked her head back, eyes blinking from the twin effects of seeing him and snow spiraling in. She spoke a long tumble of words about how long it had been and how concerned she was as he looked away, staring at the bushes beside the door, the bushes that now drooped in all directions under the weight of snow to the point that branches would soon snap. "Oh, this blizzard," she crowed, then saw the damage too. "It's flattening my bushes." She told him to wait a moment then disappeared into the house, a minute later charging out in galoshes and winter coat thrown over a bathrobe. Armed with scissors and twine she got down on all fours grunting like a wrestler. She dug into the bushes until her head was practically buried, elbows extended (also like a wrestler). He couldn't resist, taking up the spool of twine. Down on hands and knees he tied a knot around a gutter spout, handed her the spool, then motioned her down the length of hedge.

In the effort of tying up branches, snow swirling its stitch around them, all the guilt, years, cultural demons between them felt pushed off, like a boat. Something else trembled there between them. That sweet naughty trembling that had been lying dormant now fell over them like a detective's shadow. For a moment he couldn't move, to pursue or flee, imagining the bath she'd draw for him and her eyes narrowing at the sight of his string of rings. *There was no stopping it.*

[1986]

Six Encounters

DONALD RICHIE

ONE

Aiko's class had practiced long and hard and now they were all out in the steaming park, standing in their costumes under the hot sun, waiting their turn. The girls were in dirndl skirts and tight little jackets. The boys wore leggings, heavy leather vests and little fur hats. It was very hot.

Even hotter for Aiko's friend, Ryo, whom she was making practice since he hadn't got the steps down yet and here it was almost their turn.

— No, no, no, she said, irritated. Once more she put her hands smartly akimbo, rested her heel, toe in the air, and said: *Won-tu bukuru mai shu.*

— *Won-tu*, once more began Ryo, tired, hands limply on hips. He was perspiring heavily. Sweat ran down his cheeks, made damp patches under both arms.

— No, no, no, said Aiko. Really. You'll never learn. And it's so simple.

— It's the dumb words, said Ryo. Then, in scorn: *Bukuru mai shu!*

— Those are the words to the song, she explained.

— What do they mean?

She thought, then said: I don't know. Something about putting your shoes on, I think.

— If it were *tai mai shu*, I'd get it. But, *bukuru, bukuru, bukuru.*

— Oh, no. Look. We're going to be called next. See, the Bulgarians are going into their final set.

So they were, soaked boys in fur leggings, limp girls in tight bodices, lining up yet once again under the blazing sun.

— Who are the Bulgarians this year? asked Ryo.

— Koishikawa Junior High.

— Oh, it's so hot, he cried, snatching off his fur cap. Why do they always hold it when it's so hot. Why don't they hold it in the winter?

— This is a spring festival, said Aiko reprovingly. It's always held on May twenty-fifth. No matter what.

— No matter what, repeated Ryo, gazing as though in despair at the banners overhead. One said, in English: *International Friendship Folkdance Exhibition.* The other, in Japanese: Let's Be International!

— Hey, he suddenly said, hurriedly putting back on his fur cap: Look. There's a foreigner over there.

Sure enough. A large, blond person, very white under the sun, was looking at the last of the Bulgarians. He bounced slightly, keeping time with the recorded accordion and the sweating children. Then he noticed he was being stared at.

— Oh, no, said Aiko as he started toward them, toward her.

— *Hello,* he said.

— Haro.

— *Very pretty.*

— Sank yu.

The polka was rising to new fury as the sweating Bulgarians flung themselves about in the dust. Soon it would be the pert strains of the "Cuckoo Waltz" and the turn of the Austrians and here she was in conversation with this foreigner.

While Ryo stared, the foreigner talked on. He asked who they were in their costumes, where they were from. When Aiko told him he laughed and said that he was himself Austrian.

Aiko paled. A real Austrian. He was going to watch, judge, their pitiful efforts. He was going to publicly point out faults in their execution. He was going to laugh at them. Her class would be dishonored and everyone would think it was her fault.

The last of the Bulgarians shuffled off, the dust glittered in the sun, the well-known preamble to the "Cuckoo Waltz" sounded, and the Austrians, already bedraggled in their fur and leather, assembled.

— *Won-tu bukuru mai shu.*

She kicked Ryo in the shin having put out the wrong foot. Then, seeing her error, she quickly shifted and kicked him again. He smiled bravely, put his hands smartly akimbo, rested his heel, toe in the air, then limped about in a circle.

Sweat ran down her back as she continued dancing in the dust. The foreigner was still there. Staring at her. At any moment he was going to rush at them. Complaining. Singling her out for a grave error in international folk dancing.

But this did not occur. The bright blue gaze remained benign and at last the "Cuckoo Waltz" came to an end. The weary Austrians, heads down, sweat falling, left the field, and the Romanians trouped on.

Ryo was being talked to by the foreigner now. Perhaps he was being lectured, told not to bring the name of Austria to further shame. But no, they were shaking hands. Ryo returned and said: Nice foreigner. Friendly.

She nodded warily.

— Even knows a little Japanese. *Shideni.* Lots of Japanese there.

— No, he's *Asuturian.*

— No, he's *Asuturairian.*

Aiko colored, but refused to admit her mistake, shook her head, positive. The sweat flew.

— He's *Asuturian*.

Ryo merely smiled and said: *Bukuru mai shu*.

Two

Mrs. Shirai hated Koreans. Even though they had been born here, even though their parents had been born here, they were still Korean as far as she was concerned.

So far as the government was concerned as well. This was why they had to carry their registration certificates at all times, why they were penalized if they didn't, why they were fingerprinted along with the rest of the aliens though they were, in fact, citizens.

— It makes no difference, said Mrs. Shirai, strong in her beliefs. These people are not like us. They don't really belong here.

Many of her neighbors disagreed with Mrs. Shirai but none of them said so. And she was, after all, moderate. She didn't go around saying that Koreans smelled bad or that they were really animals—all things that people used to say. In a way Mrs. Shirai was an improvement.

She merely said unpleasant things and refused to shop at the best green-grocers in the neighborhood—best quality, best service, best prices and, despite everything, unfailingly cheerful—because it was run by people of Korean ancestry.

Then, the labor market discovered the attractions of cheap foreign workers. Mrs. Shirai first noticed this when she found herself looking at a construction workman employed on a new building in her neighborhood.

He moved strangely—loose-limbed, gangly, not at all Japanese. She stopped and stared and just then he took off his helmet to wipe away the sweat. Coal black he was.

— Senegal, said Mrs. Shirai later. I even asked. The foreman told me. Can you imagine that? And not a tourist, mind you. But working. In our neighborhood.

Then: Really, they're worse than the Koreans. At least they look like us. I just don't know what the government is thinking of, allowing this.

Her opinions were further tried a while later when various boat peoples began drifting to her shores. These she saw on television.

— Look at that. Not even invited and coming right in. What are they anyway? Vietnamese? What are they saying? No one here can understand that. At least the Koreans here speak our language properly.

Then, as the tube further informed, it turned out that amid the Vietnamese there were more than a handful of Chinese. Soon, many of the boat-people turned out to be of this suspicious brand. They were not, it was thought, proper political refugees. They were simple people trying to make a good living and coming where it seemed likely.

— They cheated, they lied. They entered our country illegally. They have absolutely no right to be here. They should be put back in their boats and sent away. But, no, the Government wouldn't do anything like that. It puts them up in shelters. At the taxpayer's expense.

— There, look, she hissed, staring at the screen: One of them is eating ice cream.

Observing these new events she gained a number of new prejudices. But in doing so she lost at least one of the old. She was to be seen shopping at the Korean green-grocer's.

— Well, why not? It's good and it's cheap. And after all they look and talk just like us. Can't really tell the difference. Why not? What's the matter with it?

THREE

Akiko was surprised. She had gone to this store and bought something and when the boy gave her the change he looked at her and said, very slowly: This is your change. Three—hundred—thirty—two yen. She must have looked strange at that because he then said it over again, just as slowly, but in English.

— I was surprised, said Akiko. He didn't think I was Japanese.

— So what did he think you were? asked her friend Sumiko.

— I wonder.

— Probably thought you were a Filipina bargirl, come here to get rich.

— Stop it.

— No, seriously. You got sort of brownish glints in your hair. You perm it. You got those big round brown eyes you're so proud of, and you like bright colors. Instant Filipina.

Though Akiko took care to appear offended, she knew that Sumiko was right. All those southeast Asians in their neighborhood now, all from the Philippines or from China or worse. All of them looking for work. All of them finding it. She had been mistaken for one of them.

What to do about it. She could get her hair dyed really black, get it straightened. And she could wear different colors, and fewer of them. But that meant she wouldn't be able to look as she wanted to look.

She wanted to look rather modern, mildly adventurous, somewhat original. Not too much, of course. Nothing common. No real make-up either, just a touch around the eyes.

And she had always been praised upon this appearance. Her husband said she looked really up-to-date. Her boy's teacher said she scarcely looked her age. And Sumiko said that she had a *good image*, using English to say so.

And now, all these new immigrants, illegal at that—all of these boat people. . . . But now, she caught herself, she should not think that. It was no way for a person to think—still, to be thought some Filipina whore was too much, and in her own neighborhood.

— Well, just don't tell your husband, said Sumiko, smiling. He might get ideas. Then, now laughing: On the other hand, might not be a bad idea, might keep him interested.

Akiko looked disapproving at this. At the same time she was thinking that, well, it had only happened once, it wouldn't happen again. But if it did then she was going to speak right out. After all, she was Japanese.

It happened again. She was in a different store and was looking at the mangos. She had picked up two, was going to the cashier, was just going to say these two please, when someone bustled up and began speaking to her in English.

It was the manager. He was smiling, unhappy, and trying. The English kept tumbling out and she gathered that he was trying to tell her how much the mangos cost. And above that wide smile those desperate eyes pleaded with her to understand.

And she did. Even though she had told herself that the next time this occurred she would draw herself up and announce politely that she was neither hard of hearing nor mentally retarded, when it did again occur she behaved quite differently.

She acted as she thought a Filipina would act. She smiled hesitantly, showed some relief that she could understand, nodded a lot.

He is trying so hard, she thought. And if I tell him I am Japanese they will laugh at him and make his life miserable and it looks miserable enough already.

So she smiled a lot, then picked up her mangos, paid, said thank you in English and left.

Then she told Sumiko. At first her friend was disappointed that a scene had not taken place and that the officious manager was not flattened. Then she thought and said: But, you know, Akiko, you really showed him, though he didn't know it. You really showed him that you were really Japanese.

And Akiko slowly nodded in agreement.

FOUR

Kimiko shopped a long time for a husband. Her friends told her that she'd better hurry up. That time was running out. That past thirty you're shopworn and no one will have you because everyone will think you've been refused.

But she just smiled. She was in no hurry, she said. She was going to take her time and get just what she wanted.

Eventually she decided upon a foreigner, an American. He was older, taller, had money, apparently loved her. Her friends were surprised at her choice. She just smiled and said she had looked over the market, that her new husband represented—she laughed lightly—the best buy.

Well, they said dubiously, they certainly wished her all happiness.

And happy she was.

— You certainly look happy.

— Absolutely, replied Kimiko, and then they went shopping.

Later in the month they were looking in at Mikimoto's and Mariko said: Just lots of girls marry foreigners now. It's enough to make me jealous. Stuck with that pokey husband of mine.

— How can you say that? asked Kimiko. He's just marvelous—for a Japanese man.

There was silence. A pearl was examined and then Mariko said: Yes, foreigners are better. The girls all marry Europeans now—Italians, Frenchmen. Even Germans.

Back home with her American, Kimiko began to doubt. Maybe she ought to have married a European so long as she was marrying a foreigner. Maybe marrying Americans was like buying a product with an expired shelf life.

Later in the year, turning over handkerchiefs at Hanae Mori's, she looked at a well-dressed black.

— They're very popular now, observed her friend. Attentive, kind, and naturally wonderful lovers.

Kimiko looked at the broad, retreating back: They're good at music too, she said.

Hers wasn't good at much. Inattentive, lazy. You could see why American products were getting a bad name.

Maybe she should have married earlier if she was going to marry one of them. Back then, she remembered, Americans had been very popular. Everyone wanted one. Not like now. Maybe she'd waited too late.

— Maybe I waited too late, she said to Mariko as they were looking over the scarves at Sonia Rykiel's.

— Oh, no, not at all. He's not that old. He's lovely. Not like that creep I have.

— I know, said Kimiko with a mollified smile: But I was just wondering.

— Look, said Mariko firmly. Even though he is American, he is a jewel.

There was silence. A scarf was replaced. Now Kimiko knew for certain. Tears formed. She had gone and acquired a product past its prime, a brand no one wanted any more.

FIVE

Harold and Ken met in a bar. They got along very well. Ken came back with Harold and soon they were seeing each other twice a week— Monday and Friday.

— We ought to see each other more often, said Harold, and you ought to stay over—like on Saturday night.

But Ken wouldn't. Saturday was for his mother. She always made a nice dinner for him and his sister and they watched TV, which was better on Saturday. And as for staying over, she would worry.

Ken was twenty-three, Harold reminded him.

— Yes, but . . . said Ken, whose English was getting better.

— Well, then, said Harold, the only thing for me to do is to meet your mother.

Ken wasn't so sure. They were all so busy and they had their obligations, like any family. Harold couldn't understand what it was like, he said— obligations.

Nevertheless, Harold invited Ken and his mother to a *shakuhachi* concert that a foreign acquaintance of his was giving and said he planned to take them to have *okonomiyaki*—cheap but filling—afterward. Also he said, he was going to charm the pants off the mother.

Before this even could take place, however, Ken's mother—having received and accepted the invitation—offered one of her own. That very day, Ken said, Harold would have to cancel anything else he might have planned because his mother had gotten them tickets for a foreign chamber group—and was taking them to a French-style restaurant afterward.

Harold canceled various plans, put on a necktie, and showed up at the concert hall, and there they were: Ken and his mother, and his sister, Sumire.

After the Mozart, Ken explained that his mother would have felt strange accepting an invitation unless she had invited first and Harold nodded as though he understood. And, as for Sumire, well, she needed some cheering up because her arranged marriage had not gone through and here she was, thirty. Again Harold nodded.

For the Schubert, mother and daughter changed seats so that Harold found himself next to Sumire, with the mother on the other side of her daughter and Ken on the other side of her.

After the Beethoven and during the French-style dinner, with wine and extra forks, Harold tried to talk to the mother but always found himself talking to the sister. He learned, through Ken, that Sumire was good at sports but liked staying home, was a fine cook but also read a lot, had graduated high in her class but loved to dance.

When they parted, all three members of the family waved until Ken was out of sight. Home, he got a call from Ken who told him that he had certainly charmed the pants off of his sister.

— I was hoping you would come back here with me, said Harold.

— Oh, no, my family.

— Did your mother like me? he asked.

— Oh, yes. Very much.

— Do you think she will let you stay over here now that she knows me?

— I can't talk now.

— Why not? This is English. She can't understand you.

— Later, he said and hung up.

At the *shakuhachi* concert, Sumire again appeared and Harold had to buy another ticket. Then they sat on the tatami for several hours and listened to Harold's foreign acquaintance play.

After it was over Sumire had some difficulty standing. The mother smiled and said something.

— What did she say? asked Harold.

— That she was very modern. Like a foreign lady. Can't sit Japanese-style very well.

At the *okonomiyaki* restaurant, Harold again found Sumire next to him. As he took charge with the spatula and pushed the mess about on the hot plate, he this time ignored her but kept smiling widely at the mother.

She, however, included her daughter in whatever she was saying and then, according to Ken, began to speak of her dead husband and how difficult it was: No man in the house except, of course, Ken here.

Again the trio waved until Harold was out of sight, and again the phone rang.

— You charm off pants again, said Ken.

— Look, when can I see you? It's been weeks.

— You saw me tonight.

— Come on. You know what I mean.
— We have many obligations. Very busy.
— How about Saturday?
— Oh, no. Saturday is for my mother. Television is better on Saturday.
— Look, Ken—
— Anyhow, I think my mother maybe asks you here this Saturday.

So she did. Harold put on the tie again, took flowers, and Ken came over to take him there.

— Why don't you come back with me afterward?
— Oh, no. My mother would be all alone and worry.
— She's got Sumire.
— But Sumire will get married.
— Not tonight she won't.

A large meal, half Western, half not, had been prepared—by Sumire it was said. But, first, tea and sweet beancakes. And after, TV, all four sitting in front of the set.

Ken and his mother took the two armchairs, leaving the sofa for Harold and Sumire. They watched a game show and a detective drama and a dubbed American film with Robert Stack in it. Then Harold said he had to go home.

— But I would like Ken to come back with me. I have so much work and I need him to help me with it. I will send him back to you tomorrow, he said and smiled his most charming smile.

After this had been unwillingly translated, the mother also smiled. The sister was not addressed. She stood by the now dead TV.

— Why did you do that? asked Ken when they were alone. He seemed angry.

— It was the only way to get you to come.
— But it was Saturday. I have my obligations.
— Well, how about your obligations to me then, if we're going to talk about obligations.
— I am the only man in the house, he said.
— Well, so was I, said Harold, and look—I'm half the world away.
— I must be a good son.
— You mean I'm not?

But Ken did not mean that and once in bed seemed over his anger. My mother, she is charmed, he said. My sister too. Maybe I can stay over sometimes.

Then, after some thought: You can stay over.

Harold was interested. There? In your house?

— Maybe, said Ken.

Then slowly he explained what he meant.

— Oh, no, said Harold. Never. Not on your life. How could you? I never heard anything like this.

— But we could live together, like what you wanted.

— I just don't think it would work, Ken. Look, I know you have your obligations and all, but—

— I am an only son.

— But what would your mother think?

— I don't know. But she wouldn't say.

— Well, your sister certainly would.

— No, I think not.

But Harold was not going to find out. No way.

— You say you want to see more of me, said Ken.

— I mean more often, not—well, not in depth like that.

— What? Then: You can't understand what it is like—obligations.

— No, I guess I can't.

Harold continued to see Ken from time to time but entertained no more thoughts of their living together, not even Saturday nights.

Then they saw each other less and less, and before long Harold was back at the bar. He never again saw Sumire or her mother.

Six

Saburo should not have taken the job. This he knew from the first afternoon. All dressed up he sat there and held the squirming children, one by one, on his lap. Some were distrustful, some were afraid, and none of them wanted to talk.

Yet that was what he was being paid for, to talk. And he needed the job. Fairly good money and it used his talent—English.

When he asked why they hadn't hired a foreigner. One certainly would have been more appropriate, the manager said, but you also had to speak Japanese, too, and he didn't know any foreigners who did. When Saburo asked why they needed someone who spoke English at all then, the man said it was because foreign kids came and anyway it would make a good impression.

So, all dressed up in red and white and in an uncomfortable and unconvincing beard, Saburo sat every afternoon on the first floor of Child's Play and tried to cope with the kids.

They stared and squirmed and writhed. Some of them cried. One of them wet her, and his, pants. Few of them were foreign, all of them thought he looked funny, and some of them said so.

— You're not Santa, one small boy accused. You're some student doing part-time work.

— Ho, ho, ho. I speak English, said Santa, in English.

— What's your university? asked the child.

Then, when Santa did not answer: I bet it's not very good. I bet it's not Tokyo University.

The child then climbed off Santa's lap and joined his smiling mother, remarking as they walked away: That Santa's a big fake.

Saburo too felt he was a big fake. Though he tried to act jovial and laugh a lot when the manager came around, he knew he was not convincing. The manager knew it too. At first he said maybe if he used a pillow, or maybe if he blinked when he smiled. But now he just shook his head and went back to his office. Saburo stayed on, however. He needed the money.

What had he expected, he now wondered, sitting up there impersonating a foreigner, someone little Japanese kids didn't know anything about, didn't care anything about, just a part of the X-mas sales campaign.

Perhaps if he'd been dressed up like Rambo. . . . But in that silly red and white suit no one cared anything about him. You could tell. No timidity, no hope, no awe. They just didn't believe in him.

One day, however, near Christmas, a child came who looked up to the dressed-up Saburo with timidity and some hope. He was a foreign child, a little boy, quite small, no more than three or four. His large mother lifted him up and put him in Santa's lap and there he sat, awed.

— Ho, ho, ho, said Saburo hesitantly. Then, continuing in English: What do you want for Christmas?

The child peered up at him and Santa beamed down through his beard.

— First you got to promise, said the child in a whisper.

— Promise what?

— That you'll really give me what I ask for.

Another difficult child. Saburo smiled and nodded and wished he would go away. But of course he wouldn't and his mother was standing there smiling and here came the manager to look at the sweet sight—little blond kid in an obviously black-haired Santa's lap.

— Promise? whispered the boy.

— OK, said Santa.

Then the child leaned up to Santa's ear and said: I want you to make people stop making my father sick.

— Is your father sick?

— Yes. He says that the Japanese just make him sick.

Saburo, familiar with English but unfamiliar with its idioms, was surprised.

— Sick with what? he asked. Like sushi?—voicing the first likely cause.

— I don't know, said the child. But I want you to make them stop. He says he can't even do business here, and if he can't do business it would be terrible—we'll starve.

Here the boy dramatically flung out his arms, as he had perhaps seen his father do.

— We did not make your father sick, said Saburo in a low voice, a bit too sternly for Santa. Maybe he made himself sick.

— No, said the child, retreating, sensing severity.

— We did not, said Santa Claus. Not our fault. His fault. Maybe.

This came out more forcibly than Saburo had intended. Faced with a suddenly irate Santa the child began to weep. The mother moved closer, the manager started forward.

— OK, OK, said Santa, sweating. I'll tell them to stop. Don't cry. Stop.

The child stopped in mid-sob and a large, grateful smile appeared. He snuggled against Saburo and whispered: Thank you, Santa.

The earlier tears had made everyone look, but now this affectionate scene, little American kid rubbing up against a red and embarrassed Japanese Santa, made everyone smile. The mother fondly laughed and even the manager grinned.

Finally the child left, led away, still looking back, smiling and waving. The manager gave an approving nod and went back into the office, and Saburo was left alone for a time.

Now I'm really a phony, he thought. Going around promising things like that. I'm pretty bad.

Then he stopped and wondered why he did not feel bad. He didn't. He felt good. Then he realized why. No matter how phony he was, the little kid had believed in him—had thought he was really Santa.

Thinking this, Santa sat up straighter, looked around for further youngsters, even smiled a bit. Maybe he shouldn't have taken the job, but there were worse. Besides, he needed the money.

[1985–93]

Biographical Notes

AL ALONZO is a native of the American Southwest. He has taught Spanish and Latin American studies at several universities, both in America and Japan. He has also worked as a salaryman in a large Japanese corporation and as an employee of a Japanese government ministry.

KAREN HILL ANTON, born in New York City, has lived in Japan since 1975. Her bimonthly column is a popular feature of the *Japan Times*, and her collection *Crossing Cultures* was published in 1993. "Summertime" is excerpted from her unpublished novel, *Ava's Story*. She is Director of the Intercultural Communication Center, Temple University Japan. A permanent resident of Japan, she lives with her husband and their four children in Tenryu, Shizuoka Prefecture.

ELIZABETH BALESTRIERI was born in Detroit, Michigan. She came to Japan in 1987 as Foreign Lecturer in English Language and Literature at Toyama University. She is now Professor of English and Woman's Studies at Josai International University. Her books include *The Woman Who Dreamed Japan: Stories & Poems* (1994) and *Beatitudes/Poems* (1997).

PHYLLIS BIRNBAUM is the translator of *Rabbits, Crabs, Etc: Stories by Japanese Women* and *Confessions of Love*. She is author of the novel *An Eastern Tradition* and has written about Japan for the *New Yorker* and other publications. Her collection of essays about Japanese women will be published in 1998.

CHRISTOPHER BLASDEL is a shakuhachi performer and researcher into Japanese music. He arrived in Japan in 1972 and attended Waseda University. He later returned to Japan on a Monbusho scholarship and finished graduate studies in ethnomusicology at Tokyo Geidai. He presently performs, writes, and teaches in Tokyo.

CATHERINE BROWDER is the author of *The Clay That Breathes*, a collection of stories and a novella, as well as stories and prize-winning plays. She is the recipient of an NEA Fiction Fellowship and a Writer's Award from the Missouri Arts Council.

ALAN BROWN first came to Japan as a Fulbright journalist in 1987 and stayed for seven years. His novel *Audrey Hepburn's Neck* (Pocket Books/Washington Square Press), which is set in Japan, was the winner of the Kiriyama Pacific Rim Book Prize in 1996 and has been translated into seven languages. His forthcoming novel, *Landscape with Avocado*, will be published by Pocket Books in early 1999. He now lives in New York City, where he is a contributing editor to *Travel & Leisure* magazine and a cultural correspondent for BBC Radio.

Australian JOHN BRYSON's first published work was a travel piece about a journey to Japan written while he was a law student. He is the author of *Evil Angels*, which was made into the film *A Cry in the Dark* starring Meryl Streep and Sam Neill, and *Whoring Around*, a short story collection. His most recent novel is *To The Death, Amic*.

DAVID BURLEIGH was born in 1950 in the North of Ireland. He came to Japan in 1978 and has since then lived in Tokyo. He teaches at a women's college in Yokohama and also at Waseda University. He has published essays, textbooks, and two books of haiku, *Winter Sunlight* and *A Wandering Fly*, and has collaborated on poetry translations.

MEIRA CHAND was born in London to a Swiss-British mother and Indian father. She has lived in Japan since 1962 except for five years in India. She is the author of six novels including *The Gossamer Fly*, *The Bonsai Tree*, and *House of the Sun*. The latter was the first Asian play with an all-Asian cast and production team to be staged in London and was voted Critic's Choice by *Time Out*. In 1997 it was adapted for BBC Radio 4. Her most recent novel is *A Choice of Evils*.

CHERYL CHOW is a naturalized American citizen. She was born in Tokyo to Chinese parents who fled their country just before the Communist takeover. She attended the American School in Japan as a child and returned to Japan as an adult in 1991. She now works as a free-lance writer, translator, and editor.

MICHAEL FESSLER was born in Kansas and brought up in Kentucky. He came to Japan in 1986 and is now living in Kanagawa Prefecture. His work has been published in many magazines and newspapers including *Kyoto Journal*, *Wingspan*, *Hawaii Review*, *Ikebana International*, *Kamakura Monogatari*, *New Orleans Review*, *Modern Haiku*, and *Wheel of Dharma*.

MORGAN GIBSON first came to Japan in 1975 to teach at Osaka University and is now a professor at Kanda University of International Studies, where his wife, the poet, translator, and essayist Keiko Matsui Gibson, also teaches. He is author of *Among Buddhas in Japan*, *Tantric Poetry of Kukai* (with Hiroshi Murakami), *Revolutionary Rexroth: Poet of East-West Wisdom*, and several books of poetry. He is also a contributing editor and columnist for *Kyoto Journal* and *Printed Matter (Tokyo)* and poetry editor of *Japan Environment Monitor*.

SANFORD GOLDSTEIN is an American poet, writer and translator. He first taught at Niigata University from 1953 to 1955, and often returned while on sabbaticals from Purdue University. He is now Professor of American Literature at Keiwa College in Shibata. He has published many short stories on Japan-related themes, as well as four books of tanka and translations of novels by Soseki Natsume, Yasushi Inoue, Harumi Setouchi, and others. Works on the Zen poet Ryokan and Shiki Masaoka are forthcoming.

JOHN HAYLOCK was educated at Aldenham School in France and at Cambridge University. In the periods 1958–60 and 1962–65 he taught at Waseda University, Tokyo, and from 1975 to 1984 he was visiting professor of English Literature at Rikkyo University, Tokyo. His publications include *See You Again, One Hot Summer in Kyoto* (Stone Bridge Press, 1993), *Tokyo Sketchbook, Japanese Excursions, Japanese Memories, A Touch of the Orient, Uneasy Relations,* and *Eastern Exchange.* He is a Fellow of the Royal Society of Literature and regularly reviews books for the *Japan Times* and *London Magazine.* He visits Japan annually.

SUZANNE KAMATA was born in Michigan and is most recently from South Carolina. She now lives with her husband in Matsushige on the island of Shikoku. Her fiction has appeared in *International Quarterly, Wingspan, Japanophile, Mississippi Review Web,* and elsewhere. She is the editor of *Yomimono,* an English-language literary magazine.

ALEX KERR first came to Japan with his family in 1964. He studied Japanese at Yale and Chinese at Oxford, returning to Japan in 1977, where he lives in Kameoka, near Kyoto. In 1994 he became the first foreigner to win the Shincho Literary Award for his book, written in Japanese and published in English in 1996 as *Lost Japan.*

Novelist and critic FRANCIS KING lived for four and a half years in Japan, where he was Regional Director of the British Council in Kyoto. He is the author of three works of fiction about the country--*The Custom House, The Waves Behind the Boat* and *The Japanese Umbrella*--and of the non-fiction *Japan.* He also edited and introduced *Writings from Japan* by Lafcadio Hearn.

JAMES KIRKUP has written many books about Japan. His most recent are *Gaijin on the Ginza* (a novel), *Burning Giraffes* (an anthology of contemporary Japanese poetry), and several volumes of haiku and tanka, including *A Book of Tanka,* which was awarded the 1997 Japan Festival Foundation Prize. He wrote the libretto for the first Kabuki opera, *An Actor's Revenge,* based on Kon Ichikawa's film, with music by Minoru Miki, performed in Britain, Japan, and Germany. His translations are from a variety of European languages and from Japanese and Chinese. He lives in Andorra but returns to Japan for a few months every year.

JOSEPH LAPENTA, born in New York, has lived in Japan since 1974, where he has worked as a teacher, writer, editor, and translator. His articles, short stories, and book reviews have appeared in major English-language publications in Japan. He is a First Rank Master of the Ohara School of Ikebana and works for the school's International Division where, among other things, he teaches Japanese teachers of ikebana how to teach the art in English.

DAVID LAZARUS, who has lived in Tokyo since 1989, has written for *Time, Fortune, Reader's Digest, The International Herald Tribune,* and *National Geographic News Service*, and he has worked as a columnist for the *Japan Times*. He is a two-time winner of the annual ANA Wingspan Fiction Contest and the author of *Japan, Seriously*, a collection of columns and essays, and of *The Secret Sushi Society*, a book of short stories.

Writer, poet, and illustrator MICHELLE LEIGH was born in Port-au-Prince, Haiti, and is an American citizen. She has lived in the Americas, Africa, Europe, and Asia, with nearly a decade in Japan. She is the author of two non-fiction books, and her fiction and poetry have appeared in literary journals and anthologies in the U.S. and Asia. She is currently living in England, where she is working on her third book.

LEZA LOWITZ is coeditor of the anthologies *A Long Rainy Season* and *Other Side River* (Stone Bridge Press, 1994/95), author of the poetry collection *Old Ways to Fold New Paper* (Wandering Mind, 1996), and coauthor of the film *Milk* (Fischer Film, Vienna, 1997). She has received an NEA Fellowship in Poetry Translation, a California Arts Council poetry grant, the PEN Syndicated Fiction Award, and an NEH Fellowship. In 1990–94 she lived in Japan, where she was a freelance writer and taught at Tokyo University. She now lives in a small coastal village in northern California.

American ERIC MADEEN first visited Japan in 1983 on his way home from a two-year stint in the Peace Corps in Gabon. He has lived in Japan off and on since 1985. An assistant professor of English at a small private college in Tokyo, he resides on the bluff in Yokohama, where he is at work on his fourth novel. His advertising copy has appeared in the *Economist, Time,* and *Asia Week*, and his journalism has appeared in *The Pretentious Idea, Tokyo Journal, The Daily Yomiuri,* and *The East*.

RALPH MCCARTHY was born in San Mateo, California in 1950 and has lived in Japan since 1981. He is the translator of two collections of stories by Osamu Dazai, *Self Portraits* and *Blue Bamboo*, and Ryu Murakami's novel *69*. He has also translated ten children's books and written song lyrics for Pat Benatar, Rita Coolidge, and Celine Dion among others. *One Hundred Views of Raoul* is a series of 100 stories, 51 of which were originally published in Japan.

LAUREL OSTROW is a teacher, nurse, and writer. She lived in Kobe until her family was forced to return to the United States by the Great Hanshin Earthquake. Her fiction and poetry have appeared in *Sunday Afternoon*, the journal of the Kansai Writer's Association.

HAL PORTER (1911-1984) was born in Melbourne. His first novel, *A Handful of Pennies*, is based on his experiences teaching the children of the Australian Occupation Forces. He later served as a Lecturer for the Australian Department of External Affairs in Japan. His other Japan-related writings include a collection of short fiction, *Mr. Butterfry and Other Tales of New Japan*; *The Professor*, a play; and a work of non-fiction, *The Actors: An Image of the New Japan*.

VIKI RADDEN, an American, was born in Germany. She has worked as an assistant English teacher in Japan. Her fiction has been anthologized in *SISTERFIRE: A Black Womanist Anthology* and *Catholic Girls and Boys*. Other essays and stories have appeared in the *Abiko Literary Rag*, *Off Our Backs*, and *Women Travel*. She is the recipient of a Hawthornden International Fellowship for Writers and currently resides in California.

DONALD RICHIE is known internationally as the foremost Western authority on Japanese films. He has also written widely on other aspects of Japan, which has been his home since 1947. Other works include *The Inland Sea*, *Different People*, *A Lateral View*, and *Companion of the Holiday*.

DANIEL ROSENBLUM has lived a total of thirteen years in Japan—first as the child of American diplomats and more recently as a financial journalist. He attended Oberlin College, where he majored in Japanese language and literature. He currently lives in Hong Kong with his wife Tamima and daughter Hannah, where he holds down his day job and continues to write fiction.

EDWARD SEIDENSTICKER is one of the finest translators of Japanese literature. His other works include *Very Few People Come This Way: Lyrical Episodes from the Year of the Rabbit*, *Low City High City: Tokyo From Edo to the Earthquake*, *This Country, Japan*, and *Genji Days*, a diary kept while at work on his translation of *The Tale of Genji*.

ALEX SHISHIN is Associate Professor at Kobe Women's University. He has published fiction, non-fiction, and photography in a variety of journals, including *Prairie Schooner*, *Kyoto Journal*, *Edge*, *Struggle*, *Abiko Quarterly*, *Asahi Evening News*, *Printed Matter*, the *Mainichi Daily News*, and the *Japan Times*.

KATE THE SLOPS is the pseudonym of a Canadian-American writer who has lived in Japan for fourteen years. Formerly a rewriter for the *Mainichi Daily News*, she is now living in Abiko where she works as an Assistant Language Teacher at the Abiko Board of Education. Her work appears frequently in literary journals in Japan.

HOLLY THOMPSON lived in Fujisawa City, Kanagawa Prefecture, from 1983 to 1986 and has made several trips to Japan since then for research on her fiction and nonfiction works. She received an M.A. in fiction writing from New York University. Her fiction has appeared in *Wingspan*, *Potato Eyes*, *Printed Matter*, and other publications.

FRANK TUOHY was born in England in 1925. He has written three novels, three books of stories, and a biography of Yeats. His first book of stories, *The Admiral and the Nun*, was awarded the Katherine Mansfield Short Story Prize in 1960. His novel *The Ice Saints* won the James Tait Black Memorial Prize. He has also received the E. M. Forster Award of the American Institute of Arts and Letters and The Bennet Award. He currently resides in Somerset.

WILLIAM WETHERALL was born in San Francisco in 1941, settled in Japan in 1975, and became a permanent resident in 1983. Since then he has been active as a free-lance researcher, journalist, and writer, specializing in mental health, ethnic minorities, and popular culture. He has translated short stories by Seicho Matsumoto, Kenzaburo Oe, and Nobuko Takagi and is a cotranslator of Oe's *A Quiet Life* (Grove Press, 1996). Two of his own short stories appear in *Prizewinning Asian Fiction* (Hong Kong University Press, 1991). He is currently working on a novel.

PHILIP WHALEN first moved to Japan in 1965 after receiving a grant from the National Academy of Arts and Letters. Although best known for his poetry, he wrote the novel *Imaginary Speeches for a Brazen Head* in 1966-67 while living in Kyoto. In 1972 he moved to the Zen Center, San Francisco, and in 1973 was ordained a Zen Buddhist monk.

OTHER FICTION AND POETRY TITLES
ABOUT JAPAN FROM STONE BRIDGE PRESS

One Hot Summer in Kyoto by John Haylock

Death March on Mount Hakkoda by Jiro Nitta

Wind and Stone by Masaaki Tachihara

Still Life and Other Stories by Junzo Shono

Right under the big sky, I don't wear a hat by Hosai Ozaki

The Name of the Flower by Kuniko Mukoda

CONTEMPORARY JAPANESE WOMEN'S POETRY
A Long Rainy Season: Haiku and Tanka
Other Side River: Free Verse
edited by Leza Lowitz, Miyuki Aoyama, and Akemi Tomioka

Basho's Narrow Road: Spring and Autumn Passages
by Matsuo Basho, with commentary by Hiroaki Sato

Naked: Poems by Shuntaro Tanikawa

Hojoki by Kamo-no-Chomei

Milky Way Railroad by Kenji Miyazawa

Ravine and Other Stories by Yoshikichi Furui